MURDER
RIDES
A GALE FORCE
WIND

SEAROSE

MURDER
RIDES
A GALE FORCE
WIND

YVONNE MAXIMCHUK

I acknowledge I live in and deeply cherish the unceded territory of the Kwikwasut'inuxw Haxwa'mis First Nation.

This book was printed on 100% post-consumer recycled paper.

Library and Archives Canada Cataloguing in Publication
ISBN 978-1-7779585-0-3
Maximchuk, Yvonne, 1952-   Murder Rides A Gale Force Wind:
An Island Mystery

Editor ~ Pam Robertson
Cover art, map, and illustrations ~ Yvonne Maximchuk
Cover Design ~ Iryna Spica, SpicaBookDesign and Yvonne Maximchuk
Book Design ~ Iryna Spica, SpicaBookDesign
Printed in Canada by Island Blue Book Printing, Victoria, BC

Published by SeaRose Publishing

Dedicated to
James Maximchuk (1933-2021)
My dear Uncle Jimmy, best uncle ever.

You always liked to tell a good story and
I'm so sad you didn't get to read this one

Illustrations

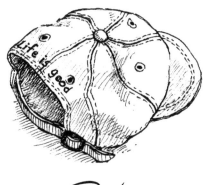

Prologue

hostly veils of mist drift and cling to low-swept cedar branches. The tide gently rises to greet them. Like a transient killer whale, the unornamented hull of a former rumrunner hugs the shoreline. It's motor produces a low, powerful throb. Could be any old water rat with a quiet vee of wake rippling away behind it. At this dusky hour, two coats of paint in 'creek-robber grey' render it nearly invisible; the vessel merges with the muted green foliage and the seaweed covered rocks of the intertidal zone. Making its way up Indian Passage, across Fife Sound, by Trivett Rock, past the green-tinted Copper Bluffs; eventually the boat enters Simoom Sound, still hugging the shore, and proceeds up the dogleg to a small group of islets.

There it slows, stops, drifts. A spotlight beam hits the water and short bursts of light circle the boat...searching.

"There it is," a low hiss.

"Yeah, yeah, 'kay."

The boat is put in gear and makes a small turn, heads toward a gently bobbing piece of driftwood, pulls alongside. A gloved hand reaches over, grabs it.

"Need some help here."

"Hold yer horses."

The stick is a couple feet long and about six inches in diameter; nothing distinguishes it from any other piece of driftwood floating around, except it doesn't float around. It stays right there, swirling slowly in a little back eddy formed by the configuration of low rocks and islets.

The two gather up the stick and bring it onto the deck, taking care not to tangle the line attached to a log salvager's dog pounded into the underside. Clipped onto the anchor line, a second, shorter line ends around a well-tied packet sealed in a kayaker's waterproof bag.

Quickly the packet is laid on the deck, opened and unrolled. Inside lies the expected waterproof wallet, full of money.

"Should we count it?"

"Nah, he always pays right. Load it and let's get out of here. Place gives me the creeps. We'll change the stick next trip."

The prepared package is sealed into the kitbag with care, then reattached to the end of the short line. The whole contraption is slid back over the side.

River Lass is the name on the bow, painted in the smallest of letters underneath the edge of the wide sweep of upper deck. A shadow among shadows, the boat motors away from the rockpile and turns back down the dogleg toward the opening of the sound.

One

Sunlight quivered tentatively through the mist wreathing Echo Bay Park. Broken into thin fingers by the hemlock trees' curved tips crowning the hill on the park's eastern side, it crept across the water, trembled in the vapour rising off the sea. Slowly it felt its way along the top floor back windows of Woody Debris's lodge and marina. The warm spring light settled confidently on a lighthouse-shaped building which long ago had housed a bakery, then onto the pitched roof of an adjacent floathouse.

Moments later it gained a corner, and in a sudden dash spread itself across a long section of dock. Secured to four acres of land on the bay's western side, where the generator, workshop and hot tub sat, the docks and fingers of the marina lay exposed to the morning sun.

Under that warm caress, the buildings' colours lit up: green and white on the main lodge, bold red and white on the lighthouse and chestnut brown siding on the floathouse.

Woodward DesBrisay, nicknamed Woody Debris by loggers unwilling to use his real name—a high-falutin' French name to them—strolled out his front door, gazed appreciatively around his domain and swelled his chest with a draught of sweet, clean air. All he had in mind was the work to do on the place, but on this sweet morning he basked for a moment in what he'd accomplished. Dressed in old blue jeans and a threadbare plaid shirt, he stroked his beard and tugged on the long ends of his mustache.

'Woody's Marina, Store and Post Office' proclaimed the sign on the concrete barge at the entrance to Echo Bay. Originally part of a bridge across the Hood Canal, it wasn't particularly attractive but it was functional, big enough for the store/post office, and the dining room he'd built. The fuel dock faced south into the head of the bay, the square bulk of the barge protecting it from winter's north winds. The long fingers of dock, empty now, awaited the boats of summer. A Canadian flag hung limp in the calm air, along with an American one. Even though he'd come west to British Columbia a long time ago, Woody celebrated his heritage by flying a third flag, that of Quebec.

Four boats coming in this week, he thought, *that's a lot for May.* There was still much he wanted to get done before the thousands of boaters showed up. His big hand fell to his right hip and he pressed his fist into the joint. The pain never went away, but it was somewhat manageable. As long as he had a toke or two every once in a while he'd be alright.

Woody's uncovered head registered the cool air. He noted the call from his bladder, unzipped and let go, then went back inside to tackle the paperwork.

Quick-stepping out to the sunny corner of her balcony on the lodge's second-storey apartment, Woody's general manager and cook, Carol Ann Murchison, looped the ties of her flowered dressing gown around her generous figure. Fine flyaway hair haloed her face in the morning light. She, too, gazed at the bay and sighed with satisfaction. *Another day in paradise. Sure made the right decision to not marry that lazy bum Herb.* So many choices and yet, here she was.

Some people may have thought that life in a tiny backwater on the Pacific coast of British Columbia was somewhat of a comedown from a career as a cordon bleu chef in the finest of the world's restaurants. Carol Ann didn't share that opinion. Succeeding in that career had been barely achievable; the brutal hours, infighting and back-stabbing had all taken their toll, but in the end she'd triumphed.

Seventeen vicious years to parlay a talent for flavour into a position at the top of her profession and then she'd surprised the hell out of her peers by walking away for a grand love with a French hotelier. In a romantic splurge at the end of a year of travelling the world they'd bought a floathouse in BC. It had proved to be more annoying than romantic and Henri had returned to France.

But something about the rugged landscape and life on the continental edge had appealed to Carol Ann. She'd traded in the floathouse for a smaller one that had been yarded onto a new cedar log float and accepted a job cooking in a logging camp in Smith Sound. A man here and there until she'd met Herb and liked him, a lot, but it turned out she'd been his ticket to ride. Twenty years of logging camp shift work passed until, needing a life less bound by erratic schedules, she'd found out Woody needed a hand, and here she was, quite content, in Echo Bay.

"Not a bad place to be, all in all," she smiled and stretched her arms high.

Carol Ann didn't linger. She swallowed a glass of water, dressed efficiently in navy cotton chinos and a purple sweatshirt with 'Woody's Marine Resort' emblazoned on it and trotted down the long flight of steps carrying a bucket and a travel mug of coffee. Not too gracefully but without accident she climbed into her rowboat and pushed away from the dock. She'd set the crab trap the night before and the red buoy marking its spot was visible on the shallow water near the long white shell midden.

Carol Ann rowed energetically. She always had a long to-do list and was eager to get at it. Violet-green swallows swooped in great circles overhead, snagging early morning mosquitoes, and she gave them an appreciative nod as she pulled on the oars.

3

"Good work, Birds."

A soaring bluff capped with graceful pine and fir trees encircled the eastern shore. Textured by time with a range of lichen, mosses and small flowers, and painted long ago with cryptic pictographs, the high granite wall was the source of the echo for which the bay was named. At the cliff base, half a dozen houses perched on log rafts, called floats, were strung together with logs and wooden walkways in varying degrees of disrepair. The row of floating homes ran from the bay's outer edge all the way to the huge midden now named Echo Bay Marine Park.

The bay's east side lay in blue shadow, and the houses had yet to come to life. Window blinds and drapes were pulled closed on most. From the small brown house in the middle, a thin stream of smoke wafted up. Solidly built in the sixties with fir milled at Deacon Bay by long-time resident William Deacon—known as Back Eddy—the well-maintained house sat high on the decking above the log float. A second sturdy float laden with tidy rows of split fir and hemlock firewood nestled beside it. Out in front, alongside the rickety boardwalk dock connecting all the houses, a timeworn west coast troller bobbed patiently against the rail.

Doramay might be old but she had a lot of life in her, Nathan Tolvanen thought fondly, as he unzipped beside his boat. Like Woody, he relished the freedom to do his business with no one to offend. A tall, gaunt Finnlander—half, anyway—his mother was a Rasmussen whose family had homesteaded at Cape Scott. His father, well, who knew? Mom had told him she'd had a flaming affair with a 'big brute of a Finnish logger' one summer and her son was the result—a most welcome one, she'd added.

Nathan's long arms ended in big hands; size extra-large in the glove department. He stood tall to counteract the slight stoop that seemed to be overtaking him lately. Above his broad forehead, a shock of white hair rose stiffly upright until he got around to laying it flat with a swipe of his palm. Above piercing blue eyes, unruly white brows arced and curled to each side. His beard and hair glowed white on the shaded deck.

As was his habit, Nathan surveyed the bay. Beginning with the provincial marine park at the south end, he took in Woody's Marina, where the bay opened to the northwest, then beyond that to Baker Island. Always hopeful he'd see a pod of orca or a humpback—his survey was rewarded often these days. The big baleen whales had multiplied rapidly in the last ten years and now their documented population numbered over a hundred. If he saw one, he'd radio Kit Sampson, a little jog north over toward Scott Cove. She was always eager to jump in her boat and run out to see if she could get an identifying tail shot to send off to the Vancouver Aquarium or the Marine Education and Research Society.

Nathan was happy to leave it to the young ones. His range of motion the last year or two had decreased with the onset of arthritis. Getting in his yearly supply of firewood, setting a crab trap, dragging a line for a salmon or jigging up a cod once in a while was enough activity for him.

Below his feet, pale and sockless this brilliant May morning, half a dozen Barrow's goldeneyes popped out from under the dock, followed by a pair of buffleheads and a hooded merganser.

Nathan liked the water birds. They kept him company, although these ones would be gone soon, returning in October. He liked the spring arrivals almost as much, and each year cleaned and prepared the feeders for the hummingbirds. He'd built houses for the various swallows and three were occupied by breeding pairs this year. He admired their efforts to keep the babies fed.

He wished he wasn't colour blind when he watched the violet-greens. Carol Ann tried to describe to him how their two colours looked different but, try as he might, he couldn't see it.

Nathan stepped over to his wood float and grasped chunks of split hemlock in his big hands, piling them against the once bulging muscles of his left arm. Those muscles he'd once been so proud of had gone somewhat ropy in the last few years but he was still a powerful man...*and don't you forget it.* He laughed, amused by his own macho thought.

He'd built those muscles in the seventies tree-planting with 'the Swede' at Head Bay—fifteen hundred bare-root trees a day. He still could feel the mattock, pointy end up, blade end slicing the soil, pulling it forward, grabbing the baby tree from the big bag hanging off his back, bending over, slipping it into the newly made crevice.

Then there were the two years falling the big timber. He'd survived that in one piece, praise be. Falling hadn't suited him like planting had—too much risk. Killing those great big beautiful trees just hadn't felt right, in spite of the incredible money he'd made. The best years had been when he'd put a licence on *Doramay* and went crabbing. That had been a good way to make an independent life and get to know the coast.

All washed up now in this quiet backwater of a settlement, he thought ruefully. Nobody here but a few old cruds, one old—well, late middle-aged—woman, plus a few young ones. It wasn't much of a population for a place that had once been home to over a hundred people—and that was right here in this one bay. He himself was a product of those tough pioneers who had come to this land of colossal trees and endless possibility, running from persecution and poverty in their natal countries.

Nathan's mind rambled from past to present and back again. Back Eddy, or 'Willy' as friends called him, had told him that the midden's depth, the accumulated pile of broken shells that formed the beach, attested to thousands of years of occupation by generations of people who, like him, albeit in the distant past, had made the long journey to this continent.

Then, as now, this bay had been appreciated and valued for its many attributes, especially the protected harbour and cedar-tinted stream where salmon arrived and returned with the seasons. The forest had flourished in the plentiful rain after the glaciers melted. Nathan often tried to imagine what life must have been like for those long ago people as they made homes and fed themselves on the abundance of their world.

This led him down the inevitable pathway to Annie, his long-lost love, his 'Indian Princess,' as he'd called her. It wouldn't be politically correct to call her that these days, no matter how much love he'd felt for her, and anyway, he did *not* want to dredge up that buried pain. He pushed his thoughts forward into the day and admonished himself for the slip.

"Now don't go gettin' all hang-dog," Nathan lectured himself. "This here is a number one, class A morning and it is going to be a real good day. Again."

Arms full of firewood he went back in to stoke the woodstove, enough to give his aging bones a shot of warmth to move through the cool morning. So far this month the afternoons had been unseasonably hot. The cedar trees and other conifers clinging to the rocky islets would pay the price over the next two years.

The water birds gabbled amongst themselves and paddled officiously westward across the bay. The mussels on the boomsticks over there were plentiful and for once, there were no crows around to compete with the goldeneyes. A blue heron released a raucous squawk as it surged off the log by its fishing hole near the midden. Three otters ran up from the strand of broken white shell along the same log and slid into the ocean, swimming fast toward deep water.

Silent on padded paws, a sinuous, tawny shape with an ink-tipped tail stole along the beach and disappeared, low and swift into the dappled forest.

A raven cried once, then again, its watery gargle messaging to those who knew its language.

Two

The morning sun climbed higher, its light played over the marina. Steam rose from the water's surface and the float-house roofs. It was 9:30 a.m. and Carol Ann's bread and buns were rising in the lodge's warm kitchen. Four big hard crab halves sat in a yellow bowl on the counter. Woody finished the batch of email business in his cluttered office area, got up, stretched and looked out the big front window to the fuel pumps. His eye travelled up the ramp to the barge where the store and dining room occupied the majority of floor space.

"Looks like Kit's here," he shouted to Carol Ann.

"Oh, she's probably bringing some mail to go out, Woody. Want me to go see?"

"Yah, she got fuel yesterday so she don' need any today, I guess."

Carol Ann rinsed her hands at the sink and wiped them on her blue flowered apron. She left the kitchen and strode along the dock, swinging her arms. It might look goofy to an observer from the city but you've got to get exercise whenever you can. Living out here in the coastal wilderness for so long had rendered her immune to what anyone might think of her. She revelled in the warmth and brilliance, enjoyed the eagle pair chittering high in the big fir trees on the slope where the old hotel once stood.

"Mornin' Carol Ann," called Kit as she neatly turned her rowboat in to the dock.

"And a real beauty, Kit. You got mail this morning?"

"I do. And I'm jonesing for a loaf of your 'whole-wheat-special-grains-properly-raised' bread. What're the chances?"

"Oh you know me, girl, don't I always have some bread going? And it's fresh today, but you'll have to get it when you come back after the mail plane comes in."

Kit shipped the oars, slipped the bowline up through the oarlock shaft and wrapped it around the cleat on the dock. She put her two hands onto the planks and catapulted her five foot seven inches onto her feet.

"Okay, thanks. That'll work. Go with my fish stew tonight."

"Lordy Kit, you're only wearing a t-shirt. Forgot your jacket?"

Kit looked down at her bright crimson t-shirt and black jeans.

"Carol Ann, it's *so sunny*! I figured I'd take a chance. Besides, rowing warms me up and grows muscles!" Kit turned toward the east and raised both arms high, saluting the sun. "Just look at it; have you *seen* a nicer day?"

She laughed, shook the auburn ponytail hanging out the back of her black baseball cap, flexed her right arm until the bicep bunched up, and grinned at Carol Ann.

"Look here. I felt so good this morning I put on my fancy earrings." She turned her head sideways and pushed her jaw forward to show the gold earrings, red-feathered and tipped with beads.

"Ooh, fancy! What's the occasion?"

"Oh, you know, Carol Ann. When do we ever get to dress up nice? Sometimes I am so sick of looking like a frump. Always jeans, grease, grubbiness. I even painted my toenails but you can't see them, of course." She stuck out her dingy running shoe. "I have no plans to get dirty today."

"I guess we'll see how long that lasts."

"Yah," Kit sighed. "Well, I'm doing a bit of paperwork and going to putter with the paints. There should be a new brush and some good paper coming in today. So, check this out—I got the name painted on the skiff."

She flourished a hand toward the stern of the old wooden rowing boat. Carol Ann leaned over to admire the artful letters.

"*Merbaby*. Cute, goes with *Mermaid Lady*." She smiled at the younger woman.

"Yah, that's what I was thinking."

Kit had rechristened her recently acquired boat, a 25-foot aluminum crew boat once named *Hector Three*. She ran freight and passengers between Port McNeill, Alert Bay and Sointula, Gilford Village and Kingcome Village, on a 'make it up as you go along' schedule. 'Not predictable but always reliable' was her watchword, and so far, while not making a million, she'd done alright.

Sometimes there were customers who asked for what she called a 'joy ride,' who wanted to run around in the boat all day, wherever she'd take them. This was her favourite sort of tour.

She'd make the run out to the west end of Fife Sound, to the sea lion haul-out where the gigantic males and alluring females lolled about, like royal sultans with a harem of beautiful dark ladies. They might see a pod of orca or a humpback whale or two at the mouth of Arrow Pass. Or she'd take them to the islands of the Burdwood Group, to the little bay where the seals gathered, their dark bodies contrasted against the white shell sea bottom as they swam beneath the boat.

A run up Viner Sound when the tide was high might result in a bear sighting, although you sure didn't want to get stuck in the 'loon shit' in that long shallow estuary when the tide dropped. There were now two grizzlies on Gilford Island, where once there had been only black bears. It added an interesting edge to life when you laid eyes on one.

As Carol Ann and Kit looked up from admiring the lettering, Willy Deacon, nicknamed 'Back Eddy' for his fabled skill at fishing salmon in the back eddies, motored into the narrow waterway between the barge and the land. Tie-up line in hand, he stepped carefully out of his beat-up blue speedboat. His barking dog tried to jump out the same time.

"Shut up, Buster! Stay! Get back in there. Stay, Buster."

Finally Buster obeyed.

"Damn dog. God, he's stubborn."

Back Eddy was an old-timer, still fishing and salvaging logs—the only local who hadn't come from somewhere else. Delivered by a midwife in Port Neville eighty-six years ago, he loved this land of channels, reefs and rocky islets, and knew it intimately.

He sauntered over to Kit and Carol Ann and leaned over to look at the painted name.

"Well, you finally got it done. Kind of a stupid name for a boat. Looks nice though," he added grudgingly.

Kit and Carol Ann exchanged a grin. Back Eddy had never approved of any of her boat names and she'd been pretty sure he wouldn't approve of this one, either.

"Hey Willy," she talked to his back as they followed Carol Ann single file up the mesh metal ramp to the concrete barge, "I need to go on the ways, maybe slap on some bottom paint, check a few things. Can you put me up tomorrow or the next day?"

11

He nodded. "There's a good tide Saturday morning. Come about nine. Plenty of water to get you off when you're ready."

"That's perfect, thanks. I've gotta run over to McNeill on Tuesday and pick up some freight for Gwayasdums and that young fella who's coming out here."

"Who's comin' out here?" He half turned toward her.

Kit was surprised. Although he didn't hear well, he somehow usually knew what was going on.

"You know, some young kid wants to come out here for a while, name's Cole Calder or Callum or something. I've got it written down. He's going to give Woody a hand. Jeez, I thought Back Eddy sees all, knows all." She raised her hands, palms out and waggled her fingers, widened her slanted green eyes and made a 'woo-woo' look at him.

He laughed, tilted the brim of his cap.

"Hah. Not *every* thing. Just most stuff."

Carol Ann fired up the small red generator, flipped the switch to power and unlocked the door. She took Back Eddy's heap of letters, set it on the Post Office counter and went to the back office where the individual mailboxes were stacked up against the wall. She dragged out the plastic mail bin and set it up on the counter by the scale, then changed the date stamp and reset it for May 9. Only then did she turn to his pile of letters.

"You might need more postage for this fat letter," she told him as she placed the thick letter on the scale and weighed it. "I think it's over the regular mail weight. Thirty grams is all you get for your stamp."

"Oh for Chrissake," huffed Back Eddy.

"Yup, sorry. You need thirty-seven more cents to bring it up to the right amount."

Carol Ann smiled at him as she pulled out the stamps packet and sorted through it. She knew he didn't like his postage calculations to be wrong. He always had his letters stamped and ready to go.

"I got some change here," he replied, digging around in his jeans pockets, "if it didn't slip out a hole."

"Bring it in next time, that's okay. I can use up some of these small stamps." She counted out several three's, two's, and one's.

"Oh and I've got a very formal letter here for Mr. William Edward Deacon. That you?" said Carol Ann playfully.

"I guess." Back Eddy was not fond of people knowing his middle name.

Kit glanced up and saw Benny, who blinked from the brilliance outside as he entered the room, then paused and removed his worn red cap.

"Benny Thompson!" she exclaimed. "Just the man I want to see today. How are you making out with my sign? And how is the prawning? Did you get the transmission repaired on *Thunder Chieftain?*"

"Good grief, what a pain that was! Opening day and I get the gear out and *boom!* There she goes, transmission is done for. I got that old one from Harry Bellows couple years ago so I put that in. We'll see how she holds up."

"Mornin' Carol Ann, Back Eddy." He nodded to both and smiled at Carol Ann. "I brought the money I owe you for fuel." He pulled a small stack of twenties out of his pocket and fanned them out with one hand. "And a bag of prawns." A big grin lit up his face as he plonked it on the counter.

She smiled back. "What a treat! Thanks a lot, Benny. Let me finish up here and get Kit's mail and then it's your turn, 'kay?"

Back Eddy observed the wad of money in the prawn fisher's hand and commented, "You must be feelin' pretty steaky, Benny. Packin' a wad like that around...prawning must be pretty good."

"Oh, it is, Back Eddy, it's real good. Ain't seen nothin' like it in five or six years. At least I have the money to pay the fuel and the freight; buyer says the price should be going up later in the season." Benny was a happy man.

"Huh," said Back Eddy. "Hope so. When I was ling cod fishing they'd quote you a price and you go out and fish the west coast for ten days, then run all the way in to Coal Harbour, and when you get there the bastards have suddenly dropped the price a buck a pound. What're ya gonna do? Can't go back out to sea and stuff a few more in the live well."

"Yah, I know what you mean. All them buyers are bastards. They got the fisherman over a barrel, then you got the government and bloody fish cops always on your ass."

"Whoa—just chill you guys," Kit chimed in. "That's my boyfriend you're slagging, Benny. Tim's not so bad. Doing his job, right? Trying to look after the health of the stocks, hey? Something you fishermen should have at the top of your mind, right? Right?"

"Yah, yah, that's right, Kit. Anyways, how's about I bring your sign over this afternoon after I pull the gear? I got 'er done and all varnished. Looks right pretty."

"Yes! That would be great. I'll make you some lunch. A late lunch," she amended, "about two, or is that too early? We can put the sign up, I'll come get the mail and my bread after."

"I should be done by then, it's slowed down around here, might move the gear tomorrow and let it build up for a day or two."

"Okay, sounds good."

Kit caught Back Eddy's eye as she turned to Carol Ann with her mail. His eyebrows had lifted at Benny's last remark. She passed over her small pile of letters.

"They're all stamped today. Oh, if you want to put in a grocery order I can bring it out Tuesday."

"Okay, thanks. Oh, Kit, I was meaning to ask you, did you hear about that girl who OD'd in Sointula yesterday?"

"No, who? What happened?"

"I think her name was Trudy something. OD'd on fentanyl at a party out Kaleva Road."

"Trudy Trauble? That Trudy?"

Carol Ann nodded. "That sounds right. One of the prawn fishermen told me. Did you know her?"

"I met her a few times; she was fun to party with but kinda crazy. Trudy Trouble, that's what they called her. Jeez. I almost went to that party. Darrell Henderson off *White Bird* invited me."

Back Eddy put in his two bits worth. "It took me a while to get used to the hippies smoking dope when they showed up here in the seventies, but at least it didn't kill them. Some of them turned out to be pretty good guys. Makes ya wonder, who's bringing in marijuana that's going to kill someone?"

"Maybe its coke or speed or something, who knows what all fentanyl can be in these days?" said Kit. "I'm sure sorry to hear that anyway. She was a nice person and a great singer; she could really rock it when she got on stage."

"Sorry to be the bearer of bad news, but it's downright creepy," said Carol Ann. "It means you never know when someone you happen to like is going to fall down dead and you won't be able to help them. Poof, gone." She snapped her fingers. "Like that. Anyway, I've got to get this mail ready before the plane comes in."

"And I better get a move on. Things to do, places to go. See you later, Benny, and you Saturday morning, Willy."

Kit waved and strolled out the door, hips swaying in her snug jeans. Benny watched her go. "What a woman," he said, shaking his head from side to side. "That girl is something."

Carol Ann grinned at him. "Too young for an old crud like you, Benny. Considering the shortage of eligible men around here she's doing all right with Tim."

"Well *you're* not too young for me, Carol Ann, although you sure look like you could be." Benny mimed an exaggerated leer and she cracked up.

"What a card. You just back off, y'old letch. Give me that pile of dough you got there and I'll write up your fuel bill."

"You know deep in your heart you're crazy for me, Carol Ann. I'm never giving up."

"Jesus," said Back Eddy, "I'm outta here."

Down the ramp he went and there was Buster, wagging his tail and hoping his human hadn't noticed he'd been all over the dock in the last ten minutes.

"Get in the boat, Buster. Get in the boat, come on now." The dog jumped in obediently; good when he wanted to be.

Back Eddy leaned to the tie-up line, but stood straight again as a trim gill-netter pulled in to the fuel dock. He left his boat and walked over to grab the bowline of Ritchie Wilson's boat, *Ahta River*. Buster bounded up behind him.

Preceded by the loud rumbling of the motor and wheels on the wooden dock, Woody was headed this way as well, towing a cartload of lumber with his yellow and green quad.

"You sure keep that boat looking good, Ritchie," Back Eddy shouted over the noise. "What's new in Kingcome?"

"Morning, Back Eddy. Same old, same old. What's new with you? Gotta be something interesting you can tell me about."

"We-elll, saw a grizzly up in Viner when Kit and I went around counting birds last month. Might be the third one on Gilford. I couldn't quite tell if it was one of the two we already have or a different one. Tide was low so we couldn't get up the creek. Sure don't want to get stuck in that muck for ten hours."

"Huh. Yah, lots of them buggers up Kingcome. Between the bears and the cougars kids aren't safe to run around anymore. A cougar took my grandfather's dog last week. Sure don't know what they're all eating, no fish to speak of, no raccoons or otters either."

"Yah, pets I guess."

Ritchie Wilson swept his hand over his forehead, pushing his fingers through the lock of straight black hair above his brow.

Black eyes inspected the dock as he leaned over the side to the stern tie-up.

Woody pulled up in the quad as Ritchie swung over the side, catlike in his dark grace. The resort owner turned off the loud machine, leaned his arms forward onto the steering wheel, happy to see both men.

"Mornin', Willy. You need fuel, Ritchie?"

"Yup, thanks. How're you Woody? Got some boaters coming in soon?"

"Four this week that are booked, maybe somebody who isn't, who knows? Feel like giving me a hand with this lumber? It's my last load up to the barge for the deck and the cover."

"Sure."

"Guess I'll go see what kind of trouble I can get into," said Back Eddy. "See you guys later."

"Later," the other two said with a nod and then watched as the old fisherman got in the speedboat, patted his dog, fired up the motor and roared off.

Ritchie reached into his boat for a pair of gloves, slid them over his callused hands, then he and Woody packed the 16-foot two-by-fours up the ramp to the barge's deck. Ritchie set down the lengths of lumber and rolled his shoulders. His muscular arms and back stretched the letters of the grey t-shirt he wore.

Woody noticed and grinned. "Hah, I see you left the Red Power shirt behind today for the Kingcome Wolves. You guys got any games going this year?"

"Well no, we don't seem to get together like we used to. I miss the action but all the youngsters, they don't want to stay in the village anymore so it's hard to organize any soccer games."

"Yah, it's the same here. They shut down the school ten years ago and burned it up a few years later. No young ones anymore. They're like unicorns. How 'bout that group you set up for the kids, to get them learning the old ways, dances and songs and all that? Making any headway?"

17

"Hard to tear them away from their phones, to tell you the truth." Ritchie grinned. "More addictive than drugs. A few are interested and learning. Have to get the right person's permission, though, or feathers get ruffled. They all like the drumming."

"Ayuh, prob'ly universal."

"Yup."

Woody poked his head in the store and asked Carol Ann to turn on the fuel pump. Benny came out the door and lurched to a stop when he saw Ritchie stacking the pile of lumber. "Well if it ain't Ritchie Wilson. I see you bin settin' yer net over to Embley Lagoon again."

"Where do you come up with your bullshit, Benny?"

Ritchie was easy; he was used to provocation from entitled white guys who resented the privileges recently garnered by Indigenous people. He didn't want to fight, just make the most of any opportunities coming his way.

Woody exited the store and headed down the ramp to the fuel pumps. Ritchie followed and Benny stomped after them, unwilling to quit badgering.

"I seen your boat there two times since Christmas."

Ritchie tamped down the thin flame of anger that licked up his spine. He'd had a big problem for a long time with that flame exploding into a bonfire.

"You got your head up your ass, Benny. Time to pull it out and look reality in the face. Or maybe that is reality for you."

He took in a slow calming breath like they'd taught him at anger management training, let it out; then inhaled deeply again. The image of a fire-breathing dragon came to mind. He imagined Benny the size of Donald Duck, quack quack quacking, and incinerated Benny with his next exhale. Not exactly what they'd taught him but it worked for him, put a grin on his face.

"I suppose you think it's funny," the fisherman continued.

Woody interrupted, "You gonna want fuel, Benny?"

"Nope, not today, Woody." An afterthought, "Thanks."

With a heavy step Benny leaned into a space-invading shoulder nudge as he passed Ritchie on the dock.

"Just sayin', Wilson. I see you there again and I'm turnin' you in to Fisheries."

Ritchie suppressed the fury that rose from Benny's taunts and turned away to the diesel pump. Refusing to react to the goading, nevertheless he felt a righteous indignation at the accusations.

"You keep shut about bullshit like that, Thompson. I haven't been there."

Three

Staying close to the shore Kit rowed back to her float-house. She contemplated the light glowing through the droplets falling off the oars, and the ripples that spread with each stroke. She spotted Benny's boat heading for his fishing gear, wondered what he was doing for a deckhand these days. She'd meant to ask if he'd got a new one since the last young fellow had bailed. Hard to get good help, she knew. Maybe that young fellow who was coming out would be interested in giving him a hand.

Like a jet, an eagle roared down from above her, swung its talons forward to grasp a fish, then soared upward with its prey firmly clasped. A feather fell from its tail and spiralled down to the water's surface. Kit rowed hard, slipped up alongside it, shipped the oar and leaned over to capture the pristine white tail feather. A smile lit up her face as she raised it to the proud bird, now perched on a big branch and tearing at the fish.

"Thank you, Great Feathered One, thank you for your gift."

At the floathouse she left the little white rowboat tied to the rail. She inventoried her many boats, laughing to herself about how she had once marvelled at the number of vessels everybody had around their floathouses. She was proud of her new work boat, *Mermaid Lady*, resting alongside the front rail. The speedboat was around the far side and the kayak and the rowboat were pulled up on the landing deck. Satisfied that her 'coastie' status was secure as to the number and quality of boats she owned, she wondered how she'd manage when the day came she had to maintain them without Back Eddy's help.

In the house she threw her hat onto the hook by the living room French doors and opened all the other doors and windows. The sun was so welcome, so dazzling, she wanted to expose all the dark corners of the house today. A monumental sense of well-being flooded her. Life was good. Sunshine and a time out from work left a gap in her to-do list. She aimed to fill that gap with a couple hours of *plein-air* sketching.

Kit didn't have any big ambitions to be an artist, but she loved to draw and had always loved flowers. That had grown into wanting to paint everything in her world, from the smallest sea creatures to wild sea-to-sky-scapes. Like anyone who loved the coast, she'd been inspired by the art that portrayed it. Her two favourite painters, W.J. Phillips, a prairie artist, and Emily Carr, from the coast, had both travelled to the Broughton Archipelago. Kit had studied their work, trying to identify how the artists were able to express the power of 'place' she felt here.

Everywhere on this windswept coast, Emily Carr had translated the rhythm and flow of the great cedar forest. The resulting paintings had shaped people's view of it all forevermore. Almost ninety years after Carr and Phillips had made their way here, the villages those two had been inspired to paint were long gone. There was little left standing but a few house posts of Aboriginal origin or mouldy Western-style houses from the early nineteenth century, enveloped in alder and blackberry canes. A few totems still stood, gooseberries growing out of their decaying tops. Many had toppled and, overwhelmed by salal, were well along the organic journey back to soil.

21

Kit felt an imperative she couldn't explain—to sketch what was left of these remnants. One by one she was documenting the pictographs painted by ancient First Nations people on overhanging rock faces. Some images were literal and self-explanatory but some were bizarre and inexplicable. Marks people made on the landscape echoed into stories for her, but it wasn't anything she paraded out to the world or discussed in public. It was her private passion; a fragile thing she didn't want scrutinized.

The history of people and place had been her one obsession in school, and she'd wanted to become an archaeologist. When she was nine, her stepdad, Drake, who worked in the Forest Service, accepted a transfer to the coast and she and her mother, Peggy, had moved with him. Leaving the snug cabin her mom had built in the woods near Hope had been a hard transition; but they'd arrived in Alert Bay, rented a house and settled in. They'd all embraced and enjoyed life in the coastal rainforest. Her mom had built up a following for her work as an herbal healer and doula, and Kit, in spite of school, had enough free time to run around in the woods learning the plants and the animals' ways. Drake had rented a floathouse in Echo Bay and the family divided their time between the two communities.

As Kit got into her teens and made friends, her stepdad had given her an old speedboat in need of some TLC. Kit had lavished that on the old boat, grinding and fibreglassing until it was as good as, or better than, new. She'd saved up gifts and handyperson earnings to power it with a second-hand 50-horse Merc. She was all set to explore the nearby islands.

During the last two years of high school in Port McNeill, any fine-weather weekend she'd be off to camp on some deserted island. Her love of the past had been inspired by and nurtured in this forest solitude. Once she'd been thrilled to stumble on an intact stone mortar and pestle.

Excited with first-year studies in archeology at UBC in Vancouver, she'd returned for the second year, but right after Christmas her enthusiasm had been eclipsed by the illness and swift death of her mother. Drake's subsequent descent into grief drinking had so consumed her energy and attention she'd never completed the program.

She'd run into Back Eddy one day when she'd crossed Blackfish Sound to poke around Freshwater Bay and the islands on the mainland side. His parents had moved there when he was very young and his mom had stayed after the death of his father, continuing to run the fish-buying business. From time to time he'd run down from his home in Echo Bay to split firewood for the current owner.

Back Eddy had been surprised to see another boat ashore on Flower Island, but wasn't surprised when it turned out to be Kit. It had been a few years since her family had lived in Echo Bay; they'd sat for a couple hours and caught up. He remembered the ten-year-old who had eagerly helped build the boat shed and had always liked her inquisitiveness and spirit of adventure. He'd needed a deckhand that summer to go fish the west coast of Haida Gwaii and offered her the job. It sounded just the thing to Kit; get away, go fishing, and see some new ocean.

That work had taken her from the wild, west coast of Vancouver Island to Triangle Island and northwest to Haida Gwaii on eighteen-hour runs. They'd fished Langara on the north end all the way down that fierce coast to Cape St. James, then southeast to the long inlets and tidal waters of the BC mainland. She'd made a good stake over the eight years she'd deck-handed for Back Eddy and was torn between going back to university and establishing a home. She decided to settle, bought a floathouse, and spent the next year renovating the house. Drake finally got sober, and Kit felt secure in having Back Eddy tow the floathouse to its present anchorage in the small bay north of Echo Bay.

It had taken ten years but at last, Kit's obsessive motion had slowed to a stop and she'd come to terms with her own immeasurable loss. Like a gopher peering out of its burrow, she'd climbed out, sat up and looked around, then asked, "What next?"

She noticed there was a need for small-scale local transport and freight delivery. It took a couple years to get her Transport Canada tickets to run increasingly larger vessels but she'd begun to fill the small niche of providing freight and transportation for the community the way old airlines like Orca Air had once done it—making up a 'sched' on a day-to-day basis as calls came in, and charging reasonable fees.

The business is going pretty good, she thought as she checked out the contents of the propane fridge. Some of yesterday's crab in a salad would make a nice lunch for her and Benny. That left enough time for an hour or two of painting and maybe she could even weed the planter boxes on the front deck. Clear out around the lettuce greens and the shooting arugula.

Last winter she'd built the planter boxes then decided she needed a small shed to stow the chainsaw, jerry cans, axe and gardening tools, life jackets, fishing gear and a couple crab traps. It sat at the back of the house, closest to the shore behind the float. She'd taken the time to make hangers for individual tools and every time she went to the shed she got a little rush of pleasure from her own orderliness. The sign Benny made would hang on the house's west side, facing the entrance to the bay.

Afternoon plan in place, she was ready to go paint. The calypso orchids she'd come upon last year would be in radiant bloom right about now. A fine-point pencil and the small notebook for flower paintings sat in a zip-lock bag on her desk. If she could find any orchids, with their delicate pinkish-purple petals, she would draw them, then return to the floathouse and lay on the colours later. She had her eye out for a patch of single delight or goblin flowers as well.

O happy May, the month of flowers.

It might be silly, but the tender wild blooms of May spoke to the meaning of life for her, which she was not much given to musing about. Generally Kit defined herself by what she did, rather than by what moved her.

Anticipating a happy hour of sketching the orchids she was sure to find in the dappled forest glade, Kit climbed back into *Merbaby* and headed for the shore, a few quick strokes along from her floathouse.

An hour later, she yarded the small skiff back up onto the lower deck and turned it upside down. Better than bailing it out every time it rained. She heard the motor before she saw Benny's boat, *Thunder Chieftain*, turn into the bay.

She reached up for the bowline as the fishboat slid alongside her dock.

"Benny, hi!" she said, as he exited the wheelhouse. "I'm so excited to see the sign, thank you so much for making it!"

"Hey, hey, it's just a little sign, no big deal, Kit. It's great to have a project to do once in a while. Kinda slow, ya know, not much social life these days. Not like the old days when we partied hard and there was always something going on."

"Oh, I know," said Kit. "Didn't we used to have fun at the bingo fundraisers for the school, the cake walks and going to Scott's house and playing the adjective game?"

"We-elll, my fun was kinda more rambunctious than that, I have to admit. So many guys here from the logging camps, all crazy drinkers. I remember one guy, he'd get so drunk at every party the other guys took turns being his minder so he wouldn't get too aggressive with the single ladies."

"Must have been a tough world for the women."

Benny agreed. "I guess that's true, the place was hard on them. But it wasn't always the men's fault. Some of the wives...! Whoo-ee, a man could get himself into a lot of trouble without even looking." He let out a long whistle and rolled his eyes.

Kit gazed at him steadily and said, "Okay...so, um...let's see my sign."

The sign, four feet long by two feet wide, was made of sanded cedar, image and words carved in relief, painted and varnished. Kit gasped when Benny held it up.

"Whad'ya think?"

"Omigod! I love it, Benny, I just love it!"

A willowy mermaid with flowing hair reclined across the top half and below her graceful form, curving letters scrolled out the words ~Mermaid Sea Cave~.

With a pleased smile Benny handed her the sign. "I'll get the hammer and the hanging chain."

"I've got one right here, Benny. We don't need the hanging chain."

"See here, Kit. I made up two pieces of chain with a hook on each end and we can attach them at the corners to hang it. Let's take a look at your eaves, should be somewhere we can hook it up."

He walked across the front deck, gazed up at the eaves, searching for just the right spot. "Don't want it banging around in the wind," he muttered.

"I've already figured out where I want it to go," said Kit. "Right here, on the wood shed, it faces out so it can be seen and we can screw it down to the siding. I've got everything ready. Do I need to put any more varnish on it?"

"Nope, it's all done."

Annoyed at her resistance to his plans at first, he softened when she said again, "It's so beautiful, Benny. I love it. Bet you're ready for lunch right about now. Want to eat first then get it up?"

Benny leered at her but let his expression morph into a hearty grin as he caught her eye. "Sure, sure, Kit. You got it. I could do with some lunch all right, thanks. Then we'll put the dang thing right where you want it."

He just couldn't resist.

Four

ong, tall and blond, Staff Sergeant Margaret Morris left her little house up the hill in Alert Bay and locked it behind her. As regional commander of the RCMP's North Island Division, she was neatly decked out in her freshly laundered uniform.

She liked this view from above the bay and always paused a moment to enjoy it. Her hazel eyes glowed bluish this bright morning. The color changed with the influence of the sky, her clothing, and her mood. Those eyes sat, large and intelligent, over sharp cheekbones. Her slightly long nose and wide narrow mouth expressed the very essence of a smart, intense, tenacious person. A good cop. You could read her like a book. At least you might think you could.

What you couldn't see was the deep wound in need of healing, unless you got to know her. And that was the hard part.

It was 6:30 a.m. and the sun was not yet risen over the hill behind her. Dew quivered on every leaf. Each branch and twig shimmered in the faint breeze dancing across the narrow strip of Broughton Strait from the Nimpkish River valley, and up the slope to ruffle her hair. Margaret sniffed the wind, redolent with the tang of low tide and wood smoke from houses downslope. She wheeled her new blue bicycle out of the shed and swung into the saddle. A good day for a bike ride. She was not unhappy as she rode down the hill toward the Seine Boat Inn and walked the bike into the flower-garlanded entryway where Colin, the inn's owner, let her leave it.

Margaret ambled down the ramp to the public dock beside the ferry terminal and stepped onto the RCMP's BWT—Basic Water Transport— as it is known in the force. She called it 'the boat,' but it did have a name as well as the official number, 17-G-1. She checked the fuel supply and fired up both motors of *Sea Wolf* before she untied the lines. Proceeding alongside the fingers, Margaret's quick glance inspected the vessels she passed. One by one, she catalogued the condition and circumstance— whether someone was on board or not, where a plume of smoke emanated from a woodstove or exhaust from a stack. Who was there and who was not.

Herbie Nelson's kid Robbie lay on his belly by his father's boat dreaming over the side at the fishing line and lure resting on the sea floor. Herbie was probably asleep in the bunk but his six-year-old lived to fish. Margaret thought fondly of the kids from the First Nations school, and especially of Robbie, whose entry had won the contest to name the cop boat.

Once out of the harbour she pushed the throttle forward and, in seconds, the twin 200's surge of power put the boat up on the step. She patted the console.

"Attagirl," she said, enjoying the small craft's power. Even though she was ticketed with 350–3,000 ton designation she still preferred to run this 28-foot Zodiac. It responded to the slightest touch on the steering wheel and rose elegantly to the challenge of wave, tide and current. A sigh billowed up from her belly...going to work. Thank goodness it had been quiet the last couple months, or at least somewhat. Running the Serious Crime Unit in Prince George the last three years had taxed her spirit.

She'd always wanted to be a cop, one of the good guys—like her dad. She had managed to build a tough enough carapace to withstand being stained by years of interaction with the most calloused beings on the planet. But one day she'd cracked—had just caved in. Couldn't pull the trigger to save one of her team. She'd been paralyzed when action was most needed.

Once again, shame and embarrassment swept over her as she angled *Sea Wolf* into the ferry wake. *God, will you never get over it? You should be happy to still have a job, live in this beautiful country and run around in a boat, doing good.* Aloud, she told herself, "Margaret, you're still doing good."

Firmly switching gears, she reviewed her activities for the day. Look at the toxicology reports on the woman brought in to Port McNeill Hospital who had died Friday night. Talk to the doctor on call who confirmed her death. Somebody else had died, too. Right—a man from Fort Rupert. She was going to Port Hardy anyway to attend the Rotary Club Thursday lunch; she'd talk to the sergeant in the Port Hardy detachment and go from there. A little twinge of anxiety bubbled in the recesses of her intuition. Her spidey sense was always on alert and it tingled when she thought about those two deaths.

Margaret docked the boat in Port McNeill Harbour, secured it to the huge railing on the concrete loading dock. She grabbed her case and walked up the pedestrian ramp to her car. It was a short drive up the main drag to the detachment office. She parked, locked up and pushed open the station door.

Quiet reigned in the office, except for the steady rhythm of soft keyboard clicks as Erika Mayfield, the steno, typed up the previous day's reports. Fingers stilled, she smiled cheerfully. "Goodness Margaret, you look pretty this morning. Nice crossing?"

"Thank you!" Surprised, Margaret got a little buzz. You don't get many compliments when you're a forty-two-year-old female cop. She often felt invisible as a person and as a woman—just a faceless uniform.

"Yes, it was beautiful. Good for the soul."

"Well, you need that, don't you? I would never live anywhere else on this planet than right here on the north island." Erika handed Margaret a paper. "This came across the desk, a fisherman up in Port Hardy Hospital. They think he overdosed on something, but he's alive."

Margaret's little bubble let off a wisp of steam. Another thing on the must-do list, and maybe a connection? A year ago, she remembered, the local newspaper reported a Campbell River man had been found dead of a suspected fentanyl overdose in the washroom at the small craft harbour there, but the tox report had been inconclusive. She shrugged off her jacket onto a chair and reached for the paper.

"Thanks Erika. I've got some phone calls to make and then gotta run up to Hardy. They invited me to the Rotary Lunch this week. I'm supposed to give a progress report on what's being put in place to deal with liaising between the RCMP and the Tribal Police. What a topic, way too big and convoluted to even think about. Hurts my brain." She flung a dramatic hand up to her forehead.

"What will you tell them?"

"I don't know," was her despondent reply. "I'll think of something...I hope."

Margaret hung up her jacket and entered the office. What *will* she tell them? That liaising as a *thing* was unrealistic? That there were too many agendas and too many tribal groups jockeying for prestige, position and power? That the area was way too huge and no amount of money or talk would address the past or aid the future? That the hopeful objectives were getting left in the dust? That no matter how well-meaning everyone was, from the RCMP, the government of Canada, the leaders of the different bands, no recompense could ever erase the wounds of the past? That the two peoples would never ever reconcile, forgive, accept or work in harmony with each other? *Okay, stop.*

Sighing, she channelled her grade five teacher, Mrs. Rhodes, and said firmly, "You are going to have to do better than that, Staff Sergeant Morris. To work."

Plonked herself down and opened the computer.

Margaret went down to the corner café and grabbed a coffee to go. She leaned forward to pay but swung around with a snarl when she felt a hand slide down her hip. Tim Connolly, ex-lover and erstwhile friend, grinned at her with his charming smile and flirtatious eyes. Acting like nothing had ever happened. Like he hadn't broken her heart when he dumped her for his new girlfriend. Acting like they still had some kind of relationship.

"Margaret! Great to see you! How're you doing?"

"Tim. Hi. I'd prefer it if you said hello to my face, not my ass."

He had no right to touch her, especially with such familiarity. The way he'd dumped her—not to mention the simple fact that he had—still burned in her heart like a hot coal. He should have told her to her face he'd met someone else. The very least he could have done was phone. So cruel, when she was all dressed up and ready for their date, to send a text message with the bare minimum—*So sorry Maggie, I can't see you anymore, I've met someone else.*

Nice.

But still he had the power to soften her anger. In less than a minute he'd coaxed her into having dinner with him that evening. Although she'd promised herself she wouldn't ever speak to him again, and despite an early meeting the next day, she gave in and accepted his invitation. Driving to Port Hardy she wondered why he even wanted to. And why did she accept after the way he'd treated her? Margaret rationalized that he was now in the 'old friend' category.

Hmm. Maybe he'd have something interesting to share about what's going on in DFO, or some tidbit of coastal gossip. They'd always had lots to talk about and she'd valued his 'eye on the coast' and insight into a variety of issues. Pulling into the restaurant parking lot she resolutely put him out of her mind.

The Rotary Club lunch was about what she'd figured—many well-meaning people wrestling with seemingly insurmountable social and economic difficulties. The town's mayor and the woman who owned a combination coffee shop, bookstore and art gallery both had some thoughtful suggestions. She did her best to sound optimistic as they discussed RCMP and community initiatives aimed at bridging the gap between the First Nations and non–First Nations communities.

When the meeting ended Margaret headed for the Port Hardy Hospital and asked the admitting clerk where to find the fisherman who'd overdosed, and if the attending doctor was on duty. Of course she wasn't. Margaret made a note to follow up.

"I'd like to see him anyway, if he's able," she said to the clerk. "Do you have a phone number for Doctor," checked her notes, "...Margulies?"

The clerk pulled up the file and gave her the doctor's number. "She's an intern, Officer. And the fisherman's name is Frank Hamilton. It's Room 6, down the hall on the left."

"Thank you," said Margaret and headed down the brightly lit hallway. She had no expectation of cooperation but was taken aback when she knocked lightly on the half-open door and peeked around it. A round, bald head over a weathered, red face and hot eyes burning with...fear? His rough voice assaulted her ears with bitter indignation.

"What the hell do you want? What's a cop doing coming in here? I know my rights! I don't have to talk to you. Fug d'ya want? Get out! Get out!"

Margaret looked at the burly man in the bed as if she hadn't registered his outburst. She'd encountered lots of guys like him in her job, and a few women, too. A calm, non-confrontational demeanour was frequently disarming to fearful or angry people.

In her most warm and compassionate voice she said, "Please don't be upset, Mr. Hamilton. You absolutely don't have to speak with me. I'm Staff Sergeant Margaret Morris. I heard you'd been brought in and nearly died, possibly of an overdose. I'd like to do what I can to help you and prevent this from happening to others. I'd appreciate it if you'd spare me a few minutes."

The scorch of the man's eyes was quickly shuttered by lowered lids. "I'm perfectly fine," he muttered.

"May I sit down?" Appearing hesitant, Margaret stepped inside the room and looked around for a chair.

"Oh, go ahead if you must. I guess I'm lucky I didn't die."

"So Frank, may I call you Frank?"

At his nod, she carried on. "I'm sure you'll understand that we're very interested in the source of the drugs you took. I'm so concerned about the fentanyl that's showing up these days. You're not the first who's ended up in the hospital in the last week or two and there's one person who didn't make it. You know, it always seemed like a pretty safe place up here in the north island but now I'm starting to not have that 'safe' feeling, y'know what I mean?"

Frank Hamilton nodded vigorously and then caught himself. He wasn't going to be charmed by the cop no matter how good she was at sweet talking people.

"I guess so," he muttered. "I'm not much of a druggie. Just, you know, it was a bit of a party and a guy offered me a line or two of cocaine. So...I did it, that's all. Then it got bad and somebody called the ambulance."

"So who you were with?"

Frank hesitated, "Just some guys we met."

"In the harbour or a bar? Who had the coke?"

"I told ya, some guys we were shooting pool with."

"You and who? Who's we?"

"Just fishermen, just guys. Nobody!"

Margaret sat back in her chair. "You know, Frank, this is kind of serious. I bet you didn't think you would almost die from snorting a line of coke. No big deal, right?"

Frank worked his jaw back and forth a few times as if he was holding on to something he wanted to spit out. Margaret waited patiently and then took out her card, handed it to the fisherman. He didn't reach for it so she laid it on the bedside table.

"What are you fishing, Frank? Is being in the hospital going to be a problem?"

"Nah, the skipper can do without me for a day or two. I'll be back sorting bugs in no time. He's got a guy who can fill in until I get back. Be soon, anyway, I'm okay."

"Ah, prawns."

"Ayuh."

"What boat're you on?"

"I been on most of them. *White Bird* right now but I got another boat lined up in a couple weeks when it slows down."

"You take my card, okay? Keep it, Frank. If you decide you have something more you can share with me, I'll take your call, anytime of the day or night."

Frank raised his eyes to her. "Really? You that worried about an old fisherman?"

"Ayuh." She copied his intonation, gazing straight into his eyes, "Yes. I am worried about an old fisherman."

All the way back to Port McNeill, Margaret gnawed at the problem, trying to make sense of what she'd gleaned from her short conversation with the 'old' fisherman. As she parked at the Haidaway Restaurant, she finally registered the exhaustion that had set in as she drove. Heavy head weighing down her shoulders, she slumped in the seat, then stretched and arched her back. Maybe she should tell Tim she'd take a rain check, go home and get some sleep. One more breath as she considered that obviously ridiculous idea. She puffed out a little snort—*like that's going to happen*—and opened the car door.

Of course, when she entered the restaurant and looked around, Tim wasn't even there. Typical, she thought ruefully, adding more heat to her ire. Same old, same old. But as the hostess escorted her to a window table he rushed in, apologizing repeatedly.

"Sorry, sorry, Margaret, I'm not late am I?"

He zipped ahead to pull out a chair for her and swept his arm to indicate she should sit. As she did he said to the hostess, "Please bring us a bottle of Sauvignon Blanc if you have one."

"We do," she answered brightly. "Your server will bring it right away, with your menus. We hope you enjoy your dinner."

Tim smiled at her and she smiled right back, holding the smile as she looked at Margaret. Wryly acknowledging the hostess's professionalism, it occurred to Margaret how few women had ever looked at her when she was with Tim. He was tall and slim with smooth muscles close to the bone. A neatly trimmed dark gold beard and mustache surrounded his well-shaped lips. So good-looking, she thought with resentment. It isn't fair.

Tim was charming and attentive to women, had always been a 'chick magnet.' To be fair, the recipient of his attentiveness was unfailingly warmed by contact with him, no matter how brief. He brought his entire being to the conversation and was never distracted. He never reacted to his cellphone, and wouldn't turn his head if someone else butted in. He listened to the end when she was telling him something and didn't leap in with a presupposed assumption—a quality she admired. She often wondered how he'd picked up such good listening skills and once had asked him.

"Girls liked it, they liked me when I did it, made it easier to... you know..."

"Get in their pants?"

He'd blushed and looked away, "Kind of. Yah, I guess," he confessed. "But then I discovered girls were pretty interesting. Like you, for instance."

And with this, had won her heart.

Now, as Margaret and Tim ate and talked, she felt so cared for. His blue eyes caressed her with the intent focus she remembered so well. She was touched that he recalled what she liked to drink even as she struggled with knowing the alcohol would weaken her defences.

By the time their plates were empty they were caught up in the spell of what had drawn and kept them together in the first place—the mental stimulus of a good conversation, her work, his work, the community, fishing and so much else. Neither mentioned his relationship with Kit, the obvious elephant in the room. Eventually she told him about the woman from Sointula who had died and her concern that there was now fentanyl in the drugs on the north island. He nodded solemnly, agreeing that was definitely something to be concerned about these days.

"I'll let you know if I hear anything in my travels," he assured her. "It's so good to talk to you, Margaret, I've missed you a lot."

She felt the deepened intensity of his gaze as the waitress cleared their plates and left, dabbed her mouth with the white linen napkin and laid it on the table. She looked at her hand resting on the white cloth, it looked fragile and lonely. "Guess I can't lie, Tim, never could. I've missed you, too, but I've been working hard to move forward."

Tim leaned over, took her hand between his and spoke with heartfelt sincerity.

"I am so sorry about the way I broke up with you. It was cowardly, but I was afraid I wouldn't be able to do it if I came for our date. Kit just...I don't know, she really...she seemed like the girl for me when we met. It hit me like a ton of bricks, and I knew I couldn't keep seeing you and be with her. But I've missed you, truly. I'd like to come home with you tonight, if you'll let me."

Margaret was helpless in the face of her own longing. She has dreamed often and long of this moment. Warmed by the wine, melted by the heat of his focus on her and her own desire, she surrendered with barely a sigh. Even as she despised herself for being willing to take what she could get, and the tiny voice of reason bleated unheeded in the distance, she was nodding yes.

"Yes, let's go."

Five

im is dreaming. In his dream he is walking up a river. It's rough and wild and he can't see around the next turn. A bear jumps out of the bushes but ignores him.

"The bear is my friend," he narrates as he walks, "although it gives me a pretend growl to threaten me. I wish I was in my flat speedy riverboat, I wouldn't feel so vulnerable."

He's walking up the river and there's a dipper bobbing along underwater. It bobs up and then dips down. The dipper bobs and says, "What are you doing, fool, don't you know they are out to get you?"

Tim realized he was in the middle of a dream. He tried to wake himself up, and he did; he woke up.

But now he's in the bunk of his boat. How did he get here? Shouldn't he be with Margaret in her bed? The dream is still happening, he *is* in the bunk of his boat, but it belongs to a very rich man. Tim raises his hand in the half light from the porthole. It is green. "Am I dead and mouldering in a grave?"

Tim's inner narration continues. "Someone knocks on the door, it's a beautiful woman. I don't know her. She is stunningly gorgeous and she likes me, she slides into bed with me and I'm excited. If this is a dream, I don't want to wake up from it."

Another knock at the door and a man calls out, "Helen, come out of there right now," and she does.

The woman leaves him cold and alone, shivering in the bed. Outside the porthole it is not daylight, rather, a light from the dock shines yellow in the window. He looks at his hands again and they are red and hot, burning. He jumps from the bed and wearing shoes but nothing else, looks frantically about for some clothes. He is bending over, peering under the bunk when the stateroom door opens.

The same man's voice cries, "Wake up ya silly bugger, this ain't a hotel, ya know."

He does, Tim woke up—again, shocked by the man's voice. But again he was still in the dream. This time he is lying by the side of a road, there is a long hill and traffic streams by, blinding headlights flashing. His narrative continues—a strange voice-over like David Attenborough in the Blue Planet movies.

"Evidently I've found my clothes, but now I've got roller skates on my feet and I peer out at the traffic from the bushes by the side of the road. Lights from cars whiz by me at dizzying speed and I fall back gasping. It's all too fast and I remember the warmth of Helen, the woman who climbed into and out of bed."

Tim's body convulsed with pain and he couldn't stop it, he stretched and woke up—for real this time—outflung arms taut above his head. He breathed a sigh of relief. Except for the muscle cramp in his legs his body was flooded with energy and satisfaction, but the dream mystified him. He tried to make sense of the flickering scraps captured while he massaged his calves.

He didn't know anybody called Helen, had only the association from school of the beauteous Helen of Troy. And what about those crazy drivers, car lights flashing past at a dizzying rate as he fell back from the fast lane? He recalled the way his bare backside was exposed to the man who came into the cabin. What was up with *that*?

Tim's thoughts drifted toward coffee and a joint as the pain in his legs eased. He smelled coffee then and realized where he was—in Margaret's bed. It might be legal now but a joint was out of the question.

Already fully dressed and ready to go, she entered the room as he was pulling on his pants. He felt her reserve as she looked at him with raised eyebrows. He knew why. The inevitable question—what does this mean for us, if anything?

"Margaret...," he started, "thank you for a wonderful night."

"But?" she said, hand on hip, widening her eyes.

Tim looked down and pulled on his socks while she stood there, remembering in the dream he'd already had his shoes on when he rolled out of bed—so he could run faster?

"Well yes, but. So. Margaret, you know I care for you. I probably shouldn't have come here. You know I want to be with Kit... but she's...she's kind of slippery, hard to get ahold of."

"Kind of elusive and noncommittal, you mean?" said Margaret.

"Exactly, yes!" said Tim, relieved she understood.

"Okay, no biggie. Good luck with it." Margaret turned on her heel, left the room. She'd been through this once already and had relinquished all hope of a future for them. And a very small part of her, really small, truly, felt a little shot of glee that maybe there'd be some suffering in his future. Payback, so to speak.

A practical woman and a responsible cop, she had a lot on her mind and Tim hadn't had much to offer when she'd queried him about drugs in the Broughton. Even though he wasn't overt about his marijuana use she knew he toked up. From time to time she'd caught a whiff of it on his clothes or skin. No big deal. She'd hoped he would have maybe given her a little something to work into the annoyingly muddy mix.

For his part, Tim was a little nonplussed by Margaret's reaction. He'd felt guilty and defensive, ready to sweet talk her, but it had been she who had come to terms with reality the quickest; she who had walked, not him. He was equal parts relieved and affronted.

Six

Nine a.m. Kit pulled into Deacon Bay and idled her boat overtop the big beams of the cradle Back Eddy had let slide down the railroad track into the sea. Her boat floated beside the scaffold on the cradle. She secured the port side centre line to the main vertical post, and then tied the stern line more loosely to the back post.

Back Eddy yelled, "Ready?"

"Yup." Thumbs up. "Go ahead on 'er."

He fired up the putt motor and engaged the winch. The cradle jerked and slowly, slowly the winch reeled in the cable. *Mermaid Lady* settled firmly on the crossbeams as the cradle rose from the water. Like a leviathan it inched and rumbled its way up the track and under the roof of the boat shed. Back Eddy kept the motor running and the winch reeling in the cradle until it came to a halt at the top end of the track.

Kit carefully climbed over the gunwale onto the slippery wet cradle deck, walked to the bow of the boat, leaped down to ground level and grabbed the bowline. She tied it to the first crossbeam—just in case. No boat she'd ever put up here had slipped off, but securing the bowline ensured it never would.

Together, they undid the screws in the motor's lower unit and drained the used leg oil into a container. Back Eddy rubbed a smear of oil between thumb and forefinger. "Looks okay," he said. "Not cloudy with water."

Kit was relieved. She'd worried the older motor would need replacing sooner than she could afford it. She held the top screw ready in place while Back Eddy pumped new leg oil into the lower hole, then tightened up both screws when the pumped oil pressed out the top hole. That done, she slid off the deck and underneath the boat. She lowered herself to her belly and rolled around checking the transducer housing and assessing barnacle growth. Not too bad this time, the paint job could wait. She climbed out from under and checked that the deck drain plug was tightened up.

The last thing was to gather up the tools. Kit went to the stern, climbed up from the beach onto the cradle and over the side into her boat.

"Can you hand me the oil bin, Willy? I'll take care of it."

"Don't worry about it," he told Kit. "I'll throw it on the burn pile."

She watched him walk across the floor, dodging piles of lumber, coils of rope, a planer and other woodworking tools, then tilted her head back to look up at the gaping holes in the roof. Plywood patches had been nailed over gaps in the end wall. *It's so run down*, she thought sadly.

It didn't seem that long ago that she and her family had come to help a week after Back Eddy had begun building the boat shed. He'd finished putting up the arches that framed the building and one of the locals had offered them a place to stay if they'd come and help. Kit had been only ten but immediately felt embraced and welcomed into the community. She'd run up and down the scaffolding with bags of nails and bundles of shingles, laughing and chatting with new friends over the banging of hammers.

Thirty years later, all those neighbours were long gone and the boat shed was decrepit, long overdue for demolition, either by a big windstorm or human hand. Over the years this boat shed had seen a lot of vessels slide up and down its track. Some of the names were painted on scraps of wood and nailed up on the walls, a kind of record, albeit with more gaps than entries.

Back Eddy broke into her reverie as he climbed back over the side. "What's next?"

"Got to replace this fuel filter, then I'm done, I think." Kit placed the wrench around the bolt holding the filter and closed it tight. She put her back into turning the rusty bolt and the wrench slipped, slamming her knuckles against the housing.

"Bastard, asshole, pig-fucker!" she yelped.

Back Eddy cried out half a breath after, "Doody butt pee stinkpee, toddy oddy!"

In spite of the tears that sprang to her eyes Kit snorted a giggle, Back Eddy snickered and then both of them were cracking up.

"Oh my god, Willy, you kill me. Where do you come up with these? Is that supposed to be a swear?"

Tears running freely down her cheeks, she pulled a limp scrap of paper towel from her pocket to wipe them, but the laughter had taken the sting out of her bruised knuckles. She retrieved the wrench and went in to the wheelhouse for work gloves.

"Do you know what a pig-fucker is, Kit?" he asked, as she pulled on the gloves and reset the wrench around the nut.

"Um, aside from the obvious?"

"Well, when the old loggers had built a fore-and-aft road, they'd be ground-yarding or maybe they'd have a team of oxen pulling the logs out of the bush and there'd be a guy, usually a young feller, he'd be sittin' in a hollowed-out log—that was the 'pig'—bein' dragged along at the back of the turn. A pair of big tongs, like those I got in the museum, that's what held on to the pig and attached it to the logs. Those great big logs were lined up one after the other and they'd be hauled along by a cable on the winch of the steam donkey a mile down the road, close to the beach. Those big logs would bump each other along and if anything got hung up, any logs and such, he'd have to leap out of the pig, and get it back on track."

Kit considered this as the sudden release of the nut gave her leverage. "So, the guy sitting in the 'pig' is the 'pig-fucker'?"

"PF man, that's what they called him."

"Would he have a peavey or anything like that? What tools?"

"Yup, a peavey; had a great big hook on the end."

"Those guys must have worked so hard all the time. All that giant machinery they got now must have put so many men out of work."

Back Eddy nodded. "I heard thirty thousand more jobs in the forest lost in the last few years. Picture it, Kit. There wasn't a bay from here to Kingcome that didn't have a show goin' on, a gyppo family outfit with the whole nine yards: the wife, the kids, the relatives. Fellas coming and going, and lots of parties at the hall and picnics sometimes on Sundays. There'd be a couple boatloads of folks go over to that little spit in Deep Harbour—you know the one."

Kit interrupted him as she turned the bolt out of the hole and started on the next one. "Yup, straight in from the entrance off Fife? The one you call Happyland?"

Back Eddy handed Kit the can of WD-40. "Give 'er a squirt, maybe it'll loosen up them other bolts. Yah, that pretty white beach with the little island on the end of it, where I took you. So they'd have picnics there, all dressed up in their Sunday clothes."

"I can picture it. It's all so empty now. I run for miles, up Sutlej or Tribune or down Fife and there's no-one here anymore, except too many fish farms and logging shows with helicopters buzzing back and forth."

"Well, if you'd find a better boyfriend than that prawn checker guy, you could make some babies for the community."

"What's wrong with Tim? You don't think he'd be a good baby daddy?"

"Kit, you know the guy's a playboy, right? Even if you settle down with him, he'll dance you a pretty tune and break your heart." Back Eddy hesitated briefly then forged ahead. "I know you don't want to believe it, Kit, but I think he smokes a lot, maybe does other drugs."

"Oh, don't be ridiculous, Willy."

He opened his mouth to say more but she carried on.

"Anyway," she put down the wrench, "I'm thinking about breaking up with him. I don't want to hurt his feelings but I don't think I love him enough to have his babies. I'm getting long in the tooth to have anybody's babies, actually. You might have better luck trying to talk Hayley into finding a baby daddy."

"Ritchie is kind of sweet on her, maybe she'll get together with him. She's a pretty nice girl and lots of smarts."

"Might be why she doesn't have any kids so far, Willy! Y'ever think of that? It takes some attention to detail to make sure you don't have children before you want them. It's too damn easy to slip up, and honestly, men mostly don't take too much care. You have to do it all yourself."

"Glad I never had that problem. One woman and that was the one I married."

Both went quiet, thinking about Eva.

"Bless the woman, nobody ever made me laugh so hard. I sure miss her."

"Me too, Kit. Anyway, if you got this thing back on, let's get you back in the water."

Back Eddy and Kit climbed out of *Mermaid Lady* and onto the cradle. He headed to the winch while Kit got down between the crossbeams and untied the bowline. After throwing it onto the bow she made her way around to the stern and double-checked that the hull drain plugs were in and no tools were lying around on the crossbeams or the beach below. Back on board, she made sure the tie-up lines would release easily, and then shouted to Back Eddy.

"Let 'er go, Willy!"

"Okey dokey!" he shouted back and released the cable.

With a whoosh the cradle carrying her boat slid down the railroad track and hit the water with a splash. Kit whooped. With a grin and a wave she released the lines and the boat floated free. She lowered the engine leg, turned the key. The motor turned over with a quiet thrum...the good sound. She backed around, put the gearshift forward and headed out of the bay. Pushing the throttle further, the boat surged up on the step and into the scintillating glitter of a rippled sea.

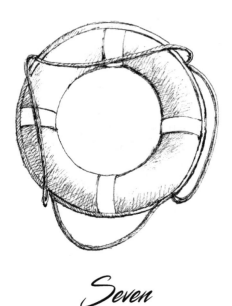

Seven

"Hooray, hooray, it's the first of May, outdoor playing begins today."

Kit hummed as she turned the bow of *Mermaid Lady* toward Cramer Pass and picked up speed. What a morning! What a day for a run to town. Good things would happen today, she just knew it.

It wasn't the first of May and the word in this particular ditty was not 'playing' but she didn't want to use it; wanted, somehow, to ennoble the happy desire running through her.

When Tim, her golden-haired lover returned…She pictured a soft mossy bed on a small secluded island, a blanket and a bottle of wine. A rising tide so the boat wouldn't go dry. So practical.

Although, when she examined her emotions about him, the surety of feeling wavered and dimmed, evaporating under the reflective scrutiny. She'd always imagined experiencing a great love, an exalting love, a love that was unreserved and true and wholehearted, and yet...Well. You've got to be, yup, practical. Evidence would indicate that there was no such thing as perfect love and you had to take the good with the bad, as they say. So Kit worked at it.

Tim was good company, adventurous and funny and a satisfying lover. Plus he was *here*, as in here on the coast, in her world, and there were far too few men who were her peers. He wanted too much, though. Or maybe she wasn't sure what it *was* that he wanted. He *said* he wants her to commit and even though she's forty, forty-one shortly, something held her back. Admittedly a subtle pressure, that age thing, but she was feeling it. He was mean sometimes, too. Oops, full stop, do not go there right now. *Just enjoy him...when I get to see him*, she thought wryly.

Which should be soon. He'd gone out for his annual pre-season update of the prawn boat checking protocols with the Prawn Sectoral Committee, along with a toothache that needed some dental work. She'd last heard from him almost a week ago and... *What's the delay? Doesn't he have work to do?*

Kit made the turn into Retreat Passage close to the rock at Islet Point, motored along the Fox Group, spared a quick glance to the right, into Grebe Cove where a pretty boat hung at anchor—one of those Monk-style classic boats with lots of wood to take care of and sleek lines. Pulled out the binoculars for a closer look. *Ooh, nice boat, whose is that?*

Three minutes later she passed Gilford Village, Gwayasdums to the Indigenous residents. Looked pretty quiet today and she wondered if Hayley Tucker, her young friend from Alert Bay, had started her job yet on the mussel testing boat.

Retreat Pass widened out and she noted a couple of vessels in places that seemed just wrong. Drawing closer to Green Rock she slowed so her wake wouldn't overwhelm the small crew boat aground on the rocks. Realized it was the Musgamagw Dzawada'enuxw Tribal Council boat, the one Hayley should be working on. Maybe she was on it right now. Or off, rather. Looked like two people on the rock, one standing knee deep in water at the stern and the other kneeling by the bow.

As Kit came in slow toward the rock, she got a closer look at the other boat bobbing nearby, a black Zodiac—a very nice black Zodiac with a brand new 60-horse Yamaha outboard. She slowly approached. The man in the boat turned to meet her. *Mermaid Lady* gently drifted alongside, he grabbed the rail and looped his line around it. Kit reversed gently, briefly, then put her boat out of gear and left the wheel, exited the cabin door.

Face to face with this new person (*a very handsome new person*), Kit observed him carefully. The man was in no way intimidated or shy under her scrutiny. He'd clearly been at sea for a while. Longish chestnut hair in need of a trim fell over black-rimmed Buddy Holly glasses. His curly reddish beard left room for a scatter of freckles across nose and cheekbones. Well-worn jeans and faded blue shirt with the cuffs cut off, no shoes.

Seriously? No shoes?

He reached up a friendly hand to shake, said, "Carson Maxwell, ex–New Yorker, world traveller, sailor and would-be artist. Pleased to meet you."

Kit grasped his warm hand for a brief moment, offered no details. "Kit Sampson, local. So what's the story here?"

She didn't reveal the small shock of delight she felt at the serendipity of his name, nor let on that his name and hers together made Kit Carson. Kit Carson—frontiersman, wilderness guide, one of her childhood heroes. Was that a sign? Probably not. She crushed the small spurt of pleasure the thought elicited.

"These guys slammed a deadhead and started taking on water, cracked a seam in the hull, damaged the prop or the shaft I think, I'm not sure. Lucky they were close to the rock, they paddled over and managed to set down on it. Tide's falling with a big current. They're from Gwayasdums." Carson pointed toward the village.

"Yah. I didn't hear them call Coast Guard...?" queried Kit.

50

"I don't think they had time, said they paddled like crazy, then I showed up. I was jigging out in the rockpile. I'm going to make the call now and see what help they can get. Said I'd run them up to the village but I think they're trying to get some rocks under the boat first to stabilize it."

"Jeez," said Kit. "Okay. Is there something I can do? I'm running over to McNeill right now, should be back in a couple hours. I can make it as speedy as possible."

Carson glanced at the beached boat, looking sad on the rocks. Both figures were now crouched down beside it. "I think they could use a jack."

"Okay, yah. I know where I can borrow one. Is Hayley on board?" asked Kit.

"Well, there *is* a girl, and a guy—maybe that's your Hayley?"

"I don't think there's any other girl working this job so I guess it's her. Tell them I'll be back and I'll radio the village my ETA so someone can meet me here."

"Sounds good. Might be me."

Kit untied his centre line from her rail and paused. "Where you headed? You on a long jaunt, a day trip or...?"

"I'm out here to paint, explore. I saw a terrific exhibition of Emily Carr work, paintings of the old villages here; made me want to come and experience it myself. I'm sort of on my way to Echo Bay."

"You paint watercolour?"

"Yeah. I'm all set up in my liveaboard so it's easy to poke around and anchor and paint. It's in Grebe Cove right now."

Kit liked his diffidence, his navy blue eyes, even his Buddy Holly glasses. If he's a painter as he said, maybe she could learn a thing or two.

"I'm up near Echo Bay, a little bay north of it before you get to Scott Cove. You could come by for coffee if you're around for a few days. My call sign is *Mermaid Lady*. I run freight and people around here but I'll be home the next few days. If you want to come over..."

Kit hesitated briefly, she was used to being friendly to everyone but this guy kind of threw her off stride. She continued when he nodded vigorously. "You could drop by after lunch one day; the whole damn neighbourhood doesn't have to know you're visiting me. Or morning, that's ok, too. I'm up early."

Carson's eyes brightened. "I'd be delighted to, thanks! See you sometime in the next few days. And I'll probably see you later when you come back with the jack," he added with a smile.

Carson pushed the Zodiac away from Kit's crew boat and she reversed with a swirl, waved at—yes, it was Hayley—and Joe with her, the regular guy on the boat, as she headed toward Queen Charlotte Strait. "I'll be back," she shouted out the window.

The strait unfolded ahead of her like a blue satin scarf, but the tide ran swift, and around Egeria Shoal it really boiled. Kit was sobered by the thought of the deadhead encounter. She did not want that for herself. Hayley and Joe could have been in so much more trouble if the weather had been foul or if they had been further from the rock. Lately, higher than usual high tides had brought big driftwood off the beaches and spring runoff had floated some recently fallen trees out of the Wakeman and Kingcome Inlets. She ran her boat fast and never took her eyes off the sea ahead.

When her mind began to wander back to Tim again, and this new guy, Carson, she sternly banished them both. *I do NOT have time for you guys right now.* They were persistent though, and as she slowed to three knots around the breakwater in to Port McNeill Harbour, she had to force herself to focus. *Control your slippery thoughts and land the boat, Skipper.*

Kit smoothly reversed *Mermaid Lady* into position alongside the dock below the covered walkway and leaned to wrap the stern line around the rail.

"Like she knows how to land a boat..."

A sun-browned hand took the centre line from the gunwale. Kit looked up into Tim's familiar face. Below a lock of golden hair, his blue eyes twinkled at her and his loose lazy grin sent a frisson of desire down her back.

"Hey, cowboy! I hoped you'd show up today! Good to see you. Why didn't you get ahold of me?"

Tim wrapped a clove hitch and a half hitch, the way she liked it tied. Leaping out of the boat she stretched up to his embrace. He stooped to wrap his arms tight and kissed her. Kit wiggled loose, uncomfortable at his overt affection. She noticed he hadn't replied to her question and decided not to press.

"Not here, okay? I've got plans for us out in the Burdwoods…"

Tim was miffed but recovered quickly. Her 'plans' were usually pretty exciting. "Okey dokey, Loretta Katherine, my darling, Lotty, Lori, Letty, let me, let me…" He chanted the love-names in her ear, already into the foreplay, pressing his pelvis against her.

"Jeez, Tim, I told you not to call me that. Any of those! Call me Kit."

Footsteps on the dock and a quiet throat clearing startled them out of the embrace and Kit pushed away from Tim. A young man stood quietly, looked away and then tentatively extended his hand. Slightly frizzy dark hair, pulled up into a knot at the top of his head, somehow made him look more masculine rather than less. Brown eyes that didn't hold a direct gaze but Kit put it down to innate bashfulness rather than evasiveness. The young man wore a dark red windbreaker over a black knit sweater and black jeans, fancy running shoes. Looked like going-to-town clothes.

The second handsome man I've met today, she thought. Suddenly they're everywhere.

"I'm Cole Harrison, your passenger? Are you Kit? Ms. Sampson?"

She smiled, hand out in return; noticed the weightlessness of the young man's grasp. "Yes, I'm Kit, nice to meet you. I'm confused, I've got Callum written down."

"Oh. Yeah, that's my other name, both names are mine. It's a long story." Lids lowered as his eyes slid away.

Kit paused for a beat. *Guess that's about it, all he's going to say.*

"This is Tim Connolly, once was a Fisheries officer, now he's the prawn checker guy for the season."

"Okay, nice to meet you." Tim and Cole shook.

"Hey, same here. You heading for Echo Bay?"

"Yeah."

"Okay," Kit cut in, "so, we have to keep the social niceties to a minimum right now. The tribal council mussel testing boat is laid up on Green Rock and I need to get a jack and get the hell out of here. Tim, could you run up to IGA and pick up the grocery order for Carol Ann, load your stuff—you are coming over?" Raised her eyebrows in question and continued at his nod.

"Cole, can you get your bags and stuff loaded, too? Put it in the cabin, maybe you can give Tim a hand with the groceries?"

Cole nodded. Kit carried on.

"Have you got a car here, at the dock? Can I borrow it? I'll be back quick, got to run up to Micron and borrow that jack."

Cole pulled out a set of car keys and pointed up to the parking lot, "The blue Dodge. I already got my gear out."

Kit looked at him approvingly as she stuffed the keys in her pocket. "Good man. Okay, see you both tout suite."

Kit ran up the dock. Tim and Cole followed more slowly, loaded Cole's gear then got in Tim's car and headed for the grocery store.

At Micron, Mike the owner readily obliged. He went in the back and returned with the jack. She thanked him. With the heavy tool held firm against her chest, she bolted out the door and promptly slammed into someone entering the shop.

"Oh my god, so sorry, I'm rushing too much, so sorry."

Kit knew immediately who she'd run into. Margaret Morris, head cop at the detachment. Ex-girlfriend of Tim. Knocked on her butt. Oops.

"I hope you're not high on speed or something," said Margaret caustically, as she picked herself up off the gravel.

"Margaret. Of course I'm not! I'm in a hurry, got to get back out there, there's a boat on Green Rock needs some help. I am SO sorry."

Margaret was chastened. "Okay, no worries. Sorry I was snotty. Not very professional."

Kit tried to pat some of the dust off Margaret's shoulder but let her hand fall at the police woman's look, which went from unyielding to thoughtful. Kit picked up the fallen jack, stood again with it in her arms.

"I don't usually do this but there's been some...troubling things in this area lately, Kit. Deaths. Could you...oh, I don't know."

She looked away. Kit's mouth opened into a round O, as she immediately comprehended Margaret's meaning. "Troubling... you mean like drug deaths? Like fentanyl?" she asked. She'd heard all about the massive increase in fentanyl overdoses, but had thought it restricted to big cities: Vancouver, Victoria. Except she had just heard that story about Trudy...were there more?

"Yes," said Margaret, now decisive. "Could you let me know if you, you know, hear anything?" She handed Kit her card. "Just call my cellphone."

"Okay, I will. I don't think anyone does any serious drugs out there but, if I get any...twinges, I'll call you."

"Thanks. It hasn't made the news yet, so maybe you could keep it to yourself? And it doesn't have to be serious drugs either."

"Okay, well, I will...um...will do. I guess."

Margaret turned, walked away waggling her fingers over her shoulder in a goodbye wave. Kit remembered she was on a mission. Heaving the jack onto the passenger seat she jumped in, turned the key and, throwing gravel as she accelerated, headed for the harbour. Halfway down the hill it occurred to her that Margaret hadn't gone back into Micron. Briefly she considered possible scenarios. Had the cop seen her and entered the shop for the sole purpose of asking her to keep an eye out for funny stuff in the Broughton? Seemed unlikely. *Why then?*

Tim was already at the dock when Kit pulled in to the harbour parking lot. He whipped open the door and seized the jack before she got out of the car. Cole opened the driver's side for her; she opened her mouth, about to instruct him on the parking scene at this harbour. He beat her to it. "No worries, Kit, I'm on it. I'll run the car over to the lot I got sorted out and park it."

Again she was impressed. This young one seemed a lot more capable and independent than most of the twenty-something's she encountered. She fired up the boat, and then it was all aboard for an agonizingly lengthy stop at the fuel dock. Finally *Mermaid Lady* with her crew of three departed the harbour, pedal to the metal after they turned out of the breakwater. The boat had a clean hull and a tuned-up motor and was eager to run.

A paying run for Kit, too, and Tim headed home with her. She whistled a cheerful tune. It was gratifying being the heroine of a story, helping out other mariners, especially neighbours, when there was trouble. The young fellow seemed like he should work out well for Woody. She already thought highly of him in spite of not knowing one thing about him. She looked back, caught Cole's eye and gestured for him to come up front.

"You get a better view here," she told him when he was close enough for conversation.

Cole, holding the back bar of each of the seats he passed to come up beside her, gazed out the windshield at the swiftly changing view. He volunteered nothing and, although Kit generally didn't pry, there was something mysterious about this young fellow. She was curious—nothing new about that.

"So, what brings you to Echo Bay? I didn't know Woody was looking to hire anyone, till he mentioned you were coming."

Cole turned to Kit, paused. "He wasn't that I know of. I worked as a guide on a whale-watching boat last summer with Stubbs Island Charters. People were always talking about Echo Bay."

"How'd you get that job? There's a ton of locals vying for those spots all the time."

Cole looked at her again, like he wasn't used to people pressing for his story, but he decided to give, part of it anyway.

"Easy to figure I'm not local, I guess," he said. "The north island has been...calling me, for a long time. I worked a few years in Vancouver as a lighting designer for movie sets. I loved it but I got tired of the city, so I came out here and went to all the boats and talked to people. I got lucky because the girl that was going to work at Stubbs got to go on a research project to Antarctica, and I was right there the day she came in to Telegraph Cove to tell them."

"So...?" prompted Kit.

"So, one day, I was on the boat and we couldn't find any whales that day, no orca I mean. We saw some humpbacks and watched them for an hour. Then the skipper radioed a guy called Back Eddy to see if we could bring the passengers out to his museum. Then after the museum we went around to Echo Bay to fuel up. Looked to me like the place could use some help. I could see a place like that needs a lot of work, all the time, so I found out who to talk to and I emailed him. I told him I can work hard, and do lots of different things and he said he liked that."

"Woody."

"Yeah, only I heard it was Woodward DesBrisay, so I don't know what to expect. Sounds kind of fancy."

"He's got a bum leg and he's recovering from hernia surgery so your arrival is well timed."

"Anytime might be well timed at the marina," commented Cole, with a wry grin.

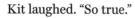

Kit laughed. "So true."

Cole's gestures and phrasing reminded her of someone but she couldn't quite place it. Perhaps the cadence of voice, or the slow way he spoke, or something in the tilt of his shoulders. Maybe it was the curly eyebrows. She filed it and put out what she called a mental APB on it. Usually those all-points bulletins popped something up pretty quickly.

Halfway across Queen Charlotte Strait she texted the Gwayasdums village office. *Mermaid Lady ETA Green Rock, ten/twelve minutes.*

Leah Harvey, the office manager texted back. *Hayley and Joe leaving with Carson for Green Rock in three minutes.*

One hundred and seventeen minutes from when they departed Green Rock, Kit returned, with the jack, hoping it would be useful and not too late.

Approaching the rock, she raised the prop somewhat, crept in slow. She noted Carson's Zodiac, resting lightly against a bed of popweed, and the encircling rocks. The mussel testing boat sat at a precarious lean. Carson met the bow of the boat, this time wearing boots.

Tim carried the jack along the gunwale up to the bow, knelt down and passed it to Carson, who grinned up at him, "Wow! That was fast, Kit must have been givin' 'er."

Startled by the stranger's familiarity (*How does he know Kit?*), Tim shifted as Carson quickly took the jack from him and turned to place it in Joe's outreaching hands. Right then the first little swell from a passing vessel bumped *Mermaid Lady* against the rock and Kit eased into reverse. Tim lost his balance, shot his hand out to the rail but missed. He fell forward and bashed his jaw instead.

"Shit! Ouch!"

Tim righted himself and then stood, turned. Firmly holding the rail on the cabin roof with one hand and cradling his chin with the other, he walked alongside the cabin to the stern deck and stormed in the door. Carson turned back to wave at the departing boat and called out, "Thanks Kit, see you later." She fluttered her hand out the window.

"What the hell, Kit! I could have fallen overboard!"

Tim was rattled but also annoyed, for no apparent reason. Kit looked over her shoulder as she backed off from Green Rock. She didn't respond immediately and Tim's ire heated up.

"Who is that guy? Do you know him? 'Fuck is going on?"

Kit looked at him coolly. She'd been pretty busy bringing the boat in gently and close enough to deliver the jack without banging it around too much or dumping Tim off the bow.

"New rule, Tim, you only get one swear on my boat. You better chill out, RFN. Sit down and take a breath."

She put the boat in gear, pushed the throttle half forward. *Mermaid Lady* sped up but not too much.

"Tim." She looked back at him. "So how bad did you get banged around when you slipped? Your jaw broken or anything? I'm truly sorry that happened, kind of circumstantial though, right? I didn't back up very fast, but I knew that swell was going to build. A crew boat went flying by and I tried to work it so you had enough time to pass the jack before I backed away from the rocks, but it was pretty tight timing."

Kit didn't wait for Tim's reply, she put the throttle full forward and the boat picked up speed as they passed Gwayasdums and roared up Retreat Passage. Tim sulked for another minute, but grudgingly respected her authority. Her vessel, her rules. He pressed his jaw back and forth a time or two, got up and walked forward to stand beside her at the helm.

"Prob'ly be okay. Not broken anyway. So who is that guy, what's he doing here? And why is he going to see you later?"

"His name is Carson, and...," here she hedged a bit, "see you later, that's just what people say."

"Carson who?" Tim interjected. "Carson from where?"

"Carson Maxwell, from New York."

"Huh. City boy."

"He seemed pretty competent to me."

"Oh, how friendly we are," sneered Tim.

Kit noted the tone of his voice, withheld her first response as she rounded Islet Point and headed up Cramer Pass. "So, when I was coming out, I saw the mussel testing boat on the rocks and another boat nearby, a black Zodiac. I went up to see what was what, which was that he was helping them, and I met him. That's it. You know the rest."

"Maybe he's a drug dealer," Tim speculated.

"He's not a drug dealer! Why would you think that? That's ridiculous!"

Kit was vehement, but honestly, how would she know? Maybe this was the kind of thing Margaret wanted her to watch out for.

"Well, we don't know, do we? Apparently there've been some fentanyl deaths in the north isl..." Tim's voice petered out, and Kit suddenly couldn't breathe. Her ears rang, a red mist materialized in front of her eyes as she instantly made the connection. Her pupils blazed black as she turned a laser gaze on Tim.

"For Chrissake, Kit, don't look at me like that!"

"I am kind of wondering how it is you happen to know this little piece of information, Tim."

He blustered, looked away as he muttered, "I hear things. Somebody mentioned it at the café."

"Somebody who? Somebody Margaret?"

"No, of course not. Well maybe. Yes, I ran into her in town and we had a coffee at the corner cafe."

Kit leapt on the about face. "When? When did you 'run into' her?" Taking both hands off the wheel, she made air quotes with her fingers, then grabbed back the wheel as the boat veered.

"Okay." She took a deep calming breath. "So maybe you ran into her, then what?"

"Then nothing, Kit. Don't go getting all paranoid."

"Liar! You slept with her, didn't you? When did you get into town, anyway? That's why you didn't call me. I bet you've been there for days. Bastard!" Kit yelled furiously.

She knew in her gut the truth of it. So angry she could barely see straight, her ears were ringing now and her head was about to explode.

"Kit, no! I did not sleep with her! I didn't!" Tim grabbed her arm and she shook him off. The boat veered wildly.

Cole jumped up out of his seat. If this was how people behaved out here, he was having none of it. "Hey, hey, Kit! Tim! Don't mean to, like, horn in, but you're freakin' me out here. You guys are getting kind of crazy."

Now Cole was in the line of Kit's laser beam eyes and she snarled at him, "You'd best sit down and shut up!"

Hands raised in appeasement he backed up to his seat, but Kit had heard him. Here they were at Echo Bay anyway. She barely remembered the run up Cramer Pass. Reducing speed to dead slow at the entrance to the bay, she sedately passed the big barge with the store on it, then the docks, pulled in and reversed the boat to a stop in front of Woody's lodge. Outwardly she looked calm, but inside boiled a volcanic stew of resentment, betrayal, rage, relief.

Relief?

Woody was on the dock with Carol Ann, both smiling wide. Kit grabbed Tim's bag and surged out of the cabin. With a visceral grunt she heaved it into the chuck. Woody and Carol Ann's faces went from happy greeting to horror as she went back in and grabbed Tim's jacket sleeve. Dragging at him, then pushing, she shoved him off her boat onto the dock.

"Bastard, bastard! Fuck you Tim!" she shrieked. "Get off my boat and never, ever speak to me again. You are so lucky I don't throw you in after your bloody baggage."

As quick as he was able with his bad leg, Woody hobbled over, grabbed the pike pole from its mount on Kit's boat, and with one sure thrust hooked the handle of the sinking bag. He swept it toward the edge of the dock, then clumsily knelt and scooped it up. He and Carol Ann stood there, mouths agape, as Tim turned and pushed Kit right back. She staggered as he shouted.

"You are one cold, mean bitch, always holding out for somebody better! No wonder I want to be with somebody else! Anybody will do, it doesn't have to be Margaret but at least she really wants me! Maybe I'd stick with you if you tried to make me feel good once in a while. You're always holding back and never do anything nice for me...You think you're so hot running your boat with your little black hat and your sexy little pouts."

"I DO NOT DO sexy little pouts, asshole, and if I did they wouldn't be aimed at you. Ever again."

As abruptly as her rage had flared, it fizzled out. Kit, worn out with her own histrionics and thoroughly embarrassed to be providing such a show—usually she was in the audience rather than being the main feature—deflated like a worn out wheelbarrow tire under a load of firewood. She put her hand on the doorway of the boat and leaned her head into her elbow for a long moment. No crying right now, get calm, breathe...

No one spoke.

Silently Cole slipped past her, bestowing an apologetically gentle pat on her shoulder as he passed and faced the two on the dock. "Hi. I'm Cole...um, Callum, er, Harrison," he stuttered. "I'm here to give you a hand for a while? Are you Woodward DesBrisay?"

Carol Ann quickly pulled herself together as Woody handed Tim his dripping bag.

"Callum? I thought it was Harrison."

"Yeah, Harrison, yeah."

"Well, whatever, Cole. Welcome to Woody's at Echo Bay. I'm Carol Ann Murchison, chief cook and bottle washer. Welcome."

Rattled by the fight between Kit and Tim—she'd never seen Kit lose it like that—she stumbled in her greeting to Cole, turned to Woody at a loss for words.

Woody, much more composed than Carol Ann, stepped up and extended Cole a warm welcome. "C'mon up, got your bag? Let's give Kit a minute to pull herself together, den we unload dose groceries. Folks around here jus' call me Woody Debris. It's an inside joke, to do wit' cleaning streams and what's good for de salmon. Also sort of my las' name but you'll hear about dat later."

"DesBrisay, right," Cole replied with a smile.

Woody led the way up the dock to the lodge. Carol Ann headed for the kitchen to heat up the coffee, thinking Kit for sure was going to need it, even if no one else did.

Woody told Cole, "I show you 'round after, dere's a good bunk for you and we'll get along jus' fine. I'll introduce you to the neighbours, not too many here. You already met half of dem. Usually nobody is so crazy."

"I heard there's only old guys around here."

"Pretty much true. Back Eddy is over to de other side; dere's a pathway from here to his museum. And Nathan across de bay, he used to be a tree planter, and a crab fisherman; he's in a float-house over dere. He might be over any minute; he smell dat coffee before we put de pot on. Coupla fishermen and some folks from Indian villages around here. Not many women. Kit and Carol Ann, an' dere's a young one and her husband who manage de research station, a couple up Tribune Channel run a summer resort, coupla artists, potters actually and a salmon fishing lodge. A girl from the village, Hayley, she's a friend of Kit's."

He clapped his hand on Cole's shoulder. "Dere's lots to do around here; it'll be good to have a young and energetic helper. T'anks for coming."

Cole wore a small grin. "I'm pretty handy," he said laconically.

Tim had left his liveaboard, a rebuilt BC Forestry boat named *Valiant Two*, tied in front of the brown house next to the lodge.

He packed his half-soaked bag over and threw it on the boat, then went back to *Mermaid Lady*, squatted down by the gunwale, said softly, "Kit, forgive me. Please forgive me. I want to come see you and talk. Kit, I love you. I don't want to be with Margaret or anyone, only you."

Kit could barely reply she was still so choked. And confused. Was she *that* upset, or surprised? She raised stony eyes, no longer obsidian, to Tim. "Maybe by Saturday I'll feel calmer. I'm going to need a few days to settle down, I think. Give me some space, then we'll talk."

Tim waited a few more seconds, wanted to say more, didn't know what. Finally, "Okay. I'll call you."

"Yah. Call me." She entered the cabin and quietly shut the door.

So this is Tuesday, what a bust, she thought. *I am going home and have a bath, drink some wine and pull the covers up over my head.* Out loud, "Right after I unload the grub."

Kit looked around for a helping hand but everyone had disappeared, thanks to the fireworks on their arrival. She cringed at her behaviour, but began to drag the boxes out the cabin door, piling them on the open stern. From inside the lodge Cole noticed her purposeful activity.

Carol Ann came in with the coffee pot and some cups. Cole turned to Woody, "I'll go give Kit a hand first, okay?"

"Yah, yah, do that. Jus' get the boxes in the door of the dining room dere, so the ravens don' steal all the meat; we'll get to them after. Tell her to come in for coffee before she goes home. If she wants."

"Yes, sir," said Cole. Woody and Carol Ann both laughed out loud. Cole looked up, the obvious question in his eyes, *What?*

"We say *okey dokey*, here," said Woody.

"And sometimes, *roger*." chimed in Carol Ann.

"Okey dokey, roger," repeated Cole. He tipped his cap with his forefinger and headed out smiling. In spite of being in the eye of Kit and Tim's storm he already loved it here so much he could hardly contain himself. Cole appraised the row of floathomes across the bay, the tall cliff behind them rising protectively. He stopped short and raised his hands to cup his mouth. Throat stretched, he shouted, "Echo, echo, I'm here. It's me, Cole."

He listened carefully and sure enough, half a second later, there it was, the echo of his call, *Cole, Cole, Cole*, ringing back faintly, and once more, even softer. Pleased, Cole jumped in Kit's boat and started slinging boxes onto the dock.

Across the bay, Nathan on his own deck heard the call. "It's me, Cole. It's me, Cole..." A little shiver travelled his back but he shrugged it off. His thought was how good it would be to have someone young in the bay and that it must be about time for coffee, now there were a few folks to share it with. Nathan grabbed his jacket and climbed into his rowing skiff, headed across the bay for Woody's.

Grateful for the cheerful face of the young man, Kit said, "I can see you're going to fit right in here, Cole. Woody needs somebody young and energetic, there's so much to do around this place."

"That's the second time I've heard that and I've only been here ten minutes! Must be true. Woody says come in for coffee if you want."

"Maybe. See how I feel in five minutes. I may need to crawl into a hole for a while."

Kit's anger had flashed explosively but just as quickly it had seeped away, leaving her with the scummy residue of her outburst. Like bats in a tower, thoughts and emotions flittered around in her brain and she ducked them all. *Not now.*

Heaving the last couple boxes up the steps to the lodge's patio deck, they got them up inside the dining room door and both went in for that coffee.

"I don't want to talk about it," she announced as she followed Cole through the door.

Woody was relieved. He didn't either. He liked it when things were calm and preferred to ignore friction and hope it would go away quickly. It usually did, near as he could make out. The fallout from this dust-up could have an impact on him. He got his smoke from Tim, a fact that he believed was not widely known, and he and Tim both wanted to keep it that way. Woody toked up in the morning usually, and at night to help him sleep when the pain from his leg heated up. A fight between Kit and Tim could have an impact but it would probably take a lot more than a fight for Tim to pack up and move out of the community. Not likely that happening while he had the prawn checking job.

Carol Ann, of course, had a different take on things. Being a woman—one of the very few in the neighbourhood—carried a responsibility to be there for the others, and listen and reflect. She took her role as senior female seriously.

"Kit honey, anytime you want to talk..."

"Not now anyway, Carol Ann, but thanks. I'd love a cup of that coffee though. Then I'm going home to pout for a week or two." She managed a rueful smile.

"Knock, knock," called out Nathan as he entered Woody's. He joined the others at the picnic table in the small kitchen, giving Carol Ann a little nudge with his hip as he slid onto the bench beside her. "Ah, Carol Ann, the coffee pot queen, purtiest gal I've ever seen."

"You're cheery," she commented happily.

"And when am I not?"

"True. I have to say, cheery is a good thing in a man, in anyone! Meet Cole over there. He's the young fellow Woody hired to give him a hand with stuff."

Nathan reached his big hand across the table and grabbed Cole's almost equally large hand. Bright blue eyes met brown and Nathan said, "Well, that's just jim dandy! Woody needs someone young and..."

Cole, Kit, and Carol Ann chorused as one: "...energetic around here."

"So what's new and exciting from the town that passes for a metropolis, Kit?" This from Nathan.

Before she drew breath to reply he turned to Cole with a wry grin, "We have to get our social excitement from people who go to town more often than I do. Nothin' much happens here anymore. Why in the old days...You're gonna hear some of Back Eddy's stories. Like the one about the guy who used to get so drunk he'd run from one end of the community hall to the other and dive forward and slam his head against the wall. Kind of crazy in them days, lots of drinking and carrying on."

Cole's eyes widened.

Nathan went to town as little as possible, about once a month at most, usually with Woody or Back Eddy, sometimes with Kit when she looked like she could use a paying passenger. She always refused to take his money but his insistence brooked no resistance.

"How 'bout I tell you about the mussel testing boat that comes down to Salmon Coast Field Station. They hit a deadhead near Green Rock and had to paddle to get to the rock to beach the boat. Hayley and Joe were on it and there was this guy..."

Kit was off on the story of her day, relaxing in the company and comfort of these old friends. Later she'd think about Tim and what, if anything, their fight meant to the relationship. She'd been putting off doing that thinking, clearly wouldn't be putting it off much longer.

An hour later Kit was feeling much better. She got up to head for home and Carol Ann invited her for dinner. "Back Eddy's coming over pretty quick to eat with us."

"Tim, too?"

"We didn't know he was coming today or I would've invited him..." she trailed off, remembering. "Anyway, no."

"Yah, no Carol Ann, thanks, but I've got a date with my bathtub and a glass of wine."

"Come and visit soon."

"Of course. See you soon, bye all." Smiles and waves all around as Kit left.

Suddenly Cole was in the spotlight as three pairs of eyes turned to him. Like vultures they pounced with equal parts concern and curiosity.

"So? Tell all." Carol Ann commanded.

Cole nearly spit his coffee. "Not my story," he muttered.

Eight

im was well liked by the other locals but he didn't have the same access to the companionship that anchored Kit to the community. Her straightforward warmth and the cheerful reliability with which she responded to people's freight and transportation needs had helped her forge strong bonds with everyone within a 70-mile radius. She'd been his conduit to that source of warmth. He and Woody did their bit of business very privately, and they were friendly, but not *friends*.

Tim believed that Kit would be turned off by knowing he was, in Margaret's terms, a drug dealer. He thought of it as helping people with what ailed them. Truth was Kit had never said word one about her attitude toward marijuana; somehow in his mind it went with the territory. One of the things that attracted him to her (*like Margaret*, he suddenly realized) was the strength of her character, the principled way she made choices. He revelled in the reflected glory of that light, imagining that people admired him, thought more highly of him because he was Kit's boyfriend—and had been Margaret's.

But it had been so frustrating. She'd totally resisted his pleas for commitment. He believed he wanted that but knew it would be hard to hide his business pursuits if they did move in together. He'd have to come clean, or maybe even quit. Tim thought about that as he let the motor warm up.

He wouldn't stay in Echo Bay tonight. The storm of emotion had unsettled him completely, following his encounter with Margaret, not to mention the toothache and his subsequent search for an available dentist. Too much trauma, plus he was going to have to hustle to catch up with his prawn checking duties. He untied and pulled away from the dock.

Tim shook off his dismal thoughts, rustled around in his kit for the baggie and rolled a joint as he entered the narrows to Shoal Harbour. Tonight he'd tie up at the mooring buoy that was securely anchored behind the island near the entrance. And before he hooked on to the anchor buoy he'd see if he could jig up a rock cod or two.

Hadn't eaten fish for a week; *that* was something he could rectify.

And tomorrow, he thought grimly, *there's someone I've got to see.*

Wednesday morning the sky glowed red with its warning to sailors. Tim put on the coffee and watched obese purple clouds shadow box each other across the sky. The VHF radio spouted the robotic female voice of the newly automated weathers with cautionary information. *Queen Charlotte Strait storm warning in effect. Wind southeast 30 to 40 knots increasing to southeast*

40 to 50 early this morning then diminishing to southeast 30 to 40 late this afternoon. Wind diminishing to southeast 20 to 30 early this evening and to southeast 10 to 20 Thursday morning. Rain beginning late overnight.

Tim sat for a while, relaxing, watching the sky. The boat swung gently on the mooring buoy. He'd planned to go see Benny today along with a couple other prawn boats, get started on the first check in of the season. Likely they wouldn't even be fishing though.

He keyed the mike on the VHF. *"Thunder Chieftain, Thunder Chieftain, Valiant Two."* No answer. Tried one more time, just to follow radio protocol, then called another boat.

"White Bird, White Bird, Valiant Two." No answer from Darrell either. In the ensuing silence he briefly debated trying Escobar on the *Helga Marin* but hung the mike back on the hook. Tim stretched, swigged the last mouthful of coffee and went back to his bunk. Might as well stay put today. He could find their locations anytime he wanted to; calling was simply a courtesy.

Fully expecting to easily fall into sleep, as was his habit, he was surprised to find himself still awake a half hour later, brain cycling like a washing machine through the events of the last few days. Rain drummed on the roof of the vessel as the wind rocked it harder. "Dammit." Tim heaved a sigh.

He'd been doing his best to avoid thinking and focus only on the job. Clearly, however, avoiding thinking was not going well. Tim wasn't used to being introspective. Mostly he was the kind of guy who took each day as it came, but even he could see that there were some days coming down the pike that were not going to be pleasant.

Heavy like a bullfrog, Kit sat in his mind, glaring at him. Behind the irate Kit was the passionate and humorous Kit, she who took him to deserted islands and rolled around with him on the mossy banks, she who was always interesting and lit up his mind with ideas. Kit with her wholehearted love of the coast, the people who inhabited it and her motivational 'get up and do it' attitude.

Was it a good sign that she was so mad when she concluded he'd slept with Margaret? Or was it just her pride? What about *his* pride, when he overreacted at the moment he handed that Carson character the jack and fell against the rail?

In a rare moment of insight Tim admitted he'd been jealous, not an emotion he was very familiar with. Women had always come to *him* and adored *him* and been broken-hearted when *he* left *them*. He'd mostly gotten off scot-free. He didn't much like this new feeling.

After he resolved to go to Kit and tell her of his newfound awareness, confident she'd understand and forgive him, his eyes finally closed. She liked it when he expressed his feelings to her and would appreciate his sincerity. At last he slept.

Hours later Tim woke up to the wind singing a rigging song. Four in the afternoon, he was rested and calm from his day of snoozing. The quillback he'd jigged up outside the entrance to the harbour, chased with a can of beer, made for a great dinner and afterwards he finished up some paperwork and got his thoughts in order. He was ready for whatever happened next with Kit.

But first, duty called. Got to get cracking checking some of those prawn fishers to make up for the time he'd lost. Be good to give Kit a few days to cool down, anyway.

Kit, for her part, having spent her Tuesday evening mostly in the bathtub drinking a bottle of wine, and writing in her journal until four in the morning, was similarly ready.

She didn't know when she'd see Tim but she did know what she'd tell him.

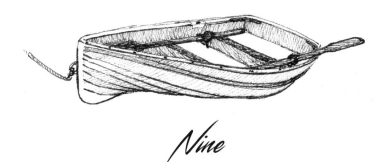

Nine

After three weeks of simmering heat, the humid southeast wind had carried a big dump of warm rain. *Inlet Transporter*, the fuel barge, arrived at Woody's Marina with an immense sling of wood and dropped it on the dock at 6:30 a.m. By mid-morning Woody and Cole had moved most of the lumber up to the land and re-stacked it. The mail plane wasn't due for a couple hours. Carol Ann had the mail box ready to go but open for any last minute outgoing letters.

In Woody's private kitchen a fresh pot of coffee sat ready to pour, along with hot chocolate for Back Eddy. Reliable as the tide, Nathan was on his way, having smelled the strong coffee all the way across the bay. Piles of dripping rain gear hung in green wings over the clothesline above the stove. Steam rose gently, fogging up all the windows as the wet bodies settled in at the picnic table to warm up.

Back Eddy leaned forward in his chair, cupped his hot chocolate in his meaty fingers. "Well, Woody, how goes the shed up the hill? Got everything you need for it now?"

"Sure do. And I got a pretty good worker here this time, too."

"Yah, it's hard to get good help, especially when it's a city boy." Back Eddy took a friendly poke at Cole.

"Don't you get ragging on Cole, I'm telling you. I know you t'ink the girls are the best workers and like dem for deckhands and help them out and all, but dis young fella is a good 'un and I don' want anyone to give him a hard time and drive him away."

"Okay, okay, Woody, relax. So, Cole, how'd ya get to be a good enough carpenter to impress Woody here?"

So far, Cole hadn't turned out to be much of a talker. The men sat silent, curious to see what, if anything, he'd tell them about himself. He hesitated but they waited. Finally he figured he'd better spit it out.

"I'm adopted," he said. "I was lucky, though, I had good parents and they loved me, still do. But I got itchy to find out, you know, my roots and all that. When I was a kid my dad, he's a carpenter; he always took me to work with him, to carry tools and stuff. I started with my own little tool belt, they gave it to me when I was ten. I followed my dad around everywhere and did what he did, pretty much. After I graduated I worked as a lighting designer for movie companies in Vancouver. Did a lot of carpentry on that job."

"Huh. Well you're pretty good at it, alright. But why the heck did you come here when you could be working in a dozen places paying a whole lot more?" inquired Nathan. Maybe too many questions but Cole seemed to be opening up a little and they all wanted to crack open the door a bit wider.

"It took me years, and my parents even helped, but only last year I found out my birth name was Callum. My birth mom was seventeen, her name was Jeannette Callum, and she died delivering me in Vancouver, at Grace Hospital. I think she'd been living in the Downtown Eastside. And I think she was Indian, Indigenous I mean."

The door opened, wide.

"Knock, knock, hey. Possible for a man to get a cup of coffee or a tankful of fuel, whichever comes first?" Benny grinned around at the seated men. His face revealed a slight questioning at overhearing Cole's last remark. Nathan, though, he froze like a stunned rabbit and his ears began to buzz.

Carol Ann came in from the kitchen, "Hey Benny, what a morning! I'm so grateful for that rain! It'll fill up the dam and the water tank. Too early in the season to be running short of water. I'll bring you a cup of coffee, got one more in Woody's potful here. I'll make another for you fellas. Then we'll get your fuel, if you're not in a rush?"

"Sure, sounds good," he replied.

Woody turned toward Benny. Both he and Back Eddy greeted the fisherman with the relaxed friendliness of men who've known each other a long time. "Have you met Cole, here, Benny? My new helper."

"Good to meet you, great, great." Benny reached across and shook the younger man's hand. Nathan said nothing as he regarded Cole. Carol Ann watched Nathan, wondered what was up with him. For a heartbeat or two no one said a word.

Woody broke the silence, started on a story. He wasn't sure what had just happened but he could feel it. He deliberately exaggerated his Quebecois accent, garbling his English even more, to lighten the sudden shift in mood.

"Somet'ing interesting dat be, alright. To be finding who you are from. Twenty year ago a man come here and he tell me dat I am a member of his family. So I say to him, 'Who is dis family you say I am from?' Den he tell me about Merrill DesBrisay, dis guy wit' a very long family tree. 'E come here from Nova Scotia at the turn of the century and he buy a cannery, Hidden Inlet Cannery. But dis cannery ends up on de Alaska side of de boundary line when dey finally decide where it goes." He paused, swallowed a mouthful of coffee.

"But dere was another cannery nearby, so he sell de first cannery and buys de second cannery, Wales Island Cannery, in 1910, because now it's in Canada. It's been decided. Dis man tells me—he say to me, 'I am your great-uncle' and he stay for two days telling me all about dat DesBrisay family, stuff I know nothing.

"'E give me some labels from the salmon, 'Lacrosse' brand was de name, 50,000 cases of salmon dey put up in 1924."

Back Eddy said, "That's one hell of a lot of salmon. Must have been pretty good for a few more years. I started fishing in 1943, out in my little rowboat. I had a friend, Sam Charlie, he lived in the summer village at White Beach Pass. He took me out in his beautiful dugout canoe when I was five years old. It was all carved with thunderbird and salmon designs, I still remember it. He showed me where the kelp patch was and how to tie the dugout to kelp, when the tide was running full flood. Sam wouldn't let me talk once we started fishing; he said it would scare the fish."

The stove popped and the floathouse creaked. The men sat quiet but for Benny's slurp of his coffee and satisfied sigh of pleasure. Back Eddy let more of his story surface. "Sam always admired his catch; me, too—the fish were so strong and beautiful. For so many years it seemed like they'd never stop coming. Sam told me if we upset the salmon spirits at a certain place the salmon would stop coming to that place."

He raised his eyes to the men around the table.

"I think we've upset the salmon in too many places."

Woody and Back Eddy's eyes met, both thinking of the innumerable hours spent on the community salmon enhancement project the two of them and other neighbours had committed to. For twenty years they'd planted salmon fry to enhance Scott Cove Creek and several other systems in the area. All these systems had been ruined by logging over a hundred years ago as the newcomers had taken out the easiest and largest timber, the trees of every watershed on the coast.

Nobody had put it together for a long time, that the largest and easiest timber was the product of the rotting flesh of millions of returning salmon. So much time and energy spent on it. Hard to swallow that their effort hadn't seemed to make much difference, just delayed the inevitable. Like reeling in a fish, Woody picked up the thread of his story.

"DesBrisay and Co. ran that cannery for fourteen years, den dey sell it in 1925 to Canadian Fishing Company. A crazy t'ing to sell the cannery when it's doing so good and making lots of money. Canadian Fishing Company, dey make de final pack—26,000 cases in 1949, a few years after de war. It was de very last cannery to close in the Nass River–Portland Canal area. Dey had eleven canneries. Eleven," he repeated.

Woody got up and poked around in one of his desk drawers. "Here, look what he give me, it's a label for Lacrosse Brand. See dat?"

The label was in a clear plastic sleeve and showed artwork of typical lacrosse players of the day. Back Eddy reached for it and admired the label, it was in pristine shape. "I've got some nice cannery labels in the museum," he said, "but I got to admit this looks as good as new. Pretty nice." He handed the label to Cole who took a look and passed it over to Nathan.

Somehow by tacit agreement the conversation about Cole's heritage had been tabled. Back Eddy searched his memory to make another contribution.

"Funny thing happened to me the other day. I was out running around in Simoom and I'm moseying along the shore, checking things out, watching for bears or logs, whatever. I hear this buzzing and look around, can't see anything but it sounds like a faraway helicopter. So it gets louder and I look around and all over and the thing gets louder like it's right on top of me and finally I look up and there's a frigging tiny helicopter! I figured out right away it's a drone, but what the hell! Who has a drone out here and what the hell for? Anyway I lean under the bow and grab my little orange bin, you know, with the useless flash-light and throwing thing for getting someone back on board if they fall over. So I root around while this thing is humming overhead, I'm damn sure it's filming me, pissed me right off. I finally find my bin of flares and get the flare gun out and aim at the little bastard thing but before I can get off a shot, it zips away over the trees.

"Any of you guys got a drone?"

Silence. Benny's shoulders shake with an exaggerated shudder. "Can't do nothin' out here anymore 'thout someone hanging around with an eye in the sky. Shit."

Back Eddy rubbed his nose, gave his head a slow shake. "Yah, well, I'm packin' my shotgun. Next time I see that thing it's going down. I'm gonna blow it out of the sky. I don't care who it belongs to, it's a damn invasion of privacy. It's bad enough with so many helicopters from the logging outfits or government up there all the time. Ya can't get a minute of peace in the wilderness anymore."

"No argument here," said Woody. Nathan nodded agreement. Made no difference to him, but Back Eddy was born in this country and was used to the peaceful solitude of his daily run. From Tribune to Sutlej Pass, sometimes he'd run right out to the edge of the strait, looking for stray logs to salvage.

Done with the drone story, Back Eddy moved on, pulled another tale from his endless supply.

"Here's a story for you, Woody, it's about your marina. We had a guy here once who built a bomb shelter. Bill Boyd was his name but everyone called him the 'Hindoo Prince' cause his hair was a big Afro. Tight black curls all over his head. I guess he was a Fiji Islander. He worked for my wife's father for a time on his logging show.

"Anyway, he builds this bomb shelter about 1968 out of 12-inch square timbers, right up the hill there behind where the hotel was. Had a toilet and running water and he put in enough food for a whole year. He was sure they were going to drop the big one and figured he could survive okay after the radiation drifted away."

The men sat soberly ruminating on the decades-old memories of the cold war and its distant but overwhelming threat. Benny broke the silence with a characteristic guffaw. "Haw, it wouldn't be that bad if you had a woman to warm your bed."

Carol Ann walked back in on the conversation packing a plate of cinnamon buns, fresh out of the oven. "That's all you ever got on your mind, isn't it Benny?" She slapped him lightly on the back of his head. He ducked the slap easily and grinned up at her.

"How 'bout you, Carol Ann? You are one big armful of woman…I don't have a bomb shelter but I got a real nice bunk in my boat."

"You get all those rude thoughts right out of your head, Benny, or I'll be putting rat poison in your cinnamon buns."

"You tell him, Carol Ann," said Nathan, glaring at the unrepentant fisherman. "Keep a civil tongue in your head, ya jerk."

"Oh ho," cried Benny, he wasn't intimidated. "What's cooking here?"

He flashed a salacious grin at Carol Ann who flushed hot pink and walked out the door, still carrying the plate of buns.

"Now see what ya done," said Back Eddy, disgusted. "Guess you won't be getting any of those. Us neither, thanks to you."

"Back to work for me," said Woody Debris, rising.

"And me." Cole followed Woody, scooping up his tool belt and buckling it around his hips as they walked out the door.

"Guess I got one or two things to attend to on my float." Nathan slid his long legs over the bench and he and Back Eddy followed the other men out the door. Benny remained alone in the precipitously vacated room, pushed back from the table. "Well, shit," he muttered. "What the hell, can't take a joke."

He departed Woody's dining table and poked his head in the kitchen. Carol Ann stood at the sink, hands deep in soapy dishwater scrubbing furiously on the baking dishes. Benny cleared his throat but Carol Ann beat him to it.

"Don't even talk to me," she snapped.

"What about my fuel?"

"You don't even deserve it. Why should I bother my little head about what you need?"

"C'mon, Carol Ann. Please?"

She flicked the soapy water off her hands, grabbed a towel to dry them and stomped past him.

Coming up behind Cole on the slippery wet deck outside, Nathan was at a loss for words. Briefly the deck occupied his attention, then, "D'you happen to be colour blind, son?" he asked abruptly.

Cole stopped short and Nathan bumped into him. "Why? I mean I am, but why would you ask that?"

The older man paused for a long moment while Cole waited impatiently, then said, "I might know someone who, is, ah...also colour blind. Maybe you're related."

Cole turned, his eyes sparked. "Really, Nathan? Who? Someone around here?"

Raindrops gathered on the older man's long eyebrows and dripped from his white hair, he remembered he was carrying his ball cap and slapped it on his head. "How 'bout you borrow Woody's skiff and come across the bay for dinner in a day or two?"

"You coming, Cole? Let's get to it," called Woody, now ten steps ahead. "The sooner we get this lumber done, the sooner we get out of this downpour."

"Coming, Woody, be right there." Cole turned back to Nathan. "Say when, I'll be there."

"Okay, good. I'll let you know real soon." He was going to have to go home and think about this for a while. In fact, he might even have to go and have a long overdue talk with his old friend Vera Harvey, down the pass at Gwayasdums.

Benny and Carol Ann were both out the door now, suited up in Helly Hansen rain gear. In spite of her wrath Carol Ann knew something was up. She addressed Nathan: "I'm going to pump some fuel for this bonehead. I don't know how I'm going to get him to keep a civil tongue. Just rude."

She glared at Benny, who looked chastened and slightly befuddled, too. Benny turned to Cole, staring hard at the young man, who squatted down to retie a bootlace. Cole felt his gaze. Lace in hand he looked up, met the fisherman's eyes.

"Young feller, you look like a good hard worker. Have you had any fun so far? Nothin' but work, work, am I right? Been out fishing around here yet?"

"No, not yet." Cole was polite. "Hoping to soon, though. Woody says he'll get a motor tuned up for me and put it on one of the skiffs on the sinky float over there."

"Ah, yah, maybe you'd like a mess of prawns or something? Or I could take you out fishing."

"Sure, Benny, that'd be great, thanks." He finished tying his bootlace and stood, "Gotta go. Woody's waiting for me." Offered a small salute with a big smile to Benny.

"Yup, yup, you bet, son."

Benny watched the boy—the young man—walk away, his youthful strength apparent in every gesture; the swing of his arms, the spring in his stride. He couldn't tear his eyes away from Cole.

Nathan bent his head toward Carol Ann. With his attention torn between his thoughts and her words, her tiny voice seemed to come from far away.

"Someone dropped off three boxes of books to the store the other day. You want to stay and go through them with me?" she repeated. "Looks like there might be a few good ones."

"Maybe later, Carol Ann. I've got...I've got a few things to do this afternoon, I better get at them. Don't worry; I'll help you sort them out. Maybe tomorrow, okay?"

She shot him a quizzical look. "I certainly am not worried, Nathan. See you whenever."

Men. Huh.

Carol Ann huffed down the long wet dock to the fuel pumps, two steps ahead of Benny all the way, clearly not amused. She pumped his gas and then stomped up the ramp to the store to ring up the sale, took his money and handed him the receipt.

At the counter he attempted an apology. She rebuffed him firmly. For once they were alone and she took the opportunity to confront him with his actions. "Benny," she said, "*what* is *wrong* with you? You can't keep on behaving like that. It is not funny, or pleasant. I have always been nice to you, but you're getting on my nerves. I've been trying to ignore those things you say. You've been good to me and helped me out a time or two, but you have to quit it. It must stop, do you hear me?"

"Loud and clear, Carol Ann, loud and clear. No more." Hand on chest, he solemnly swore, "Never again."

"Good. Now go away."

As she locked up the store she wondered if he was making fun of her. He seemed really out of it. All the men seemed out of it today. There was a weird energy disturbing the tranquil peace she'd grown used to. Maybe it was simply a case of one or two of them getting bushed. She knew from experience how contagious that could be. Too much time alone with too little human interaction, plus poor eating habits and too much coffee often caused visibly inappropriate behaviour. Out here it was called 'bushed' or 'cabin fever' and often it was hard to know how to help someone. One time an old fisherman had gotten scurvy and she'd made him a rich stew loaded with vegetables and beef; that had been an easy fix.

But Benny. Now that was a different sort of problem. The sort of guy he was had become a total dinosaur these days, thank goodness. None of the men she knew were as ill-mannered and overtly lewd as Benny. He didn't seem to get it. In fact he seemed to be getting worse.

Walking down the ramp from the deck, she caught sight of the back end of Nathan's old fishing boat disappearing out of the bay. He was definitely on some kind of mission and her curiosity knew no bounds. "You're certainly interested in that man's activities," she scolded herself. "A little too—no, quite a lot too—interested, my girl. Didn't you learn your lesson with Herb?"

Carol Ann was at a happy moment in her life. At Woody's Marina she had a good home in a beautiful part of the world, a steady job and a paycheck. She'd managed to avoid most of the afflictions of her peer group such as breast cancer, heart attack and surgeries of knee, hip or shoulder. She had no children—a mixed blessing—no grandchildren to take pleasure in but no aggravation, worry or disappointment there, either. At this stage of her life, interest in a man could only unsettle her hard won peace. Even the possibility of love—or, dare she think it, sex—would only upset her equilibrium. There was no upside.

Really?

Ten

Doramay trundled down Cramer Pass. It took the old motor a while to blow out the settled oil but eventually the black smoke pouring from the stack mellowed to a less alarming grey. The rain drumming on the roof thinned to a light patter and a weak sun peeped through the misted air. Sea and sky shimmered with silver luminosity.

For no reason at all, Nathan was suddenly flooded with well-being, was possibly even feeling...jaunty. Standing at the wheel he gave a little jig with his left foot, then a jog with his right. Might be some kick in the old rooster yet. Felt like some things were going to break wide open right now. He was up for it.

The one time in his life he hadn't pushed when he should have, he'd lost everything. As he steered his reliable old boat down the pass he resolved that was not going to happen this time. Pawing around through the box of tapes he found one of his old favourites, *Paradise by the Dashboard Light*. He cranked it up and vigorously bellowed along with Meatloaf, relishing the memory of being seventeen and barely dressed.

I oughta do this more often, he thought, slapping his thigh to the music as the village came into sight. He steered in to the dock, climbed out and looped the lines around the rail. Up the ramp he went, pausing for a good look at the old D'Sonoqua totem pole. This wasn't the same wild woman of the woods Emily Carr had painted but she had the same power to frighten the young ones. Nathan chuckled as he passed it and nodded hello to the demolition crew taking down the old mouldy houses. New houses were going up and people were moving in as fast as each one was completed.

At the village office, Leah greeted him with her cautious smile and soft voice. "Mr. Tolvanen, hi! Haven't seen you for so long, how are you doing?"

Nathan had taught the kids often over the years, when there was a school at Echo Bay and the kids from the village, along with the rest of the local kids, had attended. He missed those days, when the common goals of the two communities had bound them in a stable camaraderie. He'd played his guitar and taught them songs, helped them find their voices. He and the kids had written and produced plays for the Christmas and school year end celebrations; he'd nearly been brought to unmanly tears watching the kindergarten kids stand on the makeshift stage bravely uttering their lines.

"I'm doing well, Leah, thank you. You got a good job here." He looked around the brightly lit office, then back at the young woman and smiled. "Nice to see you grew up and stayed here, instead of running off to the big city. Guess you're not doing much about that acting career?" He raised his eyebrows.

Leah giggled. "Very funny, Mr. Tolvanen. You know I was never cut out for an acting career."

It was true. She had been a quiet little mouse afraid of her own shadow when she started school. He'd worked hard to help build her confidence. "You can call me Nathan now, I think, Leah. You're all grown up and I'm not your teacher anymore."

85

She looked down at the counter then back up. "Okay, I'll try, Mr. ...Nathan."

"Atta girl. So, I was thinking I'd like to see Vera, she around today?"

"Yes! Yes, she just got back from Yalis. Want me to phone her and tell her you want to come up?"

"Yah, that'd be great, thank you. Which is her house, has she got moved into a new one yet?"

Leah nodded as she phoned; the call only took a minute. She put down the phone and said, "Okay, she's got a golf cart up there, says she'll send her grandson, Harry, to come get you. Be four or five minutes. And yes, she was the first one to move in, says she's happy in the house but wishes they could have built communal homes like the old days in the longhouse her Granny told her about."

And an afterthought with a more open smile, "But she loves the washing machine."

Nathan laughed. "Yup, I can see that. I love my washing machine, too. Don't think I could handle having to wear my long johns until they stand up on their own, like in my tree-planting days. Anyway, thanks a lot, Leah, you take care now. I'm glad to see you doing well."

"Bye Mr. ...by Nathan. It's nice to see you again. You...it was fun learning songs with you at school. I always remember it."

Nathan was surprised. He remembered her as having a hard time expressing any kind of feelings, whether upset or joyousness. Her admission surprised and moved him. He turned away quickly, then back again. "Well, it was sure fun teaching you kids. I better go." He whipped out the door. *Anymore of this emotional stuff and I'm gonna bust out crying.*

Vera's grandson arrived in the golf cart, a surly fellow in his late teens. His rage sat right on the surface and it was a shock after the deep emotional chord struck in his interaction with Leah. Nathan climbed into the cart beside the young man and stuck out his hand, saying, "Nathan Tolvanen. I've known your grandmother almost sixty years."

The boy refused his hand, looked at it scornfully as if to say, *So what?*

Nathan sat back, calmly withdrawing the hand, said, "I appreciate the ride, thank you."

He didn't blame the boy. While they trundled up the road he reflected again on those years when all the kids from both the village and the Echo Bay community attended the school, how that had created ties between the two groups that—if the school were still standing and families with kids were still living in the community—might have continued to build understanding and mutual respect.

Vera was still the same regal character. She didn't beat around the bush being pleasant. Sitting straight-backed in an armchair draped with old woven goat hair blankets, she pierced him with her black eyes. "Ah," she said. "Nathan Tolvanen has come to visit. What will I be doing for you after all these years?"

"Vera, hello. The years sit lightly on you. Maybe you'd be good enough to talk with me and, ah, hear me out."

"Do you need me to stay, Ada?" asked Harry.

"No, no. You go see if your Auntie Lou needs help with that bed she wants to move."

"You sure?" Harry threw a suspicious look at Nathan.

She waved her hand imperiously. "There will be no harm to me from this man. Go." Snapped her attention back on Nathan, then relented. "I made tea before Leah called, would you like a cup?"

"That would be very nice, thank you, Vera."

Nathan was relieved. Worst-case scenario, Vera would have tossed him out on his ear, or not even let him make it as far as her doorstep. He returned her aloof formality with equanimity.

As the woman clattered cups and spoons onto a tray, he couldn't stop the memories of their youth—didn't even try—from surfacing. Unseeing, he looked out the window of Vera's new house while the scenes took form in his mind's eye. They'd been constant companions when young; friends since early childhood.

He'd been a lonely white boy with his parents assigned to teach school in a remote coastal village, and lucky for him Vera and her cousin, Annie Callum, had befriended him. They'd dug clams on the evening low tides, run around the islands in an old skiff with a nine-horse outboard motor in need of continual monkey-wrenching, whispered ghost stories to each other under the cedar canopy.

When they got to be teenagers they'd spent the long summer days drumming and playing music, drinking in secret and dancing all night. But the foundation of the friendship had cracked when he'd been so drawn to Annie, and they'd slipped away from Vera into the mossy undergrowth and made love until dawn lit the mountain with pink light. Those times Vera had slept alone in her blanket, trying not to imagine their murmured joy.

Vera had continued to hang out with Nathan and Annie even after their relationship had moved into that more intimate stage but she'd fought them mightily, trying to persuade her cousin that loving this white guy would only bring her a big hurt. She'd tried exploiting Nathan's honorableness in an attempt to convince him that he should let Annie alone and have a life with her own people. And she'd been right, hadn't she?

Even so they'd remained unconvinced. Their passion, conviction, and mutual desire had swept away every argument. They'd planned to marry when they turned nineteen, figured they'd be able to convince the elders that their love was real and mature, they weren't moon-eyed teenagers. And look what happened.

Well, what *had* happened? The truth was, Nathan didn't know.

Vera's soft step brought him back to the present as she returned with a carved cedar tea tray, set it down on the table beside her chair. She remembered how he liked his tea, assumed his taste hadn't changed. She had it right. He sipped the strong well-sugared tea appreciatively.

"Vera," he began. "I got to tell you first, I am sorry. I think you know this, and I learned the hard way. I was feckless."

"Feckless." Vera repeated the word without inflection.

"I just lived for...for me, for what I wanted, and when I got that tree-planting job at Head Bay out there by Tahsis, it was great, I'd finally found my calling. One job led to another and pretty soon five months passed, but I'd made good money. I wrote her, all the time I wrote her and she never wrote me back, not one word."

"And?"

"Well you know *and*, Vera. Don't 'And?' me. I came back here and she was gone and not one of you would tell me where she was or what was going on. So it couldn't have been any surprise why I never talked to you again. Someone, *you* Vera, you should have told me what happened to her. We were friends but I know you didn't think I was good enough for her. Maybe you were right, I don't know. But it wasn't up to you to decide or to manipulate our lives. She made me a better man."

Vera flipped up her hands, palms out, "Oh, and what affect did you have on her life?"

"I loved her! What do you think? I had two thousand dollars and a ring and every single one of you acted like I was...nothing, like I was nobody. So, it's time, Vera. I think you should tell me, I have a right to know. You obviously have an opinion, and you most certainly do know."

Nathan was pretty heated up by now. He'd buried his grief and the pain, his guilt and the unanswered questions, but it was welling up to the surface now; it wasn't staying submerged any longer.

He went on, "And now there's a young one, he showed up, says his name is Callum."

Vera contemplated Nathan, obviously making up her mind. "Tell me more. When did he arrive and when did he reveal this name to you?"

"Yah, well, just now, I mean a couple hours ago, at Woody's. He told us he's adopted, then he tells us his birth mother's name, Jeannette Callum. He came to work for Woody a week or two ago but we didn't know how he knew to come to Echo Bay or why he would do that. So today we're all sittin' around Woody's and he finally tells us what's on his mind, what his real name is. So maybe that name means something to you, it sure does to me."

He glared at her, saw her proud face melt, watched grief suffuse the angular face and melt the stiff shoulders.

"And, he's colour blind." As if this was proof positive.

Softly Vera repeated the name. "Jeannette Callum." She leaned forward and lifted Nathan's hands into hers. "Annie's baby."

"My baby?"

"Of course your baby, Nathan. Annie loved no other. I didn't know at the time but her parents were taking your letters. She was waiting to hear from you so she would know where to write you. She never received any letters and after you left for the tree-planting job she realized she was pregnant and she was so happy. But scared, too, because she never heard from you and her mother convinced her you weren't coming back and would never marry her. The truth is they didn't want her to marry you. Her mother said she should have the baby and they would raise it, the child could be raised as her sister, so she moved with them to Campbell River, never came back here."

"Jesus." Nathan bowed his head into his hands. "God help me, I never knew."

"It was bad for them in Campbell River. Her father started drinking again because he couldn't get a job and her mother had all those children to look after. You know Annie's mom, she could never admit she was wrong or made a mistake or ever did anyone harm. Oh, she was irreproachable that one. But she was still my auntie and it wasn't my place to talk truth to her when she didn't want to hear me. She wouldn't come back here, either. Anyway, she died. They almost all died."

"How?" asked Nathan staring at the floor, not seeing the beautifully woven old cedar mats.

It had been hard with Annie's mother, no question. She had lied, both outright and by omission. She had kept his letters hidden from Annie. She'd always believed that what she thought was right, *must* be right, just because she thought it. He'd never met anyone with such an overweening sense of her own righteous blamelessness. Likely he would have never heard an apology from her even if she'd been alive to be called to account.

"I heard she had the baby, a girl, and she did her best, but as the years went on they all got sick. Bad food I think, all the time eating chips, pop and crap, garbage like that, bad food. No oolichan grease or clams," Vera went on. "Annie's mom had a gall bladder operation and they think maybe too much anesthetic. She never woke up and no one ever investigated it. By the time she reached her teens, Annie's daughter, Jeannette—your daughter," she acknowledged, "ran off to Vancouver and was never heard from again. Somebody in the city told Annie that Jeanette was in the Downtown Eastside selling..." Vera paused, and swallowed.

"Selling herself for drugs. And it destroyed her, it just...killed Annie. She went down to Vancouver and walked around all over and asked people and she finally found her but Jeannette was so deep into the drugs, and the guy she got them from, he was awful to her. It broke Annie's heart. She finally swallowed a bunch of pills and they couldn't save her."

The Kwakwaka'wakw woman and the Caucasian man, united in their pain, leaned toward each other, hands grasping. Nathan squeezed, too hard, and Vera freed her fingers. Tears flowed. The truth was made visible, the scabs were ripped off, a tide of anguish inundated the room.

Nathan dropped his head into his hands and sobbed, great heaving cries from his belly and heart. His shoulders shook, and he reached for Vera, who took his hands again. "Vera, Vera, oh my god, what did I do, I didn't look hard enough for them. I was so hurt and mad, I put her out, I *tried* to put her out, of my mind and after a few years I just got on with my life, what could I do?"

"It is true that no one helped you, Nathan. We actively tried to prevent you from finding her, we blamed you for everything. Eventually I saw that she had some part in causing this too, she wasn't the only one living in pain. And...me. I, too, am guilty."

Unfocused eyes set deeply in her gaunt face, Vera looked straight at the truth she'd concealed in her heart. Through his tears, Nathan suddenly saw the woman his childhood companion had become. She, like him, was profoundly shaken. The strength of her personal bearing had made her appear serenely ageless until this moment, but now he saw the way the pain of life had marked her.

The two sat silently for several minutes, locked in agonizing memories of the past. The clock on the wall ticked officiously, marking off its metered seconds. Nathan pulled a wad of paper towel out of his pocket and wiped his reddened eyes. Vera broke the silence.

"Nathan, it is I who owe you an apology," she admitted. "I believed Annie's life would be better without you. It wasn't mine to decide how her life should be, but we were always like that. I decreed what we should do and she was happy to do it, until the two of you fell in love. I was jealous."

Vera looked down at her hands, now lying one on the other in her lap. "And then finally when I...was rethinking it and wanted to tell Annie, to apologize, to get her to seek you out, her mother forbade me. I had to respect her wishes. Annie wouldn't have anything to do with me anyway. She cut me out of her life when she moved to Campbell River with her mom and would never speak to me again. I thought it was cruel, but it was I who was the cruel one."

"Did you even hold a potlatch for her?" he inquired softly.

She shook her head slowly, tears sliding down the grooves in her wrinkled cheeks.

"No, never. We should have. There was no one in her family here to do it. I couldn't, it was too much to bear, to organize it all, and who was there to dance their dances and sing their songs?

There were too many losses, when so many died, and so many sad stories."

Vera's voice dwindled and she looked up sadly.

"Is it too late?" asked Nathan.

After a moment, Vera whispered, "Maybe not."

Wrung out with the explosion of grief and truth-telling, Nathan picked up the cold cup of tea. He sipped and let the tea loosen the thickness in his throat, looked at Vera with a calmer gaze. He was a forgiving man—he was old, she was old. Annie and her parents, siblings and her child were all gone—gone to wherever one went when they leave this existence.

"Well," he said, "now there is Cole. My grandson."

While Nathan and Vera had been re-twining their shared history, Vera's granddaughter Hayley lay on the beach at Gwayasdums on a grey sleeping bag that had seen better days. She'd been waiting for the sun. When the heavy rain diminished to the last few silvery drops and the pale sun peeked through the thinning grey clouds she'd grabbed the bag and a tarp to lay it on and headed for her hideout, a moss-covered depression between two cedars a short walk along the shoreline from the village. This was her place for deep meditation, for communion with herself and her world. Since childhood Hayley had sought and found answers to all her questions in the wind that shook the sweeping branches, the watery call of the raven and the soft shush of the waves on the shore.

Now that she'd finally made it out to Gilford Island, Hayley was uncharacteristically relaxed. She didn't quite know what to do with this unaccustomed feeling. Her first shift on the tribal council boat was done. It had been pretty traumatic when they'd hit the deadhead, but exciting, too, and she was thrilled to have the job.

One of the older village dogs snuffed her neck and curled up beside her, she absently stroked its furry warmth. Hayley regarded the nearby totem, eagle wings outstretched. Although she felt those wings like a protective blessing she knew the old carving would not stand much longer. She turned her gaze toward Retreat Passage and the many passing boats: crew boats, fishing boats, motor boats and kayaks—two never-ending streams heading east and west in Retreat Passage.

Against the busy backdrop of the boat traffic, she spotted the quick small dorsal fins of a pair of harbour porpoises. Once, twice, and then again they appeared and were gone; so quickly. A small rush of joy drifted through Hayley when she saw the small marine mammals. It was only anecdotal, as the scientists say, but it seemed to her there weren't so many around lately. Hard to say though because she had spent most of the past three years away getting an education and trying to figure out what to do with it. Maybe she'd start making notes of when she saw them, join that Marine Education group and report her sightings.

Hayley stretched luxuriously, happy to have completed her degree in marine biology and be done with university, and even happier because she had a job—even if just for the summer.

Just lucky, she thought, *I ran into Stevie Hunt.*

Stevie had told her the Musgamagw Dzawada'enuxw Tribal Council, or MDTC, was looking for a summer replacement crew member on their fisheries boat. The work was interesting: monitoring for red tide alerts, mussel and clam surveys, and identifying ancient midden sites and clam gardens. She'd spent the last week at home with her family in Yalis and hitched a ride to Gwayasdums to see her old ada for a few days. Ritchie, too, would be running down from Kingcome to see her.

Right now that family of hers was on her mind. Hayley's face reflected a mixed heritage. Her First Nations father was from Gwayasdums, her mother was the granddaughter of an English missionary in Yalis. Her eyes were a light golden brown like her mother's, almost topaz, yet her eyebrows were strong and black like the upswept wing of Raven. Her hair, like her father's, hung long, black, and straight down her back. Her rounded body had the sturdy torso of his people, and the fine long fingers and feet of her mother's. All her brothers and sisters revealed a variety of the characteristics of those two parents, none the same, yet all bound by powerful family ties.

Hayley pulled her sunglasses from her coat pocket and put them on as the sunbeams swelled like bright music. She'd known when she came to her spot planning to contemplate her family that it wouldn't be easy. A flood of mixed feelings boiled through her and she clutched the fur of the mongrel companion beside her to anchor the swirling thoughts. The dog whined and snuggled closer.

Love first, of course, but never pure and heartwarming. It was a love that was companion to pain. *Maybe that's true for everyone*, she thought in a brief moment of detachment, *one way or another.*

Invoking his memory she said out loud the name of her younger brother: "Sammy." Dead these past two years, he'd been bullied and dragged into a car by other drunken youth, pressured to do drugs that he hadn't wanted. The whole community suffered the anguish of the loss of three of those boys when the driver crashed the car later that night. Hayley let the tears flow as the image of her beaming baby brother rose in her inner vision. She let her love thought grow and surround him, envisioned pink clouds from her heart to his and enveloping his image within, before letting it dissolve. Her heart eased. Sammy might not be here but he was alright. And so was she.

Hayley couldn't understand how her parents could still be together in the face of so many challenges. Their mixed race marriage for starters, although not uncommon, had resulted in five surviving children. Except for Sammy, the kids had all made it to adulthood in spite of the many pitfalls along the way, particularly the allure of a life of drugs and alcohol in either the small island town or the big unknown city.

At twenty-six Hayley was the oldest. She sorely grieved the loss of Sammy, and lived in constant anxiety that that her littlest brother, Josh, would follow him into an early death. He was thin, artistic and bookish, and was learning carving skills with the old carvers at U'Mista. There was hope for him.

But Sondra, Josh's twin, oh my goodness, sweet loving Sondra at eighteen was on the path to hell—or early motherhood, maybe—if she could even stick with one guy. No studies or education for her, she had already had and dumped at least three boyfriends. Hayley figured she worried more about Sondra than their mother did. She would only say comfortably, "She'll find her way. Hayley, honey, don't worry so much. It's not your job." *But whose job is it then?* Her mother was still the hippie she'd become in rebellion against her strict religious upbringing.

In contrast, Holly, the second daughter, had sought out her devout grandfather from an early age and followed all the religious teachings of the Pentecostal ministry.

Hard to say what would happen with the youngest daughter, Lally. To some folks she appeared kind of simple. She liked to wander off into the woods and dig around for roots with a cedar digging stick and dry berries to add to their meals—not exactly celebrated behaviour in this day and age, although Ada said Lally was finding the old ways. To Hayley it was a healthier choice than indiscriminate screwing or alcohol and drugs, or even religion for that matter.

And where did she, Hayley, fit in? Always kind of tomboyish from an early age, she preferred to hang around with the men and do what they did. Unlike most young women she'd asked for and worked for her own skiff at an early age, and spent weeks exploring the nearby islands, learning the ways of the water and the marine inhabitants. She'd split wood for her grandmother out at the village, and secretly followed her uncles around memorizing the dances, the gestures and words of rituals she knew were forbidden to her.

She'd got herself a white man's education, too—had lots of support for that and did well. She wanted to help restore the salmon. Combining the old ways and new technology might be an answer.

She could even have a husband if she wanted. Ritchie kept coming around, said he adored her, kissed and pressed her for a response, for an answer. She liked him alright. But he was quite a lot older than her, thirty-five to her twenty-six. Sometimes she felt like a kid around him, like she should grow up. Often unable to name or define precisely what she felt, she was pretty surprised sometimes at what lurked inside her.

Late afternoon cooled with the approach of sundown, a light breeze lifted her hair, and a soft voice brushed her ear; her grandmother, Vera. "Thinking serious thoughts, are you, lovely child?"

Hayley sat up as Vera pushed the mutt aside and settled beside her with a small groan. Looking into the deep-set eyes of her old granny she knew something had happened. She'd never felt able to penetrate the imperial armour Vera wore, but had never doubted her ada's steadfast love and support.

"Looks like you've been doing the same." she ventured, "What's happened to you? You look...spent." Hayley reached out her young strong hand and enfolded Vera's within it.

The old woman sighed heavily and regarded their linked hands. For a long time she simply watched the thin evening clouds light up with the lowering sun. Finally she spoke, hesitating over each word. Her voice broke with the strain of the unaccustomed task of speaking out loud such shame and guilt.

"Granddaughter, long ago, when I was younger than you are now, I made a big mistake in my life. I held it in my heart and could not ever tell anyone or make it better."

Hayley was shocked at this confession from the woman who has been her idol, her mentor, her vision of the perfect person. What would Vera say next?

"This mistake hurt many people; it has hurt my own heart and made me guarded and bitter."

Another long pause before Vera continued. "Today, a man from Echo Bay, Nathan, came to see me."

"I know him, Ada. He taught us music at the school when I went that year I lived with you, he's Kit's friend."

"Yes, darling, and he was once my friend, a long time ago."

"Oh!" Hayley took this in, pondering. "I don't think I've ever seen you be friendly to him." She searched her memory and added, "Not that I've seen him down here very often but when I was in school we had the Christmas do at the community hall, fundraisers and stuff like that. I can't remember you ever speaking to him. Not one time."

"There were reasons for that, I thought. But mostly it was my own fault. I had a cousin, Annie Callum. She and Nathan and I were inseparable for years. But they fell in love and I felt left out. I...I was not good to Annie. Or to Nathan."

Like stones the words fell from her mouth, thudding on the ground around them.

Hayley held steady, her warm hands conveying support, love and forgiveness to her grandmother. So much could happen in a few words. Her sense of her grandmother was shifting like a melting iceberg, a feeling of what she could offer gathering strength. Like a fat wind, a change was coming and her grandmother's confidences were precipitating it.

"Nathan has met a young man; we believe he is Nathan's grandson, from Vancouver. Annie and Nathan's grandson."

Pretty quick Hayley pieced it all together. Although, like Joe, she'd been fully preoccupied dealing with the crew boat when they had to beach it on Green Rock, she hadn't missed the young man on board Kit's boat when she'd returned with the jack. In spite of the Caucasian cast of his features, his 'Indian-ness' had been immediately apparent to her.

Maybe he'd be someone she would know.

Eleven

Kit was in a mood this Monday morning. Daylight had been slow to brighten a thick impenetrable fog and although it likely would clear by eleven she was still annoyed. She'd planned to kayak over to Nickless Islet and sketch while the tide rose. So much for that plan.

She still hadn't heard from Tim although she knew he was around somewhere, catching up with his prawn survey, boarding the numerous boats and running up to Kingcome and down to Knight Inlet and Clio Channel to locate some of them. She'd been hoping to see that guy Carson as well but he'd been noticeable by his absence.

While dumping yesterday's coffee grounds she fumbled the coffee pot strainer and cursed when it flew out of her hand into the chuck. Stomped around to the back of the shed to find what she needed to fish it up.

She didn't have a magnet, a good tool for reclaiming axes and other metal items that fell overboard, but she did have a primitive tool that worked. A fellow who'd lived in a shack in Echo Bay years ago had dropped his false teeth overboard one morning and after having no luck finding a diver he'd nailed a can to a stick and handily fished them up. Kit had nailed together her own can-on-a-stick and figured chances were good she could easily retrieve the strainer.

She lay belly-down on the damp planks and leaned over the water. Extending her arm, she attempted the delicate operation of slipping the can under the coffee strainer. Twice she adjusted the angle of the can but finally got it right. Head hanging over the deck, she had just gently manoeuvred the coffee strainer to the lip of the can when she heard the quiet putt of a small motor rounding the point. She could tell by the sound it was no one she knew. Rather than running north straight across the opening, the vessel turned into the inlet.

Great. Must be coming here. With a grumpy scowl, she twisted her head to look and promptly lost the strainer. Pulling herself up and blinking through unbrushed hair, she peered through the thick fog. An amorphous black lump materialized into a Zodiac. *Seven a.m., for a visit?*

Second thought. *I must look like the D'Sonoqua, the wild woman of the woods.*

As the black Zodiac putted up to her dock she scrambled to her feet, stick with can in hand.

A smiling face, friendly eyes, warm behind the square, black glasses. "Am I too early for coffee?" asked Carson.

Kit was silent, mortified. She'd hoped he'd come visit, of course, but when he finally had, here she was in a damp t-shirt and ratty long johns with a primordial tool in hand and no coffee in her veins. At least she wasn't stark naked, which was sometimes the case when she dumped the coffee grounds. A small blessing.

"Give me ten minutes. Do not enter the house one second sooner. See if you can scoop up the coffee strainer."

She dropped the stick on the deck, pointed down at the thing lying on the sea floor, turned on her heel and tried to walk nonchalantly into the house.

Carson obliged, reached up to the deck for the tool and leaned over the side of his boat. In one smooth motion he scooped up the coffee strainer and dropped it into the Zodiac. Fifteen seconds.

Nine minutes and forty-five seconds to go. He turned off the motor, kneeled in the bow and used his paddle to propel the Zodiac silently along the shoreline, admiring the million drops of water hanging from the old man's beard draping the cedar foliage. He startled a kingfisher, which chattered away, and got a good look at a pair of hooded mergansers before they realized they were being observed. Turning to look back at Kit's float-house he noted the harmonious and economic design of it, and studied how the boomsticks tied to the shore were attached to a large cedar log that ran across the length of the front. Easy to see how the whole thing would go up and down with the tide, keeping the house from going dry at tides as low as this one. Maybe he should have a floathouse.

A rosy tinge flushed the fog. It brightened and spread, staining the blue white mist shades of pink and violet.

In her bedroom, Kit whipped off the long johns and replaced them with a pair of cut-offs and a clean, white t-shirt, all the while berating herself. "White? Seriously? It'll be dirty in thirty seconds. Wear the blue or the green one." She extracted three tops from the drawer, settled finally on the sea green with the mermaid, stuffed the others back in.

"Can this be such a huge problem? It's not like you've never had a man visit you before," Kit muttered as she put the kettle on the propane stove and fired up the burner, then strolled out to the deck.

All for nothing, as he wasn't quietly sitting by the dock as she'd imagined. She looked around and spotted a misty shape near the inside curve of the bay, watched him for a moment and perceived the instant he realized she was there waiting for him. Kit inhaled a lungful of moist air and suddenly the crap morning took on new light. A wave of anticipation flooded her as she watched the man come out of the fog and into focus. It was a 'be here now' moment; she caught it and aimed a big warm smile in his direction.

The smile was returned as he flourished the coffee strainer triumphantly. "Got it! What an extremely sophisticated tool!"

She laughed and reached for his bowline. "Welcome to the mermaid's cave," she grinned and accepted the coffee strainer. "What offering is this you bring? Ah, the coffee strainer. More valued than rubies, more highly prized than the riches of the seven undersea kingdoms."

"You look nice." No comment on her previous look, she liked that. "Pretty."

Carson followed Kit in, looked around her home; observed the window sills lined with moon snail and sea urchin shells, various items of corroded copper. He admired the smoothly planed yellow cedar on two walls, pale yellow paint on the other two. The doorways to the bedroom, bathroom and outside back kitchen door were framed in planed and varnished red cedar, painted mermaids in kelp twined up each side and across the top.

"You do these?"

She held up a finger, 'one sec,' and ground the coffee beans, then dumped them into the strainer and placed it on the water reservoir. "Yes, it's called rosemaling, an old fashioned decorative art; folk art."

He walked over to the desk where her sketches lay open to view. She poured the boiling water into the coffee pot. "Mind if I look?"

Kit hesitated, shrugged. *What the heck, sure, why not...* no point in hiding anything. If he was critical or dismissive, he wouldn't be a person she would ever get close to. Might as well find out right now. Cups from the cupboard, milk and sugar, spoons, her ears were tuned for a comment. None came

"We can sit over her by the heater, its warmer; you want to get the pot?" She led the way to the easy chair and couch, placed the cups and other items on the table between them, moved a small cedar mat while motioning for him to set the coffee pot on it.

"Or I can pour," he said, and did.

He sat then, in the easy chair. She noticed how he surreptitiously brushed his butt to make sure there was no debris on his jeans. She dumped milk and sugar in her cup, stirred it. Carson did the same, neither of them spoke, savouring that first mouthful.

"Mm-mm. Damn! Good coffee. I didn't expect anything like that out here. Mostly it's been boiled."

She laughed, "Yah, fishermen's coffee. Not the coffee of connoisseurs."

"So you're a coffee snob, hmm?"

Stung, she leaned back. "No. No, I don't think so. I just like it to taste...rich. I roast my own beans in the frying pan."

Now Kit wished he would go away. She couldn't think of anything to say, an unusual state of affairs. And, she remembered, she knew nothing—not one thing—about this guy. Yet here was, sitting in her house drinking coffee like they were old buddies. She'd spent a lot of time on her own out here and just to be safe, no man got in the house without her feeling pretty comfortable with him. *How did this one get in?*

"Do you like to paint on location?" His question broke the silence. "I'm going around here painting the coastal scene, following in the footsteps of Emily Carr. Be great to go paint together. Maybe you could show me where some of these places are. I know she painted at Village Island and other First Nations villages when there were still longhouses and totems."

"There's another artist from the thirties who came out here, too, W. J. Phillips. Have you heard of him?"

"Nope. What'd he do?"

"I have a book of his work, wood block prints and watercolours. He came from the prairies, and visited the old villages and the settlements, too. Old Simoom Sound out here where a guy called Dunseith had a big dock, a store and a trading post. The steamships came in on their route up and down the coast."

"Sounds interesting. Maybe you could show me some places, we could sketch together."

"You want me to come and paint with you? Sounds like you're pretty professional. I'm not, but I like to dabble and paint the wildflowers and stuff like that...some scenes."

"Looks like you're good enough to me; we could hang out and, you know, sketch. Visit. You clearly have brushes, paint and paper. Don't need much else. I'm always glad to find a painting companion, it's nicer than painting alone all the time."

"I've never had anyone to paint with," Kit smiled, sadly. "No one out here but me paints so I've always worked alone. I'm thinking about taking a workshop somewhere. Anyway, what about you? You're what—tooling around here, staying in the area for a while? Where are you from, if you don't mind me asking?"

Carson paused. Generally he preferred not to reveal a lot about himself, figured people would see who he was by what he did. This was not a fast process and because of it, he didn't have a lot of friends, but the ones he had were tried and true. He hoped she would be one of them, but something about her told him that he wouldn't be seeing much of her if he stuck to his usual taciturn practice.

"I'm...from...Toronto, and Seattle. Um, my last job was in New York but it was a terrible job, I hated it."

She settled in, wondered why the hesitation. Most people had no problem putting it out there: where they were from, what they were doing, what brought them to this point of present. Too often you couldn't shut them up.

She raised her eyebrows and let the silence pulse.

"I'm quite rich," he blurted.

Kit threw herself back against the couch, "Oh no!" she gasped.

Carson didn't quite know what to make of this until she rolled sideways laughing. "You're kidding, right?"

"I'm not, but sounds like you are," he accused.

She sat up, slurped another mouthful of coffee. "Is this, like, true confessions or something? You made that sound like a bad thing so I had to do it. Seriously, you're really rich? How? Born with the silver spoon?"

"No, I made a bucket of money with a combination of skill, maybe more good luck than skill, working for a dot-com company that set up some of the first internet communication networks. I got out before the bubble burst and had—have—a good friend who luckily has turned out not to be a thief. She invested my money for me and here I am, letting the wind blow me wherever I want to go and doing what I want. Sucks, right?"

"Wow." Kit was silenced. "So, you're simply an ordinary guy who got lucky. Honestly?"

"Yes, truly. I've been in BC for four months now, I bought my boat..."

She interjected, "The antique launch I saw in Grebe Cove."

"Right, I bought that at the wooden boat show on Whidbey Island. I fell in love with it. I don't know anything about boats but I'm learning fast."

"Hmm." She regarded her visitor with a level gaze, that last ingenuous admission seemed way too good to be true. "So, what's the downside?"

"What do you mean?"

Carson knew exactly what she meant.

"You know what I mean—what's the fly in the ointment? The big reveal at the end when the hero loves 'em and leaves 'em?"

Why she was being so pugnacious and adversarial? Her feelings were all over the place, swirling like the tide over a sea mount. The guy had come—as he had said he would—respectfully and quietly so the whole neighbourhood didn't get to speculate about her. He'd been perfectly agreeable and helpfully retrieved the coffee pot strainer. Now he was sitting here smiling at her and not arguing or getting reactive.

Agitated, she jumped up and went to the wood box, stuffed a few pieces of split hemlock into the heater.

Carson asked, "Should I go? You seem upset and I don't know what I've done to cause that. I was hoping we could get to know each other while I'm here."

Through the window she saw the fog had thinned. Drifting arcs and threads of mist trailed along the treetops. Taking a cue from the peaceful nature of the scene, Kit inhaled deeply once, then again. Releasing the whole breath in a long exhalation she released all her pique, felt it dissipate like that fog.

"Okay, sorry, not your fault. I'm going to cook up some breakfast, want some? I don't have any bookings today. If you aren't busy I could take you over to Scott Cove and we could walk up to Mini-hump Creek, give it a shot." Anticipating his question she went on, "So-called because there is a species of land-locked sockeye in the creek, they're really small; we call them 'mini-humps.'"

She turned to smile at him and their eyes locked, briefly, time stopped and the surroundings faded away. Kit shook loose first, averted her face, walked to the fridge and took out the egg carton. She put two frying pans on the stove. "How many eggs?"

"Two please. Can I help?"

"You can shake some salt on the frying pan. That's how I make toast 'cause I don't have enough juice in the battery bank to run a toaster. It's just as good anyway, maybe better this way." She pointed to the box of pickling salt on the shelf above the stove.

"Pretty sure I could do toast on my boat like this, I've had to do without for the same reason."

"I learned it from fishing with my neighbour, Back Eddy. That's how the fishermen do their toast, but on the surface of the oil stove. They keep the stove going all the time to heat the boat and to cook on. Bread's in that box."

He picked up the loaf from the bread box, opened the bag and sniffed. "Mmm, homemade?"

"Yes, but not by me. It's Carol Ann at Echo Bay makes it. I try to make sure I never run out."

They fell into a comfortable rhythm in her compact kitchen. Breakfast was served on the yellow and red cedar striped dining table Back Eddy had made for her as a housewarming gift when she'd finished the floathouse renovation. Not much talk while they ate and cleaned up the table and dishes after.

Whatever transpired, Kit decided, she's in. He was sensitive to mood, attractive (*practically a god!*), pleasant company, helpful, rich (*he says*), and seemed interested in her. *Who am I to blow against the wind?* Until proven otherwise, the man seemed perfect. Even if he only hung around for a week or two then took off, she decided to enjoy it while she could.

And Tim? At this point, that looked like a 'wait-and-see.'

"What about lunch? Should we take something to nibble on?" She turned to her cupboard. "I've got a couple baking powder biscuits stuffed with salmon and cheese that need to be eaten. An orange, and water, we'll need water." She wrapped the biscuits and filled a shiny container, screwed on the cap and put everything in with the small paint kit in her shoulder bag.

"Sounds good to me." Evidently she was preparing for a longer, rather than a shorter, visit.

Loaded with the necessities they left the house. "Gimme that lunch," he said and she pulled it out of her bag. His paints were stored in a cedar box beneath the seat of the Zodiac and he tucked the food in with them. She turned to watch her floathouse melt into the mist and, beautiful surprise, a fog bow lay glowing with pearly light; a perfect, reflected arch above and below her home.

A good omen.

The first time Kit had seen a fog bow she'd known it instantly for what it was: a magic doorway into another realm. She touched Carson's arm and he turned to follow her pointing finger, eyes widening as he took in the scene. They motored close along the shoreline, and turned in to the once bustling logging camp at Scott Cove.

"We used to come here at Hallowe'en, when there were families and the bunkhouse was full of loggers and they all had a ton of candy and chocolate bars for us, sometimes even comic books. The camp closed down because they kicked out the families and brought in a big barge for housing single men. Jack Scott used to bring us here in his boat, *Soozee*. He and his wife moved to Comox when they got old and Back Eddy took over taking the kids around on his fishing boat to everybody's house for trick or treat."

"Sounds like fun. What happens now? Do you do Hallowe'en?"

Saddened by her memories, Kit answered slowly, "Well, there're no kids here now, they all grew up and moved away. But Back Eddy still has a big bonfire and potluck dinner, for whoever's here, and he blows off a few hundred dollars' worth of fireworks. That's always fun."

They tied up the Zodiac and she led the way to the hatchery building. Tall grass and young alder shoots pressed close against the walls, working hard to reclaim the territory. In an effort to build up the depleted salmon runs, the community had once raised coho fry here to plant in the local streams. Kit pushed hard to open the swollen door. Carson followed her into the building, breathing the musty air. The egg trays and water troughs, once so useful and bright with promise, sat sulking under layers of dust and spider webs.

"It bums me out coming in here. We all worked so hard, the whole community, from the kids to the old guys. Back Eddy was the moving force; he wanted to get the salmon going again, to give back what had given so much. We had a hatchery manager and volunteers. It all closed down when the kids got too big for the school and four families moved away, including our manager."

"Anyway," Kit said as she turned decisively, "it was great while it lasted. Let's go on our walk. It's cold in here. Too many salmon ghosts."

Up the logging road they strolled, packing their paint kits and lunch. A fragile sun broke through the forest cover. The fog steadily dissipated and the forest warmed up. Fox sparrows flittered in the branches. Dangling from every limb and leaf a million drops of water lit up as one. Two ravens approached above the roadway, passing close overhead. One called when right above them and a varied thrush trilled a sweet song from deep in the woods. Kit was transported, every single sound and sight spoke to her inner being.

"This is amazing, so beautiful." Carson echoed her thoughts.

"And it's only a beat-up old logging area, right?!" She turned toward him. "I used to walk up this road three days a week with the wife of the caretaker but then the company didn't need them anymore so...bye-bye to them. I don't feel safe walking up the road alone, especially with all the cougars on Gilford Island now. Once we encountered a wolf and walked backwards for half a kilometre until we got to the dock. It followed us but never came close."

"Huh, that's an experience."

"Yah."

No need to hurry up the rutted road. From time to time their arms brushed against each other, the fine hairs of Kit's forearm quivering in response. She'd move away but then slowly find herself right back beside him, matching the pace. Scott Cove Creek ribboned along beside the road, slipping close and narrow along the bank then disappearing under overhanging hemlock and cedar.

"So what about you, were you born here?" asked Carson.

"No, I was born in Hope. As my mom used to say—with emphasis." Kit smiled at the memory. "My mom, Peggy, she was always independent; she got pregnant when she ran off to a music festival in Florida or somewhere and had me against my grandparents' wishes. They thought she should give me up for adoption, that raising a child alone and unmarried would be too hard for her, but everyone was doing it by then. She built a cabin by herself in Hope when I was a baby and she studied herbal medicine and became an herbal healer. She did massage too, then she hooked up with her guy, Drake, and that was it, he was her man. They had my brother Cody and we moved here, to Alert Bay, when I was a kid. My dad—Drake—got a job with a logging company but then switched to forest management, just after they shut down the forestry station up in Echo Bay Park. He had a cool boat, kind of like yours, we used to spend a lot of time out here with him."

"Your mom seems to have had some kind of cowboy thing going," he observed.

Kit burst out a little laugh, "You noticed, huh? She read a lot of cowboy stories, Zane Grey and all. My full name is Loretta Katherine but she called me Kit. Then my brother got named Cody. I'd read Mom's books when she was done with them, they were all stories about the wild west and the pioneer days, and she let me have riding lessons when I was eight but then we moved here. I was crazy for horses, lots of girls are, I guess. Part of the time we lived in one of those houses that used to be up in the park at Echo Bay, but was yarded onto a float. There's a concrete sidewalk a little way up from the dock, the houses used to sit along it, but they all got pulled off over the years. So I went to the school here and Alert Bay and then high school in Port McNeill. Then the boarding residence closed down so I had to look around for other housing and did more correspondence.

"The coolest was grade eight, which I did by mail. Government paid for a 'flying teacher.' Once a month she came to the homes of all the correspondence kids. I loved it when she showed up, she'd stay with us and boy—did we work hard to impress her! I loved having the teacher devote all her attention to just me. My dad taught me how to whittle, run a boat and a chain saw, and clean and shoot a gun. Also, how to drive a truck on the logging roads here. I'm still not too good in the city."

"And then along comes Carson," said Carson, slipping her a twinkling look.

"I know! Seems too good to be true, doesn't it?"

Carson threw his head back, let out a big guffaw. The road turned and he took her hand in his, happy when she didn't withdraw it. They walked along in the morning sunshine, hands swinging forward and back.

A lumpy mess on the road stopped Kit in her tracks. "Oho, what have we here?"

"What *do* we have here?" he asked quizzically, seeing nothing but a pile of animal leavings.

She searched the roadside for a short stick and squashed the mess. "See, look here. There's fur and some small fine bones. I think its wolf."

Carson leaned down for a closer look. "Huh. I guess I'm kind of a city boy. Got a lot to learn about animal poo."

"It's true, there is a lot can be learned. For starters, 'scat' is the proper terminology. And if it *is* wolf, which I do think it is, it tells me there are still wolves around here and that they haven't been totally driven off the island by the cougars. We used to hear wolves howling all the time. I miss that so much." She looked right at him and continued with mock sternness. "And furthermore, you won't get your 'coast boy' designation unless you find poking at piles of animal fecal material absolutely compelling."

"I do! Absolutely compelling! What else do I need to get my designation?"

"Oh, there's a long list. Don't park in the middle of a dock, be willing to go looking for a lost or broke down neighbour the moment you sit down to dinner, or in a snowstorm. Let your neighbour know you're going to town, stuff like that. I'll make you a list. But we should get going."

He held out his hand to raise her up. She didn't need it but took it anyway. Kit felt trepidation spiced with a surprising joy that seemed so foreign, so unbelievable; she couldn't quite take it in. A little further up the road they halted again, his hand pulling her to a standstill. His eyes were raised to the high blue sky where two eagles wheeled and turned and plummeted, talons grasping and releasing. Heads tilted back, they watched, then he lowered his eyes to her upraised face and unable to hold back another second, he leaned in and kissed her.

"God, I've wanted to do that for hours."

A tidal wave of feeling prevented her from uttering a single word. She turned, led him forward up the road and across a small bridge where she stopped briefly, then returned.

"It's this side, I think," she said.

"What is?"

Her reply was muffled as she stepped off the road, broke through a stand of thimbleberry bush and disappeared. He dove into the bush behind her. Shady green forest enveloped them as they descended a damp slope and ten steps later broke out into sunshine again. Carson looked around at the small grassy meadow bounded on three sides by the meandering stream.

"Mini-hump Creek." Kit found her voice, presented the small creek. A light wind breathed over the sunlit surface, setting off a dizzying riffle-glitter. Clouds of midges and small blue damselflies danced above the stream.

"Water striders!" Carson exclaimed. "I love those guys, the little dimples the surface tension makes and the way they scoot along." They both kneeled on the bank, watching the little creatures working their way between grasses and miniature islets of mud clots. Bubbles drifted up and popped, small fish swirled and leaped for low flying midges.

"We have arrived. Tiny, unique land-locked salmon, kokanee actually, inhabit this stream. The mini-humps."

She flopped down by the bank of the slow stream and Carson sat beside her. She opened her mouth to go on about the mini-humps and he leaned over and kissed her again, a soft questioning kiss. Once again she was surprised by both the kiss and her own response. She opened her eyes wide, then closed them and leaned into the kiss. He drew back six inches. Past the black frames of his glasses she saw long dark lashes with matching brows above, and in his eyes intelligence and kindness. Desire burned in the navy blue irises.

"Blue eyes like the indigo line on the sea when the wind is picking up in the distance," she murmured, then slid the glasses off and tossed them up the bank. She pressed her fingers into his curly beard and traced his upper lip with her forefinger. He leaned forward once more and laid his lips against hers. With her finger caught in between, she slipped it into his mouth and against his teeth. He pressed his tongue against her finger, drawing it in. She lay back on the grass and Carson eased his length against her, hard against her thigh. A shiver swept her whole body, than another, bringing to life the fine hairs of her cheeks, shoulders and back, her breasts.

Deep inside, her need unfurled. As when a tsunami overwhelms the beach, Kit surrendered to the irresistible surge of desire.

Carson slid a cool hand under her shirt and caressed her hot belly in slow widening circles. No going back now. He felt for the button and zipper and she helped him slide down her jeans. The grass prickled the back of her legs and bottom, his hands and face were hot against her thighs. He kissed her again and hovered over her, his torso sliding against hers, shirt buttons rubbing rough against soft skin.

Kit couldn't wait; in an unanticipated shockwave of release her body claimed its own pleasure. An exultant shout of laughter erupted from her throat.

"That was quick!" said Carson, smiling down at her. "I'm not even started yet..."

"Oh my god, oh my golly goodness, I can't believe that...wow!"

"Wow? How wow?"

"Really, really wow!" They laughed hysterically, hugged each other. Carson's pants hung around his knees and she laughed harder. "But there is something we haven't attended to and we must," she said soberly as she sat up, tugged his jeans up his hips then wiggled back into her own clothing.

"I know, I know. I don't suppose you have any condoms on you?"

"Well, not exactly on me, but I have some at the floathouse." She raised her eyebrows inquiringly. "I wasn't anticipating a creekside encounter on our very first visit. Maybe we should slow this mustang down. Where did your glasses get to anyway?"

Kit buttoned her shirt. Looking at the sky above and the glittering creek she suddenly laughed. She said with a slant-eyed sideways look, "Mini-hump Creek...seems aptly named, hmm?" More snickering.

Upslope a ways Carson spotted his glasses, reached to pick them up. "Lucky I didn't crush them in my seduction of the water maid," he said. "D'you want to stay and paint, go and come back or just go?"

"Hmm, well, let's stick to the plan, gets some painting done, okay? Eat lunch, then let us depart, see what happens."

"Works for me."

The afternoon passed in companionable quiet, but the flare of passion they'd shared simmered between them. While painting she mulled it over and concluded she'd best rein in her impulsiveness and get to know the guy. There remained the not-so-small matter of Tim, which she'd rather complete with some finesse. It didn't feel right to engage with someone new without first wrapping it up with him. Be better than giving him something to hook a grievance onto, in any case.

Twelve

athan had been airborne ever since he got back from seeing Vera. His thoughts crashed furiously, one into another, like the bumper cars he'd once ridden with his big brother in Vancouver. He relived his conversation with Vera and from time to time stifled another upwelling sob.

Tonight Cole was coming for dinner. Seawater was boiling on the stove for the crabs he'd pulled; prawns were thawing in the sink. His special mashed potatoes with onion and parmesan cheese sat warm in the oven. Fresh green broccoli Carol Ann had given him rounded out the meal he was preparing. While cutting the broccoli another groundswell of grief surged through him and this time he laid down the knife, held on to the counter and let it pummel him.

Clearly, resistance was futile.

That thought-phrase triggered a childhood memory. He and the girls shouting phrases from comic books, good guys and bad guys, followed by a montage of scenes from the beautiful days, when he and Annie and Vera had run free all over the Broughton Archipelago.

Those were happy years, long before love-making, before the agony of loss, before a baby born into a world of pain. Innocent years until awareness grew, of a not-so-beautiful world full of betrayal, racism and violence, the massacre of trees and fish, and of a people.

Nathan recovered from the first wave and the second. He shook out his arms and fingers and straightened his shoulders. Now there was Cole, his grandson, and he was overcome by the intensity of feeling swelling in his breast. His heart literally felt torn open, thumping double-time. He could see his chest shake with each beat, the old grey sweater telegraphing his pulse; even the blood vessels in his eyes marked the rhythm.

Nathan breathed in deeply, released the breath. A long time ago he'd meditated daily. He'd forgotten how calming that had been, but there it was, kicking right in, lowering his heart rate and helping him feel grounded and centred.

He formulated a plan. He would tell Cole the story from the beginning, then end it with who he thought Cole was. No, scratch that. Maybe better tell him first thing, and then back up to the beginning.

The putt of the outboard motor on Woody's old skiff cut in to his thoughts. Cole was here. Suddenly Nathan remembered the call he heard the day the young man had arrived, the portentous way it had echoed.

He went out to greet the boy, tied up the boat. Cole jumped out of the skiff, barely rocking it. Nathan envied the sure-footed balance of youth, he who once had walked the aerial pathway of

116

the fallen trees high-stacked like pick-up sticks, searching for gaps to climb into and re-plant the forest.

Cole rushed two steps forward, stopped, turned; he'd gone right past the lanky old man. They bumped and Cole steadied Nathan, one hand on his shoulder, the other against his bicep. Nathan couldn't help it, he wrapped his long arms around the boy, blurted it out straightaway.

"Cole, I'm your grandfather. That's it. I'm your grandfather."

Shocked Cole pushed against him, although he didn't let go. His big hands gripped Nathan's shoulders as he swayed back. There was no doubt of the truth of it. He'd been waiting for this moment; so ready to hear the words he's been longing for. The young man and the old stood, looking at each other, then Nathan remembered he had three pots boiling on the stove, jerked away and plunged through the doorway.

"Come on, come on in. No, don't worry about your shoes, the floor's cold and I sweep it every day, anyway."

He fussed around Cole like a hen around its chick. Took the boy's jacket and tossed it on the easy chair, rushed to the stove and checked the state of each pot. He threw the prawns into the boiling water, heaved the crabs out with the lifters and flung them into a bowl. Towelled his big hands dry, squeezed the towel hard to still his quivering hands. *Steady on, old fellow.*

Cole stood by the doorway, curious eyes taking in the room, inhaling the scent of seafood and wood smoke. Not a cluttered room but lots to capture the eye, interesting and comfortable. In the kitchen an expanse of yellow cedar counter, propane stove and fridge and a hand-hewn table with driftwood legs. Wood heater by the back door with a neatly piled boxful of firewood, a small TV and a shelf stacked with DVD's and books. Between a saggy blue-grey couch and a brown cracked-leather easy chair another wooden table held a kerosene lamp, a blue ceramic glass and a book. Cole read the title, Ondaatje's *The Cat's Table*. Through a wide doorway he saw a neatly made double bed covered by a navy blue quilt with a pattern of white fish undulating across it. Another doorway led to a bathroom. The homey space invited.

Aware of Nathan's agitation Cole wandered toward a wall of photos, looked at them one by one as the older man set bright blue placemats and wooden dishes on the table, and the pots onto a yew wood cutting board.

"It's ready."

Nathan's voice was gruff and he cleared his throat. "Pretty simple dinner; crabs and prawns, spuds and some green stuff. I'll tell you all about those photos after."

Cole sat down as Nathan pulled up a second chair, the two sat for a minute, watching the steam rise from the food in the pots. Cole's stomach rumbled loudly, breaking the silence. He grinned at Nathan.

"Looks awesome. I'm starving. 'Course, I'm starving pretty much all the time."

Nathan laughed, and his eyes filled again but suddenly his whole body relaxed and his shoulders involuntarily dropped from their hunched up position. Both men reached for crab and a dish of garlic butter, piled potatoes, prawns and broccoli on their plates and began to eat. Nathan, lightheaded with joy, couldn't take his eyes off Cole. He barely tasted the beautiful seafood. Cole kept giving him goofy grins while wiping his chin and dunking more crab in the butter, slurping it out of the shell, twisting open the prawns and inhaling them.

Long past the time when Nathan had pushed his plate away and leaned back in his chair, Cole had finally eaten enough. A pot of tea now sat beside two ceramic mugs.

"Let's take it to the easy chairs and we'll talk."

Cole nodded.

Thirteen

*A*t owl light when all is shadowy blue, Tim motored into the bay to visit Kit. *Finally.* She came out and wrapped the centre line around the cleat. "Hey, Tim," she greeted him without warmth.

Oh oh, not the tone he'd anticipated. "Kit, hey, how're you doing?"

"Okay. I'm okay."

"Can I come in? So we can talk?"

"There's not much to say, Tim, but come in for a few minutes."

He climbed off his boat and reached to hug her but she slipped away from his grasp. Soberly he followed her into the house. Too late in the day for coffee, but she didn't want him to stay long enough to drink a beer.

"How 'bout tea? You want a cup of tea? I've got some wild mint from Bond Sound."

"Sure, thanks."

So formal. Kit fussed in the kitchen, returned to the table with cups and teapot. Tim was still standing as she set the tea items on the coffee table.

"Kit, I..."

"Tim, we..."

Both stopped as abruptly as they'd begun. "Go ahead," said Tim.

"No, you first."

"Kit, I've done a lot of thinking." She waited out his pause and he continued.

"I was jealous, about that guy and I was...I wasn't very nice. I'm truly sorry. I'm sorry I yelled at you, sorry for what I said at Echo Bay, and honest to god, I am so sorry about Margaret. You were right, I did spend the night with her, and it was wrong, both to you and to her. I promise you I will never again, that was the last time. Ever. The last time with anyone but you."

Kit watched him for a heartbeat or two. She was moved by his sincerity, she wanted to believe him. But what did that mean, *the last time with anyone but you...*? Does that mean he'd been with Margaret more than the one time, or with other women, too? Could she trust a thing he said? Could she be with someone she couldn't trust? And what about Carson, now?

"Oh Tim, I'm sorry, too, I was a bitch, but..."

"But?"

"Well, I think we should...like, quit."

"Quit?" Tim's eyes widened.

"Yes. As in, not be together."

"You're kidding! Kit! We can work it out, I promise I'll do better, we have a good relationship, we like the same things. I want to marry you," he blurted.

Her stifled laugh came out as a snort. "It has to be mutual, Tim." Then she realized what she'd said. "Oh! I didn't mean that the way it sounds, I'm sorry." She had no desire to hurt, nor antagonize Tim. They *have* had a good relationship and she has enjoyed it thoroughly. Until recently. She touched his arm, then put her arms around him and hugged gently. He tightened his arms but she stepped out of the embrace.

Quickly he said, "Okay, you're right. Look, don't decide right now, please? Let me come over Saturday. I'm sorry I can't come any sooner, got to go most of the way up Knight Inlet. I'm a little behind."

"Oh right, playing catch-up."

"Yah, yah, with my tooth and all." He rushed through this last bit, remembering what 'all' entailed. "I'll make you dinner on the boat and we'll talk. People get through stuff like this; it can make the relationship stronger. We're good together, Kit. I know you're Miss 'She who can do everything' but people get old and they need company and…help…and, you know, they need to have love in their lives. How many people can make a life out here? We're good together. Please give it some more thought, okay?"

He sounded so reasonable, so calm and sincere. Kit didn't want to fight. She didn't want to have a long talk with him right this minute either, although she was relieved that he hadn't thrown a fit when she'd said they should quit.

Reluctantly she agreed. He deserved a chance to make his case. "Okay, dinner Saturday. What time?"

"Six okay?"

"Yah, no, maybe later. I've got something on that day, I think." Kit went to the wall and checked her calendar. "Right. A day tour for some people from Sointula, they have a friend from Germany. I'll be home by seven, seven thirty. I'll radio you if I'm going to be later."

Tim his hands on either side of her face, looked deep into her eyes. "Kit, I truly am deeply sorry. I do love you so much."

In spite of the intensity of her day with Carson, Kit tried to keep a level head, as her stepdad, Drake, used to say. She was moved by Tim's declaration. She would have dinner with him Saturday and see how she felt. She could get her thoughts and feelings in order and be better equipped to know how to proceed.

She didn't resist when he moved in for a kiss, but barely responded. Tim didn't press. Sensitive to her mood, he got his coat and said, "Thanks for the tea. See you on Saturday."

He looked at her with all the sincerity and charm he could muster. "I'll be back." He was pleased to see he'd earned a small smile as he gently closed the door.

Kit sat down, stood up, and sat again. They hadn't even drunk the tea. She poured a cup, stirred in a spoonful of honey. Alone at her table she watched the running lights of Tim's boat mark his departure.

Fourteen

Wednesday morning. Breathless quiet at 6:00 a.m. with a promise of heat.

After the good night's sleep he'd enjoyed, Tim felt a fresh optimism. Through the porthole by his bunk the sky dawned a transparent greenish colour. From the galley window, savouring his coffee, he watched as a small breeze delicately fondled the cottonwood leaves on shore. Small pink clouds drifted aimlessly in the brightening sky.

Getting Kit to agree to dinner had been masterful. He was ready to give up other women, even Margaret, although he deeply felt the appeal of her unshakeable love. Hard to admit to himself that he was holding that in his back pocket. It hadn't been easy breaking up with her and sometimes an unwelcome thought sneaked in to the middle of his dramatic relationship with Kit—a little voice that reminded him how calming and restful and satisfying Margaret's love had been. He felt a tremor of loss at giving her up forever.

Maybe he shouldn't go off the deep end here, but the thought of losing Kit made his stomach hurt. If that's what it took to keep her, that's what he'd give her. He really meant it this time. It was the right thing to do.

And now to work.

Tim tried Benny on the VHF and this time he responded with, "I'm in the dogleg." He expected Tim to comprehend fisherman's code for his location, although everyone knew where he and all the prawn fishers were anyway. Tim chuckled, thinking of his salmon-fishing days, when all the skippers were so secretive with their codes and sideband radios. How they'd threatened to throw their deckhands off at the nearest harbour, without pay, if they so much as breathed a word revealing location, catch or gear type.

The prawn checkers were not supposed to plan their boat visits, so typically Tim just showed up to board a vessel, and check the catch. He'd been away long enough that he wasn't sure where the various boats were, although it wouldn't be too difficult to track down the three he wanted to check today. He'd be busy.

The dogleg was up Simoom Sound. Easy to find Benny in there and he could buzz some of the other spots to see where *White Bird* was. Tim clipped on his life vest and gathered his five white sorting buckets, the four blue trays they fit into, his clipboard and the more-valuable-than-gold waterproof data sheets. He loaded everything carefully into his skiff.

The skiff was tough, strengthened by built-in bumpers he'd installed when he began this job. These boats got banged around pretty good sometimes, bumping up against and being dragged around by fishing vessels. Firmly putting away all thoughts of women, Tim fired up the Merc and motored away from his liveaboard, headed for Simoom Sound.

By 7:10 a.m. Benny had two strings of fifty traps set in the mouth of the sound and was almost through pulling the first line. Tim hung back while he waited for Benny to complete the string and noted the time in his logbook. Prawn fishers were permitted to pull gear from 7:00 a.m. to 7:00 p.m. Almost through the line in ten minutes was fast, but maybe there hadn't been many prawns. It seemed obvious to Tim the fisherman had been pulling gear before seven. He figured Benny would have begun even earlier if he hadn't known the prawn checker was coming. In any case, at this point he was within the regulations.

He watched as Benny hauled in each trap, opened it, shook the contents into the bin, and rapidly sorted through the catch. Crabs, the odd fish or shell, and all undersize prawns went over the side. It didn't take long to fish the remaining traps. Tim concluded the catch here was meager, but he'd know for sure when he was on board. Benny motored further in to Simoom Sound to reset the traps.

When Benny was done Tim went alongside *Thunder Chieftain* and tied his skiff to the port side. He was careful to make sure his boat was clear of the bilge pump hose. He'd had scummy water pumped into his boat once, well, twice in fact. Now he was careful to locate the pump hose and be clear of it on every single vessel. From time to time unfriendly skippers had pretended not to notice his boat was tied alongside and thrown their bycatch into his boat, with the notable inclusion once of an octopus. Tim climbed up over the gunwale of the boat. Benny greeted him with a friendly handshake.

"Benny, how're you doing?"

"Pretty good, pretty good, Tim. You? Ya get that tooth all fixed up?"

"Sure did, yup. Thought I was going to lose it, had to go to Campbell River to see a specialist but she fixed me up good."

"Yah, no, that's great, Tim."

Both men looked up at the sky for a second and Benny commented, "Kinda looks like a weather-breeder, don't it?"

Tim agreed, "Sure does. Going to be another big wind any day now. It's been so hot and quiet. Except for yesterday."

Usually Benny offered him a cup of coffee, but not today. Instead he said, "Well, let me get this line going." Tim noticed the omission and mentally shrugged. Eventually they'd get around to the other business, he was in no rush.

"Got to take a look at the logbook first, Benny, you got it handy?" The logbook ought to be handy because every prawn fisher knew this was part of the drill for the first visit of the season. Tim headed for the wheelhouse, remembering the time he'd entered Benny's cabin and seen him surreptitiously tuck something into the drawer. He'd known right away it was marijuana, none of *his* business. At least, not then.

The logbook looked okay, filled out and up to date. Tim checked the time of Benny's hail in to fisheries. He could get a good idea of the spawner index, and if a guy was pounding an area, simply by looking at the logbook. If the average size ratios dropped from large to medium suddenly and the fisherman hadn't set elsewhere he'd usually suggest the gear be moved. The catches were not large but the average size ratios hadn't changed much.

Benny hovered over his shoulder, "It'll get better when the tides settle down, real big tides this week." No comment from Tim as he closed the book and they left the cabin.

Benny went to the starboard side steering station outside the cabin door and slid the pike pole from its loop in the rigging. He leaned over and hooked the line with the pole, scooped up the round, pink scotchman. Benny expertly snaked the attached line around the power block, activated it and began to coil it into a big green bucket as the power block reeled up the line.

"You better get a good felt marker and fix up your boat name and number, Benny. It's getting pretty hard to read."

"Oh? Yah eh, never noticed. I'll do them all for you."

Tim heard the subtle dig, didn't respond. Benny knew the regulations as well as anyone and that it was his responsibility to stay on top of the clear identification of his fishing gear. Tim didn't want to be too nitpicky about what the fisherman should be doing nor did he like to overstep his authority. But if you couldn't read the boat name or number...*Don't do me no favours*, he thought.

"How many sets have you made in this spot?" asked Tim.

"Mmm, this is the third one so it might be starting to thin out."

Tim watched as Benny grabbed the snap of the surfacing weight and heaved it in to the boat. The first trap came up quick after that and there were a few in there. The mesh trap bellied out with the weight of the rosy prawns. Benny unsnapped it from the line, handily opened it, turned the trap upside down and shook the prawns into the sorting bin. Tim took the trap and checked that the tag was on and in good shape and that the mesh size was no smaller than the legal limit.

It was a pain to have to check all these little things but he kept careful watch for infractions of the rules. A few fishers tried to get around them, sometimes pulling their gear twice in one day, or using another species of fish as bait—something which was common practice before this fast-maturing and abundant species began to show signs of depletion. Double hauling was the worst, an activity that prawn fishers resented mightily in their cohorts. The regulations were designed to promote stock conservation, but often quick money in the present moment overruled the long-term objective of rebuilding the stocks.

"Looks pretty good here," commented Benny.

Tim sensed the fisherman's relief, but it was only the first trap. He said nothing as the next three came up empty except for hermit crabs, new occupants of emptied hairy triton shells. The fifth contained a male ling cod, occupying half of the circumference of the trap.

"Pass me the gaff, Benny."

"Ain't got one, need to get a new one, dang it. Forgot when I was in town."

"'Kay. I'll tip it out, hold the top open."

The two men watched the ling cod flip its tail and swim deep, and after that, up came a dozen traps each with a couple pounds. Clipboard and data sheet handy, Tim sampled every third trap, beginning with the second one, marking a zero for the empty ones.

"Whyn't ya start with that first one? It had lots of prawns!" Benny was peeved.

"You know I always start with the second, then number five, eight, eleven, and on like that. Benny. It's how we get an accurate average from the survey. If I sampled only the ones with lots of prawns it would skew the data."

Benny grunted and grabbed the next trap, emptied it into the bin. This time there were more to sort and Tim stepped forward to put the smaller two- to three-year-old males into one bucket, the huge three- to four-year-old egg-laying females—barren of eggs this time of year—into another and the transitional ones into the third. He flipped the prawns on their backs and lifted the second swimmeret to reveal the sex organ.

He could easily tell now which were the immature males, only a year old, and which were sexually mature at one and a half to two years. Somewhere along the way, maybe half a year later after having delivered their life-engendering sperm to a female, the males would grow much larger and transition to female.

Tim loved this process, distinguishing which and at what stage the prawns were in their life cycle. It was a continual miracle to him. Checking each one individually, he could tell by the smooth large plates enclosing the belly that these large ones would be jam-packed with pinky-orange eggs this coming winter. If he found a big space empty of eggs he was happy the big mama prawn had already delivered. It pleased him to find these empty prawns, even though little was known about what happened after they spawned.

Later he would total the number of females and transitionals and divide by seventeen—roughly one-third of each fifty-trap string—to get the spawner index, the figure by which it would be decided if or when to close an area.

So bright and hot today, Tim took care to handle the prawns quickly. They were okay for a few minutes out of salt water but too long on too hot a day would deprive them of vital oxygen and inevitably cause death. Not a desirable outcome for a fisher who worked a 'live' boat and hoped to deliver the prawns to the buyer in healthy flipping condition.

Benny ran one of these live boats and had always been anxious and irritable about the checking. He'd learned to bite his tongue and not hassle the checker though. He'd gotten pinched one year for pulling his gear twice and been careful ever since to stay on the right side of the checker. Of course he pretty much had to stay on the right side of this particular checker. Maybe he should invite Tim for dinner or something, would that be too weird?

He was surprised when Tim enthusiastically responded to his awkward invitation.

"Sure, when?"

"Oh, uh, Friday? I should still be here. You got to go up Tribune?" All the fishermen liked to keep tabs on where the checker was and whose boat he'd been on.

"Yah, first thing that morning, but I can come back down this way late afternoon."

"Okay."

Benny pulled at his ball cap, smiling. He was going to get things clear with Tim once and for all, no more of this silent dance around their other business. Maybe he could act like they were good buddies. He knew Tim was a sucker for the friendly overture.

Tim, too, was relieved. Benny seemed as eager as he to hash things out. He'd tell him about the deaths of the folks on the islands and the fentanyl in the drugs. He was certain Benny would do something about it to protect his buyers and make sure his product was safe.

Benny hasn't forgotten the awful dread he'd felt the day Tim snuck up on him up the head of Simoom Sound and had taken photos of him retrieving the drugs the crew from the

River Lass had stashed in the sealed packet. He'd thought it was a pretty good set-up, hanging the packet from an anchored chunk of driftwood instead of a buoy. It waited there for him to pick it up when he was able. He'd leave money in the waterproof bag, whatever the note they left him said to pay, never had any trouble.

That is, until the day Tim had pushed himself onto *Thunder Chieftain* under the pretense of boarding him to check prawns. Kind of ironic that the 'line' Benny had set that day was a decoy to make it look like his business there was legitimate. He was still filled with resentment and enraged confusion at how things had unfolded. Getting caught by Tim had turned out to be a whole lot better than getting caught by just about anyone else, though. He hadn't immediately been dragged off to jail.

Unfortunately Tim had pressured him for more than just a good buying price. He wanted Benny to cut him in for a share of the profits in return for not turning him over to the police.

What harm was he doing anyway? People wanted and needed what he brought them. Benny hadn't had much choice but to comply with Tim's demands, which varied according to his whim. Sometimes it was money; sometimes it was marijuana and once in a while ecstasy, speed or a little bit of cocaine in one form or another. It was never too much and not quite enough to prompt Benny into trying to formulate how to leverage freedom from the overzealous and snoopy prawn checker.

Then there was that time a couple weeks ago, he was pretty sure he'd seen a drone down the sound a ways but it hadn't hung around long. It had zipped over the trees back toward Moore Bay, as he was watching it. Good thing or he'd have shot it out of the sky. Hearing Back Eddy's story about the drone had shaken him up pretty good. Benny hadn't seen the old-timer's blue speedboat but he couldn't have been too far away; maybe just around the turn.

From time to time Tim motored up the dogleg to confirm that the ever-present anchored stick was still in place. He wanted to be sure that if Benny changed the delivery set-up he'd know about it. Usually he ran over there in the fog or at dusk when most folks—especially Back Eddy, who was known to head for the bunk by 7:00—were in for the night.

They both knew Back Eddy was everywhere, all the time, and his curious mind was always busy piecing things together. For sure he was someone to be avoided. Benny had hoped that his own activities way up the dogleg, not to mention the driftwood that never moved, would not be noticed.

Tim finished making his notes and gathered up his equipment. Benny hovered, trying to work out something he wanted to say. Tim looked up as he prepared to climb over the side of the boat onto his own.

"What?" he inquired. "Did I miss something? Something you want to ask?"

"I wanna know what you guys are gonna do about those Indians?"

"What do you mean, what 'Indians'?"

"Dammit, Tim, everybody acts like it's okay for them guys to be setting their gear and fishing everything in sight, no licence or anything. I keep seeing Ritchie Wilson's boat up at Embley, they got a set out in front, hanging the net all night and there's hardly any fish left up there anymore. Environmentalists be hanged! Those bastards are nothing but greedy. Conservators of the fish, pah!" He spat over the side of the boat.

"You got any photos, Benny?"

"Nah," he muttered. "Too far away."

"I don't know," said Tim. "Nothing I can do about it unless the fish cops see 'em."

"Can't ya at least give him a warning or tell him ya know and to quit it?"

Tim didn't want to antagonize Benny but he didn't 'know' just because Benny said so. Maybe he could think of a discreet way to let Ritchie know he was on the radar.

"I'll see what I can do," Tim said. "Oh, one last thing. I've got somebody I need to deliver some smoke to, you got a couple ounces? I'll settle up with you Friday."

"Mighta known." Benny didn't argue; he headed for the cabin to dig out his stash.

Fifteen

Regular as clockwork it's Thursday, mail day, again. Before she even opened her eyes Carol Ann heard wind singing in the trees, knew it is still blowing westerly. It had come up in the late afternoon and increased as night fell. She'd woken up when Back Eddy had motored into the bay at two o'clock in the morning. His homestead faced directly on Cramer Pass and when the west wind got to thumping his fishing boat, *Ocean Dawn*, too vigorously against the dock he would bring it around to Echo Bay, no matter what the time.

Carol Ann got up, looked out the window to confirm if it was still tied to the park dock. Happy to see it there, she whipped up a batch of pancake batter and took a half pound of bacon from the fridge. He'd have the oil stove cranked and be scribbling away in one of his many notebooks. Breakfast with Back Eddy was infrequent but always fun.

She'd been one of his deckhands, too; one of a long string of Back Eddy's deckhands, all female since the eighties, except for his grandsons and Kit's brother Cody. Might have been over twenty-five years ago now but you never forgot an experience like that. Those three seasons with Back Eddy had been about the most fun she'd had in her life among the islands. Too bad Herb had been such a shit about her going. Mentally she shrugged; his loss. She never could tolerate jealousy in a man. Come to think of it, she couldn't think of a single woman presently living on the coast that would. Maybe it was something in the water, or that there were so many more men than women you could snag another one anytime you wanted.

Whipping across the bay in her little rowboat Carol Ann enjoyed watching the cat's paws finger-painting blue swirls on the sea surface as she rowed by Nathan's float on her way to the park dock. Unlike his very tidy float, the dock was looking pretty tough, in spite of the repair work Back Eddy had done on it.

She tied up the boat and gingerly stepped across the rotten planks to board *Ocean Dawn*. She was right. Seated at the galley table, Back Eddy was pushing aside his notebooks as she entered the cabin.

"Thought you'd never get here! I been gettin' kind of hungry waitin' for you."

"I see you already got the pan hot," she laughed as she set the bacon and the bowl of batter on the counter.

It was cozy in the warm galley. Steam hissed gently from the kettle on the stove and the smell of the frying bacon watered her mouth. The boat rocked gently and the wind whistled through the rigging. She could easily imagine they were a hundred miles out to sea on a tuna trip.

No surprise when Back Eddy started on his rant about the state of the dock, he brought her back to the present with a thump. Angry about the shape it was in, he waved his fork over his breakfast. "We got to get together and fix it up properly but there's hardly anybody left here and we're all so damn busy all the time. Parks Board has been threatening for years now to spend fifty grand to demolish the dock. Why don't they spend fifty grand and fix it up instead?"

Carol Ann shrugged. She didn't have the answer to that.

"Government used to keep that dock in real good shape, now they let everything go to hell, then spend money tearing it down."

"What are you writing about now? Getting some more stories down?" She hoped to get his mind off unresolvable problems and on to something interesting.

"Not really," he said dismissively. "How's Woody's leg?"

"Okay I guess. He's self-medicating with marijuana but it doesn't seem to have any bad effect on him. Except for hobbling around he does some of the cooking, runs around picking up tree-planters, works on that shack with Cole and a million other things around here."

"I think I know where he's getting it."

"Oh? I have to admit I never wonder about that sort of thing. You know, Back Eddy, it's no big deal."

"Maybe not. But that fentanyl stuff is and maybe some of those drugs can get mixed up."

"He probably just gets it down island somewhere," she said comfortably. "There's lots of Vancouver Island marijuana available. Anyway, Back Eddy, it's legal now," she said pursing her mouth primly.

"Yah, well, that don't make it good for you." Back Eddy got the last word.

Rowing back to the marina Carol Ann felt fortified for her Thursday post mistress duties. She, like Woody, was always as busy as a one-armed paper-hanger, especially on Thursday. In spite of the fact that she always waited until the absolute last minute before the plane came in to snap the lid on the box and finalize the details on the flight dispatch sheet, there was always someone running in begging her to re-open it, re-weigh it and re-write the information.

On top of that there were the prawn boats coming in to fuel up and now tourist boats arriving who all needed to be registered and a tab begun for their purchases. Thank goodness it wasn't yet time for the pig roasts and dinners that were held in the high season. Woody always hired more staff for that; Carol Ann had enough on her plate. As she scrambled out of her little rowboat at the marina dock she remembered what Back Eddy had said and wondered why she'd acted like she wasn't interested. Just who did he think was providing marijuana for Woody? Must be someone local if Back Eddy thought he knew.

She fired up the generator and walked up the ramp to the concrete bridge, unlocked the door. She was open for business and here it came right behind her: first customer of the day, Ritchie Wilson from Kingcome.

"Give me a minute, Ritchie, just got to change the date stamp."

"No rush, Carol Ann."

She bustled around behind the counter then said, "We got a package here that was supposed to go to somebody in Kingcome last week. Do you want to take it up there or shall I return it to Port Hardy?"

"I can take it. Kind of a pain when the sorting gets screwed up. Two weeks to get it to the right place."

"It's a pain in the butt when the pilot drops off our mail box at Kingcome or Minstrel Island. Got to catch them right at the dock and look carefully every single time. Kit had a box of stuff delivered to Kingcome and the pilot swore he dropped it here. She had to phone Canada Post and talk to some guy in Quebec, can you believe it? Finally got it back two months later."

Ritchie chuckled. "It's worse when you get a letter saying 'Sorry, due to circumstances beyond our control, your mail got wet when the plane crashed.'"

"Really?"

"Yup, true story."

The door of the post office opened and Tim entered. He tipped his cap to Carol Ann and nodded politely to Ritchie. "How's life up the river, Ritchie?"

"Number one, Tim. How 'bout you? Looking like a pretty good season for the prawners, I hear."

Carol Ann interjected, "You guys got any mail? The plane's coming in, I just heard it go over and they'll be landing in a sec. I've got to get this box sealed up."

"Sure, sorry Carol Ann. Kind of early today, isn't it? I've got some letters for you, they're all ready to go."

She reached out her hand for them, authoritatively stamped each one with the Simoom Sound Post Office date stamp and dropped the letters in the box. She quickly entered the weight on the waybill.

"I just need to pick up that parcel you got, it can wait while you get organized. Plus I'll need a couple chocolate bars," said Ritchie.

They heard the distinctive change in propeller pitch as the plane hit the water and taxied toward the dock.

"Okay. There it is, gotta run." Carol Ann snapped shut the box, placed the paperwork on top and whipped out the door.

Dust motes drifted in the air and whirled up in the current stirred by her swift departure. They glimmered in the sudden quiet, lit up by the sun beaming in the window facing east. Tim was anxious; this was his chance to have a quiet word with Ritchie, plus he's got the marijuana to deliver.

Ritchie looked at him inquiringly. "Any chance you got that bit of smoke I could buy?"

Tim was already pulling it out of his pocket. "Yah, no problem, got it yesterday. Should be the usual good stuff."

"Yup, thanks." Ritchie pulled out his wallet.

Tim was torn; he couldn't decide whether to tackle giving Ritchie a heads up about the fentanyl thing or the illegal fishing thing. One after the other I guess, he thought; but he started with the wrong one. "Listen Ritchie, I..."

Ritchie raised his steady dark eyes to Tim's nervous ones as he pulled four fifty dollar bills out of his wallet. He said nothing while Tim stumbled to find the right words.

"I, ah, I got a report that there's been some illegal fishing going on up at Embley and, uh, thought you should know, ah, you're kind of on the radar."

"What the fuck, sorry, what the hell for? It's not me fishing up there. Who told you that? That damned Benny bastard I bet. Damn, he's getting to be a pain in the ass."

"Yah, no, sorry, Ritchie. I just thought it would be better if you knew, so, there it is. Now you know."

Tim felt like an idiot, he'd overstepped his authority in this confusing mix of business. Maybe he should apologize to Ritchie but before he could decide Carol Ann was thumping up the stairs with a bag of mail and Ritchie was opening the door for her. "Any more to get down there?" he asked. She nodded, yes.

Tim stood for a minute, gathering himself. Carol Ann regarded him carefully, taking inventory. "So, how're *you* doing, Tim. Got the teeth all fixed up?"

For a brief moment he was at a loss; so much had happened since he had gotten the emergency root canal that it felt like a year ago. "For sure, yah, thanks. Getting busy around here yet?"

She gazed out the window toward the marina, snorted. "Look for yourself! Not so much yet, a couple boats in and out, but it won't get real busy until July. The lodge is full of the last tree-planting crew right now. Got twelve young folks in there. They sure keep us hopping, and cooking. Pays the bills, I guess."

"Yah, I bet. Better get going, I guess, I've got a few things to do."

"Uh huh. You really okay, Tim?"

He twitched at that inquiry, knew precisely the nature of her interest. Replied with a tinge of bitterness, "I'm sure Kit told you the whole story, Carol Ann."

"Not actually," she said. "And we care about you, too. So I'm asking, how are you doing? Are you alright?"

Chastened, Tim muttered. "I'm fine, Carol Ann. Just fine. Thanks."

Tim had another stop to make and he headed down the ramp and along the dock. One more delivery, he'd hand off the marijuana to Woody and give him a heads up about the fentanyl; remembered then, he hadn't a chance to mention it to Ritchie.

Sixteen

im was gearing up for his visit with Benny. Leaning in to the mirror over the sink in the tiny head in his liveaboard he carefully drew the razor along his jaw. Finishing the shave he slapped on some aftershave, then washed it off with a couple splashes of water. Mostly he was used to dressing up for fine dining with women. Not that necessary to get all dressed up to eat with Benny. He was nervous and not sure why. His dressing ritual calmed him as he looked through the clothes in the hanging locker; kind of felt like putting on armour.

Bunch of fuss for no damn good reason. He wished it was Saturday so he could be dressing up for Kit. Good thing he had a lot of prawn boats to catch up on or he'd be going crazy waiting for the days to pass before he could see her. He'd got it all worked out, what he'd cook for her. Caesar salad, a nice wine, butterflied prawns fried in butter, garlic and soy sauce sprinkled on at the hot finish. The hot finish would end the evening just right.

Margaret popped into his mind then, the most recent hot finish he'd experienced. He saw her face, the way her eyes had glowed golden in the candlelight with tenderness and sorrow as they lay entwined in her bed. He pushed her out of his mind. It's done, over. It has to be if he's to have a future with Kit. He was determined to have a future with her and vowed, again, to do whatever it took to make that happen.

Reaching into the hanging locker he fingered the new blue shirt he'd bought in the Fields store at McNeill. Rejected it for the green and brown cotton plaid he'd worn on his date with Margaret; he'd save the new one for when he saw Kit. Tim indecisively pulled out his brown corduroy jacket, held it up. *What is wrong with me? For Pete's sake, I'm going to eat with Benny.*

He felt more confident when he pulled on the jacket, slipped his feet into his go-to-town shoes, and climbed into his skiff. Tim looked around at the scenery as he motored out of Wahkana Bay. He liked the anchorage here; it was beautiful, protected, shielded from view unless someone entered the narrow passage. Some of the anxiety he'd been feeling lifted as he focused his attention on the evening light and the colours of the passing scene.

A few water birds puddled around by the shore, mommy mergansers with a string of babies. He watched them, smiling, until a sudden rush of wings signalled the swoop and clutch of an eagle picking off the ninth and last loitering baby merg. It was chilling when you saw that and realized how few baby birds survived to maturity.

Tim shook off the shiver that rushed up his back and pushed the throttle forward. Dinner with Benny, coming up.

And Benny was friendly when Tim arrived: putting his best foot forward, welcoming Tim onto *Thunder Chieftain* and inviting him into the warm cabin.

"Whew, what a day."

"Pretty hot, that's for sure," agreed Tim.

"Look at you, all dressed up! That for me?" inquired Benny.

Self-consciously Tim stumbled, "'Course not. I just like to get into clean clothes once in a while, even if it's not a woman I'm visiting with."

"Ayuh, like Kit, I guess. She's worth getting cleaned up for."

"Uh huh." Tim was short; he didn't want to discuss Kit with his current host.

"Yah, I had lunch with her a few days ago, she invited me over."

Right away Tim's hackles went up. Why would Kit have Benny over for lunch? A little green devil whispered in his ear... find out about this. He could just ask Kit but the little green devil wouldn't leave him alone, poked at him, inciting him to just ask. Just ask; he resisted.

Benny pulled a joint from out behind his ear and a lighter from his pocket. He raised the joint to his lips, thumbed the lighter, sucked until the sparks fired up. The warm scent of the burning joint distracted Tim from the voice. He reached for the joint as Benny exhaled and passed it over. "Aaah, always good for what ails ya."

"So true."

So much comfort in lighting up a joint with someone, even if he had a complicated relationship with that someone. He and Benny went back a long way. They'd been around this neigh-bourhood for ten or twelve years, helped out with the salmon enhancement, fished or partied together. And now...well, now Benny's independent spirit bucked against Tim's role as the prawn checker. Plus this new element that needed to be dealt with.

But the joint mellowed the two men and they talked about fishing for a while, the weather, and the other prawn boats. Benny rolled another and the marijuana haze thickened in the cabin. Tim looked out the window: the sky was blueing deeper into indigo while paler blue clouds appeared to be stuck here and there on the hills.

The clouds over by Mount Read began to look like a circus train. First an elephant rolled slowly across the sky and in front of the mountain, then the long trunk uncoiled and stretched up into a giraffe neck. The top of the giraffe neck and head turned pink in the late sun, as they rose skyward, and a big hippopot-amus followed. Behind it trailed a couple of slinking cats, they shifted into a horsey gallop, long sprawling legs melting as they ran. Tim was transfixed. At long last, he relaxed into enjoying the evening and this fabulous show.

He nudged Benny's foot with his, said with a chuckle, "Lookit those crazy animal clouds. D'ya see them? Trippy, man." Aware he had dissolved into stoner platitudes.

Benny looked and laughed right along with him. "Far out, man. Got the munchies yet?" He pulled on oven mitts and opened the door of the oil stove, extracted a cast-iron pot, and placed it on a hotplate on the table. Tim was wide-eyed in amazement at Benny's coordination.

"Boy, you didn't spill a drop."

"Or burn myself."

Both found this hilarious and sputtered with laughter. "Made ya seafood stew; shrimp and crab and cod. Wanna grab a couple bowls and spoons?"

Tim knew exactly where to find the bowls and spoons, same place they were in every other fishing boat galley: top drawer in the stack at the end of the counter, by the door. He didn't even have to get up from his place on the settee, just leaned over to open the drawer. The table was quickly set and the seafood stew scooped into the bowls. Benny plopped a loaf of bread on the table and a knife.

"Help yourself."

Slurps and burps from hungry men while Neil Young sang in the background about a heart of gold. Benny offered a second bowlful, Tim accepted. Finally he leaned against the settee and swiped the back of his hand across his mouth. "Excellent, thank you; quite a lot better than sardines and crackers."

"That what you usually eat? Guess that's why you're so skinny."

Tim released a comfortable sigh and patted the round bulge of full belly, fumbled in his pocket. "Guess it's my turn to roll up."

"I got a nice bit of coke, let's do that."

"I dunno, man. You sure it's not laced with something? Fentanyl or whatever."

"It's fine, Tim. Don't be a wuss."

"Yah, no, I'll just roll this one then head out."

Benny didn't reply. He cleared the dishes off the table, and standing up in the alley between the table and the galley counter, put the dishes in the sink. He threw a couple tea bags in the teapot and lifting the heavy kettle, poured the boiling water.

He set the kettle back down on the hot stove and reached for a small cedar box from the shelf by the window, set it on the table. Tim watched as he took out a hundred dollar bill and a bag of white powder and carefully arranged them in front of him. With ritualistic movements he sprinkled out a small amount of the powder and cut it with a razor blade, then carefully rolled up the bill. Benny blew out his breath and then put the tube to his nose and with a swift inhalation, sucked in half the powder. With one last 'you sure?' invitation he looked up at Tim, who shook his head.

Benny changed the tube to his left nostril and finished off the line. Nodded his head in satisfaction and then sneezed mightily.

He turned on the cabin light, brought tea. He offered canned milk and sugar and poured both liberally into his own cup. Tim rolled the joint, lit it, toked deeply and passed it to Benny.

The sky was dark, the galloping clouds blending into the night sky. A few stars twinkled here and there. Getting late. The atmosphere had changed somehow, nothing abnormal when you're smoking. And snorting.

Uh oh, thought Tim. He was hypersensitive but calm, ready for anything. He hadn't forgotten that he and Benny had to talk. *Have to talk, what a phrase. Brain still tripping, better get it together.*

"So Benny," Tim began. "I saw the RCMP sergeant in town, before I came out."

Benny interjected rudely. "You fuckin' her?"

"Jesus, man, what the hell? None of your business! 'Course not!"

"What then? What're you doin' with her?"

"Talking, Benny. Talking, if it's any of your beeswax. She told me there've been some problems, asked me to keep an eye out."

"Fuck ya talking about? What kinda problems?"

Tim toked again from the smouldering joint, handed it back to Benny. "Like I said, fentanyl problems. People dying or overdosing."

Benny raised his eyebrows in disbelief. "In the north island? I don't believe you."

"It's not me, Benny; it's Margaret Morris, chief cop? She should know. It's here. Fentanyl's here. Some chick from Sointula just died and there's a fisherman in the Port Hardy Hospital, they got some naloxone into him quick enough."

"What's that got to do with me?"

"Jesus, Benny, don't be an ass. You—" Tim pointed his finger emphatically, "are dealing drugs, and you don't even know the guys you are getting it from or where it comes from or anything!"

"I guess that makes two of us, don't it?" drawled Benny carelessly. "I suppose you never snooped around in *White Bird*'s wheelhouse."

"Oh, is he in the same business as you? Well, with the risk going up like that I kinda think my cut should go up. Maybe I'll see what he can cut me in for," Tim dared.

Like a sea monster breaching Benny erupted from his seat, face distorted with fury. Leaning across the table he grabbed Tim by the shirt, pulled hard enough that the collar tore away from the shoulder seam.

"You greedy sonofabitch! Ya think ya got me over a barrel, dontcha? Lemme share a thing or two with ya! You try this shit on with Henderson, you'll be sorry; you don't know what you're messing with."

Eyes compressed into tiny slits and spraying spit he shook Tim back and forth, banging his head against the wall behind the galley bench. Tim grabbed Benny's wrists but couldn't break the unyielding clutch on his shirt.

"Calm down, calm down!" he shouted.

Benny foamed at the mouth; he twisted his hands to grab Tim's and squeezed, felt the bones give. He dragged Tim out of the seat, pushed him against the blistering heat of the stove.

"Christ!" Tim heaved himself sideways toward the door, grasped the doorknob with his good hand, turned it and flung open the door. "You're fucking nuts, man! You burned my hand, broke my fingers!"

Tim fell out the door and then Benny was above him screaming about Kit. "Lemme tell you what your girlfriend's been doing! Hah, with me! Yah, that's right. She let me in her pants and now I seen some other guy over to her place."

"Liar! Liar! You fucker Benny, you just can't leave anyone alone, can you!" bellowed Tim, but his bravado only got him a short distance across the deck. Hand throbbing mightily, Tim scuttled for the rail and fumbled with the tie-up lines as Benny rushed him.

He leaped.

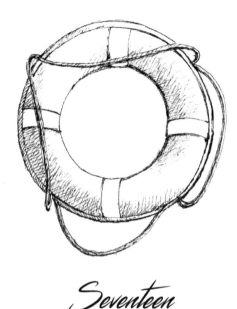

Seventeen

Cocooned in her blankets, Kit snuggled cozy, relaxed—and wide awake. She lay quietly, absorbing the tranquility, stretching her awareness beyond the bedroom, out to the float-house's deck and beyond to the narrow inlet. Except for the distant call and return of an owl, all was silent. No light pierced the velvet dark.

What had roused her? The unusual silence of this highwater slack tide? Or a familiar noise—perhaps a motor? A receding sound, becoming quieter, nevertheless it had percolated into her sleeping brain.

In any case, she was now alert. No use trying to go back to sleep with her senses fired up and longing for action. Kit stretched luxuriously, relishing the power in her biceps and back muscles, the elasticity of muscle over bone in her hips and thighs. She snaked an arm out from under the covers and felt around for her clothing. Swinging her feet out of bed and onto the fishnet rug, she pulled on a lacy T-shirt and panties, then black jeans and a sweatshirt.

Fumbling at the bedside table in the dark her hands found an elastic band, and swiftly ponytailed her auburn curls.

Kit walked barefoot across the floor, watched her feet appear in the elongated squares of glowing moonlight cast from the window onto the cool fir planks. She opened the French doors off the bedroom, stepped onto the front deck.

No wind stirred the coniferous foliage; no noise broke the soundless dark. But as she listened hard, Kit heard the faint susurrus of a boat wake, a set of small swells lapping toward her dock. The float shivered lightly as each wavelet hit the float logs.

Well.

Who could be out there in the middle of the night? Maybe a tugboat crew towing a log boom or delivering freight to a camp, or someone running up Kingcome, longing to get home after a couple weeks in the city.

Her own voice broke the stillness of the night. "Kit, stop it. You don't always need to know everything."

But she did. Always wondering, surmising, checking her conclusions against the facts as they appeared; she *did* need to know everything.

Kit went back into the house, this time through the living room door. In the darkened kitchen she walked to the sink, lifted a glass from the shelf, turned on the tap (*Oh Blessed Water*), remembering the previous winter, when it had been so cold for weeks on end that the water line froze up solid, not just once but several times. It had been a long season of careful water rationing and midnight dashes to fill the bathtub before the water slowly froze as it dribbled from the tap.

She filled the glass and drank, tasting the earthen breath of the land in the long swallow.

Her blue fleece lay over the easy chair and Kit pulled it on, grabbed the green corduroy ball cap and tucked her ponytail through the back opening. The cap was embroidered with the Seafoods Fish Cannery logo. Wearing it brought to mind the good memories of deckhanding for Back Eddy. For eight seasons they'd fished for salmon and ling cod from Cape Scott to Langara on Haida Gwaii's north shore, and points in between.

She settled the cap on her head. How extraordinary it was that the simple choice of a particular ball cap could imbue her with confidence. Back on the deck she clipped on her life jacket, slid the kayak into the sea, wiggled in and paddled away. In the breathless May night, she headed out of her own little bay and turned the bow into the moonlit swath of Fife Sound.

Kit's eyes adjusted quickly as she paddled on the still black water. She embraced the night mist with a happy sigh, admired the gauzy cloud scarves undulating along the distant shoreline. Land and sea merged, separated, and merged again, making it difficult to distinguish one from the other. With each stroke, trails of light dripped from her paddle and glistened pale silver as she lifted and dipped and pressed, left and right in a serene rhythm.

Luminous phosphorescence glittered beneath, beside, and behind. Small fish startled into action, flashed sparkles as they shot ahead of her shadowy presence. A seductive moon peeked out from behind a wisp of cloud. Stars twinkled deliriously in the high dark. Clouds of watery sparks reflected the Milky Way.

Stars above, stars below...

Resting the paddle, Kit floated in perfect silence in the midnight hour. A sleepy murrelet released a tiny squeak, then another. Her breath leaked out in a sigh of holy contentment as she leaned back against the coaming. The sea breathed, a long inhalation followed by an exhalation of swell. Her sense of self expanded into the vast immensity of the cosmos, and for this singular moment, she was one with the universe.

In harmony with it all, Kit inhaled, and then exhaled. Along with the night, the sea, the moon, mist and darkness, she experienced her being as just another element in the vast design. Oneness with the universe rarely lasted long and must, she knew, be cherished.

A strange low noise broke into her trance. She straightened and widened her range, listening intently. A muffled shout, a perceptible wave of sound swelled across the water.

Men's voices raised in anger, broken words thudding like bullets. Kit could make no sense of it. A loud bellow shattered the air. Definitely an argument, possibly a fight. More shouts, a pause. Two voices, then a thud. Silence for a long moment. A motor growled into life, then a louder rumble she identified as an anchor chain. A boat was put in gear and strained for the revs.

"What the hell?"

Now *that* was weird, not to mention creepy. Kit's first response was to paddle toward the sounds. Maybe someone needed help. Her second response was to run for home. Torn between that part of her that always wanted to *know* and the instinct for self-preservation that reminded her that a slim woman alone in a kayak—*no matter how buff she might be*—could be at risk. If she went haring after loud male voices and boats in the night she might find herself caught in the middle of much more than she'd bargained for.

Immobilized by indecision, she looked around. The mist had thickened while she'd strained to comprehend the disturbing cries. Thick clouds now obscured the moon's ephemeral half-disc. Swiftly the clamouring motor receded into the distance. From the direction and diminishment of the sound she concluded the boat was headed for Tribune Channel.

Hesitantly she dipped the kayak paddle, pausing to listen every few strokes as she glided along. Silence reigned. Should she take a look? Maybe just a bit of a look-see, just so she didn't feel a coward, shaking in her boots at a little disturbance in the night. Kit aimed for the islands, tense and anxious. She hoped to find nothing.

The motor's low throb faded until she could barely hear it. The moon leaned lower in the sky. Its light glimmered briefly until more clouds smothered it entirely. There *was* nothing to be seen as she approached the end of Denham Island, and not one single thing to see or hear, as she rounded the end and paddled along the north shore. If she didn't head for home damn quick she might have trouble finding her way back.

Kit suddenly felt so alone, so vulnerable. She hadn't even thought to bring a flashlight in her impulsive rush to embrace the night. Should she go to the fish farm and see if anyone there had heard anything?

This opened up another line of risk. She'd been actively opposing the fish farms, believing that raising thousands of Atlantic salmon in net pens was harmful to the wild salmon she and her neighbours had struggled to protect. She'd rather not wake a crew in the dead of night to ask if they'd heard strange noises out here. And if they had, or if it was them, would it be so dark and silent at the site?

"You need to think hard about this," Kit muttered. It could take two hours to paddle around all the islets that comprised this group, and most likely she'd never see a thing in the unassailable blackness. Better to go home and check things out in the big boat tomorrow—or rather, later this morning. She listened hard again, for an immeasurably long time. Floating in the hushed sea, she noticed the intensifying fog layering her skin with tiny droplets of moisture, and reluctantly made up her mind.

With the wiser (cowardly?) thoughts powering her stroke, her mind furiously engaged in the 'discretion versus valour' argument, Kit turned the kayak and made a swift journey back to her Gilford Island home. She gasped in relief as she rounded the point, sucked in a huge lungful of air and surged toward the floathouse's welcoming security.

For sure she'd get up at the first light and go cruise the islands.

In bed once again, it took her so long to let go into sleep that she finally set the alarm, uncertain if she could rely on her internal clock.

Eighteen

ayley was back in her mossy nook, daydreaming, dozing, slipping from dream to waking dream of high clouds and a sweet wind brushing her face. A warm kiss pressed against her forehead startled her out of the reverie. A small wave of shock coursed through her, was it revulsion? She shuddered and jerked her head, bumping Ritchie's nose.

"Ouch! Take it easy Hayley, it's just me..."

She sat up, rubbed her face.

"Ritchie! You snuck up on me, I'm sorry, you okay? Your nose okay? I thought you weren't coming until tonight."

He took her hand, laid it against his cheek and let the soft feel of it flood through him. He noted the fine lines the last two years had etched at the corner of her eyes, the worry showing around her mouth.

"Hayley, you're worrying again, aren't you? Let me take care of you. Please."

"Shh..." she pressed her hand against his mouth. "Don't, Ritchie."

"Dammit, Hayley. I love you. I want us to be together, I've been patient while you went to school but I want to get started on a life with you. You've got to get serious about growing up. We've got a lot to do, we need to get together and help people deal with stuff, all the history, with reconciliation."

"Oh, Ritchie, for crying out loud. I'm young! I just got out of school, I got a job, I want to just...be here, and run around in the boat and explore and learn. You know what'll happen if we get married. I'll get pregnant and the next thing you know we'll have four kids and you'll leave me and I'll start drinking or get into drugs and life will go for shit and the boys will die and the girls will end up in skid row and my life will be an unending stream of sorrow. You *know* that!"

Hayley looked at Ritchie, aghast at her own outburst. Her eyes filled with tears. *Is that what I believe?*

"Don't know where that came from, sorry."

"I'm not like that, Hayley, I'd never leave you and I'm never drinking again."

"Yes, I know, you're a good guy, Ritchie."

"Look at your parents, they've done okay, it doesn't happen to everyone," he said softly.

"But my parents *love* each other," she blurted.

A long silence as Ritchie processed her words and Hayley thought, *Uh oh*. The truth lay between them now, unadorned, and she could no longer pretend to feel something she didn't, nor hope any longer that someday she would.

"I'm truly sorry, Ritchie. You *are* a good man and you've always been good to me...but..."

"But you don't love me."

Slowly she shook her head. "I thought I could, or that I might. I have so much respect for you but I don't even know who I am. I have...feelings I cannot even name and I need...something. Something else. I don't know what but I want to find out."

Ritchie rocked back on his heels, looked toward the blue horizon. "Well," he said, "this didn't go the way I'd hoped."

Hayley snuffled beside him, rooting around in her pockets for something to wipe her nose with. The tears wouldn't stop, she cried harder, and Ritchie lay down beside her on the sleeping bag and folded her in his arms. Gently he swept the long fall of black hair from her forehead and ran his fingers down its length. His nose prickled with the pain of his understanding, tears leaked out of his own tightly scrunched eyes. He would never have this woman as his own, to love and cherish, never father her children, never be the patriarch of a small yet happy tribe. Just like that his dream of love and a future with Hayley was incinerated in her blurted truth.

A raven soared close above them, the sound of its wings like the crumbling of ashes.

Nineteen

A crackling blaze in the centre of the large room lit the Big House with a golden glow. Billowing its way out the ceiling exit above the fire, cedar smoke infused the space with mystery and solemnity. The carved and painted faces and bodies of five wolves took pride of place at the end wall opposite the entryway. Shadows of people passing between the flickering fire and the majestic wolf carvings imbued them with a vitality that appeared jovial one moment and sinister the next.

A thick layer of sand covered the floor where costumed dancers draped in woven cedar capes and headdresses adorned with feathers and abalone shell performed stylized moves around the fire. The dances—complex, compelling, hilarious and riveting—told ancient myths of Bukwus and D'Sonoqua and the Animal Kingdom. People entered and exited in a hypnotic flow of motion and colour. The fire would slow to an orange glimmer and then, as if to emphasize the action, roar up with brilliant force.

Although people of all colours and stripes were here tonight at this potlatch, the First Nations and non–First Nations communities were not as intertwined as they'd once been. When the school was open and both Echo Bay and Gwayasdums kids had attended there'd been many occasions when the two groups had gathered. The end-of-school do, their own version of Sports Day, and of course the Christmas presentations and potluck at the Echo Bay community hall had brought everyone together.

Now those ties were thin; stretched and frayed with lack of use. Since early childhood in the village with his parents, and his love affair with Annie Callum, Nathan had been immersed in the Indigenous culture. He wouldn't stay away from a feast, a naming ceremony or potlatch by or for a friend, in spite of all the years of Vera shutting him out of her life.

Not only Nathan but Carol Ann and Kit came when they could to visit with their friends and participate. And tonight Cole was with them—a special guest if he had but known—eyes all over the place as he took in the grandeur, the happy confusion of ceremony and celebration, the fire and friendliness of these people.

Benny, invited like all the Echo Bay folks, was here as well, drawn by the pull of the ceremony and the gathering of people. He had friends here, and a few customers, too. And a party is a party. He was all spruced up, looking good, looking for some fun. Like many folks at the feast he moved into and out of the Big House as he needed a break from the kaleidoscope of dancing, chanting and lengthy orations.

Kit, seated in the second row, spied Hayley as she entered, watched her weave her way through the crowd of people, waved when she saw her scanning the bleachers.

"Kit! I'm so glad you came tonight." Hayley stepped lightly up to Kit and her friends. The women leaned into the embrace. Kit felt Hayley's angst immediately.

"What's up girl?" she whispered. "You okay?"

"Yah...no. Not really."

"Oh, sweetie. Me too, not really. Want to come up and visit, have a sleepover? What're you doing Monday? I could pick you up on my way back from McNeill."

"That'd be great, thanks. I'm going back outside, was just checking to make sure you made it. Did y'all bring your cushions?"

"You bet we did. Didn't even need Nathan to remind me. My butt hurt for days after that last one."

Hayley commiserated. "The bleachers are so hard; you can't sit for more than twenty minutes before you get a numb rear end. Hey, I've got something for you."

"What? Whatcha got for me, Hayley?" Kit's interest was piqued. Not often a surprise gift came her way.

"You'll see. You have to wait a few minutes." The younger woman's eyes gleamed.

"Okay. Talk later?"

"Oh yeah, I'll be back. This thing will go on for hours."

Kit pressed her cheek against Hayley's, squeezed her arms gently as they released each other. She watched her friend step down from the bleacher seats and ease her way through the smoky atmosphere toward the darkness outside the doors.

"Who's that?" asked Cole.

"My friend, Hayley Tucker. I'll introduce you when she comes back. She seemed a little upset so I just thought I'd wait a bit. Didn't mean to be rude."

"No worries, I get it. Wow, she is beyond gorgeous."

As he listened to this exchange Nathan noted the young man's broad cheeks and strong brow in the flicker of the central firelight. Cole's brown eyes were not particularly dark. Strands of his frizzy, not-quite-black hair glittered with gold firelight reflection and contrasted with his light tan skin. He was altogether a beautiful boy, with a striking mix of his Indigenous and Scandinavian heritage. Nathan was still overwhelmed by the enormity of Cole's arrival in his life.

Carol Ann, between them, followed his lead and looked at Cole, too, then back at Nathan. He could see she was thinking the same thoughts as him. So far, Carol Ann was the only one he'd told about Cole. Although the others had got it figured anyway, they'd given him space to tell everyone when he was ready. Gently he slid his hand under hers and enfolded her fingers within his.

157

Surprised, Carol Ann turned toward Nathan. "What?!" she exclaimed softly.

"Dunno, Carol Ann," he shrugged. "I just felt like it." Sky blue eyes twinkled at her, a smile wrinkled the corners of his mouth.

How happy she suddenly felt, up a notch from her previous contentment. Pink suffused her skin and she turned her head away. No mood went unheralded by her fair complexion.

Benny was outside the Big House. He was getting some air, as he thought of it, lighting up a cigarette and contemplatively blowing the smoke. He turned when light spilled out the door, saw a female figure silhouetted briefly before it closed. She stepped out into the dark heading in his direction. He stood very still until she bumped into him, then let himself stumble and reach out. His hand brushed against her breast.

Hayley brought her hands up swiftly, pushed hard against his throat. "What the...get off!"

"Ow! Hey! No need to get huffy. I'm sorry! It was an accident. I'm sorry, okay? You're Hayley, right, the girl who works on the council boat? I've seen you around."

She stepped back and replied, cautiously, "Ye-ess..."

"Hey, you know me, I'm Benny Thompson," he said, all friendly. "From down at Echo Bay? Maybe you'd like to come fishing with me? I need a deckhand from time to time."

Hayley looked at him in disbelief. "You have got to be kidding me. You in need of a deckhand or angling for a hook-up? As you clearly know, I already have a job."

"Oh sorry, sorry, Hayley, honey, just being friendly."

Now he was trying to placate her. He'd been clumsy and gone too far, made a hash of it—again. These modern girls were just not like the ones he used to meet.

"Well, let me tell you this, pal...I don't know you well enough for you to be this friendly, and I'm pretty sure I don't want to. You better just leave me alone. And don't call me honey."

"Yah, well. Maybe you're gay or something anyway," he muttered.

"I didn't hear that," snapped Hayley as she stalked off.

Her swift forward motion brought her up hard against someone's chest, *Not again!*

"Good grief, now what?" And then at the familiar smell and feel of the man, "Ritchie?"

"You okay? Is that guy bothering you?"

"No, it's nobody, just Benny Thompson, that prawn fisherman. It's nothing."

Ritchie's hand slid to her wrist, tightened. She pulled against his grip.

"You sure? He's an asshole. I'll beat the crap out of him if he's bothering you."

"Come on, Ritchie, I said it's okay. I bumped into him in the dark. Leggo my wrist."

"You tell me if he's bothering you, I'll take care of him."

"Ritchie, no. Stop it. I'm not your girlfriend anymore; I can take care of myself, thank you very much. And you can't go around 'taking care of' guys you don't like."

Ritchie released her wrist, watched her disappear down the path, fumed.

Benny slipped around the corner of the building. He walked partway down the side of it and lit up another cigarette, stood smoking in the dark, hearing the chants and shrieks of the excited crowd responding to the story inside the Big House.

Struck down again. Hayley reminded him of someone, or something, and then it came to him. A dark, smoky bar on Hastings Street,more than twenty-five years ago now, and he'd hoped to have buried this memory—totally and completely forgotten it, forever—but like a deadhead that just bobbed up and down, it never disappeared. He'd been down to Vancouver with his pay from a big logging show and a friend from Alert Bay had introduced him to a girl, his cousin he'd said, from the North Island. A pretty girl, but thin, with brown skin and blue eyes. An Indian girl and she'd seemed to like him. He'd known she wasn't eighteen like she said, but he'd bought her drinks anyway. He hadn't been that nice with her...kind of pushed her when she'd hesitated. *What the hell had she been doing in a bar anyway?*

He cursed and threw down his cigarette, stomped on it with unnecessary force. "I wasn't that bad! Was I?"

Didn't even realize he'd spoken out loud; wished he hadn't remembered.

Benny wasn't a completely stupid man. He was a good fisherman and proud of it. He paid his debts and was helpful to women, but in his heart he knew there was something wrong with him. Every time his mind went down that path it disturbed and compelled him. That path, of course, was his childhood. Isn't it always?

Dammit, Mother, get out of my head.

He looked back at his eleven-year-old self crying by his bean-counter—according to his mother—father's grave. His erratic mother getting increasingly more weird as he grew into his teens. Always dissing the girls he liked. He'd had a big crush on Jennifer, the high school head cheerleader and thought maybe he had a chance with her. Jennifer Whatsername with her cloud of dark hair. Oh, he'd been crazy for her.

His mom insisted he brush her hair before she went to bed, would sit there in her nightgown with a few drinks under her belt and the pleasure noises she made sickened him as they turned him on. Everything turned him on at sixteen, no surprise there. But if he didn't brush her hair the way she wanted—too hard or too soft—she'd snatch the brush from his hand and wallop him. Then she'd get all wound up and take out her disappointment with her husband, lovers and life in general by whacking him harder and yelling and crying. She'd end the scene by stroking his face softly, apologizing, and saying "I love you, Benny, only you. You're the man in my life. Don't you leave me like your dad did."

Confusing as hell. He *wanted* to please her but eventually figured out that was never going to happen. He wanted to slap her, too—pay her back for all the hurt she'd laid on him.

He couldn't seem to please any of the women he'd ever wanted to, anyway. Look at Carol Ann. Didn't matter what he did or said, or how he tried to let her know she was sexy and appealing; she just laughed at him. She'd really laid it on the line after the debacle at Woody's. He'd been pretty taken aback when she'd been so direct and he'd had a hard time keeping a straight face. He so badly wanted to bust out laughing.

And Kit...he'd kind of hoped her youth would be a plus when he moved on her. Usually younger women were more malleable and responsive, but not her. Except for that one time, he remembered with a grin. They'd had a couple glasses together and he'd come on kind of pitiful and she'd gone for it. But these days, even though she was friendly, one look from her shrivelled him right up. His thick wavy hair might be going grey but the truth was, at the age of sixty he was better looking now than he'd ever been. He was strong and competent, wealthy—wealthy enough anyway—he had *something* to offer a woman.

Suddenly there was Hayley, again, returning from wherever she'd stalked off to. She didn't look at or speak to him as she swept by, cradling something in her arms. Benny was crushed and ashamed. Again. Why was he always so clumsy?

Damn women, what's the point in even trying to be nice? In disgust Benny flicked away the burnt down cigarette, didn't even bother stepping on this one.

Back inside the Big House, the dancing had paused and the lights had been turned up bright. Hayley made her way through the crowd and up the two steps to Kit. She leaned down and passed a small cedar basket to her.

"What have you brought me?" Kit was excited and pleased as she turned back a corner of the light brown blanket covering a woven cedar basket. "Oh! A little kitten. Oh my goodness, it's the cutest thing."

She reached one finger into the basket and stroked the black fur. Bright yellow eyes winked up at her and the kitten yawned, exposing its tiny teeth. "Hayley, thank you so much! Beautiful basket, too." Kit admired the complex weaving as she stroked the kitten's forehead.

"She's six weeks old, Kit. You said you wanted one a while ago and I found the litter and been looking after this one. It's kind of a runt. The rest have been all over the place. I think the eagles got a couple of them. You can keep the basket, if you want. She's been sleeping in it."

"I love her! And the basket, wow. Thank you double. I *have* been wanting a kitty. A girl kitty, that's wonderful."

"Yeah. I haven't named her, figured you'd want to."

"Kitcat," she said promptly. "What d'you think of Kitcat?"

The lights dimmed and people around were shushing them. Someone said, "Sit down, Hayley, you're blocking our view." Kit patted the seat between her and Cole and wiggled over to make room.

Cole felt Hayley squeeze into the space between himself and Kit—he hadn't thought there'd be room for one more body—and shifted toward Nathan.

The drum drum drumming of cedar sticks on cedar log began and gained power. Cole had been listening in on Kit and Hayley but now the rhythm gathered him in, as it was meant to, and swept him up and away. Like his own heartbeat, each stroke thundered in his chest. Unconsciously Cole slapped his thighs, making an emphatic fist, shaking it to amplify the energy. Beside him, he saw that Nathan was caught up in the same spell, transfixed by the constancy of the unceasing beat, the flicker of fire and smoke, punctuated at intervals by an outburst of sparks.

Nathan pressed closer to Carol Ann, noticed how soft and pillowy she felt, crushed up so close against him. *Maybe we should come to potlatches more often.* She smelled good; not too flowery but clean and sweet. He watched the revealing rosy blush flood up her neck as he squeezed closer.

162

Cole, smack dab in the middle of this dense emotional web, experienced every vibration from everyone. He felt himself as a small part of a gigantic organism. Somehow he'd been lifted out of and beyond the boundaries of self.

He turned to Hayley, met her eyes, smiled and reached his right hand around to her, said "Hi, the name's Cole." Delicately she slid her fingers against his, their eyes caught and held. She let her fingers rest against his a beat longer. Something had rattled her.

Is it me? he asked with a raised eyebrow and questioning eyes.

It's nothing. She lifted the shoulder beside his dismissively, head turned into the lifted shoulder, a small grimace, lowered lids. It's not him then, but it's something.

What? he mouthed.

Shh. She laid a finger on her pursed lips, shook her head, nodded toward the dancers, now costumed in cloaks and bird-like masks with giant beaks that clacked open and closed.

Cole returned his now unseeing gaze to the gesticulating supernatural figures. It took a few seconds before they came back into focus. Meeting this girl had filled him with an inexplicable certainty; indefinable as yet, but a certainty without precedence in his life. His adoptive parents had been good to him, tried hard to walk the line between caring for him and helping him follow his path, but they had known nothing about his heritage. Neither did he, yet, but he was hearing a clear bell-like ringing in this Big House, surrounded by these people.

He was going to follow that ringing.

Much later, after the festivities and feasting had crested, receded, and begun again, the Echo Bay group conferred and decided it was time. Hayley walked with them as they said good-night and hugged and introduced Cole to friends on their way to the exit. By the door stood Hayley's grandmother, royally garbed in her regalia, a handmade button blanket and a headpiece of woven cedar bark with a fine large abalone shell stitched in the centre. Cole felt her imperious gaze upon him, met a pair of piercing black eyes.

"Granddaughter," she commanded. "Who is your new friend? Where has he come from?"

"I don't know yet, Ada. His name is Cole."

She turned to Cole. "This is my grandmother, Cole."

He extended his hand, what was the right thing to do? Glanced at Hayley, she offered no help.

"Cole...Harrison. Ma'am."

Regally she held out her hand, barely touched his. "Mrs. Harvey, Vera. Welcome. Gilakas'la."

She shot a glance at Nathan. The question was asked and answered; he will bring Cole to her soon.

Nathan raised his hands, open palms wide. "He's come to Echo Bay to give Woody a hand, so we brought him along."

Vera nodded at Carol Ann and Nathan, bestowed a butterfly touch on Kit's shoulder in acknowledgement of her friendship with Hayley. "Take care of the cat," she smiled.

"For sure, I will. I'm so happy to have come here tonight. It was wonderful."

"I'll be back in a minute, Grandmother," said Hayley. "Just gonna see these guys to the dock."

Hayley received a nod in return. Vera turned away and the crowd parted for her passage.

Kit and Carol Ann paired up as they walked. Nathan walked a step ahead, silhouetted by the ramp lights, behind Hayley and Cole. He turned back to ask Kit, "Where's Tim tonight?"

"Don't know. He was supposed to make dinner for me yesterday but he didn't show. I told him I was done when he came over Wednesday but he wanted to talk it out, try to persuade me that we could make it work. I just don't think so but we do need to talk. It's not like him to not let me know he's not coming. I tried him a few times on the VHF, no answer."

Kit paused a moment as another thought collided.

"You know Nathan, a weird thing happened the other day, Friday. Friday night, I mean. I woke up and it was all quiet and beautiful, starry..."

Nathan interjected, "God, yah, what a night. So many stars and the moon! I sat on my deck watched the sky for a couple hours."

"Yah, so I woke up way late, and just had to go out in my kayak. It was incredible, like being upside down in the stars, a ton of phosphorescence. So I get out in the middle, you know between Echo Bay and the Burdwoods, and I hear shouting. Then the moon kind of disappeared. I heard a boat start up, it was so creepy. I mean, who's out there in the middle of the night? So I'm thinking *what*? And I start paddling over that way to see what's going on and then I hear the boat just motoring away, I think it went up Tribune, then there's no more noise."

"What did you do?" asked Carol Ann.

Now they were all stopped on the path listening, picturing Kit paddling the dark water in the middle of the night, hearing mysterious motors and shouting.

"I just got so creeped out. I thought if I went poking around... well, truth is I chickened out and went home. I was going to go back and look around yesterday morning but I had to go early on my charter so I didn't spend much time on it."

"I don't blame you one bit," said Carol Ann firmly. "Putzing around in the middle of the night in your kayak is a good way to get yourself in trouble."

Nathan pondered Kit's story as they made their way to the top of the ramp. The old D'Sonoqua figure retained its watchful power. Hayley stopped with Cole by the carving.

"Maybe you'd like to go for a little tour out and around," she asked diffidently.

"Love to," said Cole. "There's a skiff I can use, an outboard motor on it. Woody said he's going to town in the morning, gave me the day off. How 'bout then?"

"That could work, Hayley." Kit butted in. "I can run you back to the village when you're ready to go home."

"And both of you girls have dinner with me Monday!" Carol Ann was excited.

"Sounds like a plan. I can maybe hitch a ride to Echo Bay with the crew boat, they got some bigwigs coming out tomorrow and gonna tour them around, take them up to Back Eddy's museum so you won't need to pick me up here. I'll walk over to Carol Ann's from the museum."

"That'll work, see you Monday then."

Three happy people—five counting Nathan and Carol Ann.

"Night everyone, thanks for coming."

A chorus of goodnight, see you soon and thank you followed Hayley as she disappeared into the night. The Echo Bay residents headed down the ramp to Kit's boat.

"Well dang it, where could that boy have got to?" Nathan was still gnawing on Kit's story about Tim's no-show.

"Think we should report him overdue or something? Maybe we should ask Benny or some of the other prawners if they've seen him. He's probably still out there checking boats somewhere."

"Yah, no, I saw Benny here tonight but I don't want to go back and try to find him right now. I'll track him down tomorrow. I'm not sure where he's fishing right now. He had some gear up in Sutlej Channel a few days ago. Maybe he'll come in for fuel and you'll see him, Carol Ann, or one of the other boats."

"Yah, Benny's pretty regular for the fuel and *White Bird* comes in once a week, *Helga Marin*, too. I should see him tomorrow or Tuesday."

"Okay," said Kit, "we all aboard? You want to untie and push off, Cole?"

"Yup, I'm on it." Somehow Cole had become the new deckhand. Kit was pleased; one more competent helper.

"We're off," said the skipper. She turned *Mermaid Lady* away from the lights of the village and motored slowly, giving her pupils time to expand. When she could just barely distinguish the hills from the sky she progressed more swiftly into the obscurity of Retreat Passage, toward home.

Twenty

The lengthening dusk was greyed by an overcast sky but pink and gold flared briefly as the lowering sun coloured the cloud bottoms. Kit sniffed appreciatively as she and Hayley climbed the stairs to Carol Ann's apartment.

"Smells like venison stroganoff," she murmured.

"Smells good!" said Hayley. "I'm getting tired of clams, salmon, crab and grease."

"You're not!" cried Kit in mock astonishment. "Heresy!"

The porch light at the top of the stairs spilled a buttery glow onto the landing. Carol Ann appeared in the open door, her soft hair in a fluffy halo. She embraced the two younger women with welcoming hugs. "Oh what a treat!" she exclaimed. "My two favourite girls, both at once!"

More woman hugs all around; it'd been a while since they'd gotten together, and it felt like a party. Dinner was beyond Carol

Ann's usual superb offering. They started off with prawns, then stroganoff and salad, followed by her signature cinnamon buns.

"These the prawns Benny gave you?" asked Kit.

"Yup."

"So good. I'm totally stuffed," moaned Hayley, holding her belly. "Look at me, I look pregnant."

"So long as you're not. You're not, right?" Kit and Carol Ann turned to Hayley.

"Not," she said, "but why would you care?"

Carol Ann and Kit exchanged glances. *Walked into boggy territory with that one.*

Kit replied first. "We're your friends. We love you. If you want to be pregnant we want that for you. But I thought you were staying away from that. You're not married or promised...right? And being pregnant is just such a huge life change."

Confidences did not come easily to Hayley, and although she loved Kit, especially, and cared for Carol Ann, they were not family. They were not Indigenous, nor part of her culture, however she trusted their affection and felt safe in their company.

"Actually, I think I broke up with Ritchie."

Kit and Carol Ann digested this complete turnabout from what they had expected—what everyone had expected—as the outcome of Ritchie's courtship.

"So...you think? Or you did?"

"Did. I did break up with him. I didn't mean to but he was pressing me, and I said it would end up with too many kids and drinking and pain and he said my parents had a good marriage and I just blurted out, 'But they love each other!' And he looked so hurt. He cried, I nearly cried. Well I did cry, to be honest. But then he left and I felt like I was floating off the beach, so light. I knew I'd done the right thing. Is that wrong?"

"Of course not. It's your true feeling so it can't be wrong."

"How come I didn't even know I felt that way until right that very moment?"

Kit had no answer to this. Carol Ann made a feeble attempt.

"Sometimes finding your way takes time."

Kit got up and hugged Hayley. "Carol Ann is right. Things take time and especially if a guy is into you, sometimes you can't always tell how *you* feel about *him* because it feels so good to have someone love and want you. It can be hard to separate what's your own feeling."

Carol Ann turned the focus away from Hayley. "What about you, Kit? Any word from Tim?"

"Hmm. That's still kind of a mystery and I'm not sure what to do about it. He's not the most reliable guy on the planet but it's not like him to just stand me up and blow off his own invitation. So I don't know."

Carol Ann said firmly, "You need to report him missing, Kit. You've got to report him overdue. Let Coast Guard put out the call and someone will have seen him. Or what about calling up that Margaret Morris cop first thing tomorrow?"

Kit looked at Carol Ann with a hard face. "I guess I didn't tell you what the big fight on the dock was about, did I?"

"Nope. Want to talk about it?"

"Tim slept with her when he was out. And maybe he's been doing that off and on since he came after me, I don't know."

"But he's crazy for you!" Carol Ann was shocked. "I just don't think he would do that. Would he?"

"Obviously he would, because he did." Kit replied bitterly. "I just can't seem to find a good guy, or rather, one that I want to stick with," she amended more honestly.

"My dad says all relationship difficulties are from childhood wounds," Hayley commented, "and *everything* wounds us, from the journey down the birth canal to the way someone looks at you sideways when you're four years old and grabbing a peach off the table, or tells you how you bombed at the Christmas concert."

"My parents decided I was too sensitive when I was a kid so they teased me—they called it teasing, anyway," Carol Ann rolled her eyes—"unmercifully when I was, I don't know, maybe thirteen to about sixteen. Took me years to figure out that's what made me so unsure of myself. I always felt unsupported, like they were pulling the rug out from under me every chance they got. It was cruel and I vowed if I ever had kids I would always treat them with loving kindness."

"Easier said than done, I bet." Hayley laughed. "Kids are brats!"

"For sure," agreed Kit. "Funny we're all unmarried and childless living out here on the wild wet coast. I had a nice, safe upbringing with a great father—stepfather, but he was real—and a strong, kind mother. No parental angst, honestly! Don't you think there is such as a thing as an ordinary person who isn't messed up? You know, just...follow your path and try to live an honest, kind life?"

She enumerated the points one by one on her fingers. "I try to honour my word, be loyal, communicate clearly, pay fair and charge fair. What else? Oh right, pay it forward, live in gratitude...believe in the bounty of the universe."

By now they're all laughing.

"I know it sounds stupid but I honestly do. And there's no one who has wronged me that I can be bothered trying to exact vengeance from. That's a ridiculous waste of time. Except maybe Tim," she mock-growled.

"Maybe parents just do the best they can and each generation tries to do better," said Hayley.

"I don't know," said Carol Ann. "Either they try to do better or they just do the same thing. I had a really hard time when my mother cut me out of her life and wouldn't tell me why. She made it clear I was not a welcome member of the family. It hurt me deeply and messed up my life for about fifteen years. Finally

I realized it was her, not me, who was messed up. Be nice to get an apology once in a while, or an explanation, but mostly that never happens. You got to get over it if you want to have a reasonable sort of life."

Kit sighed. "It's really difficult when people who are supposed to love you obfuscate and prevaricate, and are cold and hard and...divisive."

Hayley laughed "Obfuscate! Try to use words the rest of us understand!"

"I know damn well you understand the meaning of that word, you who got a university education and graduated with honours."

Hayley grew thoughtful. "You are lucky, you know, to have the life you have. You're smart and capable and beautiful. People like you, you've never lost anything."

"That's just not true, Hayley! I've had my share of pain. I don't talk about it but I got pregnant once, my boyfriend died in a logging accident and then my baby died when she was four days old, it gutted me."

"Oh my god, I'm sorry Kit!" Hayley's eyes rounded and her hand flew to her mouth. "I shouldn't have said that. How was your family about it?"

"Mmm, well, my mother got sick right about then and my stepdad went crazy drinking for a while when she died, so neither of them had a lot left over for it. My mom had been happy about the baby, though. I had a lot of loving, kind people around to help me, thank goodness—good friends. And you're right, I *am* lucky in so many ways. No one is without sorrow, but I know some get a larger share. Anyway, Hayley, *you* are doing alright. You got a good education and you'll be able to make something of your life. You're smart, gorgeous and talented, and are from a fascinating culture coming into its own. Now's the time for the Indigenous generation."

Hayley cracked a joke, "The Indig-nation generation."

"Funny! Not sure where I'd use it though, outside of this room," said Kit.

"Likely have people think you're against Indigenous rights and reconciliation."

"Which I most certainly am not! Life is tough all over, that's for sure. Good to have a few good buddies to help solve the world's problems." Kit smiled at Hayley.

Carol Ann got up and hugged the two younger women. "You both light up my life, that's for sure, babes. Who would I mother if I didn't have you two to offer my wise council to? Everyone has their cross to bear and surprises come when you least expect them. You don't know what you are made of until life throws down the glove."

"Huh," laughed Kit. "There's got to be at least two or three more clichés you can dig up."

"Oh, you know what I'm trying to say, Kit. Anyway, that's why we have clichés to fall back on."

Hayley looked more serious, she leaned forward.

"You know what? I had a very strange encounter with that prawn fisherman, Benny. Last night? I went to get Kitcat for you, remember, Kit? I came out of the Big House and it was dark, so, I'm walking out and I bump into someone and it's him, Benny. When I bumped into him he grabbed my breast. Maybe he didn't quite grab me, it was kind of hard to tell, but it was just so weird. I bumped into him and instead of backing off, he pretended touching me was an accident. I'm sure he saw me coming."

Again Carol Ann and Kit exchanged glances, both thinking about Benny and the way they dealt with him. As mature women, while tolerant of the way many men in the male-dominated community behaved, they were used to a substantial measure of respect. They expected it, which usually had the required effect on the men with whom they interacted.

"Well that's creepy," said Kit. "Did anything else happen?"

Hayley repeated what she remembered of their encounter, getting more heated as she told it.

"He is so over the top," said Carol Ann. "I grew up in the sixties and you just got used to it. Men were rude. Not all of them, of course, but it was more accepted that it was okay to be lewd or suggestive. Like when I went to Italy—I couldn't believe those guys. You had to just keep moving, or else. They're all standing at the street corners, whistling and making awful sounds or pinching your bum. You got so you could give it right back—make it clear it was not appreciated." She shook her head ruefully. "I just laugh at Benny when he gives me the sweet talk, I'm pretty sure he doesn't mean anything by it. But I did have to chew him out the other day."

"Seems like he just can't help himself, comes on to anyone female," said Kit. "You have to keep drawing a hard line, over and over. I must say Benny's been good to me, helped me out a lot with different things. When Back Eddy wasn't available I knew Benny would help me. One time I twisted my ankle and he bucked up a whole pile of firewood, so I always try to give him the benefit of the doubt. He's given me tons of free prawns, too. But I do think if I gave him the tiniest bit of encouragement he'd be all over me. It's so pathetic. I have to give him the evil eye because any excuse, he takes the opportunity to make some kind of raunchy comment. I just don't want to go there."

Carol Ann looked at her. "But you did sleep with him."

"Yah, once." She nodded her head. "Big mistake. I had a few too many glasses of wine and he seemed so desperate and needy. Classic mercy sex. Wish I hadn't, of course, 'cause he still thinks he can get something going. I try to be friendly without encouraging him. Keep the peace in the community. You know."

Carol Ann nodded. She knew.

Hayley was listening attentively. She hadn't known Kit had once slept with Benny. She'd never even heard the phrase and realized that's what she'd been doing with Ritchie. Just trying to please him, keep him happy, but without being fully engaged herself. No more of that, he was gone—as a lover anyway.

Although that still didn't address the Benny problem. Hayley discerned the difference between the two men. Ritchie loved her, and she had been duplicitous with him. Not deliberately, but nevertheless, and irresponsibly. She hadn't taken his attentions seriously or respected his feelings even as she'd acquiesced to his amorousness. She was pretty sure that he had attributed a different meaning than she had to their intimate moments.

And now Benny. Was he just desperate to hook up with someone, or did he have a thing for Indigenous women, or what? Did he touch her by accident, by design or was it simply opportunistic?

The women considered Hayley's story and the consequences it might have for them all. Kit and Carol Ann's protectiveness of her, as younger and more vulnerable, would inevitably change how they behaved toward Benny. However they made their disapproval felt, like ripples in a pond, there would be an impact on the community.

"I'm kind of sick of him, to tell you the truth," said Carol Ann.

Kit nodded. "How're ya gonna change 'm?"

"Maybe we can come up with a way to teach him a lesson. But it might mean no more free prawns, if we get too cool toward him," mused Carol Ann.

Small price to pay. They could all get prawns several other ways.

Kit looked long at Hayley, said, "Maybe you should tell somebody, you know, like...maybe Ritchie? We don't know how bad it could get and it's true that Indigenous women are often preyed upon. If Benny is hitting on you and he's sneaky about it, maybe you ought to mention it."

"I'll think about it." Hayley was hesitant. "They're already in conflict. Benny hassles Ritchie every time he sees him and Ritchie told me the only thing keeping him from punching his lights out or drowning him on a dark night is that it gives him the moral high ground. Fomenting more trouble might not be the best thing."

"But it might make a difference in protecting you, right?"

"Yeah," said Hayley doubtfully. "Maybe. I don't think I need anyone hovering around watching out for me, though. I like to slip away by myself."

Kit claimed the last word. "Well, if I know Ritchie, I'm certain he's still your friend and would do anything to make sure you're safe."

Kit had one more thing to share. She dropped her own little romantic bombshell: "I've met a new man!" Both Hayley and Carol Ann shrieked with delight.

"Tell!"

Kit tried to play it cool but couldn't pretend to not be at least a little excited.

Carol Ann summed it up: "New men that are interesting are few and far between out here. Give with the details. No, wait. Let me fill up the glasses, I've got another bottle around here somewhere."

The other two leaned in close to Kit and she told, albeit a carefully edited version, of her encounter with Carson. When she was done, Carol Ann regarded her and said gravely, "How exciting! So...Tim?"

Kit gazed back, "Aye, there's the rub. Maybe like Drake always said, everything will unfold as it should." She smiled ruefully. "He also said I should try cultivating patience."

Excited by her friend's revelation, Carol Ann suddenly remembered the warmth of Nathan's hand as it had enfolded hers. Briefly she debated whether to share in turn and decided against it. Likely it was nothing to get all foolish about.

Twenty-One

*C*ole was ecstatic. Never before had his skin rushed with joy like this, not even when he'd crewed on the whale watching boat out of Telegraph Cove. Shivers ran up his back and rippled over his skull. He'd loved the excitement of his job as lighting designer for a gritty TV show set in the alleys of Vancouver's Downtown Eastside, but he'd never once experienced anything remotely this intense.

Cole was on a journey. He didn't know where it would take him, only that he felt like someone in a storybook his mother had read to him; someone with big boots that were too large. In spite of his youthful joy in life and gratitude for two adoptive parents who loved him, there was still a hole in his heart.

Nothing, as yet, had filled it. That hole wasn't completely empty—guilt slumbered comfortably at the bottom of it. He'd never want to hurt his mom or dad, but he was hoping to replace the guilt with something less debilitating, in fact, something nourishing and fulfilling.

In this moment, he was trying, without success, to wipe the beaming smile off his face; a face that made Hayley laugh. From his place in the bow of the tin skiff, he glanced back at her occasionally, felt communion in her easy answering grin.

Blue sky, mashed potato clouds mounded higher, one climbing the back of the next, then breaking into cauliflower florets at the top as the morning warmed. Eagles fluffed themselves big in trees along the shoreline, wings outspread to dry off yesterday's rain. Sunbeams through tree tops flashed hypnotically on/off as they ran along in Nathan's 14-foot skiff. Hayley at the stern, with tiller in hand, was giving Cole the grand tour of her people's marks on the landscape. He could tell his interest in seeing the clam gardens and pictographs and other signs of ancient occupation made her happy—all the things she planned to share with him. He was falling in love with this place, her home.

"First we'll run into Shoal Harbour, it's a perfect tide to get a real good look at the clam garden in the narrows at the entrance. Have you been over to Back Eddy's yet? That's his place over there."

To the left he spotted the fishing boat, some buildings painted green, one with an old BA gas company sign on the wall. A couple more structures up the slope; Back Eddy's house, a fenced garden and wood shed, and then further along, another house. Eventually he'd know who all was who and where, and their radio call signs. For now, he was happy to be getting to know the place, and getting to know Hayley.

The shoreline narrowed and ahead a low wall of rock encircled a beach, rough and tumble from lack of use for a century or more.

"The people used to dig clams to eat, still do, but not quite the same way. In the old days, they'd push the rocks and boulders down toward the water's edge and eventually the wall was high and the beach was clean. The tide would sweep in and over and out, creating a fertile area for the clams. Also the rock wall kept the beach from eroding, see? Low tide is the best time to dig them, the lower the better to be safe from red tide. So they'd dig the clams, with yew wood digging sticks, and hang them on racks to smoke and dry them."

Cole was all eyes, looking every which way. He imagined a busy village above the clam garden, racks of drying clams and sunbeams intermingling with smoke from the fires.

Hayley went on: "Sometimes there'd be a break in the rock wall at one side or the other where they could pull up canoes. I know an island over in Fife Sound where there's a partially carved canoe. We'll get there, not today though. But see here in this one, Back Eddy told me this clam garden was also used to trap herring. They would come in to spawn at high tide. The people would tie rocks to hemlock boughs to weight them. They'd be waiting in the canoes and when the herring were busy letting go all their eggs, the people would line up the canoes and drop the weighted ends of the hemlock boughs overboard. The herring couldn't get through the fence of hemlock boughs so the beach inside the rock wall would be full of them when the tide went out. It was called 'loxiwey,' place of rolling rocks."

Hayley ended her dissertation with another flourish, as proud as if she herself had participated in the herring capture. Drifting through on the tide it was easy to conjure up visions of that ancient communal life. Now Cole's imagined village was alive with people gathering food from the sea, some making cedar twine to tie rocks to hemlock boughs and to sticks to make drying racks. Some were weaving cedar baskets to hold the smoked fish and clams. Cole's mind reeled as Hayley listed one time-consuming activity after another. So much necessary work to be certain there was enough food for everyone through the long winter.

No phones, no cars, no huge dams creating electricity and ruining salmon rivers, no computers or satellites or men on the moon.

Cole asked, "What about clothing? Don't you think they'd always be cold? Nothing to wear but cedar mats, cloaks and skirts, barefoot on the barnacle-covered rocks? When I look at those old photos, I think they must have been so tough."

"Hard to imagine, isn't it? I guess that's why we store fat and aren't very tall. There were furs too, though, and woven blankets from mountain goat hair." She turned the tiller to enter the bay.

"So up that hillside," she pointed, "we can climb it sometime, there's a cave at the top, not very big, three rooms sort of. It's the site of a story, a tribal legend about the Animal Kingdom. The story belongs to our whole tribe, the Kwakwaka'wakw tribe, not one person. There're lots of other stories, too, but I only know this one. It's about all the animals and how the hairy Wild Man of the Woods, Bukwus, came to be."

"Wasn't he in the dance the other night?"

"Yeah, he was hustled out, remember they were restraining that wild-looking guy—he kept trying to dash toward the people on the bleachers. That was Bukwus."

"Can you tell me the story?"

"I'll ask my ada, I don't know all the details."

"Okay. What's next?"

Hayley thought for a moment. "I think we'll swing over toward Nickless Islet. There's a pictograph on the bluff near there, then we'll go to the Burdwood Group for lunch. We can run into Viner Sound after that."

"Perfect." As she turned around Cole leaned back contentedly against the port side, which immediately tilted the aluminum skiff. He scrambled back to the center of the seat, chagrined, hoped Hayley hadn't notice. Of course she had. He glanced at her, she was hiding her smile but her eyes teased.

"Hold on," she shouted as she revved up; the skiff leaped forward. They pulled out of the shadowed narrows and into the open sun, and Cramer Pass dazzled in the brilliance.

As they approached Baker Island she waved her hand again, to point out a huge old spruce log. "That's called a nurse log; see all the little trees growing up out of it?"

"Yup, little baby trees all over it. We stopping here?"

"Not yet. We've got a lot of territory to cover for your introductory tour. Some other time we'll come here."

Already the friendship had a future.

The small boat swept in toward and north along the shore, Hayley pointing out all the items of interest. A pair of eagles preened in a jagged dead tree, a kingfisher dove off a jutting limb, sounding a bird version of '*I'm going in!*' Cole laughed as it splashed under and rose with a small fish in its beak. Hayley swerved in close to the shore of an island.

"Ragged Island; used to be called Burnt Island because lightning hit it and started a fire. Good fishing here. And Pym Rocks right there. They move around so you got to watch it."

"Really...?" started Cole before he saw her gleeful smirk.

They zipped past Ragged Island and into the wide blue of Fife Sound. The tide was rising, flooding hard into the expansive waters surrounding a small archipelago to the northeast.

"Is that it, the Burdwood Group?"

"Yup. First we'll cruise by Nickless Islet, take a look at the pictograph. Back Eddy says it's a bear. Of course he saw it more than thirty years ago, but it's so darn faded I can't make it out. Lots of them have faded. I'd like to document and somehow preserve them, see if anybody knows what they mean—if anything."

Splashes and leaping bodies flashing toward them caught Cole's eye and he pointed, she looked.

"Dolphins! Pacific white sides."

Rapidly the dolphins approached the skiff, leaped and soared ahead of them and then swerved away. Moments later they're behind, hurtling the wake. Hayley kept to her course as one dolphin flashed ahead and leaped again, and yet again. Cole was dumbstruck. He pinched himself to be sure he wasn't dreaming. Not that he hadn't seen them; along with dozens of orca, humpbacks and Dall's porpoises, while working on the whale watching boat, but this was so much more up close and personal.

The dolphins were everywhere; suddenly they were gone.

"Breathtaking...but kind of a problem," commented Hayley.

"How's that?"

"We've seen them practically wipe out the pink salmon when they're coming through. They get in a big line, like a Roman phalanx, and charge across the water and there're pinks everywhere, running from them, leaping ahead, trying to hide by the boat. It's horrible to watch. The dolphins cornered, I don't know, maybe a thousand or more? I've seen it in Laura Bay and in Viner, and in front of Back Eddy's place. The pinks are on their way around Tribune Channel and up to Knight Inlet, where the grizzly bears load up on them as they spawn. So many dolphins are throwing things out of whack. The pink salmon populations are crashing and they're the backbone of the coastal ecosystem. The grizzlies don't have enough to eat and they're spreading to all the small islands looking for food...it's bad."

Even in this coastal paradise, what once seemed eternal is fragmented and diminished. Once the powerful engine of the coast, the pink salmon, so disregarded and disrespected, were now showing by their deteriorating numbers, the vital force they'd once been.

"You don't miss the water 'til the well runs dry, my dad used to say," muttered Cole.

"Okay," Hayley said firmly, "our job today is to be as happy as we can. In the face of the obvious we must see what there is to see and think about what we can do to make things better for the future," she pontificated. "But right this very minute—we fly!"

She turned up the throttle again and the skiff leaped, levelled out and surged forward. Ahead lay Nickless Islet, jewel-like with its pristine white shell beach and rocky headland, crowned with one artistically arranged tree. Cruising around the shoreline, she slowed the boat to a more sedate pace, searching the steep rock wall for the subtle rust red marks of a rock painting.

"Look for a white or light-coloured slope that goes from out to in, from the top down, and has a flattish place at the base where the painter could stand. Good thing the wall is still damp; it makes the paintings easier to see."

Cole searched the rock wall intently. They located the pictograph at the same moment and she put the motor out of gear.

"Pretty low water right now, you can feel the tide push, so we have to look way up, but there it is."

Cole craned his neck and finally discerned the faint red painted marks on the rock. Hayley put the boat in gear and backed away from the cliff face. She reversed to counteract the swift flow of the tidal push. The pictograph was fairly large, maybe three feet or more. It could be a bear. Or not; hard to tell.

"Guess we'll just have to believe Back Eddy. Haven't got a better idea from seeing it now," said Hayley. "Seen enough?"

Cole nodded. His stomach growled.

"Then we're off to the Burdwood Group and lunch. This will blow your mind."

"It's already so blown," said Cole, shaking his head. *Can this day get any better*? He raised his face to greet the breeze as they headed east toward the group of islands.

To surprise him with maximum effect, Hayley motored in the back way, rather than approaching from the south. They passed a twisted fir tree and cruised along that island's shadowed northwest side. Conifers lined a narrow passage that widened quickly. A white shell beach appeared, lustrous in the sunshine. A flock of birds flushed, running on water, and then taking flight.

"Harlequin ducks," said Hayley.

"Beautiful."

Close ahead, another island snuggled within the encircling shore of the first. Hayley guided the boat around to the far side until the white shell beach lay directly in front of them. Like sturdy sentinels standing guard, cedar and hemlock trees arose dark and erect, above the bleached strand. Fifty shades of green foliage cast dappled shadows throughout a clearing, in which sat a neat cedar cabin. Double arcs of golden brown needles, deposited on the beach by recent tides, paralleled the aquamarine sea.

Cole gasped as they approached the beach. "It's like a secret tropical island!"

"Told ya. Everyone has the same feeling, like they're the only ones who ever discovered this paradise." She ran the skiff up onto the shore, turned off the motor and raised it in one smooth motion.

He reached under the seat for his packsack with the lunch Nathan had made for them. He was pretty eager now for the crab salad sandwiches and thermos full of home-pressed apple juice, straight from Back Eddy's trees. He hung his legs over the side of the skiff and levered himself out, grabbed the packsack and offered a hand to Hayley.

She declined it. "I'm good. Been getting in and out of boats since I was four years old, so I don't need any help, thanks."

"Huh," said Cole. "Sorry for trying to be a gentleman."

"Maybe you're too much of a gentleman. How come you don't try anything?"

"Like what?" Cole was startled.

"Oh, you know, like stuff guys usually try when they're alone with a girl?"

Cole was dumbfounded. Just one more surprise, in a day full of surprises. He wasn't without interest in women in general, and Hayley in particular was fascinating, beautiful and friendly, but he wasn't the kind of guy that just jumped on someone without being certain it was mutual. And attractive as she was, he wasn't getting the vibe.

"But aren't you gay?" he blurted.

"What? Why would you say that?" But she didn't deny it and stopped mid-reply. "Do you think so?"

"Don't you think so? I mean, it's none of my business but I just thought, you know, there's something about some people, some girls, and a guy, just...he just knows. I can tell."

Hayley grabbed the bow and dragged the skiff higher up the beach, gathering her thoughts. Was that it? Benny had thrown the word at her like a dagger. Could they be right and she was simply gay and never figured it out? How was that possible? Or maybe it was more complicated than that.

She turned back to Cole and lifted her head, brushing her hair back from her brow. "I think I need some lunch," she muttered.

"I'm sorry, Hayley. I didn't think—it just came out. You're really beautiful and it would be great if you liked me enough to let me kiss you, or...or anything, but honest to god, maybe I jumped to conclusions but, well..." Cole was completely stumped; sure he'd blown it with Hayley. She wasn't going to want to be friends with him now and he was stupid to jump to conclusions about her sexuality. As if his city life had made him so street smart he could pick somebody gay out of a crowd.

"Well what?" she demanded, jerking the packsack out of his hands and delving into it for the sandwiches. She flung herself down on the beach and patted a command for him to sit beside her. She handed him a sandwich and the juice, dug deeper for a couple glasses.

Cole bit into a sandwich and chewed before he answered. "It's like this. You don't flirt, or act...sexy, or alluring around me. You're kind of just like a guy. Like I am a pal, not a man."

He beat his chest a few times and smiled at her, both to make fun of his manliness and her lack of perception of it and to take any sting out of his words. Hayley looked solemn. She was thinking it through, trying it on. Finally she laughed out loud.

"I can't believe it. I think you're right! It takes a guy from the city to show me what's been true all along. Poor Ritchie, good grief, he must have been so frustrated, wondering what was wrong with me that I wasn't as turned on by him and all excited about making babies."

She turned to him eagerly. "I have this friend, I'm crazy for her and whenever I'm in the bay we spend every minute together. My mom doesn't like her, though, and my sister, Holly, positively despises her. She's a nutso Pentecostal Christian. Not that I have anything against Christians but she walks around like she has God's right ear and he agrees with all her damning pronouncements. Could they know? Anyway, there's nothing to know."

Cole silently finished his sandwich and gazed at the trees. He'd been in a lot of uncomfortable places but this beat all.

Hayley just sat there, chewing her sandwich without another word. Finally she turned to Cole.

"Okay. So, Cole, maybe you're right. It kind of rings my inside bell, so I'm inclined to consider it a real possibility. I could never figure out why Ritchie never turned me on, and I tried. He is, from a certain point of view, incredibly hot. A good catch, as they say; you, too. But." She flashed him a wry grin.

"We have a thing called 'two-spirit,' and maybe that's where I'm headed. I'm going to have to ask my ada about that and see what she says. No one has ever thought of me as a typical girl, I mean not ever. I know some couples that are for sure 'gay,' people in the bay and in Kingcome. It's cool, but maybe 'two-spirit' is something else altogether."

"Needs more research." Cole smiled.

"Right. You done, shall we carry on?"

"Sure." He was gratified that she'd let him see her real feelings. He found most people were full of baloney; not forthcoming with what they truly believed, felt or thought. In the face of her potentially life-changing realization, she still intended to show him around the area and introduce him to her Indigenous culture: the pictographs, clam gardens and midden sites among the islands. Already impressed by this person, now he was even more so.

Hayley looked at him as she spoke. "You're not too shocked to continue on with this?"

"Jeez, of course I want to continue! I've never met anyone like you and, honest to God, I truly want to be your friend."

"Okay, then." She nodded and looked away, packed up the lunch remnants, stuffed it all into Cole's packsack and then jumped up and went for the bowline.

The skiff had nudged closer up the beach with the rising tide. It was easy to load their gear and climb over the side, push off. Hayley slid into the stern and lowered the motor, then pulled the cord to fire it up. Well maintained by Nathan, it responded instantly. She gave Cole a pleased nod and put the motor in gear.

"Last stop, Viner River," she exclaimed.

"Viner it is," agreed Cole and turned face forward.

The midday sun beamed hot on their skin. Laden with the intoxicating fragrance of wild roses and heated cedar, a light, dry wind caressed them. Cole dug around for his ball cap and sunglasses. Hayley headed east away from the picnic beach and passed the last few small islands in the archipelago, turned slightly toward Penn Island. The sea glittered as it washed under the hull and the rushing wake formed a ruffled pathway astern.

Western grebes snoozed, dramatic black and white necks arched, heads tucked under wings in the high noon sun. Cole was enchanted with them, flipped through the bird book he had tucked into his kit. From time to time a horned grebe burst into action, bouncing as it took off, and red-necked grebes dove at their approach.

Penn Island loomed closer as they ran along in the indigo sea. A big old fir tree claimed centre stage and just as he was about to ask Hayley about it, she said, "There's an eagle nest on this island, a pair lives here, they maintain the nest. Last year they hatched a baby that survived and matured."

"Cool."

She swung the boat wide around the island.

"We'll stop here on our way back. It's easier to land when the tide is higher. It should be high enough now to run up the estuary and higher here when we come back. There's a channel from the river carved into the mud but I absolutely do *not* want to get stuck in the loon shit. A ton of birds in there and I've seen plenty of bears, including one of the two grizzlies on Gilford Island. Saw one in April rooting around in the spring grasses. You know why they eat grass?" Her eyes twinkled.

"Nope. Why?"

"They form an anal plug that stops them up during hibernation; the proper word is 'torpor.' Eating the grass in the spring starts up the digestive system and out it pops."

"So, a butt plug, that's hilarious." Cole laughed out loud. "Thank you for that fascinating science fact, Professor."

"Stick around; you'll learn everything you never wanted to know about animal poo. It's called a 'tappen' or fecal plug, made of its own hair, bits of bark and pinecone. Kit and I've worked out a set of rules to get your 'authentic coast kid' certification and everyone knows that's rule number one."

"So there will be a test, right?"

"Right!"

"Hope I pass."

The estuary narrowed ahead of them and Hayley ducked into each of the small coves along the sunny north shore. She showed him the shadowed picnic area with the biffy and the red box in which campers were requested to deposit their comments and camping fees. The gloomy darkness of the site struck Cole as a poor choice of location in all this wild beauty.

"How come they didn't put the campsite in the sunshine? It's like a crypt in there, not a speck of light."

"I know, right? Maybe because it's reasonably flat and slightly separated from the animal trail that goes along the shoreline. A cougar killed a dog here, this woman was working on carving out a small wilderness camping spot along the shore, just up from the lagoon here, and while she was eating her lunch, a cougar came along, grabbed her dog and ran up a tree with it."

"Did it survive?" asked Cole, eyes round.

"Not much you can do when you are looking up a tree where the cougar has your dog by the neck—unless you have a gun. Okay, onward. Let's see how far up the channel we get." Hayley turned the skiff again and motored slowly toward the grass flats where the river vanished into the spruce forest.

A mountain rose steeply behind the estuary, divided by a valley and the coursing white track of a mountain stream. Even a city boy like Cole could see the logging cut blocks on each side of the mountain had scored deep gullies and slides down the slope.

"This was, still is, I guess, a salmon-bearing stream. Back Eddy and a bunch of other locals, and some folks from the village sometimes, have been trying for years, working on different projects to bring back the chum salmon and whatever else might grow here—but it's tough going."

"Who does all the logging?"

"Well..." Hayley paused. "The truth is—everybody. Your people, my people, big business and small. Logging has been going on for over a hundred years on this island and it's still producing big trees and big money. So the salmon, like everywhere, come a very slow second."

"Maybe I don't know who 'my people' are," said Cole, face turned away from Hayley.

"What? What do you mean?"

Cole deliberated. He hadn't wanted to reveal anything this close to his heart just yet, but he was feeling such an intuitive bond with her and already he knew so much more about her than she did about him. It was his turn to share.

"So...I'm adopted."

She raised her eyebrows. Lots of people she knew were adopted, fostered or parented by aunts, uncles and grandparents.

"Yeah, so?"

"I found out more about my birth mother, nothing about my dad though, and I am pretty sure she was from around here somewhere. Maybe even from your village."

"Seriously!"

"Yeah, so I'm not sure where to go from there, I'm just following my nose. It was amazing at the potlatch the other night, I felt...at home in there, it all was real to me, and even though I don't know anything, none of it felt alien. And Nathan is my grandfather."

Hayley whistled. "Whoo-ee! Wow. But Nathan is white."

"Yeah, well, I don't know the whole story yet but he's giving it to me in small chunks, what he knows. But he says it's not just his story."

"Huh. So white boy finds out he's adopted, comes back to home village and is renewed as brown boy, something like that?"

"Are you making fun of me?"

"No, no!" she said. "Sorry, I didn't mean to sound like that. It's just, like, so common, it's everywhere. And you're damned if you're a white who is really brown, or a little bit brown, or a brown who wants to get an education and study and work, or if you are white and brown, which how can most of us not be at this point? So if you think life is going to be better because you find your roots," she made air quotes, "believe me, you will just have a new set of troubles."

"You sure make that sound inviting. Anyway, I just want to find out. It's going to keep bugging me until I figure it out. Maybe she's alive—my mom. Or somebody that I'm related to."

Hayley's eyes rounded. She reached out and grabbed his arm. "Cole! What if we're related?"

A smile creased his cheeks, eyes compressed by its wholehearted fullness.

"That would be so fantastic, Hayley. I guess if we turn out to be related, then your ada and me would be, too, and maybe people would teach me stuff and tell me about my mom. Anyway, I don't even know for sure if she's Native. My mom, my adopted mom, said that even though the people she talked to before they got me didn't actually *say* I was an Indian baby, something they said made her think that. When they signed the adoption papers, one of the men said something like..." He paused to recall his mother's words. "She told me she was so excited about getting to adopt me that she didn't take much notice or think about it until years later, but one of the officials said something like, 'This kid, you can't tell, he just looks like he has a nice tan.' She concluded that meant I was probably Native, Indigenous I mean, and they didn't want to tell her and when she started asking them, they just clammed up. Then, when things started opening up and the adoption agencies had to help connect people, they said all they knew is my mother, my birth mother I mean, that *her* mother came from somewhere near Alert Bay. So then I got that job on the whale watching boat and started asking around and there's a pretty big community at Gwayasdums so I thought...maybe?"

"What else?"

"I know my name."

"But Cole...What is it? Aren't you using it? Is Harrison your adoptive family name?"

"Yeah. I'm kind of...hesitant. I don't want to just go announce, 'Oh here I am and my name is so and so and you have to take me in 'cause I have this name I think is mine.' It might be kind of upsetting for somebody, who knows? And I know my mother's name, too. Nothing about my dad though so I'm just working with what I have so far. Trying to work it out slow and easy, you know?"

Hayley thought about what he'd said as she steered the skiff up the channel. The shallow water was clear enough to see the silty banks of the underwater riverbed, carved a foot deeper than the rest of the muddy bottom. It took all her attention to navigate the channel without running the bow into the ledge on either side.

Uncertain whether to wait until he chose to share the rest with her, or express her fascinated interest and urge him to tell, she opted for giving it a rest and asked, "Would you like to hear the creation myth I know about this river valley?"

"Yes, please," he replied, relieved she'd changed the subject.

She began.

"The Thunderbird was living in the Upper World with his wife. The name of the Thunderbird was Too-Large. Now, Too-Large was very downcast, and he spoke to his wife, saying, 'Let us go to the Lower World, so that I can see it.' Then his wife spoke to him, 'Husband, do you know about your name, that you have the name Too-Large, for you will be too large a Chief in our Lower World?'

Despite his wife's advice, Thunderbird told her to get ready to go. Then he put on his Thunderbird mask and his wife also put on her Thunderbird mask. They came flying through the door of the Upper World. They sat down on the large mountain, Xakwikan, or Split-in-Two, near Gilford Island, and they saw a river at the bottom of it. Too-Large said, 'Let's go down and look at the river.' So they flew down to sit at the mouth of the river near a man who was working alone on his house.

The man was struggling to raise a beam and said to the Thunderbirds, 'I wish that you would become men so that you could help me with this house.' Too-Large lifted up the jaw of his Thunderbird mask and said, 'Oh, Brother, we are people!'

Then Too-Large and his wife took off their Thunderbird masks and ceased being birds forever. The man who had been Thunderbird said, 'My name is Too-Large in the Upper World, but now my name is Head-Winter-Dancer in this Lower World, and the name of my wife here is Winter-Dance-Woman.' So, Head-Winter-Dancer and Winter-Dance-Woman built a house on a hill and from them came a large tribe and much greatness."

Hayley paused, then said, "I know there's more to the story. This is from Boas and Hunt who wrote down what someone told them in 1905 or so. I memorized it word for word from U'Mista, the museum in Yalis. It said 'near' Gilford Island but it's *on* Gilford Island. It's a myth, right, so you can't be too picky about the details. Anyway, you can look on their website; all the villages have a creation story."

"I'll do that," said Cole, solemnly. "And there is Split-in-Two." He pointed to the mountain with the cleft in the middle and the river cascading down it.

"Yup," she replied. "Also known as Mount Read."

Hayley put the motor out of gear and shut it off. Bubbles rose from the mud and the river murmured. A mink ran up a log. Ravens strutted along the bank and the rising tide chuckled its way through islands of tall green grasses. A flock of Canada geese and behind them two hundred American widgeons took flight, then a dozen mallards. Hundreds of Bonaparte gulls bobbed and dipped, feeding on microscopic organisms.

A black bear ambled out of the woods, lifted her nose to the breeze. Behind her, two small cubs tumbled from the spruce forest, bumping into each other and running here and there. Cole and Hayley exchanged a glance of complicit delight. A perfect finale to their Viner River excursion.

"Used to be a big village here; my uncle lived with his grandmother in the fish-drying shack. They all decayed before I was born but Back Eddy showed me where they sat. The river's changed course since then. Several times."

Eventually Hayley pulled the cord and fired up the outboard, its roar smashing the peaceful stillness.

"Quieter in a kayak or canoe," she commented.

Swiftly they proceeded along the south shore, ducking in close to view a small overflow basin, then a rock ablaze with wild rose brambles and yellow monkey-face flower. The estuary widened out and Hayley pulled away from the shoreline. Cole let his vision expand into the long view, all the way to Fife Sound. Fifty shades of blue fringed with small scraps of lacy foam.

"Looks like the wind's up," said Hayley. "Afternoon westerly."

Cole focused on Penn Island as they approached.

"This is one of the best spots to find a flock of turnstones. It's also covered in wildflowers—'cause it's May, right, when all the flowers bloom on the rocks. Yellow monkey-face flowers here," she said, "and cinquefoil, columbine and Indian paintbrush."

With a rush of broad wing strokes three eagles and half a dozen ravens rose as the boat closed in to shore.

"Is this a seal haul-out?" inquired Cole.

"Don't think so, I've only ever seen them a couple times here."

Raising her hand to the brim of her cap to block more of the sun's glare, she peered ahead to the island. A lumpy soft shape lay draped on the rocks, but it didn't move like a seal would when a boat approached. A shivery sensation transformed rapidly into horror as the lumpen form suddenly, undeniably, became that of a human body with out-flung arms and spread legs. A torn shirt and ragged pants clung in tatters to the lifeless form.

"Whoa! What the hell?!" Hayley slowed the boat as they approached.

"Oh, jeez, I think it's Kit's boyfriend, it's Tim." He looked at her in shock. "It *is* Tim. Let me get out, Hayley, I'll go look for sure, maybe he's still alive."

In his heart he knew this was certainly not the case. The body looked too swollen, too pale and cold, too still. The flesh of the torso was torn; suddenly he comprehended the birds' behaviour. Nausea boiled in his gut.

Hayley, too, clapped her hands over her mouth and paled to a sickly greenish shade. Tears pooled in her eyes, dripped over her hands.

"Hayley!" he called sharply. "Come on. Take the boat in to the rocks, I'll go up and look."

Not that he wanted to be heroic. But what do you do when you find a body on a rock in the middle of nowhere? If he could call the Coast Guard, what would they tell him to do?

She nosed the boat into a narrow cleft and he climbed out, looped the bowline around a rock.

"Is there any rope in the boat?" he turned, called to her, noting the slippery golden popweed and black scum. He remembered the people on Green Rock where Kit had stopped to deliver the jack, how perilous their footing had appeared. Same for him now. He muttered, "Slow, slow and careful."

Hayley rooted around in the bow to see if Nathan had left any line there. *Bless him.* A spare length for the crab trap lay neatly coiled under the seat. She hefted it and carefully climbed out to join Cole on the rocks.

"This is one time I should have a radio in the boat. I really like just being completely out of touch when I'm out running around but we should've borrowed one."

"Can't be helped. Let's try to secure him somehow while we go tell somebody," said Cole. "Definitely don't want him to float away. I'm not sure if it's full flood yet."

"The night time tides are higher so he should be okay for now." Gently she touched the foot of the cold body on the rocks. "Kit is going to be so upset. Remember she said he didn't show up Saturday night? He was going over to do dinner for her."

Hayley glanced at Cole when he said, "Maybe she won't be that upset. They had a huge fight the day I got here."

"Yeah, I know. He was screwing around on her. With Margaret Morris—the cop in Port McNeill. She's the boss." Hayley considered this new horror, imagining how Kit was going to feel. "She said he wanted to kiss and make up and be only with her and marry her, yadda, yadda. And she didn't think it was going to work. And besides…"

She was babbling; snapped her mouth shut realizing how disrespectful she sounded. She'd almost blurted out to Cole what Kit had revealed about her encounter with Carson.

"It's going to be Sergeant Morris who has to deal with this. I can't believe it. I just can't believe it."

Hayley shook her head as she sorted through the complications, at once feeling, or imagining the feelings of, every single player in the scenario. Margaret Morris's personal loss—she must have feelings for Tim to have taken him into her bed—alongside the professional task she'd be faced with of figuring out if there was foul play, and if so, by whom, why and when. And Kit, who had been, until very recently, Tim's reasonably happy girlfriend, but now seemed to have something cooking with that new guy, Carson.

She freed the end of the line from its neatly tied loop and handed it to Cole. "Here ya go, hero. Let's get a line around him so he won't drift away and we can go alert the authorities."

"What about the birds? That's so gross. Let's cover him up with something, my jacket. You got a jacket?"

Hayley gathered the garments from the boat and Cole carefully tucked them around Tim's bloated body. He was nearly sick from the effort as he positioned several loose rocks overall in an effort to prevent the birds from ravaging the defenceless remains of Tim Connolly.

The run back to Echo Bay took forever. As if in harmony with the changed tenor of the day thick clouds billowed up behind Mount Stevens and boiled over in front of the sun. The sky darkened in collusion. The westerly kicked up behind them, adding a rough chop to their passage. No chatting now as they whizzed past a couple of boats near Powell Point, both with guys lolling in the stern dragging fishing lines.

Hayley looked back and saw behind them a blue speedboat bouncing over the swells coming across from Fife Sound, behind it explosions of white spray. "Looks like Back Eddy," she said. "He's heading this way. Should we go to Nathan's?"

"I don't know! I guess so, he'll know what to do."

Hayley didn't even slow as she entered the bay. Even though there was no help for the man lying dead on the rocks of Penn Island, recovering his remains was urgent. The expensive tourist boats tied at the marina had better have good bumpers.

Back Eddy came flying around the corner behind them and reduced speed abruptly. The suddenness of his stop set up a rolling swell. He followed them over to Nathan's dock, urgency radiating off him.

Hearing the motors Nathan came out wiping his hands with a dishtowel, a big grin lighting up his blue eyes as he strolled over to welcome the kids and Back Eddy.

"Got a little windy all of a sudden, didn't it? I was getting worried about ya's," he said to the kids.

Buster boinged out of the other boat to nose around Nathan's deck.

Cole and Back Eddy both burst out with their news; couldn't keep it stopped up for another millisecond.

"Found Tim's speedboat up Tribune Channel stuck on Smith Rock. So I thought I better go looking for..."

And Cole with Hayley, one echoing the other. "We found Tim, he's dead, dead."

"He's dead? Who's dead?" repeated Nathan, befuddled at getting news in stereo, waving his hands up and down. "Okay, okay, one at a time."

Back Eddy climbed out of his boat, glanced at the kids and added to his story. "I ran up Tribune to look around for some slide logs, went up the far side by Lacy Falls, then jogged into Bond Sound to check for fry, see how the creek is doing and by God, when I come out and run down the shore to home, I'll be damned if there isn't a speedboat stuck on it's side between a couple rocks and I go look and it's Tim's."

Cole and Hayley could barely contain themselves through this tale and butted right in when Back Eddy paused for breath.

"We found Tim lying on the rocks at Penn Island," Cole rushed in. "We were coming back from Viner and there were eagles and ravens, they flew up and it looked like a dead seal at first..."

"But not really," interjected Hayley. "And luckily, or good planning I guess," she nodded to Nathan, "you left a crab pot line in the bow of the boat."

Cole's turn: "So we tied the line around him and put our jackets and some rocks over him so the eagles wouldn't eat any more...of him." Trailed off, looked down.

"Lord God! Tim! God rest his soul. So what now? I guess we'd better call the police." Nathan looked at Back Eddy.

"I guess," he replied. "Nosy buggers. But when you find somebody dead and their boat miles away, well," he paused, "it's bigger than us."

"Yup, okay, gimme a sec, I got to turn off the kettle. You kids head over to Woody's, we'll catch up. I'll come with you, Back Eddy."

Nathan re-entered his house, turned off the burner, grabbed his red ball cap, then reached instead for the black one; departed. Buster leaped dutifully back into the boat. Nathan pushed past him, stepping over the pre-tied loops of log-salvage tie-up lines.

"Well that's quite a turn-up," commented Back Eddy. "I haven't heard Tim on the radio for a day or two, and he's usually calling around first thing every morning. Can't hear him when he's down Clio Channel or thereabouts, though."

"He was supposed to have gone to Kit's Saturday night and he didn't show. She told us at the potlatch Sunday night; didn't know whether to call Coast Guard or what."

"Them two been on rocky ground ever since he got back. What the hell happened? I kind of thought she was down in the dumps about him."

"We-elll..." Nathan was reluctant to gossip but he figured Back Eddy must be the only person who didn't know by now, an unusual occurrence. "He was messing around with the cop, remember, his old girlfriend?"

"Sergeant Morris?!"

Back Eddy was shocked. Not much surprised him anymore, but he hadn't expected that. Shook his head, pushed back his cap and rubbed his forehead as he brought the old blue speedboat along the rail at Woody's dock.

"She's not gonna like this news, that's for sure."

Nathan tied the stern line and both men got out, joined Cole and Hayley as they headed into the lodge.

There was Woody, in the middle of his noisy, steamy kitchen. Tunes playing loud, he and Carol Ann mixing, whirring and baking; piling up the dishes as they built a four-course meal for the tree-planting crew. He came to the kitchen doorway, scanned the four faces; with all those worried eyes and wrinkled brows he knew right away something was going on.

"What?" he said. Carol Ann peered out from behind him, wiping her floury hands on her apron, echoed the question.

"We've got to call the cops," said Nathan. "The kids found Tim, he's dead. They tied a line on him, over by Viner, at Penn Island."

"Oh!" gasped Carol Ann, her hand flew to her mouth, almost a slap. Flour puffed and whitened her cheeks. The other hand followed as she cried, "Oh! No! That poor boy, what happened?"

"Well, we don't know, Carol Ann, that's why we got to call the cops," said Back Eddy. "I found his boat high and dry on Smith Rock; the kids found his body washed up on Penn Island. Don't make any sense."

Nathan asked, "How's your phone working, Woody?"

"We give it a try," he said. "Maybe she work today, maybe not."

Woody opened the door to his living area, led the way past the picnic table to the office area where his phone and computer sat. The pack followed; barely room to fit a single other person in. Carol Ann remembered the food cooking in the kitchen and the half kneaded bread. She couldn't bear to burn the stew or ruin the bread but didn't want to miss a thing.

Woody poked around through his papers, what was he looking for? Oh right, a phone number...911? Be faster than trying to find the number of the cop shop in Port McNeill. Or maybe not; he's flustered. He remembered it was written down in his old address book, ditted it in and paused before pressing the call button.

"So, who will be de one who talk?"

Nathan looked at Cole and Hayley, "You guys found the body, you want to do it? Back Eddy can tell them about the boat...?" He raised his wild white eyebrows at Back Eddy.

"No, the kids can do it, I hate them things, can't hear a damn thing on the phone. It's just a bunch of garble."

"Who's going to tell Kit?" asked Cole.

Back Eddy's body jerked. "Dammit, I guess that'll have to be me." Looked at the floor.

Later when he pulled in to Kit's bay, she wasn't home. Relieved and irked at the same time, he dithered. He'd have to make a return trip but she'd likely hear it from someone else pretty damn quick anyway.

Twenty-Two

"RCMP North Island detachment, how can I help you?" Erika's receptionist voice was calm after the strident ringing of the phone had ruptured the silence in the quiet office. Neither of the women had spoken for over an hour, both engrossed in playing catch-up with reports on this hot, quiet afternoon. Margaret looked up, listened as Erika's tone changed with her next words.

"Who am I speaking with? Cole Harrison? And you are presently where?"

Pause. "Echo Bay, Woody's Marina; okay. Thank you, Cole. I'm going to put you through to Staff Sergeant In Charge, Sergeant Morris."

Erika gave Margaret the high sign, mouthed 'dead body' and transferred the call.

"Sergeant Morris," Margaret barked in her huskiest tone. "I understand you are reporting a death? Please tell me the details."

The colour drained from her face as she listened to the caller, and she raised stricken eyes to the ceiling. Suddenly unable to breathe, she put her hand to her heart. From dead white her face flushed to bright red as she struggled to gain control of herself.

"Okay, okay, hold on a moment, Cole. I'm going to get a new notebook and take some notes. Can you do that? Okay, I'm going to put you on hold for a minute or two. Thank you."

Her hands trembled as she pressed the hold button. She stood up and wobbled to the door of her office, pressed the backs of her hands to the door frame as she stared unseeing at the other woman.

Erika rushed from her chair. Margaret might be her boss but at this moment she was clearly in deep distress and she sagged unresisting as Erika grasped her elbows.

"What is it? Margaret, tell me what?"

Margaret straightened quickly, pushed her away. "Sorry. It's... someone I know, he's died. He's dead."

"Who?"

Deep breath, "It's a guy I used to...to go out with. A guy called Tim. Okay, I need a new notebook."

Erika rushed to the cabinet and pulled one out of the box of new ones, handed it over. "Here you go."

"Thank you, Erika. Thank you."

The first thank you was her usual polite behaviour to the staff, the second thank you was for the hug, and for not pressing her. Margaret Morris may be Staff Sergeant In Charge but she was still human and the months of policing this district hadn't significantly reconstructed the emotional armour that had been shattered at her last posting. Margaret turned back into her office and took two more deep breaths. Got back on the phone.

"Hello, Cole? Can you spell your last name for me? Okay, and who were you with when you found the body? I'm going to...oh I see."

Cole told her the phone reception at Woody's Marina was iffy, it had been fading in and out while he was on hold.

"Then please tell everyone who's there with you to be available to speak with me, and also don't discuss this with anyone until we get there, okay? No one. We'll be out in *Sea Wolf* in about an hour and a half. What? Okay, yes, tell Mr. Deacon he can head home, we'll come to his place, no problem. Okay, see you shortly. Thank you very much, Cole. I know that must have been traumatic."

Margaret hung up, then gathered her travel kit, prepared for just such an event, and jacket.

"Erika, can you get a hold of Barrett James and John Carrigan, they're on today, right? Tell them I need them to be ready to go with me to Echo Bay within thirty minutes. They may need a toothbrush and a change of underwear." A small smile; trying to be jokey.

"And get hold of Patrick Battersby and Heather Abbott and tell them, she's in and he's on call, okay, for the rest of the day, probably tomorrow, too. We may be doing an overnight somewhere in Echo Bay, not sure yet. Probably. Maybe a couple days."

The run across Queen Charlotte Strait was rough for the crew on the BWT 17-G-1. The tide was flooding with force into Knight Inlet and wayward gusts of wind over Blackfish Sound were stirring up a moveable sculpture on the sea's surface. *Sea Wolf* approached the rumpled swells like a horse running the third race of the Triple Crown. Margaret experienced the boat almost as a conscious being, exulting in its own aggressive power.

"At last! A crime! A reason to run! At last! A crime!" she heard it chanting as she steered through the roiling chaos of deep green water. She didn't share the feeling she attributed to the vessel. Staff Sergeant In Charge Margaret Morris was filled with dread, wondering if she was the right person for this job.

She'd notified Courtenay Dispatch and the dive team was on standby until further notice. The *Nadon* would be on its way at her call, with a full crew of divers/investigators. She desperately hoped that wouldn't be necessary.

Maybe it was her imagination but Echo Bay looked dismal as she pulled in to the dock in front of the lodge. The flat light reduced the shadows and gave the buildings and trees the look of an under-exposed photograph.

The last time Margaret was here she'd been with a group from the Chamber of Commerce and they'd come out on the *Naiad Explorer*, a local whale watching and Auxiliary Coast Guard vessel. The group had lunched here at the lodge and then visited Back Eddy's Museum. It had been a happier moment than now and Margaret tried to recapture the emotion of that day to counteract her current mood.

While Constable Carrigan leaped out with the tie-up line, Margaret turned off the key and stepped out of the boat, shook the tension from her neck and shoulders. Woody Debris hobbled awkwardly down the steps, trailed by Carol Ann, Cole and Hayley. Nathan stayed on the upper deck.

"Come in de lodge, chilly wind out here," Woody greeted them.

"Thank you," she said as they made their way up to the lodge. "Which of you is Cole Harrison?"

Being extra polite; she already knew who was who even though she'd only met Woody and Back Eddy. She acknowledged Cole, and then Hayley. Nathan offered his name with a reaching hand to shake and Carol Ann's mutter was barely audible.

Margaret introduced her staff to the Echo Bay group and asked if there was anyone besides Cole with some knowledge of events.

Nathan replied, "I don't think so but we just found out. The kids found Tim's body on Penn Island. And Back Eddy saw his speedboat up Tribune Channel on Smith Rock."

Margaret gestured to Constable James to note the time and place and everyone's name as she went through the preliminaries. "Guess we'd better go and retrieve the body before the tide takes him off the rock or the birds get more of him. Can you all please stay in the bay? I'd like to get the full story. You two come with us."

She gestured to Hayley and Cole while Carrigan pulled out a couple life jackets.

Hayley paled to green at this peremptory order, balked briefly, then realized she would have been thoroughly annoyed if Cole had been singled out to accompany them. Gamely she stepped into the police boat and sat where Carrigan pointed. He handed her one of the regulation life jackets and she and Cole each clipped one on.

Margaret turned to Woody before they left and inquired, "Mr. DesBrisay..."

"Jus' Woody, okay," he interjected.

"Woody," she repeated, "have you got somewhere we can be, one of the cabins maybe?"

"Yah, sure, you betcha. I'll get the brown-shingled one dere set up for you guys, plenty of rooms. Carol Ann, she'll make up de beds. We're full right up wit' tree-planters in de lodge. You'll need some privacy anyway, I'm t'inking."

Margaret nodded gratefully. "Thanks."

Sea Wolf made the jarring eight-kilometre run to Penn Island in minutes. Sergeant Morris glanced at Cole for direction. He pointed his thumb at Hayley, who guided the sergeant to the cleft they had nosed the skiff into. It was too small for the wider bow of *Sea Wolf* to navigate but Margaret eased close alongside the rocky shore. Carrigan climbed off the bow with a line and held it. Tim's body lay nearby, undisturbed.

Margaret turned to Cole and Hayley, asked, "Has anything changed since you saw him, the covering is the way you left it? Look carefully. You'll have to sign a statement when we are through your story so this is part of it. Those are your jackets, correct?"

Both nodded yes, both looked carefully, as instructed, then nodded again. The jackets and stones remained precisely where Cole had placed them. At least they had been successful in preventing more damage to Tim's body by the ravenous birds.

"Stay put."

Hayley and Cole rolled their eyes at each other. As if they wouldn't.

"Back the boat away easy when I get off, Barrett, then hang close," said Margaret, and followed Carrigan onto the rocks. She pulled on a pair of thin gloves while the constable took several photos of the scene with the digital camera.

"Best we can do without the team," Carrigan said, then carefully removed the stones and the jackets, laying them aside after inspecting them for tears in the fabric or blood. He shot several more photos, put the camera in the kitbag and pulled out the case notebook.

Margaret lifted Tim's left hand then the right. Gently she teased a remnant of bandaging off the wrinkled palm of the hand, felt the broken finger bones and closely inspected the fingernails of each. Carrigan noted down her murmured observations and was ready with the thin plastic bags to slip over the hands when she reached for them.

Margaret slowly examined the entire head, the slightly bloated torso, then the legs of her dead lover, noting each of the bruises and contusions, trying to determine if they were the result of floating around in the water for days (*and how many might that be?*) or from impact such as a fight or landing on something hard. Plaid shirt, two buttons missing, slightly torn at the collar, long sleeves, hard to tell if the dark stains were blood; over that a light quilted jac-shirt, and over all a life jacket, firmly clipped at the waist.

The words—*dead lover, dead lover, dead lover*—tolled in her head with a bone deep reverberation. Each time she firmly replaced them with the two-syllable phrase: *the vic, the vic, the vic.* Now was neither the time nor the place for emotional indulgence.

She was absolutely obsessive, using her abyssal sense of loss to propel the professionalism of her examination, not noticing that her feet were three inches deep in water.

"Sergeant, the tide is getting pretty high; we're going to have to get him off damn quick." John Carrigan helped her roll the body over and she cradled Tim's head, looking closely.

"Right, my feet are all wet. See this on the back of his head, looks like he bashed his head on something long and narrow, or was maybe whacked with something, doesn't it? You got enough pictures?"

"More than enough I think."

"Need a couple more here; back of his head."

Carrigan complied, then shot a few of the spot where Tim's body had lain.

"Going to be hard to see anything on the rock."

"Pretty sure it's not the scene of the crime anyway."

"If there is a crime," he commented.

"Okay, let's get him in the boat." She stood up and waved to James to bring the boat in close. "Tell him to pass you the tarp out of the locker. We'll roll him onto it, then wrap it around him and then lift him together. Get the kids out while we do it."

"Yes, ma'am."

Margaret appreciated Carrigan's formality, especially in front of civilians. Too many men she'd worked with had been disrespectful or dismissive but Carrigan, James and Morris had bonded into a good working team within months of her arrival as the new Staff Sergeant in Charge. She was glad they had been on shift today. She could count on them to support her decisions and add their skills to hers.

Bringing the cumbersome tarp-wrapped body onto the police vessel was awkward but accomplished fairly smoothly, and then *Sea Wolf* was underway again with its sad burden carefully secured near the stern. Cole and Hayley took comfort from their grip on each other's hand as the vessel careened back to Echo Bay.

"Now we're going to have to ask Woody if he has somewhere cool we can leave him while I talk to the neighbours. I'll have to see Kit Sampson, I think we passed her floathouse in that bay next to Scott Cove but we'll get her radio call sign from Woody. Who else? Woody and Carol Ann of course; Back Eddy. That'll do for a start."

Margaret Morris was being as efficient as she could and going by the book, too. Somewhat difficult when you couldn't leave a body in place because the tide might float it away. At the dock, Cole asked, "Okay if Nathan and me take Hayley back to Gwayasdums?"

"Can you sit with Constable Carrigan and give your statements first? Have you got a phone number?"

Both nodded, Hayley replied, "I can give you the village office number, Leah can track me down."

Margaret looked at Cole, who said, "I'm here at Woody's. Phones aren't the best out here but email works okay."

"Sounds good, thank you. You kids did well. I'm sorry you had to be the ones to find Tim." She was sympathetic; Hayley was surprised at the policewoman's warmth.

"Thank you. It's very frightening knowing someone was killed out here. I'm used to feeling so safe, not like in the city. But..."

Quick to catch her hesitation, Margaret said, "But?"

"Nothing concrete. Only, some guys make you feel...anxious."

Margaret understood how she felt; bad enough for any woman but Indigenous women were often more preyed upon than their white counterparts.

"Anytime. Any time," she emphasized, "if you need anything at all, you or anyone you know; talk to me. We want to hear what you young people experience in order to help protect you."

Hayley nodded. "For sure, I will."

"Okay, good. Work to do, right now, but anytime. Remember."

Hayley nodded. *She really means it.*

Twenty-Three

*M*argaret used Woody's semi-reliable phone to call the high-speed catamaran out of Nanaimo. The *Nadon* and crew would show up tomorrow and in the meantime she had people to talk to. *What else, what else?*

She needed to find Tim's liveaboard and secure his speedboat, so...talk to Back Eddy. Margaret dispatched Carrigan to go around to his homestead after taking Cole and Hayley's statements. James would gather everyone's radio call sign information and mark on a chart the home locations of Kit, Nathan, Back Eddy and every other member of the community.

Next...*right, Woody.* Heading into the kitchen of the lodge she discovered he was nowhere to be found, but Carol Ann was there, prepping the evening meal for the ever-hungry tree-planters.

"Knock, knock." Margaret echoed her action with the words as she broke into the music Carol Ann was dancing to.

Round-eyed with guilt, Carol Ann froze when she saw her visitor. She'd been cutting up chicken legs with a large butcher knife, she carefully laid it on the counter and turned to the sink to wash her hands.

Margaret reached out her hand and said, "We didn't get formally introduced. I'm Sergeant In Charge Margaret Morris. I guess you know why I'm here."

"Yes, yes, of course I do. Yes. I shouldn't have been dancing. It just took my mind off it, off of Tim." In sudden delayed reaction she responded to the outstretched hand, said, "Carol Ann Murchison."

"Woody here?"

Margaret looked around. Obviously Woody was not.

Carol Ann looked around, too, as if she was going to find him hiding behind the stove, then she found her tongue. "He's out to pick up the crew, the tree-planters. He won't be back for an hour."

"Oh, I see, right. Could I sit here for a few minutes? Visit a bit?"

"Sure, of course, I don't know anything though, nothing. Honestly." Carol Ann was flustered.

"That's okay, I don't expect you to figure out 'who dunnit.' I wouldn't have a job if civilians did all the work."

She smiled, offering up her warmth and charm to put the cook at ease. "I know it is terribly upsetting when a friend or neighbour is found in such appalling circumstances."

Carol Ann responded to this enthusiastically, "Oh yes, it's such a shock!" It didn't take long for her to feel right at home with Margaret. She looked into the policewoman's haggard face and led the way into Woody's private home space.

"Cuppa tea, Sergeant? You look all in, if I may say so."

Seven minutes later she set the hot strong tea on the table. "I'll join you for a cup, too. I have to admit it's been pretty crazy around here lately." She sat on the bench opposite Margaret.

"Why do you say that?"

"Mmm...lots of fights and conflict and people yelling at each other..." Carol Ann trailed off as she remembered who she was talking to.

"Go on," invited the sergeant gently. She read the woman's discomfort accurately—at least one of those fights must have included Carol Ann herself. "Don't worry about anything. I want to know the truth and I want to find out what happened to Tim. We all want that, yes? I won't be blaming anyone for anything they did or did not do that is not related to this single issue."

Margaret directed her compelling gaze to Carol Ann and spoke ever so quietly, forcing the other woman to lean closer to catch her words. "Talk to me, Carol Ann. Help me find out what happened to Tim."

"Well first, there's been a lot of trouble because of this fisherman, Benny. He hates Ritchie Wilson, he's from Kingcome. Ritchie I mean; he's a great guy but Benny keeps poking and poking trying to get him mad and one of these days they're going to be taking a swing at each other. I don't think Ritchie is going to be able to resist."

"About what? What's the problem?"

Carol Ann rolled on. "Well, Benny is mad at the natives for wanting..." flipped her hands up and out, "wanting...everything, or reparations or whatever. Thinks it should all be equal access to salmon and other resources. Says he's seen guys from Kingcome fishing prawns in the winter when they're spawning. He hates that 'cause he says they're egged up in the winter. And he says he's seen Ritchie setting a net at Embley Lagoon for salmon there. Ritchie swears it isn't him. It probably isn't, he has a terrible cousin whose boat is a sister boat to Ritchie's, but still. He..."

"He, who?"

"Benny. He told Tim what he thought and then Tim went after Ritchie, even though he has no power or right to, which pissed Ritchie off."

"How did Tim 'go after' Ritchie?"

"Oh, you know, he lectured him, shamed him, according to Ritchie. He's a proud man, that guy. And he's kind of a creep, to tell you the truth."

"Ritchie, you mean? Or Benny?"

"Oh, sorry. Benny. Benny Thompson. I don't know, he's been so weird lately."

Margaret noted all this down in her book but none of it seemed relevant at this point. Hard to tell what was relevant at such an early stage.

"How do you mean, a creep?"

"Mmm, like he's always making lewd remarks, kind of coming on to us. To women; me and Kit and Hayley. I'm more worried about her than anybody; she's young and vulnerable, and Native, right?"

"Indigenous, yes." Margaret nodded. "Did he ever do anything any of you felt you should report?"

"Not really, you just have to, you know, be firm."

Carol Ann raised her eyes as Margaret looked up from her notebook. "What else?"

Carol Ann jumped like a cat had scratched her. "What do you mean?"

Margaret leaned back and tapped her teeth with the pencil. "You mentioned other fights and yelling...?" Repeating Carol Ann's words, she made finger quotes in the air.

For about two breaths Carol Ann deliberated. Margaret waited patiently as she watched the cook conclude it was all going to come out anyway, might as well be as accurate as possible.

"Maybe you don't know this but Kit found out about you and Tim."

In spite of the thump of her heart, Margaret maintained her outward calm. "Found out what?"

She leaned forward ever so slightly and narrowed her eyes. She wanted Carol Ann to spit it out and she sure didn't want Carrigan or James to come in right that very moment.

Carol Ann pursed her lips then pressed them tight as if she couldn't or wouldn't reveal anymore. Was she betraying Kit or simply telling the truth? She could picture her friend's eyes emitting black sparks when she heard about what she said. *Too late now*. She regretted her easy confidences to the inviting questions.

"Too late," Margaret's murmur echoed the thought.

Carol Ann looked away, then back to Margaret, twisting her apron in her hands. She'd gone too far and couldn't backpedal now. Margaret waited; no signs of agitation ruffled her apparent tranquility.

"The day Kit picked up Tim in McNeill, they had a big fight on the dock here and she was yelling something horrible at him, cursing him, and she hardly ever swears. She threw his suitcase in the water and told him she never wanted to see him again. She didn't want to talk about it when she unloaded the boat and came in for coffee but a week later she was here with Hayley and she told us what happened."

"And what happened precisely?"

"Well, she guessed he had slept with you, because of him saying about the fentanyl thing and you talking to both of them about it and he admitted it and maybe there were others too." A small shock pierced Margaret.

"You mean other women?" Her voice squeaked on the last syllable and she coughed to cover it.

"I guess," said Carol Ann, taking a breath. "It was only maybe, he didn't actually say that. But then later he went to visit her and told her he loved her and wanted to marry her and only her, but what she wanted was to break up with him. So he went away but said he wanted to make her dinner later that week, but he didn't show."

"And when was that supposed to be?"

"Last Saturday."

"Did she call Coast Guard? Did anyone call them?"

"No, because she figured he was mad or down Clio Channel or somewhere checking boats and couldn't make it and she didn't want to see him anyway because, you know, what she wanted was to break up. I told her yesterday that she should call the Coast Guard and she said she was going to."

Suddenly Woody was at the door, and a burning smell wafted from the kitchen on a cloud of smoke.

Carol Ann leaped up in a tizzy as Woody exclaimed, "What d' hell, Carol Ann? What's burning? And why you are you talkin' 'bout Kit? Shouldn't you leave dat to her? Isn't it bad enough Tim is dead and nobody give a shit?"

He rushed for the kitchen, grabbed the smoking pot off the stove and dumped it in the sink. Carol Ann followed, hands fluttering. "That's not true, Woody. Everybody cares. We all want Sergeant Morris to figure it out. I was only helping as best I can."

"Yah, well, maybe she shouldn't even be de one to try to figure it out."

Margaret rose from the table, gathered up her notebook. Woody had a valid point. Maybe this wasn't such a good time to talk to him—in fact, it was the perfect time to leave.

She headed for the door, as Woody and Carol Ann bickered in the kitchen. "Thanks for your time, Carol Ann, I'll be back in a while."

Neither answered.

What next? She tapped her pencil against her teeth again as she ran through the options. First, confer with Carrigan and James, then check in with the Courtenay detachment, somehow, and find out the ETA of *Nadon*.

When she exited the lodge Carrigan was back with *Sea Wolf.* She told him to get Woody's statement as she took his place at the wheel. Margaret sat quietly in the vessel; thought about Carol

Ann's revelations and added remembered details to her notes before she put the boat in gear and pulled away from the dock. Not looking forward to her next task but it must be done. She headed for Kit's bay as the sky slid to an early evening teal and the first star appeared.

A wreath of smoke circled above the floathouse. Snug against the shore, it was backed by a curtain of dark evergreens; warm light glowed from the window; it looked so appealing. As she drew near, Margaret was surprised by a flash of envy. Epitomized by that almost storybook little house by the treed shore, Kit's life appeared so...stress free. Not like hers. Kit didn't have to deal with murderers, wife and child abusers, thieves and drug dealers, death in all the ways it could be inflicted.

Well, she does now.

Kit was friendly when she came out on deck; surprised to see Margaret, but politely invited her in for a cup of tea.

"I'll pass on the tea, thanks, just loaded up with...over at Woody's. I love your house, it's adorable and functional and kind of fairy-tale," Margaret exclaimed as she disembarked.

In turn, Kit admired the well-kept boat. "I wouldn't mind having something like this myself. Must run pretty good. C'mon in."

Kit led the way, wondered what the heck Margaret was doing here. She waved a hand toward the couch, then the chair, said, "Pick a spot, any spot."

"May I use your bathroom first?"

"Oh, sure, in there," Kit pointed.

When the sergeant returned she chose the chair; sat, waited until Kit, who didn't appear to be upset in any way, sank onto the couch. *Could she not know?*

"I need to ask you some questions."

"Okay..." Kit was quizzical. "About?"

"Well," Margaret looked down at her hands folded in her lap, "about Tim."

"Oh. Tim. What about him? I've kind of been worrying about him. He was supposed to come over for dinner on the weekend and he, um, he didn't make it."

"Did that concern you? Did he often not show up?"

"Sometimes. I never worry when he doesn't, particularly now when he's working."

Margaret paused a moment. "So you didn't call Coast Guard or report him missing?"

Kit's turn to hesitate. "I thought about it. Carol Ann said I should, but we were thinking he'd show up any day. She was going to ask some of the prawn fishermen; see who'd been checked by him and when. I didn't go over today so I don't know if she's seen any of them. Maybe I should've."

Margaret stared right into the other woman's eyes and abruptly stated, "I guess you were pretty angry about Tim being with me while he was out."

Kit reared back, throat constricted, mouth dropped open. She recovered quickly though and returned the shot. "How do you even know I knew about you two? Did you talk to Tim? The lying sack of shit," she muttered bitterly. "Is that what this is about? You come out here to get him back or something? Fight for your man? Well, guess what, Sergeant In Charge Margaret Morris, you can have him. You are welcome to the scumbag! So there you go, now get out of my house!"

Kit leaped up and stomped over to the door, wrenched it open and swept a bow to the cop as if swishing her out the door. Margaret remained seated on the couch.

"Maybe you were angry enough to do something violent in revenge?"

"What? No! What are you talking about?"

Margaret took out her notebook and pen, noted the time and Kit's name, her question and the answer.

Kit shut the door. Suddenly weak-kneed, brow furrowed, she walked back, lowered herself to the couch. Kitcat jumped onto her knees and she automatically stroked the purring ball of black fluff.

"What's going on? Did something happen to Tim? Stop playing little cop games and tell me why you're here."

"When did you last see Tim?"

"He came over a few days after we got back from town, the day I saw you, so...when was that, Monday or Tuesday? Yeah, Tuesday. So, he came over...said he had to go check prawn boats and get caught up and he wanted me to have dinner with him."

Time for the truth; maybe Kit would have more to say if she was fully informed. "Tim is...dead, Kit." No sugar coating this statement. "Cole and Hayley found him on Penn Island this afternoon. I was called and brought a team out and we went out to see, and...get him." Margaret stumbled, her emotions pressing up through her professional carapace.

Kit gasped, her lips whitened and a bright spot of red bloomed on her cheeks. Her caressing hands twitched and Kitcat leaped out of her lap like a pilot bailing from a crashing plane.

"He's dead? Honestly? How? Why didn't anyone tell me?"

More silence, then Kit gasped again as realization dawned. "You think I did it? Me? Why would I?" She can't even say the word 'kill.' "Why would you think that? I was mad that he was messing around with you and I dumped him. Anyway, I didn't even want to have dinner with him." Cruel in her pain, she added, "He told me he loved me and wanted to marry me, that he would give you up and everybody else. Of course who knows how many other women there were. I suppose he screwed around on you, too." Kit looked up to see how the other woman took that.

Conflicting thoughts raced through Margaret's mind. It was too much; sorting through her job as a cop, her emotions about her recent intimacy with Tim, and now his death. She'd jumped the gun and practically accused Kit as the perpetrator, although she was not yet certain that a crime had been committed. And even though it stung as Kit had intended, the suggestion that he hadn't been faithful to her when they were together didn't ring true. He had told *her* pretty quickly, after all, when he'd gotten together with Kit, hadn't tried to hide it.

Margaret tapped her pen on her knee and cogitated.

"This is a bad scene, Kit. You and me, and our relationships with Tim, and now he's been found dead on Penn Island."

Kit had gone from furious to plain old angry and a lot confused. Throw in dawning grief, maybe some guilt; a stew of emotion for them both.

"You were talking to Carol Ann, weren't you?" guessed Kit.

"You know I can't tell you anything about who I spoke with, right? So you'll have to think what you like, but it would be great if there was anything, any little thing at all that might be helpful in sorting this out."

Blood thumped and thundered in Kit's ears. She was certain her good friend Carol Ann had told Margaret everything she knew. *She'll be hearing about this.*

"Where is Tim...his body, I guess, where is it? What will happen to him?"

She jumped up, went to the kitchen counter and pulled a bottle off the wine rack. Holding it while her brain whirled, she fumbled for the opener, twisted out the cork with unnecessary force. Plucked a glass from the cupboard, raised the glass and her eyebrows at her visitor.

Margaret shook her head, no, then changed her mind, nodded yes.

"We've placed his body in the long freezer in the back at Woody's Marina."

Kit poured them both a glass, brought them to the table; surprised the cop with a complete change of topic. "Have you had anything to eat today?"

As Margaret sipped the wine, her stomach gurgled; she *was* hungry. "I have not. Are you...offering? Something?"

"I could. Yes. I'm offering something. Sitting here and getting all jiggled up is not going to do Tim any good and figuring out what happened with him is the most important thing."

"You'd make a good cop, Kit."

Kit snorted, "No, I wouldn't. I get too mad. I'm trying to not be so impulsive. My feelings are all over the place lately and I can't seem to control them. I mean, look at you. You're not exactly in an easy position yet you have so much self-control. I've got to think about this, see if there's anything I can come up with that might be useful."

Kit looked at Margaret and continued earnestly. "There's so much stuff goes on in a small community, and you can't tell what's real when you're in the middle of it and things are happening. Sometimes you witness events and sometimes you only hear about them, and everyone talks to everyone else. It's like this. Say someone tells Person A something they think or heard that *might* be true. Then Person A tells Person B, as if it *is* true. So Person B thinks that what they heard is a repeatable fact and that's how they present the information to the next person they talk to. I'm always looking out for that and waiting to see what is actual, accurate and factual."

"I know. I know exactly what you mean. And the smaller the community is the more completely everyone is sure of the 'truth,'" Margaret gestured finger quotes, "of what has not been shown to be true."

"Yup, like that. Okay, I'm going to make us a bite to eat. Won't take long."

"Thank you. I need to get back to check on the boys, my staff, and figure out who to talk to next."

Kit found a partial onion and some ham in the fridge, eggs from Back Eddy's chickens. She sautéed the onion, added the ham, whisked four eggs and dumped them in the pan. While the omelette cooked, she stood at the counter, thinking. Pretty clear that Margaret had truly loved Tim. It dawned on her that in the face of the sincerity of that love, her own relationship with Tim had been considerably less than authentic. She'd responded to his desire and pursuit of her because he was presentable, attractive, employed, present, and fun to be with. Proximity had been more key than true love and respect.

Flooded with shame, she acknowledged that at any point she could have been firmly honest with Tim and sent him on his way, but—here was the unvarnished truth—she'd liked having him panting after her. She'd liked having the man in her bed trying to please her, and having him on her arm to go to dinner or a party at the neighbours'. Living in a small community didn't give you a lot of choices and sometimes you had to make do with who was there. And she had.

Kit placed the plate of food, a fork and a napkin in front of Margaret, whose eyes had drifted shut.

"Margaret," Kit said softly.

Margaret's eyes popped open.

"Oh, it's getting dark. I need to get back to Woody's."

"Eat, Margaret, you've had a long day. Woody will take care of your guys."

"I don't know if I can. My mind is going around in circles."

Kit raised her fork to her mouth, her eyes to the cop across from her.

"I'll probably never say this again, Margaret, but I want you to know I'm sorry."

"For what?"

"First, I guess the thing to say is, I'm sorry for your loss, Margaret. And I truly am. I think you really loved Tim. Second, the truth is, I didn't; truly love him, that is. I'm sorry I didn't set him free. I wouldn't admit it to myself, but I *didn't* love him that much. He was right. I *was* always waiting for something better to come along—not so much *better*, but something...more deep

221

and true and heartfelt for me. That's why he yelled at me when I threw him off the boat."

Before Margaret could reply, Kit cocked her head, said, "Someone's here."

Set her plate on the coffee table, jumped up. As she opened the door, she threw her words back toward Margaret, "Ooh, it's foggy out; half an hour ago I thought it was going to be a clear starry night." Then forward to the man at the door. "Hi Carson."

Carson grasped her arms, startled Kit.

"Did you know? Kit, are you okay? I just heard about Tim."

"Um, yes. Me, too. The sergeant here is questioning me."

"Right, the cop." Carson nodded to Margaret. "Okay if I come in?"

"Might as well join the party."

"Fine by me, too." Kit rolled her eyes.

Opening the door wider Carson slipped off his coat; Kit took it, turned and introduced the two. "Carson Maxwell, meet Sergeant In Charge Margaret Morris, North Vancouver Island RCMP detachment."

Carson smiled warmly, extended his hand as Margaret rose to greet him. Perceptively he assessed the scene: two plates with unfinished mounds of omelette, two glasses of wine and the bottle on the table between them. "Not your typical interrogation, I take it?"

Margaret watched as Carson settled his length onto the couch and Kitcat leaped into his lap. Who was *this* fellow and what, if anything, was he to Kit?

Kit inclined her head toward the wine bottle in offer to Carson. He raised his palm, no, and she forked in a bite of her dinner and chewed. Nobody said a word. The floathouse lifted gently and settled. The walls creaked. An owl hooted once, another toowhoo-ed from deeper in the bush.

"Carson is new in the neighbourhood. I met him the same day I ran into you in town. He was helping the folks on the mussel testing boat; remember I was borrowing the jack? We've, ah, visited since then. Went up Scott Cove Creek together and painted."

Of course Margaret remembered. Both women also recalled the request Margaret had made to Kit: to keep her ears open for any suspicious activity that might be drug related. Kit was in no way suspicious of Carson but was pretty sure Margaret now had him on her radar as a person of interest.

"So tell me about yourself, Carson, may I call you Carson? How long have you been in the neighbourhood?"

"Mmm, been here in the Broughton almost a month now. I live on my boat and I'm poking around, exploring. It's about four months since I bought it. I've been painting some of the scenery and searching out some of the places where painters like Emily Carr went. To be clear, Sergeant Morris, I know you'll need to investigate me but I'm not a drug dealer. I'm not wanted for anything, no record except one speeding ticket in New York City when I was trying to make a plane. My life is an open book."

With a big ingenuous smile he spread his hands wide.

Margaret looked at Kit, who shrugged. "Can't vouch, I barely know him. Sorry."

The 'sorry' to Carson, who threw her a wry smile. He was comfortable with the truth. "We just met," he added, "but I like her."

Kit jumped up, poured a glass of water for Carson and some in her own, now empty, glass. Margaret placed her hand over hers and shook her head. She gathered her energy and rose.

"I'm so tired I can't see straight. I'm staying—my whole crew is staying—at Woody's. I can't believe he found space for us with a lodge full of tree-planters."

"Sergeant, I have a drone. I haven't taken time to look at the footage from the past few days yet but if you think it might be useful...?"

"For sure, Carson. That would be terrific. I'll see you, say, eight-ish? That too early?"

"No problem. I'll come to Woody's."

"Thank you. He gave us the big brown floathouse, by the lodge."

"Yup, I know it."

"See you tomorrow, then."

"Okey dokey."

"Thank you for dinner, Kit." Margaret hesitated. "This isn't standard operating procedure, but..." She turned to Kit and embraced her; a brief warm connection. Kit was stiff but softened and returned the hug. Margaret stepped away and turned to the door. "The *Nadon* is on its way, they should be here by early afternoon tomorrow. If you want to come over to Woody's and... see Tim, say your goodbyes, or anything."

"Thanks, I will."

Twenty-Four

Thick fog in the falling dark slowed Margaret as she navigated the shoreline to Echo Bay. *Kind of like my mind right now*, she thought, pulling up at the dock with a sigh of fatigue. Woody stepped out of the artfully shingled floathouse to greet her, trailed by Carrigan and James.

"Dis cabin be okay for you?" he asked. "You'll be comfortable here, dere's lots of bedrooms and de kitchen and everyt'ing. I bring you some tree-planter's dinner. Carol Ann, always she make a ton of food. Coffee and cereal for de morning. No wifi here, sorry, but use my office if you need. Tomorrow, if you stay, we talk about de groceries and all dat."

Margaret looked around, up the stairs. *How great would it be to have a holiday here.*

"Perfect." She smiled at Woody and added, "Please invoice the office when we're through here. I'll have to sign it. And is there any chance you have paper charts stashed away somewhere?"

"You betcha. Dere's rolls in de storeroom in back of your cabin, as a matter of fact."

"You've got everything, thanks a lot."

Woody waved dismissively, "No problem. For you," he said, "anyt'ing to help find out what happened to Tim. He was a pretty good guy."

John Carrigan and Barrett James apparently shared her thoughts about the cabin. "Nice place. Be great if we weren't working," commented James.

"Yah, maybe we can find five minutes to go fishing." Carrigan was wistful.

"You guys eat, hey. This looks good. I'm going to crash so I can be bright and chirpy and all detective in the morning. Wake me up at 6:30, Carrigan."

"Sure, boss. Sergeant. Good night."

Margaret fell rapidly into a fitful sleep but awakened a couple hours later. The recently laundered sheets smelled of an unaccustomed soap and irritated her skin. Used to the still quiet of her home, the creaking of the floathouse and the shrill squeaks of the docks responding to the movement of wind and tidal flow grated on her. Generally she was good at putting the day's work out of her thoughts, letting her mind sift and sort without duress. This enabled her to get the sleep she needed, but tonight—memories of Tim burned on the screen of her closed eyelids; inescapable movie-like scenes. Margaret lay rigid in the dark trying by desperate will to disappear the torturous thoughts.

At long last she slipped from memories to dreams.

She's lying in Tim's arms in her own luxurious bed. Sleepy and cuddled; Margaret knows true love in the aftermath of their love-making—until he turns to her and dumps her from the bed. He leaps out and dashes for the door, running for his life. Shocked and enraged, her love brutally snuffed out, Margaret struggles with the sheets, slides to her knees and grabs her gun from the side table drawer, rises and dashes out the bedroom door.

But there is no living room beyond that door, no Alert Bay spread below her. The derelict warehouse where she last spotted her partner, Jack Raynor, looms above her. Black eyes of splintered windows glare down accusingly. Above, a dense sky crushes down in black, white and shades of grey. A narrow alley separates her from the rest of her team but she knows they're near, she hears their shouts. Confused she looks down and sees her nakedness; what happened to her clothes, to her body armour? Where's Tim gone? Jack runs across her line of sight, he's yelling, "Shoot! Shoot! Shoot the bastard!"

Margaret freezes; her trigger finger freezes, her hand is paralyzed around the gun. She whirls and turns and whirls again, remembering...she hadn't shot and her partner had died. She can save him this time. Shoot!

Grasping the gun with both hands, she steadies her arms. A man dashes across the end of the alley, she shoots, shoots again.

She did it; she saved her partner. Margaret runs to the fallen body, rolls it over. Tim's stricken eyes are open, gazing into hers. She screams in horror and—her eyes fly open; she's sitting up in bed gasping for breath and sobbing without restraint; deep heaving sobs from an abyss of anguish.

Finally the sobs diminished; her breathing steadied. The faint nightlight from the hallway illuminated the pile of wet tissues surrounding her in the tangled bedclothes. She sniffed a couple times.

Maybe you need counselling.

Ya think?

I am so sick of you voices. You are not helping.

Margaret flopped back against her pillows, a few last tears leaked down her temples into her hair.

Was that a good cry? Feel better now?

Shut up! God, who are you?

No reply.

Dawn washed a delicate hint of violet across the sky before the sleep of exhaustion finally obliterated her grief.

Twenty-Five

Wednesday morning at Kit's floathouse, the bedroom filled softly with violet-pink light. She opened her eyes and lay there peacefully, enjoying it before the memory of Margaret's visit pitilessly claimed the space. Rosy, vaporous plumes of last night's fog drooped languidly before dematerializing altogether. Wind whipped up small circles; they eddied on the surface of the narrow bay. Hemlock rustled and cedar boughs sighed and the floathouse rocked to the rhythm of the swell.

The morning sky distracted her as she sifted through recent events: the sergeant's visit, Tim's incomprehensible death and her own guilt, now jacked up another measure by her lack of action in reporting him overdue. It was impossible to bring order to her chaotic thoughts. Coffee in hand, she went out on the deck and admired the contrast of peachy-pink clouds arranged for brief moments in sandbar-like ripples against green slopes. High in the blue, whiter clouds scudded along swiftly. Maybe a little painting time would help ease her troubled thoughts. Sometimes that worked; sometimes it was just avoiding the inevitable.

The marine weather forecast on the VHF radio didn't bring any peace to the tumult of her thoughts. *Queen Charlotte Strait – gale warning, southeast 20 to 25 knots, changing to northeast and rising to 25–35 late in the day and to northwest 45 overnight.*

Going to be windy around here. Good that her treasured home was well secured against the shore and protected from the northwesterly, thanks to Back Eddy and his expertise at setting up floathouses.

Last night Carson had finished off the glass of water after Margaret left, but sensitive to the vibe, he'd known she'd been overwhelmed and conflicted. He'd made no effort to comfort her, though. Maybe he'd heard that she and Tim had been an item. He'd left before she'd asked him to, with a warm hug and quiet assurance, "You're going to be alright."

When she'd nodded in agreement he'd said, "I'll stay if you want but—you'd probably rather be alone, right?"

She'd nodded yes again and with a casual "See you tomorrow then," he'd pulled on his coat and left.

She'd been half relieved, half annoyed and entirely confused.

Now Kit wished she'd asked Carson to show her the images on the drone, maybe something would have clicked. But the real hot button blistering her brain was Carol Ann (*pretty sure it was her*) blabbing everything to Margaret. She wanted to storm over there and give her a good slap upside the chops. Better to cool down before she confronted her, though. She sat down at her desk and pulled out her watercolours.

As she'd hoped it might, the time spent painting calmed her powerful urge to storm over and grab Carol Ann by the hair. In spite of the distress of Margaret's news, Kit felt less agitated and more clear-sighted. Tim was dead. Fact. Certainly explained why he hadn't showed up for dinner. She was sad, but not heartbroken; something she already was well aware of. He didn't need to be dead for her to figure that one out. The pertinent question was how he'd died. Figuring that out, of course, was Margaret's job, but if she put her mind to it she might be able to come up with something helpful. Maybe she ought to tell the cop about her experience the night she'd gone kayaking, except what was there to tell? She'd heard a boat and some yelling late at night. That's it. But still, it was unusual. Kit decided to talk it over with Back Eddy first and check in with Margaret later.

It was mid-afternoon before she felt in control of her emotions and ready to take action. She wanted to see Tim's body before the *Nadon* took him away, too; that was not going to be easy.

Time to go.

The fragrance of bacon sizzling in the pan filled Nathan's house and wafted out the door he opened when he heard a motor outside. Frying pan flipper in hand he poked his head out, smiled when he saw Ritchie; waved the flipper at him, turned back in, leaving the door ajar. A couple minutes passed, then came the expected knock as Ritchie entered.

"Mornin', Nathan. Got a few minutes?"

"You bet, Ritchie, how can I help?"

Nathan and Ritchie had worked together on salmon enhancement projects over the years; Viner River and Scott Cove Creek and other smaller creeks. They'd grown to trust and respect each other over the years. Ritchie knew Nathan to be a calm man, who thought before he acted; a peacemaker who worked to smooth things out when friction surfaced between the people working on the streams. Ritchie needed some of that now. Nathan waved his guest to the table and pulled out another plate; heaped bacon, toast and two eggs on it, set it in front of Ritchie.

"Didn't expect that warm a welcome."

"No reason why not, it's ready to be eaten." Nathan pulled up his own chair, tore the toast in half and swiped up some of the runny, golden yolk. "Eat first, talk later, that's what I always say."

"Thanks a lot. Boy, this is good." Ritchie lit into the bacon and eggs with gusto. The two men ate without saying much more, then sat back in their chairs.

A full stomach calmed Ritchie's seething thoughts. "Nathan, you know Benny has been harassing me about fishing at Embley Lagoon."

"Nope, didn't know that, Ritchie. I guess by the way you're framing this, it's not true."

"Yah, no. It isn't. But I think my cousin is. I think he's using my fishboat to do it and that's who Benny saw. I'm thinking maybe I should go to the cops about it. I hate that he's fishing there, but I don't want to be the one to turn him in. He doesn't listen to me. Maybe somebody else could convince him it isn't right. And I hate that Benny is such an asshole to me. I get so mad at him I'm afraid I'm going to do something crazy."

"Yah, maybe you better talk to them. Anything is possible."

Ritchie doesn't take offense. With his cousin, anything *is* possible.

"Isn't there a First Nations guy on the force, or in the bay?" asked Nathan.

"I don't know, there might be. Should be, right?"

"Yah," said Nathan, "I thought there was a First Nations police force or members or something. Probably be a good thing for folks to feel like they could talk to someone who understood the way things are from both points of view."

"You do, in any case. I appreciate that." Ritchie patted his full stomach and pushed back his chair. "Guess I better head out, got a few things to do, over at the dock. Thanks a lot for the breakfast. That hit the spot."

"Yup, most welcome." Nathan raised his hand in farewell and picked up the plates as Ritchie left. He thought over the conversation, realized he'd made no mention of Tim's death. Maybe Ritchie didn't even know. Was that even possible with the way word spread so fast in their small community? *Should have told him there were cops over at Echo Bay,* Nathan realized. Ritchie had probably noticed, in any case. Not much got past his observant eyes.

Twenty-Six

Margaret had a hard morning. Carrigan's knock on her bedroom door at 6:30 a.m. was painful. She'd stifled a snarl, and was relieved when he said the magic words.

"Coffee's ready."

Her wrinkled uniform was unappealing but she dragged it on, taking comfort from its familiarity. Dawn's violet light had left its colour in the half-moon under each eye of the face in the mirror. Not a good look.

She'd done everything she could to keep Tim's body cool, getting Woody to agree to shift everything in the freezers so Tim could be laid to rest in the biggest one. She took a quick sip of water, then crossed the wooden plank from the brown house to Woody's lodge, went around the back and in the door to the laundry room. She lifted the lid of the six-foot long freezer and took another look at the back of Tim's head, trying to imagine what he might have been struck with. She couldn't do much until the medical examiner got a good look at him.

Resting her hand on the shoulder of the dead man she noted again that he wore an odd mix of clothing. The jeans looked quite new and although salt-encrusted and torn she recognized the plaid shirt as the one he'd worn on their date. He'd been at least a bit dressed up then. But the jac-shirt overall didn't fit with the dressier clothes, looked like a throw-on, as if he'd been in a hurry to get out the door and just grabbed whatever was handy.

Margaret decided she'd keep Kit on the list a while longer in spite of her apparent sincerity.

Back in the open kitchen/living room of the floathouse, Carrigan offered her a mug and gestured to the milk and sugar. He was still rhapsodizing about fishing as he gazed out the big picture window.

"Dream on, fellas," snapped Margaret. "We've got work to do, in case you've forgotten your mission in this Shangri-La. I want you two to take the boat and cruise the shorelines in the Burdwood Group. You're looking for something like a rounded stick, maybe two or three inches across, a foot or two or three long." Her voice petered out as she realized what she was describing.

"Oh, there're maybe about ten thousand of those floating around," put in James, blue eyes laughing.

"I'm glad you think this is funny."

"Well come on, Sergeant, what are we looking for? Need a tad more than that to go on."

"Dammit, I don't know! Something that may have been used to strike the victim on the back of the head hard enough to maybe knock him overboard. What's on a boat? There's fish bonkers, and boathooks and..."

"Gaffs," said Carrigan, the fisherman.

"Yes! So you look for that and then we're going to have to look at fishing boats. How're we going to do that without a search warrant?"

"We could talk fishing with guys. Who is there, anyway?"

James filled three bowls with cereal and he and Carrigan slurped theirs down while Margaret consulted her notes.

"So, looks like there's been some friction between Ritchie Wilson, from Kingcome, and Benny Thompson, he's a local prawn fisherman. Benny would have a gaff for sure, and maybe Ritchie, too, he probably fishes."

"Yeah, and Woody, and Nathan Tolvanen across the way. My guess is most of these guys, the women, too, would have a gaff in the boat. They all fish, right?" said Carrigan.

James inquired, reasonably, "How are we going to find something that may not have been there in the first place?"

"Okay, the *Nadon* is on the way but they've been delayed in Johnstone Strait, some mechanical problem but they're on it. The medical examiner's with them, so maybe there'll be some slivers or hairs or something that can be matched up. You guys fuel up, we're running a tab here; go take a look around. Back Eddy told me he found Tim's speedboat on Smith Rock. If it's still there, get a line on it to secure it; he said it was tipped on its side so it's probably stuck there. He figured Tim's liveaboard might be up in Wakhana Bay so run up there and take a look. If the boat is there it'll likely, hopefully, be anchored and the *Nadon* can tow it out. Pull that chart over, Carrigan; let's take a look at it." As she spoke he reached for the charts he'd pulled out of the storeroom the night before and rolled out the two he'd selected.

"Look at this, Sarge. This chart was retired so many years ago I didn't think anyone even had one anymore. Chart 3576." He patted it reverentially. "This is a true antique."

"Look, it shows the whole layout for miles in every direction; everything from Echo Bay to Wakeman Sound, down to Gilford Village, over to Tribune Channel, and up Simoom Sound."

James laughed. "But it doesn't show Wahkana Bay. You old farts, there's nothing better than the nav program, we just set it and the boat goes there." Carrigan's bald head was bent over the table and Margaret blessed him for his age, his experience, his modesty and the way he'd never taken offense to her being his superior officer.

"Yah, well, you still have to know where the rocks are, and this is so detailed." commented the older man.

"I'm not an old fart yet, James. But I sure prefer these to the nav program; too bad there's no storage place for them on the boat," said Margaret.

Margaret traced her finger along the shore to Penn Island, then around King Point and up Tribune Channel.

"Guess we need another one to see Wahkana." Carrigan pulled it out of the pile and unrolled it over 3576.

"Okay, guys, get that done and come back, we'll compare notes, it's going to take a while. We'll figure out what to do after that, okay? Might have to get in a helicopter to take the body out of here, if the *Nadon* doesn't get here pretty damn quick. We'll see. I'll talk to everyone that shows up here while we wait for them. I've got that Carson fellow, Maxwell, coming with his drone memory card reader in a while, too."

She checked her watch. "Any minute, if he's on time."

Right on cue, a knock on the door. Carrigan opened it. Carson was on the doorstep, bright-eyed and wide awake. His longish chestnut brown hair was combed back and his beard neatly trimmed. He saluted the three RCMP officers with a tip of his finger to the side of his glasses.

"Good morning! Going to be a windy one today. I've got that chip, Sergeant Morris."

"Great, thank you," she said. "I'll fire up my computer." She waggled her fingers bye-bye to Carrigan and James as they pulled on jackets and boots and clomped out the door.

Carrigan turned as he stepped over the doorsill. "Eat your cereal, Sergeant."

Margaret looked out the window, then down at the screen again. Wiggled her butt in the rolling chair and settled in for the long haul. Carson dragged over a chair and loaded the drone card reader into her computer.

"It's brand new," he told her. "This is the first time I've loaded it."

They spent an hour together sorting out the program. He showed her how the various search functions worked and how to search by date.

"Lots of footage to get through, holy smokes."

It looked to her as if Carson had been developing control and guidance of the drone, seeking out streams and pausing when he spotted wildlife. They scrolled swiftly through footage of bears in estuaries, orca, a couple of humpback whales, even several minutes of a sperm whale in Johnstone Strait.

Although some vessels appeared as the drone passed over, Carson had paused but not gone close or lingered on them. It was going to be tough getting any conclusive imagery. She'd have to go through each frame that included a boat and then go in close up. Plus, there was one little problem, which was that she likely wouldn't recognize many of the boats. Maybe Back Eddy could take a look and help her identify those she was unable to.

Margaret pushed back her chair, stretched and rubbed the back of her neck. "Looks like this will take a while. Do you mind leaving it with me?"

Carson hesitated briefly, "Sure, okay. I have another chip I can use."

"Why do you have this anyway?"

"It's interesting, new, fun. I can afford it. See, this is state of the art, the technology is amazing."

Carson pulled out the drone from his kitbag along with the controller and placed them on the table.

Margaret was curious but not impressed. "What happens if you hover too close to anyone? I'd be insanely annoyed if someone's drone was hovering near me, it would feel so invasive. Worse than a helicopter, it's like a little creepy buzzing thing. Too big and maybe noisy to be good for surveillance."

"Yeah, I try to be super careful. It's pretty quiet out here, though. I was in Moore Bay and sent the drone up; it went over the hill and over some boats, a few days ago. Maybe got too close to a speedboat. I think it was Back Eddy but I haven't looked at it yet. I'm mostly looking for animals, bears and cougars, or fish in the river. It would be incredible to see a cougar or get some idea of where they travel or hang out."

"Okay well, how 'bout I get it back to you, tomorrow or something, soon as I'm done. What channel do you stand by on? Did James get your call sign?"

"Don't think so. *Restoration Point*. Channel 16, same as anyone."

Carson left. Margaret thought about him. *Drug dealer*? He seemed open, transparent even, and helpful. If she knew one thing for certain, though, it was that murder was never transparent. She was positive Tim hadn't died by ordinary accident. Carson's name got added to the bottom of the list with a question mark. Have to revisit his story in more detail.

Cole, Woody and Hayley were already crossed out. Slowly she drew a line through Kit's name and hoped that wasn't a mistake. She'd also concluded that Back Eddy was an unlikely perpetrator, although she hadn't ruled him out entirely, either. He was eighty-six after all, although an extremely vigorous and competent eighty-six. He had an up-to-date criminal check as a requirement for his log salvage licence, no history of violence, and was highly respected in the community at large. What about Woody? Ridiculous. Where would he, or Carol Ann, find a spare minute to be running around engaging in conflict with the neighbours?

The second thing she knew for certain was that there was always more to the story and it could take a lot of inquiry, and sometimes just plain old good luck to uncover it.

Time to engage with the rest of the cast of characters, do some interviews, gather some intel. *Stop*, she commanded her chatty mind, *please, stop it*. Margaret rubbed her dry, itchy eyes; not enough sleep when she needed to be sharp. She got up from the table, stretched her arms, then headed to the main lodge.

"No problem," said Woody when she told him she'd like to hang out at the store and speak to people as they came in.

The first to show up was Nathan, who rowed over with a jerry can to get some diesel. He was straightforward in his responses, telling her all that he knew, which was not very much.

His reluctance to say much about Cole sparked her curiosity and she pressed for more. He said simply, "Maybe I'm feeling kind of protective. He's my grandson, I'm pretty sure, and we're starting to get to know each other. He showed up barely a week ago and nobody knew anything about him, and I guess we still don't, but I think you can rule him out. He's got no reason to go after Tim. That I know of, anyway. 'Course, he saw the big fight between Kit and Tim, but I don't think he made anything of it, you know what I mean?"

Margaret nodded and added the sparse details to her notes.

She and Nathan both looked up as another boat putted around the end of the dock, pulled up by the fuel pumps. "Tourist," he said, glanced at Margaret and added, "Clean, white boat, total stranger."

Probably not much to be had from a total stranger tourist but Margaret spoke with the skipper anyway, to make certain. Satisfied that the couple, an American and his pretty young wife, newlyweds, wanted only to fuel up and be on their way to Alaska, she left them to go about their business.

Fretting from inaction, Margaret wandered around the marina for a while, wished she could jump in a boat and go find somebody. Maybe that drone would be a good tool, you could sit in one place and fly it around and watch everybody all the time. Too late for Tim, though. And it likely wouldn't help much at night, unless you had infrared maybe.

Woody met up with her at the bottom of the ramp up to the land.

"Phone message for you, Sargent. *Nadon* still delayed and de weather she's getting bad."

"Isn't that just great. Thanks, Woody." She rubbed her head, noticed it was throbbing. Wondered if she should call for investigative support via helicopter, or if maybe it was too windy for that already, or too late in the day. Second guessing herself.

Thoughts rambled along with her feet as she prowled the dock and up the ramp to the shore. She found the beginning of the trail to Back Eddy's homestead and wished she could walk it. Later for sure; she wanted to have a chat with him. Consulted her list and saw there were two names left on it, two she wanted to see; then she heard an incoming motor.

Not much your ears can't tell you out here. Already she'd distinguished that you could often tell who was coming by the sound of the motor. In this case, it was Ritchie. She'd noticed the gill net boat over at Nathan's earlier. Margaret walked back to the fuel dock and reached for his bowline. Noting her RCMP uniform, he gave her a quizzical smile as she bent to tie the line.

"Sergeant Margaret Morris, I'm from the RCMP over in Port McNeill, Hardy and the North Island."

"I know who you are. I'm Ritchie Wilson, from Kingcome," he responded. He had no reason to be concerned; he'd intended to seek her out in town anyway. Nevertheless, encounters with police over the years had made him wary of how he might be treated. This officer, at least, had begun with politeness and a notable lack of aggression.

"May I speak with you for a few minutes, Ritchie?"

"Sure, you want to sit on the boat?"

"Perfect," she climbed on board. "This shouldn't take too long."

Ritchie observed the long lashes that swept down over her tired eyes, the violet shadows underneath them, as she pulled her notebook from her pocket. His gaze lingered on the sharp cheekbones and wide mouth of this female officer of the law. She was a different kind of white woman—make that woman—than he was used to. His attention fully caught, he waited patiently rather than asking what she wanted or offering his own thoughts.

Margaret caught herself drifting off focus, damn she was tired. And something about this guy was so...masculine. Overwhelmingly so. With a small headshake she brought her attention to bear on the subject of the inquiry.

"Okay. So, you're from Kingcome Village, right? Did you, um, know Tim Connolly?"

"Of course. Everybody knows Tim out here." His black eyes looked directly into hers with the obvious question. She answered it.

"Maybe you haven't heard, his body was found yesterday afternoon on Penn Island."

Shock expanded his pupils as Ritchie absorbed the news. A shiver wracked his torso, and goosebumps rose on the skin of his forearms. None of this went unnoticed by Margaret.

"Damn!" He dropped his head and raised his hand, swept his fingers through his hair. "Damn. Tim! What the hell? You going to tell me how or...who found him?"

"Cole Harrison and Hayley Tucker, from Gilford Village."

"I know who she is; him, too." His eyes flicked away and back. "Was Tim murdered?"

"Why would you think that?"

"Well, Sergeant Morris, it's either that or some kind of crazy accident, and here you are, apparently investigating. So it's not exactly an unreasonable surmise, is it?"

"Mmm, you are quite correct, not an unreasonable surmise."

She's good, Ritchie thought, *didn't even let on that she didn't expect an Indian to speak as if he was educated.*

"So what was the nature of your association, Ritchie? Were you friends? Did you hang out together, party or toke up together? Did you have any altercations or friction between you?"

Back stiffened, he was slow to answer. Not certain what to say exactly, he took another look at the woman, debating whether to tell her everything or stick to the bare bones.

Like she was reading his mind, her gaze sharpened.

"Everything. Tell me everything you can, you know, or you think. That's the best." Her low voice was calm and melodious; it seemed almost to exert hypnotic power. Aware of her use of that voice he gathered his thoughts.

"Okay, well, we weren't close friends but we were cool. Sometimes I'd buy some dope from him."

"Often? Was he well known as someone to buy dope from?"

"I don't know, I guess so. Maybe Woody got some from him, I'm not sure."

"Was it good dope? Or a good selection? Did he make any other drugs available to you?"

"No, I'd buy a bit of smoke once in a while and I make it last. Never asked for anything else. I've been kind of anxious lately; had a couple friends who OD'd on fentanyl, one in Vancouver and one in the bay."

"Alert Bay."

"Yah."

"Do you have any idea about the supplier?"

"Not a clue. You don't ask stuff like that, right?"

"Okay, so, anything else? Did you get along all the time or...?"

Ritchie was reluctant to address this; part of him had hoped the marijuana would have satisfied her. Should've known better.

He let his hands swing between his knees. She waited.

"I saw him last week when I stopped here to pick up a package from the mail for Kingcome, I got some smoke from him, he..." Ritchie grimaced. "He really pissed me off. Said I shouldn't be setting my net up at Embley. So I knew he'd been listening to Benny Thompson, the prawn fisherman, who's been giving me a hard time. Every time I see him, he goes after me for fishing illegally because I'm Indigenous. I have to tell you, Sergeant, I work pretty damn hard not to punch his fat head in."

Ritchie clenched his fists, his strong neck thickened and his biceps swelled. With a little frisson of...fear *(attraction, lust?)*, Margaret thought she would prefer not to meet this guy in a dark alley. Remembered scenes from her nightmare flashed at the word alley, but she shook it away and ploughed on.

"I take it you're not fishing illegally, then. But you felt harassed by Benny and then Tim for what, giving you a warning?"

"Yeah, he warned me he'd have to mention it to fisheries so they could investigate. The thing is, I'm pretty sure it's my cousin. He uses my boat when I'm gone and I can't...there doesn't seem to be much I can do about it."

Margaret was sympathetic. Even being a cop and having procedures, tools and the might of the justice system behind you didn't make any of it easy.

"What do you do, Ritchie?" Margaret veered into more personal territory. She sensed a tangible rapport developing between them. In spite of her intention to stay focused on her investigation, a few more minutes wouldn't impede that.

Surprised, he lifted his head. "I'm just sorting that out. I've pretty much done everything a man can do around here. Logged and fished, dug clams, ran my grandfather's trap line, tried carving. I spent a lot of years screwing up my life, done with that now."

"Have you ever thought of law enforcement?"

Shook his head, slowly. "Can't say I have. Always seemed like cops were the enemy." He looked up and a little twinkle sparkled in his eyes. Margaret twinkled back.

Is he flirting? Am I? Enough of that; work to do.

Margaret abruptly stood, pulled out her card and offered it to Ritchie. To cover her visceral reaction to him she made her voice curt, very much the chiding officer of the law. "Here's my card. My contact info is all there. If you have anything to add, please let me know. And...you know, give me a call. If there's anything."

Which you already said, Margaret.

Don't lecture me.

Maybe you mean a different sort of 'anything.'

Am I losing my mind? All of you just shut up and let me get on with this.

Distracted by the interior multi-voice conversation and the squiggles of light behind her eyeballs, Margaret shook her head. She pressed her fingers to her forehead, then into her eyes. Felt like a migraine coming on.

Not now. Please.

Ritchie reacted to her change in tone, concluded that whatever fugitive spark of interest flickering between them hadn't a hope in hell of ever amounting to anything. He didn't get that her headshake had nothing to do with him. Dipping into his deep well of grievance he summoned up a scoop of indignation to counteract how attuned he thought they'd been.

Margaret felt the change in temperature she'd precipitated; regretted it, but couldn't undo it now. She was having a hard time keeping herself focused against the crescendo of drumbeats thudding in her skull. Maybe it was something about this place; it was like a, yes, like a drug. She wanted, needed to go lie down with someone strong and close her eyes.

Tendrils of hair by her temples lifted in the breeze. Her long blond braid glowed in the sun as she stepped off Ritchie's boat. Right behind her, she felt him close enough to breathe in the scent of her hair and her sleeplessness; sensed his lifted head and inhalation of a big breath of the wind.

"Going to blow pretty good, I think. It's coming up fast. Southeast right now but coming around to the north tonight."

Margaret emulated Ritchie, inhaled a deep sniff, hoping the honeyed air would alleviate the flashes. The wind did smell different, almost flowery, and warm against her cheeks.

"Southeast can smell real sweet, almost like its coming from Hawaii," Ritchie added. "Northwest gale on its way; hope they've got everything at the marina tied down real good! We only get those about once every ten or twelve years. If it blows hard enough it'll tear off anything not nailed down tight."

That's it; his last effort to be friendly, and Margaret, seeking to establish her authority and reclaim her focus ignored his weather report and picked the single hottest topic to assert herself. She turned back and looked directly at him.

"Seriously Ritchie, I would stay away from fishing at Embley. The run there can't take any more pressure."

With an inner groan, Margaret saw Ritchie's black eyes glow with the heat of insult. His eyelids closed and reopened revealing pupils gone to cold obsidian. She'd made her intent clear, but at what cost? She was supposed to engage with First Nations individuals in a way that forwarded the principles of reconciliation; she'd certainly made a hash of that.

It wasn't that he was Indigenous that motivated her assertion of position; it was that she'd found him so attractive. Yes, sexy as hell, a real grown-up man. And she had work to do, a crime to solve; could not—absolutely *not* —let herself get distracted like this. Time to get on with it.

Margaret turned on her heel, jaw clamped on the 'I'm sorry' squirming past her lips. Ritchie stomped up the ramp to the store, looking for Carol Ann to pump some gas for him. Margaret headed down the dock toward the lodge, stumbling from the increased intensity of her headache.

Hearing the deep and regular throb of another motor, she knew before she turned to look that it was a fishing vessel. The name painted on the bow of the old style troller was *Thunder*

Chieftain. Squinting at her notes through the brilliant dots swimming in her eyes, she saw that it was, indeed, the boat owned by Benny Thompson.

And there was Back Eddy pulling up to the dock on the shore side, behind the concrete float holding the post office and store. She didn't stop to greet him, although she managed to give Buster a hello pat as he pressed his head up against her leg. Cole, too, was heading for the store. He nodded to her but kept right on going up the ramp after Ritchie.

"Pumping gas for Carol Ann," he said with a smile. She nodded back and flipped her hand at him. Right now her interest was in Benny and it was all she could do to hold that thought.

Margaret fought hard to snap into focus. She'd get back to Ritchie later, for sure. She was relieved to feel her cop self resurfacing. Like a suit of armour within which the rest of her could be confused or even completely messed up, this part of her being knew what needed to be done and how to do it. Her jaw tensed a little, a bolt of pain shot up her cheek to her temple, but she turned to catch the eye of the man climbing off the boat.

And what did she know about Benny Thompson? Prawn fisherman, someone who Tim would definitely have associated with in his job as prawn checker. He nursed a strong grievance against First Nations people and targeted Ritchie with unfounded accusations. Possibly a menace to women as well, if Carol Ann was to be believed, and likely she was. She'd forgotten to ask Kit if she concurred, maybe Hayley had an opinion, too.

Margaret gathered her notebook, pencil and energy, and approached the burly fisherman.

Benny watched her come; he was all prepared for this encounter. He'd pasted on his warm and friendly smile, cautioned himself to not be *too* friendly. That was it—the thing that always got him into trouble.

So no remarks about her looks, or her great job as head honcho of the North Island District. Got to keep his story straight about the last time he saw Tim.

By the time Margaret was on Benny's boat and noting his particulars, she could hardly see through the glittering veil of migraine sparks. Benny's face guttered in and out, so that one of her best means of distinguishing truth from lies was compromised. Eyes narrowed to reduce the light, she listened carefully as he told her he'd heard about Tim's death through the grapevine and described how and when Tim came aboard to do his job checking Benny's prawns.

"And that was last Wednesday he boarded your boat? Did you move your gear out of Simoom Sound or is it all in there?"

"No, no, I just kept it where it was except for two lines I took up into Greenway Sound on Thursday. Fished up there on Friday then came back down to Simoom, then ran back and forth from Greenway to Simoom to do the rest of the gear. I'm kind of a slowpoke, this is an old boat."

"I'll take your word for it." Margaret said. She didn't know much about prawn fishing.

"Don't much like running around a hundred miles an hour like some of these guys."

"The last time you saw Tim was Wednesday when he checked you, then?" Margaret tapped her teeth with the pencil, realized she couldn't see well enough to write. Maybe she could dictate his comments when she got back to the cabin.

Should he lie? Yes. Take a chance on Tim not telling anyone about their dinner.

"Ayuh, that's right. Wednesday, yeah."

"Did he seem disturbed about anything or agitated in any way?"

Benny made an 'I'm really thinking hard' face, shook his head. "Nope. Business as usual. What the heck could've happened?"

Proud of how he made his voice sound sad and puzzled.

"So Benny, ah, apparently Tim sold marijuana to a few folks around the area, and maybe some other drugs. Were you a customer of his, too?"

Benny could barely control his laugh at this ridiculous shot in the dark, but he managed to stifle it and keep the serious, thoughtful look on his face.

"Gee, did he smoke dope? No, I didn't do that, smoke. With him."

Benny reached behind Margaret to rip a piece of paper towel off the roll over the stove. He buried his face in it, pretending to blow his nose. Maybe he was overdoing the innocent bit.

Margaret was nearly blind from the migraine by now; no way could she continue this interview. One more question and she was going to have to get off this boat and back to the cabin and do something about it.

"Did Tim give you any idea about what his plans were for the next day or two?"

"The last thing he told me was he'd be up Tribune; he had some other boats to check but I don't know who. *White Bird* was fishing up there and that high speed boat...um, it's a woman's name." Benny rolled his eyes upward, appearing to search his thoughts for the boat name.

If Margaret had been able to see, her spidey sense would have gone off like a fire alarm. Thousands of boats have a woman's name so it wasn't much help to her. The tone of his voice grated on her skin.

"Ya know, Sergeant, you might want to take a real close look at that Indian, he just went up the ramp. Have you talked to him?"

"You mean Ritchie Wilson? What about him?"

"Well, I know he's a real druggie, and he's been fishing illegally up in Embley Lagoon and I think him and Tim did business together. Maybe they had a, you know, a drug dealers bust up. A falling out."

Margaret digested this little tidbit, trying to fit it in to what she'd learned so far, but the pain throbbed in her head and the scintillating veil of light in her eyes oscillated faster. She shook her head to clear it but instead felt so dizzy she nearly retched.

Margaret reached out her hand, grasped the edge of the table; she rose and turned to the door, forgetting to thank Benny for his time. "I'd appreciate it if you'd stay in the area for a day or two, I'll talk to you again," she mumbled. "I've got to go now."

Aware of the grizzled fisherman watching her departure, she still ricocheted off the narrow doorway and stumbled inelegantly out the door. But, one last thought; she stopped abruptly, managed to turn and ask, "Do you have a gaff?"

"A gaff? 'Course. Everyone has a gaff."

"I'd like to see it."

He got up from the seat, hesitated, spread his hands. "Well, actually, I can't show it to you. I..."

Margaret interrupted him, "Why not? Where is it?"

"Well, ma'am, it's like this. I hooked on to a big ling cod a few days ago and got it up to the boat, tried to gaff it but it fought so hard I couldn't hold on. She pulled out of my hand, threw the hook and somehow broke the gaff."

Margaret gripped the stay lines by the gunwale, blurted, "Gotta go." She climbed laboriously over the side, took a few steps, then by sheer strength of will straightened up.

Benny watched her go, lurching every few steps, shook his head dubiously and said aloud, "What's her problem? All shook up about her dead boyfriend." Figured he handled that pretty well, maybe he could join the coffee crew and buffalo them, too.

Weaving like a drunk, hoping she didn't take a dive into the chuck, Margaret navigated down the long dock toward Woody's lodge and the relative safety of the cabin. She needed so badly to lie down. She'd been pummelled and pounded; by Tim's death, by her terrible dream and sleepless night, by the argumentative, spiteful multitude of voices in her head that would *not* shut up and now this damnable migraine. And she needed the *Nadon* to show up so she could share the burden of this investigation with others.

And maybe get the help she'd been resisting.

She stumbled across the uncertain footing of wood chunks and heavy planks that connected one float to another, and right in front of Woody's lodge her knees gave way and she collapsed onto the rough decking.

Ritchie Wilson, having pumped his fuel and avoided Benny, was fifty feet behind her. He saw her fall and broke into a run. "Sergeant Morris!" He fell to his knees by her, put his hand on her shoulder; she didn't move. Ritchie looked up and around. No one in sight.

Slowly Margaret got her knees under her and pushed up; paused, shoulders trembling. This close, Ritchie could see the fine blue veins pulsing in her eyelids and blond eyelashes against the curve of her cheek.

"Let me help you up, Sergeant. I'll walk you to..." He looked around. "Is it the big brown cabin?"

She nodded. "I've got a migraine, I can't see a thing. How the hell am I going to figure out what happened to Tim? I'm blind and the *Nadon*'s not here and my guys are out somewhere looking for Tim's boat."

Kneeling there, trembling and dizzy, she knew she'd missed something important, a fleeting something she tried to grasp but it was like running after a ferry pulling away from the dock... too far to jump.

"Shh, shh, never mind right now. Let's get you some painkillers."

Ritchie put his arm around Margaret and helped her to stand. She wobbled and limped, but at least he didn't have to carry her. He guided her up the steps into the floathouse and settled her on the couch.

"My bag is upstairs in the bathroom, painkillers in there," she whispered.

Pretty easy for Ritchie to figure out which was her toiletries bag, the one with the cute dogs on it. He grabbed a clean washcloth and the bag, took it down to her, opened it so she could identify the bottles and choose what she needed. He ran the tap until the water was icy cold, soaked the cloth and poured a glass of water.

She accepted the drink and the painkillers and laid the cloth over her eyes. "That feels so good, thank you."

"My mom used to get migraines. Okay, what about your leg. You were limping."

"Yes, it hurts." She raised her leg and rested it on the coffee table.

"Hmm, it's kind of a mess. Your pants are torn and you're bleeding all over the place. Splinters in your hands, too. Hold on, I'll see if there's a first aid kit somewhere."

"Bathroom."

"Good thing Woody keeps this place properly equipped. Maybe I should be a medic." Ran up the stairs again and found the first aid kit under the sink, ran back down quick.

"Doing great so far; thank you. Hey, I'm sorry about what I said."

Ritchie was surprised, but he knew exactly what she was referring to.

"Doesn't matter. Don't worry about it."

Now he's sure he hadn't imagined the blossom of feeling that had flowered between them. He finished cleaning the deep scrape on her knee and bandaged it, extracted a few of the larger cedar splinters from her palms. He rooted around in a kitchen drawer for a safety pin, with which he pinned together the torn knee of her uniform pants.

"I'm going to leave you now, Sergeant, and go tell Woody; he can tell your crew when they get here what's happened. I'll come back and check on you before I head up Kingcome, okay?"

"Okay, thanks a lot. One other thing, Ritchie. Benny Thompson is not your friend. He tried hard to point me at you as somehow responsible for Tim. Seemed like a big leap to me."

Ritchie rolled this around in his mind. Benny just wouldn't back off on his vendetta to scapegoat Ritchie for his turnabout experience of disentitlement.

"Ritchie?"

"Yeah?"

"Come see me in the bay?"

"Off duty?"

"Yeah, maybe we get a coffee or something."

"Okay."

Margaret was asleep before Ritchie had softly closed the door.

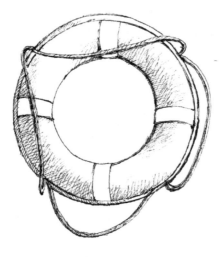

Twenty-Seven

*C*arol Ann had Nathan on her mind, along with Tim, cooking for the tree-planters, the investigation, and the fact that Woody was mad at her for talking to Margaret. Kit would be, too. But mostly it was Nathan on her mind. Possible there was something happening between them. *Kind of gives an old girl a thrill*, she thought. A smile widened her soft mouth and briefly smoothed the worry wrinkles from her brow.

Rising early, as usual, she'd fed the planters, cleaned up the dishes, thrown a load of laundry into the washer and started the cinnamon buns. Without measuring she'd mixed sugar and yeast, salt and flour, stirring until the dough attained the non-sticky consistency needed to switch from the wooden spoon to her hands.

Food is what Carol Ann knew and food is what they would get from her, and she hoped it would help. She was putting her all into those buns today. Everybody would have some, to make up for her flouncing off with them the other day. The tree-planters had been thrilled, though. Even though she'd been angry at Benny, that hadn't been fair to the others, and she felt bad about depriving them of the treats she'd made. They were her family, for good or ill, and now with Tim gone, who knew how, and Margaret's investigation causing so much disruption (including her own part in it), they needed to feel more secure with each other. She knew their idiosyncrasies and who could eat what and who did or did not—Back Eddy for example—like raisins.

When the men began to gather late in the day, she was ready. She'd managed the store, pumped gas, got the cinnamon buns in the oven, and now she removed the smeared apron and replaced it with a clean lilac flowered print, wiped the sweat off her face and smoothed her flyaway hair. Like a benediction the fragrance of the baking buns floated from the kitchen.

First to show up was Nathan. He greeted Carol Ann in the kitchen, putting a smile on her face with his comment on how pretty she looked before he entered Woody's private quarters. Woody and Cole came down from the land, removed their dirty boots and work gloves by the entrance and followed Nathan.

Here was Ritchie with news about Margaret; he stopped to tell Carol Ann before he told the other men in Woody's suite. "Got a bad migraine, then she fell on the dock coming back from the store. She's asleep; she had some painkillers I got for her. Can't do any more investigating right now."

"*Nadon* should be here before dark, or dey won' be makin' it tonight. It's startin' to blow pretty good." Woody's contribution. Right after his coffee he'd be running up Tribune to pick up the planters. "Going to be rough. Dat crew better be all down at the landing, don' want to wait long tonight."

"Wonder when her boys are going to get back in, they maybe don't know their way around here much," said Back Eddy as he entered and joined the other men at the picnic table.

"I'll keep my eye out for them," replied Woody.

One more time the door opened; Benny poked his head in, not confident of his welcome but bluffing it out. He'd play it cool but friendly today.

Back Eddy and Cole nodded at him, Nathan asked, "How's the fishing, Benny?"

The seated men had arranged themselves around the table; Ritchie and Cole facing the door, Nathan and Back Eddy across from them with a view out the window. The last to enter, Benny squeezed in beside Nathan across from Ritchie, who averted his gaze. Standing by the narrow counter that separated the table area from his compact kitchen, Woody caught the move.

"Guess you had a nice little chat with the sergeant, hey Ritchie?"

"What?" He whipped his head back and glared at the fisherman.

"You, too, I guess, Benny? She's interviewing most everyone. Going to be the only way to figure out what happened." Back Eddy, trying to be peaceable.

In the kitchen Carol Ann could hear the cadence of deep male voices rising and falling and felt hopeful. She pulled the cinnamon buns from the oven and drizzled icing on them; gave them five minutes to sit, then arranged them on the blue and white ceramic platter.

She tapped Woody's door with her foot and Nathan leaned over to open it. Carol Ann graced him with warm eyes as she entered.

At the sight of the loaded platter of cinnamon buns a baritone chorus of "Mmm-mm" rang out, music to her ears. Maybe this offering could help to reclaim some small harmony in this frayed community.

To Carol Ann, they looked like eager boys, all in need of something; something reassuring and binding to cut through the escalating mistrust, friction and suspicion. In spite of the appreciation for her offering Carol Ann realized with a sinking heart that the men's conversation had ceased when she showed up.

"Hello, fellows; have I got some goodies for you! Nice to see you here today, Ritchie." Carol Ann set the platter on the counter and served Ritchie first and then Woody

"Here you go, boss, I know you like lots of cinnamon and sugar." She slid his plate along the counter, laden with a couple of warm, thoroughly iced and spiced buns.

"What's your favourite, Cole?"

"Anything, Carol Ann, it's all great!" he said enthusiastically. In spite of his boyish levity she could feel tension in the older men.

She had a 'coffee time' rule that Woody supported and that was 'No Squabbling at the Table,' and maybe—she measured the strain in the atmosphere—maybe there'd been some squabbling. Not surprising, considering the last few days.

Ritchie knew the rule. With the thoughts boiling around in his head, maybe he shouldn't have come. It wasn't easy for him to be civil to the guy sitting across the table, smirking like he'd got him by the balls. Goddam Benny, spilling all his lying rotten beans to the cop who now, just like that, has become more than a cop to him. Whatever else he'd been about to say died in his throat as he looked at his plate of plump buns.

"Appreciate it, Carol Ann. These look great, thanks."

"And here you go, Back Eddy, no raisins; and for you, Benny, extra raisins." She was dishing them out, everyone reaching for her delicious treats; she had high hopes for her peacemaking. It *was* working; she could feel the atmosphere relax a little bit as the men chewed quietly, emitting little moans of ecstasy.

But the second she left the room the deep rumble of voices began. Benny started up again, and as the door swung closed she caught his comment to the Kingcome man.

"Seen you go into the cop's place, there, Ritchie. Making a little time, I guess, hey? You cozying up to her so she won't think you popped Tim, or you maybe want to hook up with a white woman?" So much for cool and friendly.

Woody's voice, uncharacteristically strident. "For crying out loud, give it a rest or you're outta here!" Two seconds later, shouting, "Stop it, dammit, stop. What de hell! You guys, take it outside!"

Hearing a loud crash, Carol Ann turned back, pushed open the door, saw her platter in pieces on the floor and Ritchie leaning over the table.

"You friggin' asshole. You and your big lying mouth pointing the finger at me! Not only that, you just can't keep your hands to yourself, can you?! You got to be all over everybody, don't you? You keep your hands off Hayley, and every other Native girl, you hear me?" He's half-lying across the wide table, big hands squeezing Benny's throat, shaking him back and forth. Back Eddy choked on his cinnamon bun, shock all over his face.

Benny raised his arms hard and fast, whammed Ritchie's hands off his neck. Ritchie fell back and the bench caught him behind the knees.

"What the hell is your problem, Wilson? I didn't do anything! I told that cop the truth, and as for Hay...ley," he drew out the syllables contemptuously, "I never touched her and if I did it was an accident!"

He drove himself up and followed Ritchie's arc as he fell back. Woody caught Benny from the back, wrapped his arms around the fisherman's broad chest.

"Oh no you don't, you guys get out of here! Get de hell out, right now!"

Ritchie lost his balance completely and toppled backward off the bench, Cole reached down to help him up. Ritchie pushed his hand away, then grabbed it and levered himself up. He slid out of the bench, breathing hard, fists clenched.

Spewing vitriol, along with cinnamon bun crumbs, Benny barely took a breath as Woody hustled him out the door. "Bastard, you *Indians* are raising so much shit these days, all about red power and your bullshit about saving the resources. I SEEN you at Embley with a net and you're all about fishing prawns out of season and there ain't going to be none left for the licensed boats. You could have a licensed boat anytime you want, goddam government will just give you one..."

Ritchie didn't need any help, he was right behind Benny and the second they got outside, he leaped in front of the man, threw a punch, landed it. Benny's nose blossomed a red fountain and he flopped to his knees.

Ritchie stood over him, livid with rage, punctuating every word with a hard thrust against the prawn fisher's shoulder.

"I. Don't. Ever. Fish. Out. Of. Season. Or with an illegal net. And it's not my fault the prawns are going down, you think you're entitled to everything and don't like it that maybe we can regain some of what was taken from us. You had no business lying to Tim, and getting him all riled up and siccing the cops on me. IT WASN'T ME! For the last time, asshole, it wasn't me. Get away from me, stay away, and quit your bullshit hassling me!"

Ritchie's last push exploded into an ultimate punch, knocking Benny flat on the deck. "And that's for Hayley, you horny bastard, you keep your hands to yourself or you'll wake up dead in your bed, I swear!"

"Yah, well, she's nothing to you anyway, is she? I heard she ditched you and you deserve it."

With this parting shot burning his ears, it was all Ritchie could do to resist the urge to kick the guy's head in. His thigh muscles spasmed with the strain as he towered above Benny, then he stomped off down the dock, rubbing his hand and stretching out his fingers.

Benny rolled onto his hands and knees, stumbled to stand up. He swiped his hands across his bleeding face. Cole ran into the lodge and returned holding out a damp dishtowel.

"Here, press this against it."

"That's my dishtowel!" cried Carol Ann, instantly regretting the outburst.

"Don' worry, don' worry, Carol Ann, I get you more dishtowels. Let de man wipe his face." Woody patted her shoulder.

"Mother of God, of course. I'll go and get his cinnamon buns, that'll make him feel better."

Benny shook his head to clear it. He'd had a couple tokes this morning and even done a line of coke before he came over to the bay. He'd just needed something to fortify himself. He hadn't expected Ritchie to be here, nor had he been able to resist needling him as usual. Didn't want the guy to get relaxed and think nobody was watching him. But he'd been planning to play it cool…messed that up big time. The fisherman swayed as he stood, then stumbled again and finally headed for his boat. Carol Ann ran after him.

"Benny, wait! Are you alright? Maybe sit a few minutes before you run the boat anywhere. I brought your cinnamon buns; you can eat them when you feel better."

Making nice, the buzzing voice in his head muttered scornfully, *silly old cow*, but he accepted the plate of buns with a show of appreciation. "Okay, okay, I'm alright. I will, thanks."

"You should stop harassing Ritchie. I am sure he's not doing what you think he is."

"Yah, well, it's none of yer dam business how I talk to Ritchie, is it, Carol Ann? Guys like him are gonna wreck the country."

Carol Ann reached for her dish towel then changed her mind when she saw the blood-stained cloth. He shoved it at her but she whipped her hands behind her back and stepped away.

"Keep it. Maybe it's guys like *you* who are going to wreck the country," she sniffed, turned on her heel and marched back down the dock.

Benny flung the towel down, but set the plate of buns carefully on the deck of *Thunder Chieftain* before he climbed aboard and fired it up.

Twenty-Eight

s she departed her own little bay, Kit spotted Ritchie's boat running full bore, spray flying through each swell. Maybe heading for Kingcome. She angled her bow to run through the big wake he'd set up. Something was up, that was clear. Back Eddy was at the marina, standing by Nathan and Carol Ann, Woody and Cole. Weird. Hard to concentrate on docking and tying up her boat as she watched Benny climb on his, left hand covering his nose, blood running down his chin. She could hear him moaning as he shoved off.

What now? Kit raised her eyebrows at Back Eddy as he sauntered over to greet her.

He responded to her silent question with an apparently unrelated remark. Nodding toward Nathan and Carol Ann, he commented, "She's a real Molly Hogan."

"What's that supposed to mean?"

"Well, in my logging days when you needed to secure cables and logs and such you'd wind a strand of wire on a cable back on itself to form a loop."

"So...?" she raised her eyebrows.

"It was kind of handy for holding things in place—like Nathan, for example, if you see what I mean."

After giving it a second's thought Kit nodded her head. "I do, Willy, I do see what you mean."

The two looked over at Carol Ann and Nathan, now in deep conversation. The cook wiped her hands on her apron, then, looking up at the tall Finnlander, she laid her hand on his forearm. Back Eddy and Kit locked eyes briefly, then she broke contact, feeling a flush of envy. The look that had passed between Nathan and Carol Ann had been tender and full of promise.

"I got to talk to you, Willy. It's so crazy around here all of a sudden..."

Back Eddy interrupted her, "Kit, I sure am sorry to hear about Tim. I came over to tell you but you weren't home."

"Yah, well, Margaret came over, so yah. Thanks. It's too much. Tim...and Margaret investigating and Benny being so rabid against Ritchie and...I'm kinda mad at Carol Ann."

"What'd *she* do? Christ, has everybody gone nuts around here? Ritchie just punched Benny out, had a big bust up in Woody's, ended up rolling around the dock whaling on each other. Well, Ritchie was whaling." He looked down and spat.

"Anyway, what about Carol Ann?" he inquired again, as Kit processed this bit of info. Back Eddy was puzzled; he'd only known Kit and Carol Ann to be the best of friends.

"That explains why Ritchie is hell bent for leather, halfway across Raleigh Passage already." Kit snapped back to the question of her and Carol Ann. "Oh jeez. I'll tell you but not this very second. I got to go talk to her, RFN."

Back Eddy knew what RFN meant. If he was Carol Ann he'd be running out the back door right about now. "Come have dinner with me after, I've got some clam chowder needs eating."

Kit looked at him, "Not my favourite, Willy, what else you got?"

"Picky today, aren't we? Leftover chicken, you can have a sandwich."

"Done, see you shortly."

Woody turned in to the lodge, calling for Carol Ann. "We better get at that dinner, Carol Ann. I got to leave to get de crew pretty quick. And someone should check on Sergeant Morris."

"Coming," said Carol Ann as Kit walked up to her and Nathan. Kit didn't miss the fond look on his craggy face.

But they're old, she thought. Nathan raised his eyes as she passed him, lifted one brow quizzically, like he could read her mind. Embarrassed, she looked away, chastised herself for revealing her thoughts, for even having those thoughts.

"Just got a dinner invitation," he said with a crooked grin.

"Sweet! Me, too."

Why *shouldn't* they be together if it makes them happy? They've both been alone for a very long time. She followed the cook into the lodge. "I need to talk to you, Carol Ann."

"Oh jeez, sweetie, not now, 'kay? Woody needs me to get at the planters' dinner." *First Benny and Ritchie, now Kit, who's next?*

"Yah, well, they won't be back for two hours so I think you should have time to talk to me."

Quick glance at Nathan for support, but he was clueless. Carol Ann gave in. "Five minutes, that's all I can spare."

Carol Ann didn't want Woody to witness their exchange and turning quickly, she bumped into Kit. "Let's go up to my place." She yelled into the kitchen, "I need five minutes with Kit, Woody."

"Okay, don' be long."

"C'mon upstairs." Carol Ann was regaining her calm. What turmoil, things were all in knots here.

Up in the apartment, they could feel the wind rocking the lodge, and hear a high-pitched moan as it whipped around the edge of the building. The docks were squealing and groaning as the surges rolling in grew more powerful. Carol Ann felt like squealing and groaning herself.

The second they entered her living room, Carol Ann turned and pre-empted Kit's opening blast with surrendering upraised hands.

"Kit, Kit, I am so sorry! I'm sorry, sorry, sorry! Margaret just got to me, she was so smooth and before I knew it, I'd told her everything and I know I shouldn't have betrayed your confidences. Please forgive me. Please."

"Jeez, Carol Ann, she thought maybe I'd done it!"

"How could she possibly think that? Completely ridiculous! Kit, I really do apologize, I blabbed..."

Kit snorted, "Yah! You sure did blab, holy shit."

"How long are you going to be mad at me?" Carol Ann sighed.

"Two years," snapped Kit.

Carol Ann looked at her, horrified, then giggled. Seconds later Kit caved in and giggled, too. Like that, it was over.

"Have you seen Tim yet? Margaret said you might be coming over to look at him, say your goodbyes. Do you still want to?"

"Not yet, and I don't know. He must look awful."

"I haven't seen him but I'll go with you if you want."

Kit plunked down in Carol Ann's chair, put her head in her hands. "Might be better not to look at him, just remember the good times."

"Say the word, I'll go in there with you. I sure hope they can come and take him away pretty soon. So creepy with him in the freezer back there. I've got to go help Woody; he'll be steaming by now."

"Okay, let's go."

Carol Ann led the way, Kit followed. She made up her mind, patted the other woman's shoulder. "Yes, please."

"You want me to come see him with you? Okay. We can say goodbye to him together."

Half way across Raleigh Passage, Ritchie remembered he'd told Margaret he'd come back before he went up Kingcome. He slowed the boat and put it out of gear. Still shaken from the depth of his rage against Benny and the fight, now he had a new thought. Trying to be a little objective—maybe the man was seriously messed up. Maybe 'bushed,' to use the vernacular, or more clinically, having mental health problems. Or too much drugs problems, which maybe go hand in hand. He may have been the last person to see Tim, and if Benny's temper and style of needling a person in their vulnerable places was his usual way of relating...maybe he'd been giving Tim a hard time, too, and things had erupted.

Ritchie was thoughtful as he swung wide to roll broadside through the turn. He was a man of his word and he wanted Margaret to know that about him. He steered for Echo Bay. Surveying the sea ahead, as always, he spotted *Thunder Chieftain* a half mile away by Powell Point, and was relieved they wouldn't cross paths.

Keeping a watchful eye out the wheelhouse windows, Benny grabbed a bowl from the cupboard and poured hot water into it from the simmering kettle. He took the cloth hanging over the oil stove and dunked it in the water, wiped his face. The soothing touch of the hot water helped him gather his thoughts. Better to change course and run up to Greenway Sound right now so he could pull his gear in the morning—if it wasn't too rough.

He wondered who they'd get to replace Tim as the checker. The relief he felt at not having to pay Tim anymore, either in money or in drugs, washed over him like a wave. Right behind the thought a real wave broke against the bow and sheeted the window with spray. He'd been so stricken at Tim's demand for more, and their fight and seeing Tim disappear over the side, he hadn't considered the benefits that might ensue. Even so, he'd untied the prawn checker's boat from his and shoved off, never looked back.

He wrestled the wheel and steered into the breaking swells while reviewing his impulsive decision that night to fire up the boat and take off. *Maybe he got knocked out and didn't feel anything, maybe he survived and went to check someone else the next day.*

Maybe he remembered White Bird, was his next thought and Benny shuddered. If Tim *had* survived; what then? How had he ended up dead on Penn Island?

Another wave broke over the bow and he revised his plan to head for Greenway. Probably better to anchor in the Burdwoods for the night.

He truly did feel bad about Tim drowning. Maybe he'd send an anonymous note to the sergeant. It would ruin his business but maybe it was time to let that go; Darrell kind of scared him anyway.

"It was an accident," he told himself. "Self-defense."

If anyone inquired further or found any reason to suspect him, that would be his story. He congratulated himself on feeling some remorse; thrust the memory of shoving Tim over the side right out of his mind.

Better pay attention to running the boat.

Benny looked around for the cinnamon buns Carol Ann had brought him, took a big bite.

"Silly cow," he repeated, "but nice, big buns."

He laughed aloud and pushed the throttle forward, pleased with his little joke.

Twenty-Nine

So Kit was over to Back Eddy's. Not sure how he might help, but he was her 'go to' person. In any case, he was astute, saw things others didn't. She knew he lay awake at night, thinking...about all kind of things. Like how to move a house off of or onto land, or where to look for new railroad tracks to replace the old ones for the boat ways. Or maybe he'd seen some mysterious animal interaction or a decrease or increase of animal, fish or bird population; he'd be trying to suss out the meaning of that interaction and its impact on the ecosystem.

She'd never known anyone who spent more time simply thinking than Back Eddy. He lay awake at night, trying to work it all out. Clearly it was a skill that ought to be highlighted and taught to the children of the world. Maybe it was *because* he never had an education. Whatever the reason, it was true that he didn't make many mistakes and was rarely wrong in his conclusions.

Dinner turned out to be a chunk of spring salmon, pulled from his freezer and quick-thawed in hot water. Kit was touched by the gesture. Back Eddy knew she was a total salmonaholic, he must've figured it was time she had a good feed.

"Ya don't eat enough to keep a winter wren alive," he commented.

"You should talk," she rebutted.

Kit rolled the salmon around in her mouth, savoured each bite before she swallowed, chased it with a mouthful of mashed

267

potatoes, then a spoonful of peas. She heard the poof of the propane flame in the oven cut in, asked, "You want me to turn off
the oven?"

"Nope, something in there."

"Pie?"

"You hope."

"Yes!" Kit cheered. "What a lucky girl am I. Lemon meringue?"

"'Course."

"You're amazing, Willy. Thank you so much for such a great
dinner." She burped, then continued. "I took a look at Tim; he's
in the freezer at Woody's."

"Yah, I know."

"I'm glad I did, had to say goodbye."

"Huh. How'd he look?"

"Like I would imagine someone who was dead would look.
Work clothes, except go-to-town jeans. Beat up though, but who
knows if that was from banging into rocks or what, I don't know."

"Maybe when the medical examiner gets a look at him, they'll
know more."

"Yah."

Back Eddy got up, went to the stove and took out the pie.
"Just brown enough; like Eva's." He set the pie on the table and
cleared Kit's plate away, then put the kettle on.

"We'll let it cool for a minute while I make tea."

Kit nodded her head agreeably. "You sure are treating me
good."

"You've had a shock, I guess."

The kettle sang and he poured the boiling water into the
teapot and set it on the table. Kit loaded sugar into her cup, and
cut the pie in slices while the tea steeped. In the woodstove a log

fell into ash with a soft puff and Buster came over and laid his head in Kit's lap. She sighed.

Calmer now, she forked a piece of pie into her mouth and let it rest, tasting. Back Eddy was digging steadily into his. Head down, he chewed the last bite of pie. Fiddling with the fork, he looked at his empty plate.

"Kit," he said, "how're ya doing?"

"What do you mean?" Kit twitched in her chair, surprised. He almost never broached this sort of topic, assuming if she had a problem, she'd tell him, or deal with it herself.

"Y'know what I mean, Kit." He glared at her. This was difficult for him. "You lost your boyfriend, but he was screwing around with the sergeant, maybe other women, you must be feeling a *bit* upset."

Kit gave him a long look. He was trying to be compassionate but also holding something back.

"I guess I am kind of, Willy, but it almost feels like—there's a sort of inevitable feeling about it, don't you think? Like, it was supposed to happen or something. I can't quite put my finger on it, but, the truth is, inside all this sense of loss, and grief..." She stumbled. "I *am* sorry Tim died, but in a way, a decision was taken out of my hands and honestly, I'm kind of relieved. Relieved that I don't have to make a decision that will hurt him, which sounds ridiculous, I know. Does that make me an awful person?"

"Probably. Awful, but honest, anyway."

Back Eddy didn't lift his eyes from his plate; he carefully lined up his fork beside it.

"What?" said Kit. "You're keeping something from me."

Back Eddy sighed. "Kit, I got to tell you Tim was doing some serious drugs. And I think he was dealing them too. I know Woody got his marijuana from him. I know, I know, it's not serious and it's medicinal, but I think Tim got in over his head. There's some strange doings going on around here."

"Beginning with the obvious, I guess. Tim is dead, after all. You know, Willy, I was out kayaking Friday night and I meant to tell you this, I've been so busy and also...I spent some time with Carson."

"Who?"

"You know, that guy with the old launch, *Restoration Point.*"

"Oh yeah, pretty boat, he's kept it nice."

"Well, he just got it. Anyway, he's a painter, an artist, and he's the guy I met when I stopped at Green Rock to help the mussel testing crew boat, remember? I told you."

"Oh, yah, okay. Haven't met him yet. So?"

"So nothing, too soon to tell. But I kind of like him."

The light dawned and Back Eddy leaped to an accurate conclusion.

"He the one with the goddam drone? I nearly shot that thing down with my flare gun awhile ago. I hate them things. Can't run around here anymore without a helicopter, now them damn machines, hovering over you in the middle of nowhere."

"I know, I know, Willy. But listen, I went out kayaking that night, the day before Tim didn't show up. In the middle of the night, I heard a boat and then I heard people yelling, and then it was all quiet. I wanted to go look, but..."

"Why didn't you tell me that?"

Kit sighed again. "I was ashamed to. And I've been busy. I *wanted* to go look but it started to get foggy, misty anyway, and the moon wasn't so bright anymore. I chickened out and I went home and when I went back to look the next morning, I barely had any time 'cause of my charter so I wasn't thorough but I didn't see anything. Then Tim showed up, or didn't rather, the kids found him, and you know the rest."

Back Eddy digested this for a few quiet moments. "If youda told me I coulda gone out and looked around."

"I know Willy. I'm sorry, I just like to do things myself if I can. I think I should tell Margaret, though. I'll go over and tell her after I leave here."

"She's got a terrible migraine, Ritchie said. She fell on the dock after she was talking to him and Benny. He helped get her into the floathouse."

"Oh! How bad? I still think I should go and tell her. Jeez, why didn't I?"

"It might help her figure things out. Anyway..." Back Eddy steamed on. Now he'd made up his mind he was determined to spit it out. "You're not gonna like this, Kit, but I am pretty damn sure, believe me. Tim was dealing drugs, or at least doing them himself. I think he was getting them from Benny."

"No, that's not right, he toked up sometimes, I guess, but he was helping Margaret, keeping his eyes open out here. He knew she was concerned about fentanyl and some people who died over on the island. She even asked *me* to keep an eye out."

"Kit, ya got to wise up here. Tim was not who you think he was."

"You're always down on the guys aren't you, Willy? You may be a lot of help to me and a good friend but you don't know *everything*! I suppose you've already decided that Carson is too good to be true, oh and he's got a drone so he must be an asshole and I should stay away from him, haven't you? Well, it's none of your business and you should stay out of mine!"

With this Kit flung herself out of her chair and hurled open the door so hard it bounced back against her foot as she exited. The air in the room simmered with her rage as she stormed out.

Back Eddy sat for a few minutes letting the residue of Kit's emotion settle. *Going to be fun around here until she calms down. What a turn-up.*

After a while he got up and closed the door.

Thirty

It had been a brief and lumpy ride around the point to Echo Bay but now Kit sat alone in her cabin listening to the wind rise, letting the adrenalin dissipate, attempting some clear thinking.

Clearly she needed more practice controlling her temper.

Heat vibrated the shoreline and the scorched flower-covered rocks. She smelled the welcome rain coming on the wind but it had some distance to travel before it could do its work reviving the flowers and thirsty trees. Out Fife Sound the sea was one continuous set of navy blue waves trimmed with lacy ruffles, backlit with evening gold. On the shore behind her house the tossing green boughs flipped from dark to light in impulsive dips and swirls.

In her semi-sheltered cove she heard the windrush coming from afar...a soft sound as it wove gusty fingers through the bristling trees, louder as it approached, then booming like a freight train as it swooped down into the bay. The lines attaching the floathouse to the shore stretched singing tight, relaxed and tightened again. The boomsticks resisted the push of the wind, then shifted and swayed. Her little house shuddered with each assaulting blast. Kit hoped she'd got everything tied up securely enough.

She sat motionless, thinking. Reviewing the facts.

Concluded she'd been ignoring some fairly pertinent facts. *Stupid*, she castigated herself. *Stupid, stupid.*

Angry and confused, her thoughts boiled around like kelp in a tide rip. Kit jumped up to find Kitcat; petting the kitten might help calm her. Kitcat refused to settle on her lap though and Kit carried on thinking without her. If it all added up, she'd been ignoring her instincts, been blindly loyal to Benny, not wanting to hear or believe anything really bad about someone who had been a good friend to her, even if for some unimaginable reason he did think he was irresistible. And Tim, while clearly not her knight in shining armour, had been much worse than a lying, cheating philanderer.

Was the prawn fisherman dealing drugs? Certainly the faint smell of marijuana had wafted from his boat from time to time. Someone had to be bringing it in, but maybe that was Tim? And who was responsible for Tim's death? If Tim went to see Benny when he was anchored—if he was anchored—in the Burdwood Group, maybe the shouting she heard was them? It could be true that Benny was somehow involved. But not deliberate! She couldn't believe it was deliberate; did not want to believe that.

But what if it was true?

She was damn well going to find out.

The house shuddered under another whiplash of wind. Bursting with adrenalin, Kit sat up straight, her fists clenched in her lap. She needed to know and she needed to know right now. Throwing on her floater coat she turned the door knob and the door itself whammed open with astonishing force. Kit stumbled back but was not deterred from storming out to the boat.

Mermaid Lady responded instantly to the turn of the key. *Thank you, thank you.* A butterfly thought careened through her agitated mind, *I should get Margaret.* Rejected instantly: *She's got a migraine. I'm going. Now.*

Inside her bay the sea was fidgety, ripples and cross-swells resembled a topographical map she'd built of British Columbia in her grade eight social studies class. Outside the bay, foam boiled up against the rocks on the point and threw spray with each swell.

Like a mouse from its hole, out she crept. And like a waiting cat, the tempest leaped on her with ferocious zeal.

The wind hit her boat broadside and it leaned, swerved. Muscles tensed, she wrestled the wheel tightly to stay on course. The southeast gale had veered around to the northwest; it recruited every whisp and stray billow of wind to its gathering strength. Flares of lightning popped across the horizon like the sudden illumination of a camera flash.

Each flash obscured Kit's vision with a negative after-image and she steered more by instinct than anything else. The sky darkened as the sun fell completely behind the boil of purple cloud, the dark gold light turned to cinders in seconds.

Kit stiffened her spine; no place here for the fearful. 'Kit the pilot' was at the wheel. Kit the pilot knew how to drive this sea, how to angle the bow into each oncoming upsurge, steer across the trough and up the side of each breaking swell.

Benny's favourite spot was right in the narrows at the back of the small island circled by the curving arms of the picnic beach. If she guessed right, he'd be snugged in to the anchorage with the stern line tied to an eyebolt secured in the rock long ago by tugboat operators.

The wind and waves eased up as she entered the shelter of the Burdwood Islands. There were the lights of his wheelhouse cabin glowing in the dusk, just as she'd envisioned. Kit threw over the bumpers and swung alongside *Thunder Chieftain.* Even in this protected nook the sea was rough and she was careful with her hands as she tied her centre line to the cleat on the gunwale of *Thunder Chieftain.* She took the time to secure the stern line and the bow, too. No rush, now she'd made it. Kit climbed off her boat and onto the prawn boat, surprised when Benny didn't come out to greet her. She rapped hard on the door.

"Benny," she shouted, "Benny, you in there?"

Kit opened the cabin door cautiously and peered in.

"Benny?"

She heard the pump flushing the toilet; he was in the head. Kit looked down the companionway to the bunks, a white moon of face peered up at her, surprised, and relieved.

"Kit, thank goodness you're here. I'm sick."

Kit ignored this. "You're not going to be so glad when I tell you why I'm here."

"What is *your* problem?" he snarled.

Honestly, what had she expected, Mr. Nice Guy? Well, sort of. He'd never once been anything but friendly and helpful, sometimes too much so, but never surly. Benny surged up the ladder. Reflexively, she stepped back.

The guy looked pretty tough all right. Sweat beads rolled down his brow and into the grooves in his stubbled cheeks. Kit noticed but ignored this as well.

"I need you to tell me what's going on here!" she demanded. "Are you dealing drugs? What the hell happened to Tim? Did you get him hooked on drugs?"

Holding his stomach Benny leaned over, hand on the bench seat where he sat to steer. "Oh, is that what the little weasel told you? Your nice boyfriend Tim," he jeered scornfully. "Lemme tell you what good ol' Tim was doing. You sit your nice round tush right there, Miz Kit and I'll tell you all about it."

He gave her a little push, grunting with the effort. She backed up against the passenger seat by the portside window, hoisted herself up. She wasn't scared—yet. She figured she could take on a guy who looked as rough as he did right now.

Kit reached inside her floater coat and Benny freaked out. "What're you doing? Get your hand out of your jacket!"

"Calm down, jeez Benny, just chill. I got to blow my nose, its running all over the place." This with a little grin. Making accusations wasn't working well. Better to be friendly and non-confrontational.

"So, I'm all ears. What's the story?"

Benny leaned further, peered up at her from the corner of his eyes, the whites showing below his enlarged pupils. *Completely crazy.* Kit cautiously slid her hand in her jacket again, pulled out the crumpled wad of toilet paper and wiped her nose, stuffed it back in the pocket. In spite of his paranoia she didn't have anything in there. She wished she had.

"Your dear darling *boyfriend*," again with emphasis, "was... what's the word?" Hung his head, struggling to find it, glared up at her again.

"Oh right, extorting. Yah. Extorting money. From me! Yes, I bin selling drugs, not much. It's not much of a crime. Marijuana, barbiturates, uppers and downers, stuff like that. Okay, cocaine, too; some pharmaceuticals when I get them. People need them, Kit."

Like he was pleading with her to understand.

"People *need* them," he repeated quietly, then shuddered and wrapped his arms around his midsection.

"You need the drugs, Benny?"

"Yes, dammit. I need the drugs. I got so much pain."

He groaned and then again, louder. He lurched toward the door and leaned out, swaying. Tried to step over the door sill, lost his balance and went down on his knees, crawled to the side of the boat and vomited. Kit followed him out and Benny gestured furiously at her.

"Let me help you, what's wrong with you?" Compassion outweighed caution, but then he snarled again.

"Get back in there. I ain't told you about Mister Prawn Checker, Pretty Boy, Tim."

She could practically see the capital letters. Curiosity outweighed caution as well. She turned back into the wheelhouse, noted the wind moaning in the rigging, and the shore line to the rock humming with tension. While Benny sagged by the wheelhouse door wiping his mouth she unhooked the microphone from the VHF radio and pressed the talk key. Before she could say a word, he stumbled back into the cabin, saw the mike near her lips. Red-veined eyeballs bugged out in a paroxysm of renewed rage.

"Put that down! Kit, dammit, gimme that!"

He snatched the open mike from her hand and yanked, tore it from its curly wire. The radio died. Benny grabbed Kit's arm with one hand, heaved the mike with the other. It ricocheted off the sink counter, landed on the floor quivering. Kit jerked back, struggled to peel his meaty fingers from her arm.

"You're hurting me, Benny, stop it!"

"Listen, to me, Kit, ya got to listen. Tim was taking a cut. He made me give him money so he wouldn't report me to the cops, but I'm only doing a little bit of selling, not much, right? So he comes back here after his trip and he wants MORE! He wants more; I couldn't believe it, the bastard wanted MORE."

Benny was salivating, spit dribbling down his chin; maybe going to throw up again. He swiped the back of his hand across his mouth.

She almost felt sorry for him, but…"So then what happened? Did you push him off the boat? Don't you know there are people dying of fentanyl overdoses now? Did you give him drugs with fentanyl in them? Did he OD?"

Watery red eyes staring, he swayed on his feet; shook his head.

"Are you stupid or what? I didn't have to make him take anything; he was all over it. He'd get paid and then get some… whatever, smoke or speed from me, and he'd be doing it."

Stunned, Kit froze, running this through, checking her memory for twinges. Nope, not the Tim she knew. But how could she have missed it? Maybe he'd just been so careful around her and everyone else knew and no one told her. Not entirely true, Back Eddy had tried and she'd completely blown him off.

Kit persisted, speaking sharply. "Okay! Benny, okay. Tell me what happened then. How did he end up in the water?"

For a long moment the two faced off, holding onto whatever was handy, the back of the driver's seat, the galley counter, as the boat heaved and strained at its mooring.

"What the hell, I might as well tell you. I said he should come over for dinner and he came, we smoked some dope and it was real nice to just be friendly. But then he wanted more money. And I...I got mad. I pushed him around a bit, punched him. Like Ritchie punched me." Benny touched his still swollen nose.

"And then?"

"He punched me back, and then we got into it and he tried to get out the door, and I followed him and he was trying to get into his boat and I shoved him..."

"What?! Then what?" Kit spat the words. "Did he land in his boat?"

"I don't know! Whatever! The guy was messing with me big time! He deserved it, he deserved everything he got! Anyway, then he..." Benny stopped and sucked in a big breath.

"He what?"

"Maybe he rolled over the side. I don't know!"

In disbelief, Kit gaped at him.

"You killed him, didn't you? Tell me the truth!"

Benny looked away, flicked his eyes back to her.

She knew then. This might be part of the truth but it sure wasn't the whole truth.

"I never killed him," he muttered.

278

"You let him go, didn't you?" she accused. "You just let him go, all toked up and stoned on cocaine, who knows what the hell happened to him after that. Did he get in his boat, d'you even know?"

His head fell heavily to his chest. "Don't know where he went. I left."

"Oh my god, I thought I knew you. I don't *believe* you! You're a monster."

Nauseated and dizzy, he can't make sense of anything. It's his mom standing there accusing, then she disappears and it's Kit—another woman he could never please. He flipped between trying to placate his mother, no, Kit, and berating her. He should stand up to her blazing black eyes, he wants to poke them out, make them stop looking at him.

He lunged for her and she dove for the door. Benny's knees buckled as she rolled past him and he groaned in agony again, clutching his stomach.

"Kit, Kit, ya got to help me!"

"Are you *crazy*? I'm not going to help you, I'm outta here! You can roll around in your own puking life. I'm getting Margaret. I can't believe she didn't arrest you when she talked to you!"

Benny released a guttural moan as another convulsive seizure racked his belly, but with abrupt manic strength and demented eyes he rose up and clutched Kit's leg as she leaped for the door.

"It's not true, Kit, I never killed him. Ya got to believe me, I didn't do nothing bad."

Thirty-One

After Kit's stormy exit, Back Eddy cleaned up the dishes. He filled in a few more words on the crossword puzzle, then watched TV for a while. Before sundown he was tucked into his sleeping bag on the couch. Like an animal in pain, the wind screamed around the corners of the house, preventing his customary early sleep. He tried imagining himself in his little bunk in his troller, all tucked in and safely secured to the can buoy in Sea Otter Cove. Buster snored on his cushion and the woodstove popped and crackled as it digested the last of the wood. Back Eddy was finally slipping into dreamland when the VHF radio on the windowsill at the end of the couch squawked.

Although he was getting hard of hearing these days, years of listening had honed his interpretive skills. Even half asleep, he recognized the unmistakable words '*Sea Wolf.*' Like a shot he was up off the couch, all his Auxiliary Coast Guard expertise kicking in. He keyed the mike and called, "*Sea Wolf, Sea Wolf, Ocean Dawn.*"

Waited for the comeback.

Victoria Coast Guard Radio came on. Back Eddy told them the RCMP had been out all day, looking for a local vessel. He'd fire up *Ocean Dawn*, go take a look up Tribune. He pulled on his pants, shirt and shoes, grabbed a flashlight from the table, and his coat off the hook by the door. Buster opened one eye and he patted his head. "Go back to sleep, Buster."

Outside, the wind was high and eager, panting to throw something over. Lines of black cloud streamed across a sky punctuated with lightning.

"Why don't nothin' ever happen on a calm night," he grumbled.

The troller fired up easily; he was glad he'd replaced the old motor last year. What a nightmare that had been, but clearly worth it in moments like this. Rounding the corner out of his bay he radioed Woody at the marina and asked if Cole could be ready to jump on the boat and go with him.

"Yup, he just went upstairs. I'll call him right now. I'd come with you but I got the planting crew to deal with," replied Woody.

Cole ran out the door with a flashlight as Back Eddy swept in slow alongside the dock. He put the boat out of gear for less than two seconds as Cole jumped aboard and entered the cabin.

"Where we going? Woody didn't have time to say before you were coming at the dock and I ran out the door!"

"Up Tribune I guess, I think that's where the sergeant's crew went this morning to try to get a line on Tim's boat and tow it back down here. They might've run into some trouble, seeing as they been gone the whole day."

"You gonna be able to do this? Rescue them, and Tim's boat, in *this*?"

"If I can't do it, nobody can." Back Eddy grinned, his trademark boast. "Maybe they haven't got Tim's boat hooked on. I hope," he conceded.

He had to concentrate hard though; a rough wild sea and dark. No moon tonight, it was obscured by the clouds boiled up by the gale barrelling out of the northwest.

"Tribune's going to be a real mess," he said. "Get a life jacket on before you do anything outside."

"It's on," said Cole. "Woody gave me this new one, you pull here and it blows up."

"Yup. Fancy. If they work. Never tried one."

Penn Island on the starboard side and the Burdwood Group to port, he glanced out each window. Briefly through the flying spray a light flared, cabin and running lights, in amongst the islands to port. He and Cole had slogged halfway up Tribune when a voice on the VHF radio blurted out loud and clear.

Benny. Yelling, "Put that down! Kit, dammit, gimme that!"

Back Eddy's heart jolted in his chest, and again when Benny's voice was followed by a brief crackle of static, then nothing. He keyed the mike, tried Channel 16, the communication and calling frequency.

"*Mermaid Lady, Mermaid Lady*; y'on here, Kit?"

No reply.

"*Thunder Chieftain, Thunder Chieftain; Ocean Dawn.*"

Dead air; radio silence.

Nathan came on, "You got your other one on, Willy?"

"Roger. Hold on." Back Eddy keyed the mike on his second radio, permanently set for talk on Channel Six. A moment later he was back. "You hear that? Benny yelling at Kit?"

"Yah, I heard it. Kinda worrisome."

"Yah. I'm up Tribune Channel going after the sergeant's crew. Cole's with me."

Silence while Nathan ran through the options.

"I think he's out in the Burdwoods," said Back Eddy. "By the picnic beach. I seen running lights when I went by. I think they're his."

"Okay. I'll run out there."

"Yah, okay. Nathan, it's rough."

"I'll get back to you."

"What a night."

Thirty-Two

*A*ll dressed up for his dinner date with Carol Ann, but Nathan didn't hesitate. The 60-horse Yamaha on his speedboat coughed and sputtered, then fired up. He steered out of the bay, directly north into the teeth of the gale. The marina floats bucked and banged, groaning in the direct swells. The sea was wild, as Back Eddy had meant; big rollers pushed into huge piles of salt water by 35-knot winds. Short fierce squalls struck from all directions, loaded with brief torrents of rain. Water everywhere, slapping him around. Wind ripped the tops off the waves; in an instant the bilge pump kicked in. Thunder rolled in the heavens.

Should have stuck to tree-planting, he thought, as he turned the bow into each swell. The motor sounded okay, maybe he should have tuned it up a month ago. He and the boat shuddered in unison, but Nathan steered into the swell and the speedboat sturdily ascended each wall of water, then rode down the back of it.

Plowing toward the Burdwoods, he fumbled under the bow for a life jacket; struggled into it, one hand at a time, one knee pressed against the wheel. *Shoulda done this right off the bat.* Most of his brain and energy were occupied keeping the boat headed in the right direction but he had something left to think through possible scenarios, and what he might find when he located Benny. And, presumably, Kit.

Finally he made it into the lee of the islands and the relative comfort they offered. Visualizing the 'reef which must be avoided' to his right, he carefully made his way around it toward the backside of the picnic beach. Another thunderous boom and zigzag of white fire handily lit up the narrow passage.

There she was. *Thunder Chieftain* rode tethered between her anchor line and a shore line to the island. Might or might not be secure for much longer. *Mermaid Lady* lay along the port side of the old fishing boat. The lines joining the one boat to the other repeatedly snapped tight then relaxed into a 'u,' then slammed together again with a vibrating thump and hiss.

Nathan pulled along the starboard side, no easy task with all this nauseating heaving. He reversed too hard, sea foaming around the gunwale, and bounced away. Second try did the trick and he stood up to loop the bowline over the gunwale, heaved himself over the side and kneeled on the deck of Benny's boat to secure it. *All that banging can't be good for those boats.*

The cabin door whanged open, then closed, rebounding off the latch. Nathan crawled cautiously toward the door, hands feeling everywhere for something to hold on to. Overhead, another horrific roll of thunder crashed clouds into each other, released a blinding burst of rain.

Suddenly the door slammed open again and a silhouetted shape loomed dark in the doorway of the wheelhouse. The shape expanded and fell on him. Hands clutched his jacket, then touched his face. *Who is it, who is it?*

Kit's voice, Kit's hands. "Nathan? Nathan, oh my god, thank God! He's lost his mind. He killed Tim and he's trying to kill me. Don't go in there, he'll kill you! We've got to get off the boat!"

"Kit, Kit, get out of here, get on your boat and get back to Woody's."

"I'm not leaving you here."

"Yes you are, dammit, get on your boat and go! Bring Woody, or the sergeant, if she's got her wits about her."

Nathan shoved Kit toward the gunwale, she grasped the rigging and flopped over the side, fumbled for her pocket knife, snapped open the blade and sawed through all three lines. Oh why had she done up all three so thoroughly?

Thunder Chieftain shuddered as another surge broadsided it. Strained to its limit, the shoreline snapped and the vessels swung wildly. *Mermaid Lady* scraped along the fishboat until the momentum separated them. Nathan heard the sound of the motor turning over, gained his balance, held steady for a moment, then burst into the wheelhouse.

Benny lay on the cabin floor groaning, spittle bubbling from his lips. Less of a threat than Nathan had anticipated, clearly the man needed help.

But when Benny opened his eyes and saw that Kit had been replaced by Nathan, he laughed maniacally. "Wow, what insane magic turned her into you? If it isn't Mister Wonder Grandpa."

Benny's venom hadn't deserted him; he could still sting with the scorpion tail. "Guess I got a few things to share with that boy, like who's yer daddy, hah!"

"Don't know what you're talking about, Benny, but you're looking pretty tough. Looks like you could use a hand."

"I don't need any help from you." Benny struggled up off the floor and lurched to the doorway holding his stomach, heaved again.

"Are you seasick?" asked Nathan. It was a wonder he himself wasn't.

"'Course not, I ain't never bin seasick." Benny turned to the rail, fell to his knees and threw up again. Clinging to the gunwale he hung his head between his arms.

Nathan followed him out and Benny looked up. Rain inundated his face and washed off some of the vomit.

"I figured out who Cole was a week or two ago. And I got to tell you, I'm his daddy. How d'ya like them apples?" He nodded, affirming this truth. "Yup, li'l ol' me."

Nathan listened intently; he wanted to know the when, the where and the how but instead asked, "Why should I believe a liar like you, Thompson?"

Another blast of wind and wave buffeted the vessel. Benny used its leverage to propel himself up, grabbed on to the chain that secured the stabilizer poles, swayed back and forth with each roll. His unconquerable malice gave him the strength to reach out, grab Nathan's jacket and pull his face close.

"I had a girl once, a pretty little INDIAN girl, yup. In Vancouver. She was hanging around the bar in Gastown and shining up to me so I took her out back and wham, bam, as they say."

Nathan went rigid in Benny's grasp as the crazed man glared into his eyes. Merciless images flashed one after another across his retinas. Annie, their daughter Jeannette; the daughter he never knew. Drugs, bars and Benny in the city. Jeannette's pregnancy; her lonely delivery of Cole and subsequent death. Cole's adoption and arrival in Echo Bay.

The entire, catastrophic story.

From the fundamental core of his being a furious roar erupted. "You raped her? Don't deny it, you piece of scum! Cole will *never* know who you are, I promise you!"

One gigantic heave against Benny's chest and they're both overboard, landing with a resounding thump on the bow of the speedboat. Benny bounced, Nathan didn't. His wrist was hung up over the tie-up line, his fingers spasmed clutching it. Benny's body slid to the edge of the speedboat's flat bow, his legs dangled and his boots filled instantly with water, then he was in it up to his ribs. Like a limpet he clung to Nathan—but not to save himself. Insensible in the grip of insane fury he wanted nothing more than to drag Nathan over.

With one hand Nathan tried to roll Benny up onto the speedboat. He closed his ears to the crazy rant. "That sweet little piece, she wanted it and I gave it to her, and look what came of it! Cole!" As if the end justified the means. Lightning illuminated the black holes of Benny's eyes and his yammering mouth. Nathan craved desperately to shove something into it.

Benny screamed into the black rain, "I'M his Dad! ME! I am Cole's father! He should know; it's me! You can't stop me telling him!"

The speedboat crashed up, then down, then hard against the hull of *Thunder Chieftain*, crushing Benny between the boats, then releasing him. He slid further off the slick hull of Nathan's heaving speedboat, so deep in the past he couldn't see his own end when it was staring him in the eye.

His fingers convulsed on Nathan's arms but inexorably he slid further. Nathan had been trying to save Benny; now he desired desperately to escape his clutch. Like a pinpoint of light at the end of a tunnel, Nathan's entire being narrowed to focus on the single essential thing—to survive.

Imbued with superhuman strength Benny refused let go. His body thumped with bone-crushing pressure against the hull of his fishing boat. He wanted to drown Nathan, and maybe himself. He thrashed and his fingers slipped, grasped again, clawing at Nathan's sleeve. With a last burst of effort Nathan shook him off; barely registered the astonishment on Benny's dumbfounded face as his fingers released their hold and he disappeared. Gone.

I gotta get offa here.

But getting off was easier said than done. Gasping and spent on the bow of the heaving boat, Nathan became aware that some unknown force was holding him in place. With a grunting push he tried, unsuccessfully, to get to his knees, then understood that his belt had somehow hooked over the bow cleat.

If that don't beat all. Musta done something right in this lifetime.

Clinging to the bowline he wiggled around until he could undo his belt buckle and release it from the cleat. Gauging the rhythm between the two boats, he seized a moment when the small one rose and the big boat dropped. He leapt from the speedboat to *Thunder Chieftain* and rolled over the gunwale onto the deck.

Dark smears of blood stained the wooden deck. He left more blood on the doorframe as he lurched into the wheelhouse. Nathan collapsed onto the seat, tremors quaking his entire being. Held up his trembling hands; they were smeared with blood and throbbing with pain.

"Well, fuck me with a crowbar," he muttered, borrowing one of Back Eddy's sayings. "I'm too old for this shit."

Nathan sat for more endless moments, hoping his heart rate would settle. He suddenly remembered Kit; where was she now?

The speedboat thumped against the side of the boat and he wondered if Benny had found anything to hang onto. He didn't want to know, but nothing would be worse than having the crazed man appear in the doorway of the wheelhouse again. He had to look.

Helpful sprays of lightning illuminated the black water as he crawled along the deck side, looking over wherever he could. No Benny.

Wind-whipped spume exploded off the tops of waves. Nathan listened hard, heard only the wild cacophony of wind in the trees and surf pummelling the rocks.

A fitting score for Benny.

Nathan's thoughts galloped through his brain. Maybe he should stay anchored here until it calmed down. Or maybe he should try to get the anchor up and run *Thunder Chieftain* back to Echo Bay. These old trollers were built for weather like this, yet it would be a rough ride back. And the speedboat would be tough to tow.

Again, what about Kit? Panic swept over him. He couldn't bear it, it would be simply too much, to have the death of Kit on his conscience.

The decision was made for him when the old boat took another broadside wallop and juddered as the anchor pulled loose. Speedboat thumping alongside, she suddenly was streaming west toward the narrow passageway that opened into the centre of the islands.

Got to get the hell off this rig right now!

Like a galvanized frog he leaped for the door, realizing mid-leap he'd lost his boots. He grabbed the bowline, untied and fell into the speedboat as it bounced off and away At least the wind would be behind him; he could surf the swells.

Nathan was too busy cranking the motor to watch the old troller careen off the cliff side of the narrow passage. Dim thuds and crashes added a new dimension to the screaming wind. Motor running smoothly at last, he followed the stricken fishing boat as it careened through the narrows into the calmer waters protected by the ring of islands.

Nathan gritted his teeth and turned the wheel to port, sweeping wide around the lurking rocks. Nothing for it, he'd have to leave the relative shelter of the small archipelago. He motored out of the islands' protection, wishing he hadn't had to. Another squall hit him with a dump of rain, salt water sucked around his ankles. He flicked on the bilge pump switch. Nothing.

Tears leaked from Nathan's salt- and rain-burned eyes. He ploughed through the tumultuous night, crying for the loss of Annie, mourning her and grieving the daughter he'd never known.

"I'll *never* tell Cole, I promise you Benny, whatever hell I hope you find," he muttered. "He'd be ashamed to have a scumbag like you for a father."

Grinding the heels of his palms into his eyes, he leaned over the windshield, straining to distinguish the black slope of Gilford Island. The further he got from the smaller islands the more monumental grew the rolling swells. Taking it on the stern, the speedboat valiantly climbed one wall of water after another. Each time he made it to the top he was sure he'd be going over, but each time he slid down the lee side. A childhood memory surfaced...the little engine that could. *I think I can, I think I can.*

The lights of Woody's lodge flickered in his vision, his knees shook. And then the unthinkable happened.

The bow dove into a trough, the water slopping around in the speedboat poured forward and filled the bow. A muscular wave shoved its liquid fist under the stern and flipped the boat.

An enormous flash lit up the roofs and docks of Echo Bay as Nathan hurtled forward. He hit the sea hard, flailing and gasping; gulped salt water, spitting and coughing as a wave engulfed him.

And right there, the heavens opened up, an awe-inspiring light blazed all around and he was ready, he was going on home now. A voice reached him through the surf and thunder, "Nathan, reach up! Nathan! Nathan, for God's sake, reach up!"

It must be God. He reached up as he was told. *Does God scream at you?*

But it wasn't God. It was Kit and she was leaning over the side ready to fling a rope with a life ring. Her boat was bounding up and down and she was trying to get that life ring to him. He'd better snap to it. Nathan reached out as hard as he could, the ring slid into his hands like a Frisbee and he clutched for dear life.

Dear life.

There was her white face and black eyes, her strong arms dragging him up over the side of *Mermaid Lady.*

"Told you to get back to Echo Bay," was all he could muster as he lay, landed like a salmon, gasping on the wheelhouse floor.

"Damn good thing I didn't listen to you then, isn't it? Shut up and let me drive, this is crazy wild."

Nathan shut up.

Thirty-Three

It had been quite the day, week actually, and where was Nathan, anyway? She'd expected him some time ago, had radioed twice. The dinner sat cold and uneaten upstairs in her apartment and she was miffed. She'd checked on the sergeant, who was still in a deep drug-induced sleep, and Woody had told her Cole was off with Back Eddy to track down the other two cops.

Carol Ann opened her door and gulped as the wind, like ten intruders with mayhem on their mind, forced itself in. Down to Woody's kitchen, there were a few little things to take care of. She'd make a cup of tea for them and find out if he had a clue where Nathan was.

She filled the kettle, turned on the burner, waited. She was pouring the water into the teapot when the side door opened. A sweep of wind and rain whistled in and was quickly snuffed as a raingear-cloaked body stepped in and pulled shut the door.

"It's me, Carson; can I come in, Carol Ann? It's crazy wild out there!"

"Of course, come in, come in. I'm making tea, want some?"

"I went over to Kit's place and she's not there; where would she be on a night like this?"

"Oh my god, Kit! I have no idea! Nathan was supposed to be over for dinner but he's an hour late. What on earth is going on?" Carol Ann flung her hands in the air.

In came Woody through the back door with an armful of firewood. "Carson, hi. What's up now?" He looked from Carson to Carol Ann and back again.

She turned to him, rounded eyes fear-filled. "Kit's not home!"

"Okay, okay, we don' panic. Dere's enough of that going on around here. C'mon in, Carson."

He led the way into his home and Carol Ann brought the full teapot. Woody dumped the pile of wood by the stove; saw a boat enter the bay as he stood.

"Here's somebody now, maybe it's Back Eddy."

But it was Kit who eased alongside the dock. Carson dashed out, went to grab the tie-up line, Woody right behind him.

"Just hold the rail for a sec, got to get a new line on here," said Kit.

Carson held firmly to the rail while Kit grabbed her spare line, tied it and passed him the end. He leaned down, secured it to the dock cleat, then reached up and wrapped his arms around her. Soaked with rain and sweat, trembling, she held on tight for a moment, then said, "Got to get one more to tie up," and left his embrace.

Another wet body limped out of the wheelhouse. Carol Ann stood on the porch, bare-headed in the rain, eyes bugged out and questions all over her face. *Where the heck have you been?*

Nathan stumbled over the side rail, past Woody, across the

deck, up the steps and into her arms. They fell through the front door, bumping off the narrow walls. He may have been dressed for dinner with her, but he was a mess now. Blood smeared across one white eyebrow, blood on his hands; no hat, no boots.

"Nathan! Your hat! Where's your hat?"

She held him thankfully, felt him vibrating. He'd better have some answers pretty damn quick.

"I know something's happened Nathan, you don't have to tell me right now. Whatever it is, you did the right thing."

She looked intently and seriously at him, made him meet her eyes; imbuing him with her faith in his integrity. Nathan couldn't hold back, he spat it out immediately, all of it, in gasping breaths.

"I might could've saved him, Carol Ann. But I didn't. I let him go. Or he slipped away, I can't remember."

"Who, Nathan, who're you talking about?"

"Benny! He killed Tim, or let him die, at least. Said he's Cole's father, his *father*. Because he...he forced that little girl, my daughter. Jeannette, Annie's baby. When she was only seventeen. God, I can't ever tell Cole."

Nathan sagged, as the weight of his own guilt bore down on his sense of himself as a good person.

Carol Ann enfolded him in her warm softness, met his despair with her love. "It's not your fault," she said, taking his cold green-fingered hands in hers. "Maybe it's karma. He was way too messed up, too wounded and he made some pretty bad decisions. Someday you can tell Cole the whole story. It's his right to know."

Carol Ann held Nathan up, but not for long. Droplets slid off the ends of his hair, off his clothing and one remaining sock. A puddle formed where he stood. Her blouse and apron were soaked, too and she could no longer bear his weight. He stepped back, stood straight.

She remembered there was something she had to do, it had felt quite urgent. *Oh, right.*

"One second, Nathan, honey, I'll be right back."

She bolted for the kitchen and searched under the counter, patting here and there, a little anxious. *Where had she put it?*

Nathan went back down the hallway to the door. He bent over, peeled off his sodden sock, leaned out the open front door to wring it out. Woody stepped up from the lower deck, face yellow in the lights from the lodge.

"You look like you've been through the ringer, Nathan."

"You can say that again. Or I need to be put through the ringer."

In the kitchen, Carol Ann's hand fell on the plastic she'd wrapped around the old box of rat poison. She clutched the packet and slipped back into the living room where the stove was roaring. One heartbeat to open the stove door, another beat to toss the box into the flaming inferno, two to fire in a chunk of wood.

Must have been here forty years, and good riddance to it.

Relief flooded through Nathan as he saw *Ocean Dawn* enter the bay, *Sea Wolf* in tow. His boy was safe.

"That Back Eddy, he can sure pull off the rescues," he said to Woody, who grinned.

"You and Kit didn't do too bad, either. Buncha damn fools runnin' aroun' on a night like this."

"That's for sure."

A flash of lightning splashed electric blue discharge all over the sky and his scalp tingled. Nathan shut the door, went barefoot down the passage into the warm room, paused by the stairs to grasp the railing, still trembling.

"Whoa, that stove is hot enough." He shrugged out of his wet coat and Carol Ann took it, smiled up at him.

"Yes," she said, "it's hot enough."

Thirty-Four

The early morning sky arced high overhead, an inverted, blue bowl scattered with popcorn puffs of baby cloud. Nevertheless an eerie feeling simmered—a leftover remnant of catastrophe. Glowing sun swept over the forest, sweeping the peculiar energy out to sea. In the distance remnants of last night's gale stirred the sea an intense indigo but the wind had veered around to the west and the bay itself was calm.

Kit awakened in a strange bed in one of Woody's cabins. She was bundled up in unfamiliar clothes; grey long johns that Carol Ann had borrowed from a tree-planter. The memory of Carson tucking her in came to mind; her head against his chest, feeling the steady beat of his heart. She remembered his words and her last thought before sleep had claimed her.

"I'm not going anywhere," he'd said, and held her, waiting, until finally with a small sigh she'd surrendered.

Last thought: *Life is a crapshoot, might as well take another chance.*

Shoeless, she wandered out the door with a blanket around her shoulders, tangled curls all over her face. She saw Carson saunter, also barefoot, up the dock, smiling big, right at her. Warmth bloomed in her chest, heated her cheeks.

The late spring sun teased up steamy tendrils from the dew-wet decking. Carol Ann bustled out of the lodge with a tray of coffee, Cole close behind with mugs and spoons. Woody carried the canned milk and sugar to the outdoor picnic table on the deck.

Kit remembered Nathan, with an assortment of Cole's clothing in hand, being welcomed upstairs to Carol Ann's apartment, ostensibly for a late dinner. Here he sat, she noted, happily spooning sugar into the coffee Carol Ann poured for him.

"Don't want to be indoors on a morning like this."

Kit grinned at them. "Kinda chirpy this morning, aren't we?"

Cole plonked himself down on the step beside Nathan. "Can you pass me a mug, Grandpa?" he asked. "Is it always this crazy around here? I might have to go back to the big smoke for some peace and quiet!"

"Not on your life, son. Not letting you get away now," replied Nathan, gruff to disguise the squeeze of his heart at Cole's use of 'Grandpa.' "How 'bout we run down to the village later, see Hayley and Vera."

Cole nodded. "Roger that, Gramps."

Back Eddy roared in, chipper as anything after his gruelling rescue mission. Buster leaped from the boat ahead of him but not by much, joyously sniffing all over everyone. Unusually demonstrative, Back Eddy hugged Kit awkwardly and muttered, "I hope you're never gonna scare me like that again."

"I won't," she said, "I'm so sorry. I was such an idiot."

"You got that right." He turned, addressed Carson, "Pretty boat, Carson. Looks like you take good care of it."

"Thanks! Want to take a look?"

"Sure. After I talk to the Sergeant. Found pieces of Benny's boat all over the place this morning."

Carol Ann froze, then she and Nathan both turned to Back Eddy.

"His body?"

"Nope. No body, nowhere."

The police vessel, *Nadon*, had arrived at the crack of dawn after salvaging *Valiant Two* from Wahkana Bay, and was ready to depart. The black body bag containing the cold corpse of Tim Connolly had been carefully loaded and *Valiant Two* and *Sea Wolf* prepared with tow lines for the trip to Port McNeill. A pale but (almost) fully briefed Margaret Morris, along with her team, were ready to depart—for now. There was a lot more to this story, she was certain. According to Kit and Nathan it was only a maybe that Benny had, presumably accidentally, killed Tim. She'd be back; there'd be a dive team and aircraft and forensics all over this scene.

That Echo Bay crew could count on it.

Seeing Back Eddy hurrying towards them, she stopped Carrigan and the *Nadon*'s crew member from casting off.

"Morning, Sergeant Morris," said Back Eddy, "you feeling better today?"

"A bit, thanks. What's up?"

"I went on my run this morning, got out pretty early. Found pieces of Benny's boat all over the place, a couple big ones hung up on the rocks up Fife Sound a bit, west of Ragged Island. No sign of Benny."

"Oh boy." She grimaced but thanked him

"What're you gonna do?"

"I need to confer with my team, and Coast Guard, get those pieces gathered up and a search underway. I'll let you know, you going to be around?"

"Ain't going nowhere."

"Okay, thanks a lot, Mr. Deacon."

"Call me Willy."

He turned back to the group having coffee on the deck. Carson rose to join him and they headed for Carson's boat. Woody strolled down the dock behind them, turned his back to the gathered company, unzipped for a pee. He looked up to the land where the hotel had once stood, and the bomb shelter of the 'Hindoo Prince' of Back Eddy's story. His gaze drifted over the bridge to where the path to Back Eddy's began.

Golden and regal in the morning sun, a cougar stood at the trailhead. She and Woody locked eyes for a long moment. Casually she flicked her long, black-tipped tail, turned and dematerialized into the dappled green wood.

Thirty-Five

With a good night's sleep under her belt and wearing a freshly pressed new uniform, Margaret entered the RCMP office, returned Erika's welcoming smile.

"Seems like you've been gone for days!" she said. "I can hardly wait to hear the whole story."

"It's not a whole story yet, Erika. Got some more work to do to get this wrapped up. There're so many questions. There's a big search on for parts of the fishing vessel and the skipper, Benny Thompson, and I'm waiting for the autopsy report on Tim. I've got a ton of drone footage to look through, I got it from a complete newbie to the area; none of them know him from Adam. I know those Echo Bay people are keeping secrets. Damn civilians, always figure they know better than us. Something else I should let you know Erika, I'm going to take some leave."

"For the PTSD?"

"What? Why would you say that?"

"Oh, I'm sorry, Sergeant!" Erika was flustered. "It's none of my business."

"Is it that obvious?"

"I don't know about anyone else but I've been in this job almost forty years and I can tell when people have gotten messed up by it. I've been hoping you'd get some help."

Margaret turned away, shook her head, then turned back to accept the slip of paper Erika held out.

"Anyway, I've got something here that may help. Or not. You talked to a fisherman at the hospital last week, right? Frank Hamilton? So he came in yesterday and wanted to talk to you. I couldn't convince him to talk to anyone else. Told him you'd call him."

A buzz ran up her spine. "Hamilton, yes! I hope he's got something good for me."

"Mr. Hamilton? Staff Sergeant Morris here, how are you? All better?"

"Kinda, yah."

"You wanted to see me?"

"Oh, yah, huh. Well, I'm gonna need witness protection or sumpin'. Before I tell you."

"Goodness. Okay, so, you've got some significant information?"

"Yah, I guess. Maybe."

Margaret tapped her teeth with her pencil.

"Can you come in to the station, Frank?"

"Did that; you weren't there," he accused. "Don't think that'd be safe for me. Somebody'll tell."

"Could I come to you? Where are you right now? Are you safe?" She could hear his heavy breathing.

"Maybe. Could you come in...like, not a cop car? Or cop clothes? I'm staying at a friend's shack near Port Alice but I don't think I can be here long."

"Tell me where, I'll come right now."

Margaret jotted down the directions Frank gave her. She changed into the jeans and t-shirt she kept in the closet and pinned her blond braid up under a baseball cap. She drove Erika's beat-up Toyota down the logging road, peering into the bush for the faded pink ribbon tied to a tree Frank had said to watch for.

Spotting it, she pushed down the narrow turn, through brambles and thimbleberry bushes and into a small clearing; turned off the motor. She sat for a few minutes with the window rolled down. A varied thrush threw leaves right and left on a small square of grass, a song sparrow pealed out its tune. Weak sun filtered through the catkins of the alder trees, leafy green salmonberry bushes cast an underwater light on an old log building. No smoke. Door and windows closed.

Margaret adjusted her shoulder holster, opened the car door quietly and stood in the clearing for a moment. Walked to the door, raised her hand to knock.

A crack behind her, she whirled, gun in hand in an instant, balanced and ready to shoot. Frank came out of the bush, carrying a shotgun. "Don't shoot, Sergeant, it's just me."

"Put it down, Frank."

"Yah, yah..." He laid down the gun. She slowly lowered hers.

Peering around, jumpy, the fisherman said, "Follow me. Got a spot we can sit away from the house."

Margaret returned her gun to its holster and followed him up a short rise to a bluff above a small lake. He sat; indicated a flat rock beside him for her to sit. She noted the old cushion on the rock, asked, "This your sitting place?"

"My friend's. He fishes here. But y'can see the house, look."

She looked. "Right. Nice little set-up. Is he worried about something?"

"I don't know! None of my business. Listen, Sergeant, I found something, on a boat I work on."

She raised her eyebrows.

He shifted, rubbed his face. "Dammit! A prawn boat; *White Bird*. I went back to work and the crew was actin' weird. Didn't know what the hell was going on. I told them about the overdose and hospital and all that. Not you," he hastened to assure her. "They don't know I talked to you. I had to look all over for the gaff, to hook on to the line, y'know, 'n it was cracked and had, I don't know, some blood on it maybe. Anyway I told the skipper we needed a new gaff, he grabbed it from me, took the boat in to Alert Bay and told me to get my gear and get off. Just like that!"

Margaret had no pencil to tap. She watched her long fingers beating a tattoo on her knees as she listened.

A shiver ran from hips to neck at his next words. "I got the gaff."

Galvanized, she rose, hands out. "Where is it? Give it to me. I'll get that protection in place for you immediately."

304

Thirty-Six

Steam billowing around her, Carol Ann was canning a couple of last year's salmon she'd pulled out of the freezer, when she heard the plane come in. It wasn't Thursday so it couldn't be the mail plane. Woody hadn't let her know anyone was expected so who...?

Kit poked her head in the door. "Looks like the sergeant's back. She's coming down the dock. Oh. Ritchie is with her."

"What, why?"

"How would I know? Maybe came for fuel or something." Kit peered at the other woman curiously.

"No," said Carol Ann, "I mean the sergeant; why is she here?"

"Maybe she's got some news about Tim," said Kit, as Sergeant Morris entered.

"Are you looking for Woody?" asked Carol Ann.

"Ladies, good morning. I'm looking for all of you. I have news."

"Oh, want some tea while we get...oh! Nathan, what...?"

"Saw the plane. Woody and Cole are comin' down the hill," he reported. "Carson, too. Guess he's helping out. Back Eddy just pulled in. Look's like we're having a meeting." He grinned amiably.

Carol Ann flushed pink, scooted back into the kitchen and put the kettle on; she rooted around in the cupboard for some cookies. No cinnamon buns today; she'd gone off them lately, anyway. Nathan followed her as the others entered Woody's apartment.

"Carol Ann," he caught her around the waist and turned her toward him. "What the heck is going on with you?"

She leaned her forehead against his chest, rolled it back and forth, pulled away. "Nothing, nothing, I'm fine. I just want this to be over."

"As do we all, sweetheart, as do we all. Let's go see what she has to say."

Once again the picnic table in Woody's suite was crowded with bodies. Last to the table, Carson squeezed in beside Kit. Buster slipped under the table to sit at Back Eddy's feet.

Woody went behind his counter, gestured an invitation to the sergeant to join him. She surveyed the inquiring faces arrayed around the table.

"Good morning! How perfect that you all happen to be here at this moment."

"Saw the plane come in," said Back Eddy. "Good chance somebody interesting would be on it."

Margaret laughed. "Well, you'll be interested in this. We arrested Darrell Henderson this morning, charged him with assault, bodily harm. We might be able to make murder charges stick but have some work to do."

Carol Ann gasped. "So Benny didn't do it!"

Kit leaned back and closed her eyes. Ritchie crossed his hands under his chin.

"No. A source contacted us, he found a gaff with some very small samples of skin and blood that forensics was able to match with Tim, and Carson's drone showed an interaction of two boats early Saturday morning. One is *White Bird* and although the light is very poor, we're pretty sure the skiff tied alongside was Tim's. We salvaged the skiff Back Eddy reported, Tim's for sure. The hull had a small puncture and was side-slipped on the rock. It probably wouldn't have floated again but somehow it must have made several miles before it settled on the rock. Some prawn checking gear was on board. We can't know at what point Tim and the boat parted ways, but possibly when it came up against Smith Rock. Tim may have had an altercation somewhere, and then returned to his boat and then left again. We found bloodstains in the bunk of the liveaboard, *Valiant Two*, and bandage wrappers on the counter.

She paused, looked down and then said, "I am so sorry, all of you, I am so sorry for your loss."

"We're real sorry for yours, too, Sergeant," said Woody.

"Thank you. His family's been notified and we'll release his body to them in a couple days. Will you be planning a service for him?"

"Yes," Kit replied. "I called his parents and sister and we're organizing a celebration of life, sometime in late June. They'll be coming out to spread his ashes in the Broughton Archipelago." She put her head in her hands. "Why didn't I call Coast Guard when he didn't make it for dinner? It just didn't seem that...odd. I was relieved. I'm such a schmuck."

Carson patted her arm. "It wouldn't have made any difference to what happened to him, Kit."

"I guess," she said through tears, "But I'm warning you all, never be late without letting me know or there'll be a call out on you so fast."

"Okay, alright. About de celebration of life; Tim's family will stay wit' me and everyone can meet up here. We jus' have to pick a date."

"Will you come, Margaret?" invited Kit.

"I'd like to, yes. Thanks."

"We'll let you know when."

"Okay. I'd better get going, the pilot said to be quick, the wind's coming up."

"But..." Carol Ann blurted and stopped.

"Yes? But...?"

"Well, what about Benny?"

Sargent Morris looked at her a long moment, then said, "I'm sorry to say we have very little at this point, in spite of an area-wide search. We collected several pieces of his boat but it's very hard to tell if the interior damage is from the effects of the storm or what. We have an all-points bulletin out on his body and hope it will show up somewhere; but from Nathan's description of their fight, unlike Tim, he wasn't wearing a life jacket. So..." She spread her hands wide. "It's anybody's guess. If any of you have anything else to add to your statement, now is the time."

Nathan felt the tension seep out of Carol Ann's body like a slow-leaking tire. She sagged against him, slid her hand into his underneath the table.

No one spoke until finally Carol Ann broke the silence.

"Poor sad man, may he rest in peace."

"Amen to that," agreed Woody.

"I'd better get on that plane," said Sergeant Morris and she came out from behind the counter.

Back Eddy pushed up from the table to follow her out. "C'mon Buster, let's go home. Bye for now, Sergeant. Thanks for coming. I'll see the rest of you tomorrow."

"Yup, catch ya later."

Silence reigned for a few beats after Back Eddy and Margaret left. Ritchie slid off the bench and said, "Let me know the date when it's fixed. I'll be here."

"Of course," said Kit. "It'll be a big crowd, I think. See you, Woody, fellas." She stood, waggled her fingers at Cole and Carson, then turned toward the door. Nathan and Carol Ann slid off the bench behind her.

"Kit," said Carson.

She turned back, question in her face.

"I'll come by after I finish here, okay?"

"That," she smiled, "would be lovely."

Woody Debris waited until they'd closed the door, then nodded to Cole and Carson. "Got your work gloves?"

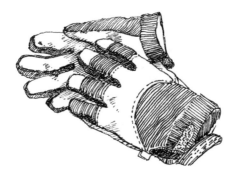

A Note From the Author

Dear Reader: I hope you enjoyed your visit to Echo Bay, and with the (novelized versions of) residents therein. It took me way too long to complete this story; I found it considerably more challenging than writing a memoir. Lucky for me the landscape of inlets and islands of the Broughton Archipelago is such a powerful and beautiful element in its own right, I was saved the difficulty of inventing one. The individuals here are so vitally unique, and so visible under the spotlight of each other's scrutiny, that it was easy to grow versions of them by mixing and matching characteristics and activities. Adding the spice of history via Bill Proctor's stories, along with cherry-picked details from a vast selection of books about BC coastal history to the unfolding present, gave me much to work with. Hanging it all together as a chain of imagined interactions and events that ended up making sense, while requiring the reader to pay attention and piece things together...that was the hard part. Wow! A zillion details and conflicting conversations and all the things you're 'supposed' to do to make a good book, well...I just hope I did.

If you found the part where Nathan was saved from certain death in the fight scene on the speedboat somewhat apocryphal, know that it is firmly rooted in truth. Years ago Bill told me this story. He was running home after a visit with a neighbour, going full bore in the dark. He smashed into a boom of logs that had been brought in while he was visiting, flew over the windshield and was caught by his belt buckle on the bow cleat; an astounding detail I was determined to find a place for in this story.

With his permission, 'Back Eddy' is closely based on my friend and neighbour, real life old-timer Bill Proctor, fondly known as BP, Doctor Proctor or the Mayor of Echo Bay (he actually has no middle name). It was he who came up with the names 'Back Eddy' and 'Woody Debris.' I thank you, Billy, for so much: the inspiration to write, the books you shared, the stories you tell and for generously allowing me to use it all to build these characters. All of the history is true, according to Bill, and to various researched sources. When I came upon the name of the DesBrisay family and their role in West Coast fishing history I laughed out loud. What a terrific way to weave together the fictional 'Woody Debris' character with a real life family story.

'Woody Debris' was a good fit with real life Pierre Landry, who also kindly gave me permission to do what I would with him. Through Gallic charm and monumental effort Pierre built Echo Bay Marina into a thriving marine resort. I'm grateful to you as well, Pierre, and to you, Alana Coon from Gwayasdums (Gilford Village), for inspiring my character Leah, the young woman who manages the band office (and so much more) at Gwayasdums.

Thank you to another good neighbour we miss since he moved, Coady Webb, co-manager at one time of Salmon Coast Field Station (who I thank for their generous use of their more reliable internet), who read parts of the text and gave me detailed feedback on the professional activities of the prawn checker. Any mistakes are, of course, my own and not his.

Although he is no longer with us, Chris Stewart of Port McNeill, a much loved member of the community, engaged in enthusiastic and informative correspondence with me about RCMP protocols. I am so sorry he is not able to read this book and tell me where I went wrong...any mistakes are on me, of course.

I appreciate so much those who took the time to read the book during its early stages: the first was my brother Frank Maximchuk, who offered useful feedback, as did my friend Kathy Cassels. Another friend, Mary Morris, printed out a copy and made extensive notes throughout the manuscript, including a couple like, "Great!" and "Love this!" Mary, this was an effort I hadn't imagined anyone would undertake.

A warm thank you to author and editor Carol Sheehan, whose insightful editorial comment reshaped the book, and to editor (of *Tide Rips and Back Eddies)* Pam Robertson, who read the fourth draft and replied with seven pages of creative and critical suggestions. It took me a while but eventually I incorporated every single one, which helped build (I hope and believe) a much better book. I especially thank you, Pam, for your swift response to my plea for an immediate copy edit as the manuscript was being transformed into an actual book.

My daughter Theda Phoenix Miller, singer of healing sound journeys, has been a wonderful resource in so many 'modern technology' arenas. I value our long inspirational conversations about communication, relating styles and healing modalities, and her assistance in dealing with websites, Facebook and PayPal...things that sometimes frighten me. Thank you BBD.

Three other dear friends have my deepest respect, gratitude and love. Peggy Hall, Vicki Auerbach and Jeanne Serrill have blessed me with twelve and a half person decades of their wisdom and unstinting personal and emotional support. Your love has significantly shaped my sense of self and unfailingly reflected to me a person I like. Love and thanks to you, my beautiful crones.

Thank you so much to those who bring to the production of this book their talent, knowledge and skill; Craig Shemilt of Island Blue Book Publishing (so calm while speaking to an anxious author) and Iryna Spica, creative artist and the book's designer. And to Jacqueline Carmichael for her detailed replies to my many questions, to Mary Shendlinger, editor of *Full Moon, Flood Tide: Bill Proctor's Raincoast,* who showed me what a good editor does, and to everyone at Harbour Publishing and Caitlin Press from whom I learned so much about what makes a good book and a book good. 'From-the-heart' thanks for being essential to my writing life, in particular, and to the wonderful world of book production in general.

My husband, Albert and I often end our day by shooting a game of pool on the table he salvaged after the shutdown of the logging camp in Shoal Harbour. His preference is to focus on the game and I, so often, wanted to talk about my book. For years,